BLIND SPOT

SPLIT IMAGE

DOUBLE TAKE

FAST FORWARD

"A riveting delight, a veritable banana split of a mystery."
—*The Washington Times*

"Wow! . . . *Fast Forward* is smooth and smart, with enough thrills to satisfy even the most jaded mystery reader. Judy Mercer's characters are so real that . . . you may have to restrain yourself from phoning them just to chat."
—Susan Isaacs, author of *Red, White and Blue*

"An action-packed thrill ride that's full of unexpected twists and turns. . . . Reminiscent of Jonathan Kellerman at his best."
—*Booklist*

"A winner. . . . Packed with puzzles within puzzles, *Fast Forward* delivers layered suspense and a heroine readers will root for."
—Nora Roberts, author of *Carolina Moon*

"*Fast Forward* is that rare thriller that delivers much more than it promises. . . . Mercer doesn't miss a beat."
—*The Orlando Sentinel* (FL)

"Suspenseful and compelling. . . . Judy Mercer fast forwards to the head of the pack of new mystery and suspense writers."
—Nancy Pickard, author of *The Whole Truth*

"Credit Mercer with a rare imagination . . . skill and wit . . . and a Machiavellian penchant for plot. . . . *Fast Forward* is a good yarn, well told."
—*Los Angeles Times Book Review*

"Engaging, fast-paced . . . with just the right combination of terror and compassion. . . . The ending, like the rest of the book, is a pleasing combination of the slick and the jagged."
—*San Francisco Chronicle*

Books by Judy Mercer

Fast Forward
Double Take
Split Image
Blind Spot

Available from POCKET BOOKS

JUDY
MERCER
BLIND
SPOT

POCKET BOOKS
New York   London   Toronto   Sydney   Singapore

POCKET BOOKS, a division of Simon & Schuster, Inc.
1230 Avenue of the Americas, New York, NY 10020

Copyright © 2000 by Judy Mercer

Originally published in hardcover in 2000 by Pocket Books

ISBN: 0-671-03425-1

First Pocket Books paperback printing March 2001

10 9 8 7 6 5 4 3 2 1

POCKET and colophon are registered trademarks of Simon & Schuster, Inc.

Front cover photo by Kirsty McLaren/Tony Stone Images

Printed in the U.S.A.

For Brad and Matthew Alper,
with love and respect

Acknowledgments

Partner, I thank you again and always for twice transforming my life.

For their questions, answers, assistance, and ideas, I am indebted to Dean A. Alper, attorney at law, for thinking of me when he thinks of murder; and to Beth Ashley, *Marin Independent Journal;* Bhavani; David H. Bryman; Cynthia Currier; Sheila Duncan, U.C. Medical Center; Damian Friary; Jeff Herschelle and Ed Gutowski; Kenneth Holmes, Marin County coroner; Grace Hughes, Marin Airporter; Debra Lehane, San Francisco Art Commission; Stacy Lynn, FitFirst, Mill Valley; Kenneth Miller; Fiona Page; John Perkey; Patricia Porter; John C. Shin, M.D.; Frank Tavel, M.D.; Mary Ellen Taylor, Federal Food and Drug Administration; and others who remain anonymous but deeply appreciated. If I've fumbled information provided by those who have been generous with their time and knowledge, it was inadvertent, and I hope to be forgiven. Or it was shameless poetic license, and I hope to be indulged.

On the subject of taking liberties, a word about the "Marin Guide Dog Academy": it is my own invention. Anything positive you read herein is, to the best of my knowledge, factual, inspired by a real and remarkable institution. Mayhem, as well as certain sites and all characters, human and canine, are utter fiction.

For information about the real school, a nonprofit charitable organization dedicated to providing skilled

x   Acknowlegments

guide dogs and training in their use to visually impaired men and women in the United States and Canada, phone or write Guide Dogs for the Blind, Inc., P.O. Box 151200, San Rafael, CA 94915-1200, (415) 499-4000, or 32901 S.E. Kelso Road, Boring, Oregon, 97009, (503) 668-2100.

We have met the enemy, and they are ours.

> —Captain Oliver Hazard Perry
> Dispatch from U.S. brig *Niagara*
> to General William Henry Harrison

We have met the enemy, and he is us.

> —Walt Kelly
> *Pogo*

BLIND
SPOT

1

GOOD NEWS DOESN'T COME AT FOUR IN THE MORNING.

For those unlucky enough to lie wakeful, that silent predawn black is a lonesome place. Worries nibble at the mind. Old regrets come home to roost. As sleep eludes, just beyond grasp, every minute stretches. The clock ticks. Fears that would seem foolish by day take hold of the imagination, and grow.

It isn't the dead of night, 4:00 A.M., but it can, nonetheless, be deadly. Ask a nurse on the graveyard shift. Ask any priest. It is the hour, you'll learn, when the body's purchase on life is at its weakest, when those sapped by age or illness will often, finally, surrender.

It is an hour when the earth itself is unreliable. Predawn—historically, quirkily, and inexplicably—is favored by earthquakes.

And when the phone rings in the last, dark hours of the night, chances are it's bringing trouble.

It wasn't the phone that woke Ariel Gold at 4:06 A.M., and it wasn't the rumble of a quake. It was, in the first disoriented second, as shocking. She'd been deeply asleep. She'd gone to bed alone. She no longer was. Something cold bumped against her cheek. She jerked awake, still half mired in a nonsensical dream. The noise she heard then was a low, anxious murmur, so close it was like a moist breath on her face, so close it almost stopped her heart. That was when the phone rang.

Later, she questioned whether she could have the sequence of events right: that her dog nudged her awake *before* the phone actually rang. How was that possible? Did telephones emit some sound undetected by human ears in the split second before the ring? Was it coincidence? Or did animals have an early warning system for tragedy on the way? The time came when Ariel stopped questioning. Weirder things were entirely, provably possible. Whatever the big German shepherd may or may not have sensed, tragedy had already happened.

"Hello?" Ariel said, her voice hardly audible over Jessie's panting. She stroked the dog's neck, invisible in the dark, but warm, softly furred, and familiar. "Hello?" she asked louder. "Who is it?"

She heard the *thwack!* of a receiver being dropped, banging against something, and snapped on the bedside lamp, squinting against the brightness of the 100-watt bulb. This wasn't a wrong number; she was somehow sure of that. It wasn't a creep of the heavy breathing variety either, although Ariel could, faintly, hear the sound of someone breathing. The receiver was evidently retrieved, for the breathing grew loud. It was ragged, the desperate, greedy mouth-breathing of a woman in labor.

"Help me! Oh, God! Help me!"

The voice was a woman's. Thin. At the very edge of a scream. It took Ariel a second to place it. She'd never heard this particular woman sound anything but serene, even detached. "Laya?" she asked. "Is that you?"

Horribly, Ariel's friend had begun to moan. *She's been attacked!* Ariel thought. *Raped.* "What's happened?" she cried, but the moaning, a litany of pain, overrode her. "Hurts!" Ariel made out, and the words "Oh!" and "Please!"

"Stop it," she ordered, "and tell me what's happened."

Laya made a strangling sound and then swallowed noisily, more than once. It sounded as though she were forcing down stones. "I can't," she said. "I can't . . ."

"You can't what?"

"See!"

"What?"

"Don't you understand English?" The hysteria broke loose then. A flood. "I can't see! I can't see anything! I'm blind!"

2

THE KINDEST THING THAT COULD BE SAID ABOUT THE HOSPITAL waiting room was that it was neutral. The muted Muzak piped in through some unseen speaker was vanilla: white noise, par for Otis ups and downs. The only other occupant of the room was a spent-looking old man. He was snoring quietly, mouth ajar, emitting delicate little puffs, as if he were blowing dandelions, and his head had dropped back at an angle that was sure to mean a crick when he woke up. Ariel had seen him earlier down in the emergency room, comforting a woman on a stretcher. A crick, she thought, might be the least of his troubles. He had her sympathy. She didn't know much about her first thirty-two years, but the last one had packed more trouble than most people faced in a lifetime.

It was 6:05. The sun was presumably up, but since there were no windows in the room, it was impossible to know what the new day looked like. Ariel was reluctant to take even a short walk outside for fear a doctor might come looking for her. Paramedics had turned Laya over to the emergency room staff over an hour ago. An hour and twenty minutes ago. Ariel had no inkling of her condition, and she still had no inkling of what had taken place before that horrifying call.

Her race to Laya's apartment had been little short of
suicidal. She'd beaten the paramedics, whom she'd
phoned en route. The front door had been locked.
Frantically, Ariel had felt above the door frame, under the
mat, the usual places people keep a spare key. She'd found
it beneath a potted plant, a fishtail palm that reigned over
a small oasis of palms and succulents in a recess beside the
door. Plants were among Laya's few indulgences. She traveled lightly, even in regard to her name.

She was a yogi: Ariel's teacher and her friend, a woman
always in possession of herself and, Ariel was sometimes
convinced, the secrets of the universe as well. Laya
seemed unaware of her quiet charisma and unconcerned
about her looks, which were arresting. (Ariel once
remarked on her resemblance to Poitier. "Poirot?" Laya
had teased. "Wrong accent," Ariel had said, straight-faced.)
There was a trace of the West Indies in the tall black
woman's cadences, as elusive as its origins. Her graying
hair was left to its natural tendencies, and cropped within
an inch of her skull, and her wardrobe was utilitarian, the
comfortable leggings and sweats of a yoga teacher, or, on
occasion, playful: some flowing garment likely to be
plucked from a secondhand rack.

Her home was as spartan as a transient's. That morning, in the dense gray predawn, it had appeared abandoned. Ariel had called out. There'd been no answer.
Reassuring herself that if anyone had been here—a burglar? a rapist? (a lover who'd turned violent? Who knew?
There were chunks of Laya's life about which Ariel knew
nothing)—they were long gone, she had made herself go
in. It was dark. She was feeling for a light switch when she
heard music, jazz, turned very low. It came, she thought,
from the bedroom. So did a faint shaft of light.

At first she saw no one but Arthur, Laya's fat mar-
malade cat. He was in the middle of an unmade bed, a

tightly tucked, unhappy-looking orange mound. Normally the most lethargic of animals, his ears were back and his eyes watchful. His tail switched once, an emphatic arc.

Then Ariel spotted Laya.

She was on the other side of the bed, on the floor with the phone beside her. She was in a sitting position, slumped against the wall, dressed in an oversized T-shirt. Her eyes were closed. She was inert. Ariel was sure for a blank bright moment that she was dead. Then a sprawled leg twitched, the tiniest contraction.

Calling her name, Ariel rushed to kneel beside her. Laya didn't stir. The eyes weren't just closed, Ariel saw; they appeared to be swollen shut. Both dark cheeks bore long scratches. In the stingy glow of the bedside lamp, Ariel could see the welts below each eye: not deep, she thought—the blood beading and beginning already to dry—but angry. There were red smears on the front of the T-shirt.

Ariel reached out, unsure what to do. "Laya!" she said sharply. There was no response at all. She touched her fingers to Laya's neck. The flesh was cool, but the pulse beat, it seemed to Ariel, strongly. Gritting her teeth, she lifted an eyelid. The eye was hideously inflamed, as if it were bleeding internally. Very gently, she let the lid close. There were no other obvious signs of injury. She stood and looked around. Other than an overturned desk chair, there was no sign that anything of a violent nature had taken place.

Ariel pulled the comforter from the bed, dislodging Arthur, who thumped gracefully to the floor and vanished. She was tucking the cover around Laya when she became aware of the sound of running water. Careful to touch nothing, she went into the bathroom. Using a tissue to handle the tap, she turned it off.

Laya was as oblivious to the noisy arrival of the paramedics as she'd been to Ariel. "Shock," guessed one of the EMTs after a swift glance.

It wasn't until they were lifting her insensible friend to the gurney that Ariel had noticed the small plastic bottle in Laya's hand. It contained eyedrops, a generic over-the-counter brand. She'd pocketed it.

In the bedlam of the emergency room, Ariel had remembered the bottle only at the last minute. The ER doctor barely glanced at it, saying that if the lady's problems stemmed from any kind of chemical burn, he hoped she'd used more than drops. "Should've irrigated with water," he'd said tersely, "and lots of it!" Thinking back to the questions he'd fired at her, Ariel surmised that he'd been more concerned at that moment about his patient's unresponsive state.

She paced the waiting room. It was six-fifteen. What were they doing that was taking so long? What had been done *to* Laya to make her this way? Every guess was less likely than the one before. Had she scratched her cornea? *Both* of them? Idiotic! Contacts! Did she wear them? Maybe the old, non-air-permeable kind that stuck to your eyeballs like glue if you fell asleep with them in? And when you tried to peel them off . . . Ariel sat down, fidgeted, and got up again. Something had to have gotten into her eyes. Had she had an allergic reaction to soap or some cosmetic? But her eyes looked flayed! An accident then . . . some household cleaning solution. Didn't every bleach and detergent and polish caution against contact with the eyes? Why, Ariel asked herself, would Laya be cleaning house at four in the morning? And, surely, even if that was what happened, she would still have been hysterical, as she was on the phone, not . . . comatose. Out of it. Or whatever she was. Just . . . gone. *Where?* It was then that Ariel recalled something she'd read in a book about yoga.

It had to do with a thing called kundalini. As nearly as she had understood, it was a force or power activated while in a profound trance state. Adepts, she'd read, could stop their own hearts. They could enter into a state of suspended animation. They could curl up on a bed of nails or stroll around on burning coals without pain. *They could escape pain!* Was Laya capable of willing herself, meditating herself, into such a trance?

If she herself were in severe pain, Ariel was sure, in severe distress, and could remove herself to oblivion or bliss or at least absence of pain, she'd be *om*-ing fit to kill.

She was clutching at straws, avoiding thinking about those facial scratches. What were those all about? *Was* Laya attacked?

What kind of attacker would scratch rather than strike? Or had she been struck? A head blow, knocking her unconscious? Impacting whatever portion of the brain affected vision? The water left running . . . Someone cleaning off blood? The evidence of attack?

The old man who shared the waiting room exhaled forcefully, one noisy snort. He woke himself up. Smiling sheepishly, he glanced at Ariel and then at the nurses' station and, then, starting slightly, at Ariel again. She smiled back, sympathetic acknowledgment of a fellow passenger in the wait-and-worry boat. He turned pink and suddenly found his fingers of interest. Lacing them together, he watched himself rub the pad of one thumb against the other. After a good thirty seconds of this fascinating exercise, he blurted, "Excuse me, but you're somebody, aren't you?"

"Pardon?"

"I'll get it in a minute. Somebody . . ."

Ariel almost turned to look behind her. Preoccupied as she'd been, dressed in last night's wrinkled clothes, her hair at odds with her head and her face bare of makeup, she honestly didn't get it for a second.

"*Open File!*" he cried. "You're the lady from that TV show! A celebrity!"

Wincing, Ariel admitted that the first part, at least, was true. She still wasn't used to being recognized. She found it incredible, at the moment, that she had been. She looked more like a gummy-eyed bag lady, she imagined, than a "celebrity."

In Los Angeles one spots them—celebrities, even legends—regularly, on the street, in the dry cleaner, at the car wash. A major box office draw blocks the grocery aisle with his cart, studying the ingredients on a cereal box. A sitcom lead sees your look of recognition and gives you a wink as he passes on the sidewalk. The woman rummaging through old linens at the next flea market stall is an Academy Award–winning singer-turned-actress. Ariel wasn't in that league. It was a fact, though, that since she'd gone from producer to correspondent on a network newsmagazine three months before, she did get surreptitious glances and even the occasional autograph request.

"My wife watches your show faithfully," the man said, patting his pockets, pulling out a pen from one and what turned out to be a phone bill from another. "She even tapes it when we go out. We square-dance." He faltered, and seemed to sink into himself. "Diabetes, she's got. Bad. They may have to amputate . . ."

Ariel took the envelope and scribbled inadequate best wishes. "Tell you what," she said. "When your wife's feeling better, you call the studio, Mr. . . ."

"Morris. Bobby Morris. Merle, that's my wife."

"Ask for me. I'll arrange a tour of the studio, if you'd like to do that." Jotting the studio number and wishing him luck, Ariel got to her feet. "I need to check on my friend," she said, and started for the nearest nurses' station.

The ER doctor intercepted her. After asking for information Ariel didn't have (like Laya's surname; hospital red tape snarled hopelessly on a patient who'd dispensed with the family name and, it was Ariel's impression, the family that shared it), he volunteered only, "An ophthalmologist is with her now. We've got saline drips going to irrigate the eyes. We'll know more later."

"Tell me what you know now, please," Ariel begged.

The doctor (whose name, Ariel later thought, she must surely have heard or read on his ID badge but didn't remember) considered his reply. Blinking rapidly and addressing his answer through half-closed lids to some point behind her (a nervous and probably unconscious habit she put down to shyness—or having delivered bad news a few times too many), he said, "Chemical burn, of course. Damage to the left eye looks like it might be limited to the outer layer of the cornea." He went through the blinking routine again. "Other eye's not so good. Cornea's cloudy."

Ariel felt herself grow cold. "Which means?"

He tried falling back on his earlier bromide. "We'll know more a little later."

"But what happened?"

He sighed. "What actually took place, you mean? Since the patient's out of it—which is something I have *never* seen in these situations—I can't answer that. We can't get any information from her. I can only tell you that some form of acid was introduced to the eyes." He blinked. "I'm having the contents of that bottle you gave me checked out."

3

"I NEED A FAVOR. THE BEST OPHTHALMOLOGIST YOU CAN GET your hands on. Fast."

Ariel didn't ask favors casually. A good three seconds passed before her grandfather said, "Come again?"

B.F. Coulter wasn't hard of hearing, but he was often a hard man to find. Ariel had run him down in Seattle. At seventy-seven, he'd slowed from the pace that made him a millionaire in his early thirties. He no longer sprinted; he merely frolicked, skipping around the globe as if it were his own personal Monopoly board. A cracker, he called himself. Born and raised in rural Georgia. Son of a sharecropper. An accent you could cut with a dull knife. It came and went, camouflaging a mind that was anything but dull.

If a million dollars was a lot of money in the postwar decade when he first amassed it, it was nothing to what he'd made since. The wheeling and dealing was a game now, but it was one he still played by the old rules. His handshake was more binding than seventy pages of legalese.

Ariel was his sole heir. She hadn't had much time to adjust to the idea, as she and B.F. had known of each other's existence for hardly more than a year. She'd found him just about the same time she'd lost her own identity. It was, Ariel had come to feel, a fair swap. She could live with amnesia. Life without her grandfather didn't bear thinking about. "I said," she began, "that I need the best—"

"I heard what you said, honey. What's wrong? Is something wrong with your eyes?"

"Not mine. It's Laya."

"Laya?" B.F. exhaled noisy relief. "God bless America, Ariel, don't scare me like that! Now what's this about Laya?"

"The ophthalmologist they've got here—Chaney, I'm told his name is—he might be adequate, I don't know. I haven't talked to him yet. But I want a second opinion to everything. A top man."

"You want to back this train up so I can get on board, too? Tell me what you're talking about. What's wrong with Laya?"

"Chemical burn. They don't know what yet or how it

got in her eyes because she's in some kind of, I don't know
. . . state. Totally nonresponsive. The ER doctor said he's
never seen anything like it with an injury like this. Can't
even imagine how somebody in that kind of pain . . . Well,
anyway, now he's talking neurological tests. The point is,
they don't know. It's as if she's gone somewhere inside
herself. *I* think she's got herself in a trance."

"What in the world?"

"I called Dave Friedman—you remember him? The
psychiatrist I saw last year after the . . . accident?"

"That was no accident, Ariel Gold. It was murder, pure
and simple, and it near about wiped out my whole family—both of you—in one God-almighty blast."

"Yes, well, at any rate, Dave's a hypnotherapist, so I
thought maybe he might . . . I called him. He's with her
now." Ariel could see the closed door to Laya's room from
the pay phone she was using. Dave had been in there
quite a while. She felt as if she were awaiting a verdict.
Was it good or bad when the jury stayed out too long?
"What if he can't get her back?" she worried aloud.

"Well, I'll get onto the eye doc. Sounds to me like you
need a different kind of medicine man for the other business. A shaman."

Dave Friedman's suggestion wasn't that far afield from
B.F.'s. "Guru," he said to Ariel a few minutes later after
confessing he'd struck out.

Ariel looked at the psychiatrist askance—and down; he
was a good two inches shorter than her five nine—but his
dark eyes were serious, and troubled. He smoothed the
crown of his head as if he still had hair there. The dense
crop of dark hairs on the back of his hand gave the momentary impression of a funky toupee. "You know, Ariel," he
said, "you're a challenging person to know. A woman with
no past who has a friend with no present. This is . . . if it's
a trance state, it's not one I can take her out of."

"But a *guru*?"

"She's a yogi, you said? Advanced? How advanced? If she's into self-induced trances and she's got any sense, she didn't normally meditate alone. She had somebody with her. A teacher. A guru."

"Well, I don't happen to have one on my Rolodex, do you? Wait a minute." Ariel sucked her lips in thought. "We need *her* teacher. I know where she goes to practice!"

It took detective work, but before the morning was over Vishnu Praviniji was on the phone. When he heard about Laya, he was on his way.

While she waited, Ariel called the *Open File* studio to apprise them of her whereabouts. Hers was a job that didn't entail regular hours, only killing hours. She'd been in a marathon lately. She didn't have a pager or cell phone with her, she told her assistant; she'd be calling in, but they shouldn't look for her until late afternoon, if then.

She hung up, mentally reorganizing her schedule. She prioritized with an ease born of more than a year of relearning her business from ground zero. Ground zero. That's exactly where she'd been when she first met Laya. It had been a week to the day after Ariel lost her memory.

Seven days before, she had awakened a stranger to herself. She'd had no recognition of the ransacked house in which she found herself or the menacing dog with which she shared it or the bruised, overweight woman she saw in the mirror. The woman named Ariel Gold was a void. The gun and filthy bloodied clothes that came with the name charged the void with sheer terror. Fighting the terror—often losing the battle—she'd set out to survive.

Ariel felt her stomach knot. It always did when she remembered the lonely desperation of those early days. She'd unraveled the basic facts of herself bit by hard-earned bit. She was stunned to discover that she was supposed to be a journalist, that she worked as a producer for a TV newsmagazine. She had no clue what a producer did. She felt even more cut off to learn that she was, apparently, a remote sort of woman, with no close friends to whom she could turn. She no longer had a husband. At thirty-one, she'd been a widow. She had no family in either direction: no children and no birth parents that she could find; even the adoptive parents who'd raised her were dead. She had good reason to believe that if she weren't careful, she would be, too.

Unsure whom to trust, she'd kept her mouth shut. Knowing nothing about her job or the story on which she'd been working, she faked it. Soaking up technical knowledge, watching and listening with a vengeance, she'd gone after the story as if her life depended on resolving it. In fact, it had. Laya had been one of her first interview subjects. Ariel remembered what the soft-spoken yogi had told her that day.

"I don't know what you think your reasons are for considering this case special, but I think you'll find there're other, much more telling reasons."

The focus of the story was Laya's friend and B.F.'s granddaughter, a woman named Jane McCaulay. Ariel had never met her and wouldn't have remembered it if she had; Jane had died precisely one week and one day before. The car bomb that killed her had been meant for Ariel. Her connection to Jane, she had eventually learned, didn't stop there.

"Ms. Gold?"

Lost in the past, Ariel didn't hear the man until he called her name a second time. He had to introduce himself before it sank in who he was. She'd half-expected a swami draped in bedsheets. She didn't know whether to be worried or relieved that Laya's teacher looked more like a lifter than a mystic. Muscles meshed sinuously under Vishnu Praviniji's black turtleneck. His hips were

narrow in stylish black pleated pants. He was slim, well
defined rather than bulky, and probably in his midfifties,
but his ponytail was still coal black, as were his eyes. They
burned with concern.

"Laya is really blind?" he asked.

"They don't know the extent of the damage yet," Ariel
said, trying to read those dark eyes, to reassure herself that
what she saw was concern and not something else
entirely, like weird. She was way over her head, and
maybe way out of line. What was she getting herself into
here? What was she getting Laya into here? "It would help
considerably if she could communicate."

"Tell me again," he said, "what's happened."

Ariel ran through what little she knew, including the
doctor's plans for neurological testing. "How long,"
Praviniji asked, "has she been in this state?"

"All I can tell you is that she called me shortly after four
this morning, and I got to her apartment no more than,
maybe, twelve minutes later. By then she was . . ." Ariel
made a vague gesture toward her head. "Listen, Mr.
Praviniji, could I be wrong? Is Laya *capable* of meditating
herself into a trance?"

"Even neophytes are capable of freeing their minds and
traveling deep within themselves, and Laya is not a neo-
phyte. What you describe, however, is beyond what I
would have said she could achieve. It's a state that, under
any but the most extraordinary circumstances, she would
never have attempted while alone."

"It's dangerous, then? I mean, where *is* she?"

"Perhaps . . . beyond pain. Where the self ceases to
exist. From where," he muttered more or less to himself,
"she may not wish to come back."

"What is that supposed—"

"Please take me to her," Praviniji said.

Ariel turned to point out Laya's room. Two white-jacketed men wheeling a gurney were about to open the door.

"Excuse me." Praviniji held up a hand to the nurses or technicians or whatever they were, and without any apparent doubt that they would do as he asked, he said, "You must wait, please." He strode into the room, leaving the two men looking at the door closing behind him, and then at each other.

If Ariel thought bringing in a patient with less than the usual quota of names shorted out the system, she quickly learned that bringing in an "alternative expert" was trickier still.

She tried to distract the gurney pushers to little avail. "Please," she begged quietly, hoping they weren't disturbing whatever procedure or ritual might be going on behind that door, trying not to think what the consequences would be if she'd brought a crackpot into the mix, "could you give him a minute? He's a friend of the patient. He might be able to help. Okay?"

One of the men gave her a narrow-eyed look. "I know you. You're on one of those TV tabloids." His head swiveled in a one-eighty, looking, Ariel guessed, for cameras. His partner was already backing away, heading, she was sure, to alert security.

"It is not a tabloid," she said firmly, "and I'm off duty. Do you think I'd go on camera looking like this?" She smiled the professional smile she'd secretly practiced in front of the mirror—inviting confidence (and confidences), and unflappable. "The patient," she said, "is my friend and the gentleman's. He's seen her through, let's say, somewhat similar episodes. It's possible he can save you work. You don't have a problem with that, do you?"

"'The patient,'" said the same narrow-eyed man, "is due downstairs. We're here to take her. We've got a schedule."

"You can't wait a minute? Listen, why don't you fetch a

doctor and I'll talk to him or her." (And say what? Ariel wondered.)

Fortunately, she was spared the challenge. The door opened, and Praviniji stood in it. Ariel's eyes darted from his expression, unrevealing, to Laya in the bed behind him. Her face was upturned. She looked as if she were staring at the ceiling, which would have been quite a feat, given the small plastic tubes dripping saline solution into her eyes. Her hands were on her chest, dark against the stark white of the bedcovers. Praviniji, Ariel gathered, had been successful in bringing their friend back from "beyond pain," for the hands were balled into tight fists. Ariel wondered whether Laya would thank Praviniji—or her.

4

ARIEL'S GRANDFATHER DELIVERED. WITH THE ARRIVAL OF B.F.'S "top man," Ariel sagged with relief. The marines had landed! The new doctor's presence had a different effect on Chaney, the resident ophthalmologist who'd been on the case since dawn. His nose, it seemed to Ariel, proceeded to get seriously out of joint. His posture got straighter and straighter. He strummed with tension. If you could have bowed him, you could have shot an arrow from his armpit. Within the hour Ariel didn't blame the younger, now redundant doctor.

Dr. Brian M. Crowne (board-certified eye physician, subspecialty corneal diseases and surgery, diplomate American Board of Ophthalmology, fellow American Academy of Ophthalmology) was a pompous ass. He'd shown up at the hospital so promptly Ariel had to wonder if he'd been in B.F.'s pocket—or hoped to be. He patronized Chaney. He brushed aside Ariel's questions as if they were fruit flies swarming over his breakfast banana. He interrogated Laya. He had the bedside manner of a czar.

"I can get a contract out on him," Ariel grimly joked when she happened to find herself alone with Chaney. "Say the word."

"Tempting," said the worn-out, worn down resident. He slumped. "Who is that lady, anyway, that she rates Crowne?"

"'Rates'?"

"Brian Crowne's a genius. He hasn't practiced in three years. He's into research. He lectures. He writes. He accepts honors and awards by the wheelbarrow load. I'd guess he's attended more banquets in his honor in the last year than any ten *mortal* physicians will in their lifetimes, and he probably owns more tuxes than I do undershorts. And since he's dispatched me on an errand . . ." Chaney snapped to, saluted, and walked away, disgruntled but, Ariel noticed, making time, his white coat flapping.

"Thank you, B.F.," Ariel murmured, speculating about what her grandfather's bait had been. She sank onto the nearest hard bench and closed her eyes, just to rest them for a second. She must actually have slipped into a light doze, for she nearly jumped out of her skin when from directly above her came, "Damn it! Couldn't you at least have said which floor you'd be on?"

"Henry?" Ariel blinked. "What are you doing here?"

Henry Heller towered over her, breathing hard and glowering. "What am *I* doing here? I've looked all over this hospital for you!" He plunked down beside her, searching her face with his eyes and then with a tentative hand. "I called the studio. They said you were here but you hadn't said why. Ariel, what's wrong? Were you in an accident or something?"

His arrival, Ariel realized, was even more of a relief than that of the eminent Dr. Crowne.

When she'd been an *Open File* producer, Henry had been her boss. When she'd gone on the air as a correspondent, he'd become her colleague. He remained her friend. He'd once been more, and if it were up to Henry, would be still. A month before, unwilling or unable to stand their daily proximity, he'd left the show, accepting the editorship of a new magazine called *Newsfront*. The first issue was due out soon, and Henry was in meetings night and day, traveling, interviewing, hiring, and, basically, busting his hump. He was happy enough, Ariel felt, to get back to his print media roots; he was reveling, she was pretty sure, in being top dog.

She hadn't seen him in two weeks. His brown eyes looked even more deeply set than usual, and his dark, neatly trimmed beard looked less dark—grayer. Was that possible in just two weeks? She'd missed him. "Is it raining?" she asked, reaching to touch damp blotches on his silly fedora. She'd missed him a lot.

"Let's get to the weather report later, okay? Now answer me! Are you—"

"I'm fine. It's not me."

"B.F.?" He took her hands. "Is it B.F.? What's happened?"

Ariel shook her head. "Laya," she said. Once again, she repeated the chain of events. The wake-up call. Laya's strange mental self-exile that for a while had been even more frightening than the injury. The parade of diverse specialists she'd spent the day roping in. The lack of a prognosis from any one of them so far. From one sentence to the next, Henry looked more horror-struck. "She can't see at all?" he croaked. "Good God! That poor woman. I can't think of anything worse!"

"I can," Ariel said. "If this wasn't an accident . . ." She looked beyond him to the open door of Laya's room.

Crowne hadn't brought her back from wherever he'd whisked her off to. "If somebody deliberately blinded her, he may decide not to stop there."

Henry frowned. "Did she say it wasn't an accident?"

"She's not talking. Not to me anyway."

They both turned when Dr. Chaney reappeared. "Crowne's on his way to speak to you," he told Ariel. "Also, the lab report's in. I just gave it to him, and he didn't say I couldn't tell you. It was something called hydrofluoric acid."

Ariel licked suddenly dry lips. "What, exactly, is that?"

"I'm not a chemist, but I'm told it's an aqueous solution of hydrogen fluoride."

That didn't sound too bad. "That sounds," Ariel said hopefully, "almost benign."

"Well . . ." Chaney was already visibly regretting his impulse to be first with the news.

"What?" Henry said. He stuck out his hand. "Henry Heller, Ariel's and Laya's friend, Dr. . . . ?"

"Chaney."

"'Well' what, Dr. Chaney?"

"Let's put it this way. Even the vapor's dangerous. You get the stuff on your skin, it can cause severe burns. Deep ulcerations. You ingest it, it can be fatal. It was in the eye-drops."

Ariel's hands flew to cover her mouth. Silently, they all took a minute to digest the unthinkable implications.

"That's why there's little disfiguration beyond the lids," Chaney added. "If it had been thrown at her eyes . . . That's the way that kind of thing's usually done, then—"

"Good God!" Henry said.

"Yeah," Chaney agreed. "A pH-one concentration. Highly corrosive."

"How highly corrosive?" Henry pressed.

"They told me in the lab . . ." He glanced at Ariel and

then back to Henry. "One of the main things the stuff's used for is to etch glass."

"You think that Crowne character's got a case of multiple personality?" Henry asked Ariel. "Did you notice the way he kept referring to himself as 'we'?"

"Hmm?" Ariel asked, dropping pasta into boiling water, scratching Jessie's ear absentmindedly, not listening.

Henry didn't care a fig about the good doctor's quirks. He was trying to distract Ariel. He'd insisted on following her, to Laya's place to see to the cat, and then home. He'd invited himself in. He'd asked if he could buy her dinner.

"Dinner's fine," Ariel had said. "I don't want to go out, though. I'll fix something." That was just about the last thing she had said. Henry had entertained himself with the dog while she spent ten minutes in a shower so hot her fair skin was still pink. Her short, light-streaked hair was damp, but (credit an expensive cut) already it was curving into the style becoming familiar to TV audiences. She was wearing a sage-colored terry cloth robe and, behind the oversized tortoiseshell glasses that kept sliding down her nose, her eyes picked up the green. They were distant. She was being entirely too quiet.

"This farm table's new, isn't it?" Henry asked, making conversation. "And these chairs? Antiques, are they?" And built for nineteenth-century midgets, he thought, shifting his long legs in an effort to get comfortable. The chair creaked threateningly.

Ariel was stirring a ragout she'd defrosted in the microwave. It had started as a frozen brick, obviously homemade. It was drawing Henry's saliva embarrassingly. "Well, I'll tell you one thing," she suddenly blurted, apparently continuing a conversation she'd been carrying on with herself. "'What is essential is invisible to the eye.'"

Henry had been reaching to pet Jessie, who'd despaired of attention from her mistress. The shepherd, Henry could have sworn, gave Ariel a look as blank as his own. "Excuse me?" he asked.

"Laya's got the most important kind of vision," Ariel said. "Inner vision. If the worst happens, if this does turn out to be a permanent thing, then she'll learn how to live with it."

Dr. Crowne's diagnosis had been couched as if he were delivering stone tablets from the mount, but it was no more heartening than that of the ER doctor.

There was "a possibility" that Laya might regain some degree of sight in the left eye. "We" would wait until the acute inflammation quieted down, and "we" would see to what extent the cornea might heal and stabilize. "The eye," Crowne had comforted, "has amazing regenerative powers."

Even that poor comfort couldn't be offered in regard to the right eye.

Ariel rescued the pasta just before the water boiled over the top of the pot. "No, really!" she assured Henry as if he'd disagreed with her pronouncement about Laya's resilience. "If anybody could conquer blindness, it's Laya. She's got incredible strength. Patience, too. Endless patience. She—"

"May be fine," Henry said. "You're getting ahead of yourself."

"She may not be fine. I'm trying to be realistic."

"Sounds more like negativism to me."

"Then you're not listening. I'm saying that I don't know a more balanced person. She'll deal with whatever happens."

"I hope you're right. Remember while you're deciding what she will and won't do, though, it's not your eyes, or your life."

Ariel had asked if she could see Laya before they'd left the hospital. No, she'd been told. The patient had been firm in her wish to be left alone.

It was one thing, Crowne had explained, when loss of vision was gradual. The victim of disease, retinitis pigmentosa, for example, or diabetic retinopathy, had months or years to adjust. To grieve. "Your friend," he'd said, "needs time." Then, with a surprising depth of feeling, he said, "Imagine it! To lose your sight in minutes. In agony. Mystified by what's happening to you. And then to learn that you're the victim of some psychopathic stranger. I've never had a case like this! Meaningless, random evil." His mouth turned down in disgust. "Sick bastard," he muttered in what Ariel imagined was a totally uncharacteristic loss of control.

"The scratches on her face?" Ariel had asked. "How did—"

"She has no memory of how she came to have them. We assume they were self-inflicted. Sheer mindless panic. The pain had to be excruciating."

Henry had scowled along with Crowne, but he looked more queasy than angry. "See, that's what I don't get," he muttered. "That stuff had to burn like fire! So, after she'd put the drops into the one eye, why in hell would she do it to the other one?"

"God only knows." Crowne had looked aggrieved not to be taken into the Almighty's confidence. "If you're adept at applying drops, we're talking about a matter of two seconds. Still . . ."

"I can answer that, actually," Chaney put in. "They said in the lab that hydrogen fluoride is 'calcium-seeking.' It goes to the bones. One of the things that makes it so dangerous is you don't necessarily know right away you've been injured. You may not immediately feel the pain. It can come later."

"She'll need counseling," Crowne had said. "We have access to the best people. Shall we arrange it?"

It had been nearly seven o'clock when Henry and Ariel left the hospital. The worst moment, in a way, came then. What they saw when they walked out was a fairy-tale sky. Despite the fact that it was raining, the sun decided to put in one last-minute appearance, just to prove it could. It burst, triumphant, from behind towering rose-lit clouds. The rain shimmered with sunlight. And then Ariel saw the rainbow: a perfect prismatic arc as clearly delineated as a child's drawing.

"Oh!" she gasped, and the sky blurred into fragmented brilliance through her sudden tears.

Henry dropped his arm across her shoulders. He knew exactly what she was thinking.

"One more beautiful thing she's missing," Ariel whispered. "Like a reminder. It's cruel."

"It's refracted light. Don't take it personally. It's right there for anybody who happens to look up."

"Anybody who can see," Ariel said miserably.

5

LOCAL AND FEDERAL AUTHORITIES HAD, OF COURSE, BEEN NOTI-fied about the doctored eyedrops. They were, as Ariel had noticed, a generic brand, marketed by a California chain. The alert went out to every hospital emergency room in the state. No similar injuries had been reported. Within hours the unfortunate company had recalled their stock and issued a public warning. Random testing of all brands was begun. No further tampering had thus far been dis-covered. Time might tell a different story but as of now, mercifully, Laya's tragedy appeared to be an isolated incident.

While the FDA did their job, the local law did theirs: treating the single known victim as a deliberate target.

At Ariel's request, Max Neely wangled himself onto the case. Widower, soon-to-be newlywed and stepfather to a teenaged daughter, LAPD detective lieutenant, Max was Ariel's professional friend from way back, from before she could remember; he was also one of the handful of people who knew how short her memory span was.

"Very buttoned up, your one-named friend," Max told Ariel when he dropped by her office after questioning Laya. He plopped his sizable self into a chair, propped his ankle onto his thigh, and began to jiggle his foot. Max ran on some kind of personal amped current that when short circuited, Ariel fancied, surged into his crinkly red hair, which looked slightly sizzled. "Tough interview," he said. "Half the time she acted like we weren't there."

"I hope you made use of your sensitivity training," Ariel said.

"I was a lamb. What's with that name business?"

"She can't call herself what she wants to?"

"Actually, she can. She changed it legally. I asked."

"Tell me about the interview."

"I probably won't be telling you anything you don't already know. I assume you've visited your—"

"Don't assume."

"Okay." Max's foot abruptly paused in its jiggling, as if it might want to kick that remark around a little. "But she is a buddy of yours, right? How well do you know her?"

"She's my teacher. I told you that. We have lunch sometimes after class. She's been to my house for dinner parties. We went to a weekend yoga retreat together. Why do you ask?"

"Why do you think? Because I need to know more

about her, and about her friends and associates. Enemies, too, if she has them."

"I can't imagine that. Laya's kind of . . . unworldly. Maybe even otherworldly at times."

"*Other*worldly? As in weird?"

"As in spiritual. Self-realization. *Ch'i.* Unity with the divine Being."

"Uh-huh." Max's expression made his opinion on those matters abundantly clear. "Any chance she could have 'united' with somebody a few bubbles out of plumb?"

"In L.A.?" Ariel snorted. "But I doubt it. Laya's sensible."

"In this world or the other one she visits?"

"She's not a kook, Max. She didn't spring from some Himalayan mountaintop. I mean, she *is* a Westerner. The thing that attracted me to yoga is the way she teaches it. Demystified. She makes it accessible. She even makes it fun."

"Yeah, well, somebody got his jollies by blinding her. Just maybe, blinding *her* on purpose. So, come on . . . friends? Enemies?"

"I know some of my classmates, but beyond that . . ."

"You're not much use, are you, Gold? How come she called *you*, anyway? How *did* she call you for that matter? She couldn't see."

"I don't know. The truth is, there's a lot I don't know about Laya; I mean about her actual life."

"Her 'actual' life? As opposed to what?"

"I'm talking about her family, Max. Her background. Her romantic relationships if she has any. I don't know how to explain it. I feel a closeness with her. I know her goodness, her calmness. I know her, but I don't know *about* her."

"My."

"Yes, well . . ." Ariel said, embarrassed and irritated at herself for being embarrassed. There was no way she'd try to explain that Laya was an old soul; that people drew from her strength. Friendship with Laya bypassed the extraneous. You didn't talk about promotions or clothes or taxes. At that moment Ariel couldn't put her finger on what they'd talked about. Breakthroughs. An *asana*, a posture, that you'd never gotten before. Feelings that came out of practice. It occurred to her that her friendship with Laya might be a bit selfish.

"I met her," she said, "when we were doing the story on Jane's murder. The two of them had a simpatico relationship. Scoff if you want to, but Laya knew before I did, before anybody did, about Jane and me. It was as if she sensed it."

"Ariel, big damn deal. You and Jane were identical twins."

"Who looked as much alike at that point as Laurel and Hardy."

"Yeah? Well, this Laya was just about the only person 'at that point' who'd been in contact with both of you, and we're talking surface differences."

"Thirty-five pounds is a lot of surface."

Max laughed. "You were a mite chunky."

"I was a mole, burrowed into flab, and you know it. 'Kind of a mutt,' I believe, is how you once delicately described me."

"I said that?" Max was tickled. "I do have a way with words."

"A mutt whose idea of makeup was Chap Stick. A mutt hiding behind oversized clothes and glasses so ugly they should've come with a mustache and fake nose."

"Yes, but—"

"And Jane was a model. Not *super* status maybe, but a—"

"Okay! But you spruced up. Once you worked your way out from under the camouflage and hit the beauty parlor and so on—"

"'Beauty parlor'? Quaint."

"Whatever. Point is, except for the odd feature, like for example your nose, which *is* fake, matter of fact—"

"It is not."

"It ain't the one you came equipped with. My point, except for the fixed schnoz—which, by the way, I have never understood—you and your sis looked enough alike that anybody who knew you both could see the resemblance. B.F. recognized you, didn't he? On some kind of gut level? And he didn't even know you existed!"

"He recognized an affinity. He did not recognize me as his granddaughter." Ariel gave Max a hard look. "Why are you making such an issue of this? Does the possibility that some people might have the ability to sense things you and I don't scare you?"

"Scare me? I'd pay money for it. Tell me where I sign up!"

"Bull."

"My sentiments exactly, about that whole subject. You're lying if you tell me nobody's ever mistaken you for your sister."

Ariel couldn't deny that it had happened. Jane had been slimmer, rail thin. She'd had a deep chin cleft, souvenir of a childhood accident. Ariel's hair was cut differently and colored lighter. And there was the nose thing. Still, she had been mistaken for her sister by people who hadn't heard about Jane's death.

There had been the teenage girl who accused Ariel of being "stuck up" when she wouldn't share modeling makeup tips. And the seriously inebriated man she'd met at a reception who claimed he had a *Playboy* issue in which she'd posed nude. (Her grandfather had howled about that one when she'd told him. He didn't find it as amusing when a wild-eyed fan who *had* heard Jane was dead insisted that Ariel was her ghost.)

"Well?" Max prodded.

"Yes, okay," Ariel admitted, "it's happened once or twice, but back when Laya and I met, I looked entirely—"

"Bowwow, right." Max's fingers, which had been splayed on his thighs, tapping out some rhythm heard only to him, suddenly shot to Ariel's desk and a small framed photo there. Angling it for a better view, he asked, "Who's this?"

"My mother. B.F. gave it to me."

"She died when you girls were born, right?"

Ariel resisted the urge to turn the photo back the way it had been.

"Hey," Max said, "did you ever find out any more about how you and Jane got separated?"

"What's to know? Our father was a flake, a flower child, above such petty concerns as proper medical care for his wife, and birth certificates, and . . . responsibility. Child Welfare got hold of me, and I ended up Baby Doe. They didn't get Jane, and she ended up with B.F." Ariel shrugged off the explanation. In fact, she fantasized about might-have-beens. If there were any way to learn the particulars, she'd have them. If there were any way to change them, to have one day, one hour, with the twin she'd last seen as an infant and would never see again, she'd turn the world upside down to do it. "How'd we get off on this? We were talking about—"

"You could hire somebody to look into it, you know."

"Max, research is what I do for a living. You think I haven't 'looked into it'?"

"What about your parents' hippie pals? Couldn't you—"

"The commune scattered. The only one I could track is *off* her track. *How* we got separated is a moot issue. What I really want to know is *why*, but I don't have a pipeline to cosmic rationale."

"Gosh, maybe your psychic buddy Laya does!" Max said slyly. "How come you don't ask her?"

Ariel gave her watch a meaningful glance. "How come you don't just tell me about your interview with her?"

"The interview, right. Okay, we've got some possibilities. Tenuous but interesting."

The drops, he told Ariel, had been purchased near Laya's home, a grocery-pharmacy chain store where she was well known, the purchase made earlier the same night on which she'd used the drops for the first and only time. "And—here's where it gets interesting—the bottle, bagged along with her other purchases, was left unattended. We're talking a good ten-minute window of opportunity."

Laya, it seems, had finished her shopping and returned to her car, only to find her keys missing. She'd gone back into the store to find them, leaving the bags in a cart beside her locked car.

"Can you believe that?" Max asked Ariel. "Where's she been living? Happyland? It's a wonder she didn't find an empty cart when she got back."

"Yeah," Ariel said softly, "too bad for Laya that nobody ran off with her purchases."

Max's beefy shoulders hunched, and his redhead's complexion grew ruddier. "I guess," he said, and cleared his throat, "she figured she'd be in and out in a flash, but the keys weren't at the checkout counter and they hadn't been turned in, so she retraced her steps. She stopped for a kibitz with a clerk she knows. Guy's daughter'd had a baby or something. Point is—and this is point one—somebody did have plenty of time to empty the little bottle and do the dirty deed."

"That," Ariel objected, "makes no sense whatsoever. This monster happened to be hanging around the parking lot with hydrofluoric acid? I mean, who's ever even *heard* of hydrofluoric acid? But he was hanging around with it? Just in case Laya went shopping that night? Just on the off chance he might have access to eyedrops she happened to buy? That's the craziest thing I ever heard."

"Well, putting acid into eyedrops isn't the picture of rosy mental health, is it? Listen, the reason we're looking at your friend as a deliberate target is because she's the only victim. The kind of nut that poisons consumer products, see, doesn't tend to stop at one. Any rate, we have to eliminate every possibility, and since it appears it was at least *possible* the drops were doctored that night, we check it out."

"Go on."

"Point two. During our search of the parking lot—in a Dumpster buried under a bunch of stinking rotten produce to be precise—we recovered an empty bottle that formerly contained a handy concoction no home should be without. Zap-O, the stuff's called. It eats rust off porcelain or metal or whatever. It'll also eat your skin if you're clumsy using it. Bottle has more warnings than a petroleum tanker, and you can buy it in your neighborhood grocery or hardware. It ain't tough to come by. Three guesses what the main ingredient is."

"Hydrofluoric—"

"In one. Lab's checking if the chemical in the eyedrops bottle is this rust eater, which, according to the price sticker, came from the store where the victim shopped. If it was sold that night, like during the same period she was doing her shopping, then nobody was 'just hanging around' with it."

"So the acid was readily available, but still . . ."

"You can buy it in shops where they work with glass. Pro-Etch, the brand I bought's called. You can even get it in one strength or another from craft shops. You can—"

"Okay, okay, you're now the reigning authority on

hydrofluoric acid availability, but still . . ." Ariel swiveled in her chair, considering. "Eyedrop bottles have awfully tiny holes. How'd this person get the acid into the bottle?"

Max's chuckle was smug. "I am also now an authority on eyedrop bottles. The little pointy top pops right off; no tools required. You know how long it took to empty the contents and squirt in Zap-O? Eighteen seconds. Three to empty, fifteen to fill."

"And this Zap-O . . . it was bought at the same store?"

"Yes, ma'am. We're getting the store's register records. See if we can pin down the purchase time."

"And," Ariel thought aloud, beginning to get excited despite her reservations, "maybe a credit card or ATM reference. Or maybe he paid by check. They'd still have a check, or the bank would!"

"Dream on. I'm not saying a perpetrator would be too smart to leave that kind of trail, you understand. Had a guy a couple of months ago that pulled a bank heist and then took a cab straight home. Cabbie took him to the address and then called us." Max chuckled again. "Bozo asked us how we found him so quick."

"Is there a point three?"

"We don't know," Max went on, not to be rushed, "that the Zap-O was actually *purchased*. A person who'll put acid in eyedrops might not be all that particular about shoplifting.

"Now, point three. The victim had a talk with the store pharmacist about drops, 'artificial tears,' as he calls them. She'd been going through them pretty good lately, he told us she said. She'd heard that constant use might not be so good for your eyes, and she wanted his opinion. They could've been overheard by the perpetrator. It might've given him the idea. But say not, say until he found the drops in the grocery bag his objective wasn't necessarily blindness, just meanness. Which brings up point . . . whatever.

"The acid would do a job if taken internally, too. If the victim bought juice or bottled water—refilled from one of those machines, say?—and *hadn't* bought drops, the creep could have had his fun causing severe internal injury. Or death."

Ariel exhaled. "Lord," she muttered. "'Evil is easy, and has infinite forms.'"

"Did you just make that up?"

"No. Max, . . . he couldn't know he'd have time to tamper with anything. He couldn't know she'd lose her keys."

"She didn't. They were in the cart basket all along. I get the idea that the lady is a bit, uh, lacking in street smarts."

"She's just not into possessions," Ariel protested, defending her friend; privately, she was thinking the behavior did sound ditsy. Laya wasn't. What had her so distracted? "Your theory is that Laya was being watched? Followed? Somebody took advantage of an opportunity—"

"What theory? I'm looking at facts and asking questions. She says nobody's got reason to be after her. She didn't notice anybody following her or acting suspicious around her. Woman that practically wears a sign saying 'Please steal from me,' though, that doesn't notice the seal on the eyedrop bottle's missing . . . ?"

"I wondered about that," Ariel said. "Did you ask why—"

"Sure. She still had a little left in her old bottle, and she just reached for the one nearest at hand. She assumed, she said, it was the old, already opened bottle. Obviously, she wasn't paying attention to what she was doing."

"It was four o'clock in the morning. She was probably half asleep." If she had been asleep, Ariel thought, wondering, not for the first time, what had her friend up before dawn.

"What I was saying is, I don't put much confidence in the lady's awareness level."

"That's not fair. That's not accurate. She is . . . usually, she's about the most—"

"She says she doesn't know anybody that's got a grudge against her? Says nobody's been following her? Woman could've had a Ku Klux Klan parade on her tail, and she wouldn't have noticed."

"You think this is a race thing?" Ariel asked incredulously.

"Not really. All I know is she couldn't have made it easier for a psycho every step of the way if she'd drawn up a plan."

"So you're thinking it is a crazy? I mean a random crazy as opposed to—"

"It's entirely possible—of course it is—that the creep that did this never laid eyes on the woman before that night. Could be she was just convenient for a sicky with a vicious idea and the chance to put it into action."

"Could it be somebody who works at the store? Or was fired by them? Somebody with a vendetta against the store instead of Laya?"

"Sure. We've got the personnel records. We're questioning everybody from the manager to the bag boys. Bag persons. The entire staff of the manufacturing firm's being questioned, too."

"But it could be somebody who wandered in off the street."

"Sure. That's what makes this job such a delightful and never-ending challenge. We got no suspect. We got no motive. We got a case like I've never seen before. Acid in eyedrops? Who goes to the considerable trouble to do that? And why? If somebody wanted to hurt your friend, there's lots more direct ways to do it, ways like I deal with every day. If somebody wanted acid in her eyes, why not do it the old-fashioned way? Throw it in."

"Because if he approached her directly," Ariel supposed aloud, "she'd recognize him?"

"Gold, I'll be frank. My personal opinion? I don't think your buddy *was* targeted. And I don't think the drops were doctored that night. I think she was just the unlucky customer who happened to take that particular bottle off the shelf." Max sighed. "You ever hear of the Tylenol killer? Laced pills with cyanide? Seven people died. They were the first victims of product tampering, did you know that? It wasn't twenty years ago. The phrase wasn't even part of the language yet. Did you know the killer was never caught?"

"Yes, and I also know *faked* tampering's been used as a cover. If Laya *was* targeted, she's vulnerable. She needs—"

"Protection, and she's got it, at least for now. We put somebody on her door." Max got to his feet. "By the way," he said. "you happen to notice the date?"

"The date?"

"Day before yesterday. When this happened."

Ariel flipped open her desk diary. Wordlessly, she looked up. Max's expression was bleak. "Yeah," he said. "April first."

6

THE COUNSELOR DR. BRIAN CROWNE SUGGESTED WAS A PSY-chologist, a woman with her own successful private practice. Ariel thought the choice was a smart one. She was even more impressed with Crowne's astuteness when she learned that Dr. Sarah Aguilar was blind.

Laya, evidently, was unimpressed. Neither the day after her admittance nor the day after that would she consent to a visit. The NO VISITORS sign was democratic; it applied to everyone, including the psychologist. It applied to family, a sister in New York who was not to be called. It applied to Bishnu Praviniji, Laya's teacher of eight years. It applied to Ariel.

She went by before and after work the first day. After talking with Max the second day, she managed to squeeze in a visit. She might as well have saved herself the trouble; the only visiting she did was with the policeman posted outside Laya's door.

While they were discussing such items of burning interest as the weather, a nurse Ariel had talked to before, a big gravel-voiced woman named Dinah, stopped to let him check out a bouquet of flowers. "Frisk 'em," she said. They'd been dropped off, she reported, by a student of Laya's. "Told me she picked out flowers that smelled good," Dinah said, "since the patient, quote, 'you know . . . can't see them.'"

Ariel turned to see a plumpish young black woman, hardly more than a teenager, waiting to board the elevator. A man her age or a little older waited, too; perhaps with her, perhaps only at the same time. He looked pressed for time, as if he had an important engagement elsewhere. "Thoughtful," Ariel said. "What's her name?"

"Just said the flowers were from 'the class.' I think . . . " The nurse made an apologetic face. "Maybe she's a little slow?"

That would be like Laya, Ariel thought: to coax the developmentally disabled into her class. "Is that fellow with her?"

"Who?" Dinah turned to look, but the two had stepped into the elevator. A last passenger hurried aboard, and the doors closed.

"Have there been other people coming by?" Ariel asked.

"Just calls, asking about her condition." Dinah inclined her head toward the guard. "I turn 'em over to the coppers."

Ariel stood aside while she took the flowers in to Laya. "Any of the calls interesting?" she asked the guard.

"All kosher," he said, "except for one guy. Shy type. When I asked his name, he hung up."

"What did he say?" Ariel asked.

"Just asked how she was. I said coming along. He said, did that mean she'd be able to see again? I said who was calling, please. End of conversation."

Ariel wasn't especially impressed by the detective work. There should be a caller ID setup. The girl who'd just left should have been questioned; the man with her, too—if he had, in fact, been with her. She swallowed criticism. She'd been surprised, frankly, that the police were providing round-the-clock protection for Laya. And who was she to judge? It wasn't as if *she* were being of any help. Except for having arranged for one of Laya's neighbors to look after Arthur, the cat, she felt utterly useless. She also felt a little hurt at being shut out, although she wouldn't admit it even to herself; it was too selfish a reaction to own up to.

That same day she made an appointment with Dr. Sarah Aguilar.

Ariel didn't know exactly what she wanted from the psychologist. Magic words? A course of action? To be told to butt out? She offered her hand before it occurred to her that the other woman couldn't see it. She was surprised when, without any noticeable hesitation or groping through the air, her hand was firmly grasped.

Dr. Aguilar gestured toward a chair opposite her desk, which might just have been delivered, so bare was it of typical desktop clutter. When she'd seated herself, she touched the face of her wristwatch and then clicked the crystal shut. The meter, Ariel gathered, was running. She used a few cents' worth of her fifty minutes to study the psychologist.

Sarah Aguilar was a short woman in her forties. She wore her dark hair in a no-fuss cut that took advantage of natural curl. Her face was plain but pleasant, the best feature an aquiline nose. On it rested opaque glasses. Ariel had the spooky notion that from behind them she was being observed in return. It was disconcerting. She crossed her legs and shifted position. Dr. Aguilar's face followed: a minute adjustment like that of a motion sensor.

The doctor broke the ice. "I understand," she said, "that it was you whom Laya . . . " She paused and inclined her head questioningly. "Laya? Am I pronouncing it correctly?"

"Long A, actually," Ariel said. "As in *day*."

"Pretty. And she uses no last name? Interesting."

Ariel wondered if that was 'interesting' as in psychologically significant. "Unusual but legal," Ariel said.

"It was you whom Laya called for help?"

"Yes."

"That must have been a frightening experience."

Ariel started to nod, caught herself, and, again, said "Yes."

"And she's refused to let you visit with her since, I'm told. How do you feel about that?"

"Sad. Concerned." Ariel smiled ruefully. "Relieved. I don't know what I'm going to say to her when—if—she does let me in." The smile fell. "Why won't she, do you think? And you . . . ," she said, opening her hands, becoming conscious in that moment of the extent to which she used her hands and facial expressions to communicate. "Even if her friends are too much for her now, why won't she at least let you in to see . . . uh, to see her?"

"Ah! The big 'see'?" Dr. Aguilar said, reading Ariel's discomfort. "Don't get hung up on that. You start trying to edit every reference to sight when you do talk to your friend, it's going to make for awkward conversation. It's natural to say, 'don't look now' or 'see what I mean' or 'want to watch TV?' We visually impaired are willing to cut you sighted folks slack."

"Okay," Ariel said. "What else?"

"What else what?"

"What else can I say without doing more harm than good? That's really what I'm here to ask. How can I help her get through this?"

Dr. Aguilar's eyebrows rose above the dark glasses and dropped again as she considered her answer. Then, rapid-fire, she went through what sounded like a catechism. "If she looks like she needs help, offer; don't push. Identify yourself when you enter the room. Let her know when you're leaving. Give clear directions. If you leave her alone someplace unfamiliar, make sure there's something nearby she can touch to orient herself; empty space can be frightening. Don't rearrange things. Don't leave doors half open. I've seen your show." She smiled. "You've got plenty of common sense. Use it. Treat her like a normal person, not a freak and not as if she's helpless. Let her know you care. Don't show pity. Listen when she's ready to talk."

"When do you think that'll be?"

"I don't know. How independent a person is she?"

"Very. Very strong in herself. Laya's a giver. I hadn't thought about it until this happened, but I've never known her to ask for anything. She's amazing. She's—"

"Human, Ms. Gold. She has human frailties, and if they're ever going to manifest themselves, it'll be now. You want to be patient, and you want to be careful not to foist your own expectations onto her. Being considered the strong one can be a burden."

"You mean 'If you are brave too often, people will come to expect it of you'?"

"Something like that." Dr. Aguilar sighed. "I'm sorry your friend isn't ready to talk, but it's early days. You know about grief stages?"

"Some. Shock and denial, anger, bargaining, depression . . . "

"And acceptance, yes. Some contend there are three stages, some four; the most popular theory currently, Kübler-Ross's, puts it at five. Laya can't even get started with the process because she's still got legitimate hope. She might regain some sight in one eye. If not, since the optic nerve and retina are healthy, there's still the option of a graft. Meantime, everything's on hold. Waiting's tough.

"Plus, she's got fear to deal with. Someone deliberately tried to blind her. If that person's unknown to Laya and bears her, as an individual, no ill will, it makes the situation even more frightening in a way. There's no way to exert control, no way to protect oneself against mindless, pointless ill fortune. There may be no resolution, either, and if that should . . . "

At that moment there came an audible growl-like murmur. Ariel was certain that it came from the other side of the desk. She thought that perhaps the psychologist had skipped lunch. Instead of ignoring the embarrassing noise, though, or apologizing, Dr. Aguilar said, "Willy, quiet. Nobody's talking to you."

Willy? Ariel didn't know what to do. Did the woman think someone else had come into the room? She glanced behind her to make sure she hadn't missed something herself. "Dr. Aguilar," she said, "there's nobody here but me."

What she heard next was, unmistakably, a yawn. It ended in a satisfied squeak and a jingle of metal on metal

familiar to Ariel. Sarah Aguilar laughed. "Willy," she said,
"would disagree with you." She rolled her chair slightly
to the side and reached down.

Ariel peered over the desk. Lying peaceably at the doctor's feet, enjoying a scratch behind the ears, was a black
German shepherd as large as Ariel's own dog. He wore a
leather harness.

"Meet Willy," said the doctor. "My eyes and my best
friend."

7

DR. AGUILAR'S TIPS ON HOW TO INTERACT WITH A BLIND PER-
son went untested. Ariel gave up going to the hospital,
which accomplished nothing more productive than reliev-
ing the guard's boredom. Over the weekend the closest
she got to her friend was the nurses' station telephone, via
which she got daily status reports from Dinah, the big,
good-natured nurse who, Ariel thought, would be right at
home slinging hash under a blinking E-A-T-S sign. ("She's
a quiet one, your bud! I keep taking her pulse, thinking
maybe she's passed over on us.") The reports didn't take
long, same-old same-old being their essence. On Tuesday
morning Dinah didn't crack any jokes; she suggested that
Ariel call Dr. Crowne.

Ariel fervently hoped he'd be gentler with Laya than he
was with her. "We're starting to get a leak of aqueous
fluid," Crowne told Ariel bluntly. Which meant what?
Ariel wanted to know. "We've given notice for donor tissue," Crowne said, "for a graft."

"A graft," Ariel repeated dumbly. "A transplant, you
mean."

"As soon as tissue's available. We'll be telling the patient this afternoon. Dr. Aguilar will be present."

Ariel felt as if she were reeling. She could hardly imagine how Laya would feel. "What are the chances it'll take?" she asked. "And when will you know if it has?"

Crowne, perhaps inadvertently, answered only the second question. "Possibly quickly. Within weeks perhaps, even days."

"I'll drop by the hospital after work," Ariel said.

She was still replaying the conversation in her mind when she looked up to see Tara Castanara trying to get her attention.

The buxom young woman had been Henry Heller's rather dilettantish assistant, quick-witted but equally quick to react to quitting time. She was far more interested, Ariel had always thought, in the length of her skirt, the state of her nails, and the color, or colors, of her quick-change hairstyles than in the news business. Consequently, Ariel hadn't been surprised when, on Henry's resignation, Tara had turned down an offer to work for the new supervising producer. She *had* been surprised when Tara finagled the creation of a new position, that of special assistant to Ariel. Ariel hadn't thought the woman especially liked her. She'd been skeptical about Tara's work ethic. In one month she'd come to wonder how she'd ever functioned without her.

"What?" she asked Tara.

"Valente's on the way down here!"

Chris Valente, executive producer of *The Open File* and Ariel's immediate superior, was like most of the show's executives, producers, and on-camera talent in that he appeared and disappeared on a schedule as erratic as El Niño weather. Story meetings were more likely to be conducted during a hallway encounter or from a cell phone in a courthouse washroom than in the studio conference room. The last time Ariel had actually seen Valente in person was when they chanced to pass each other in the airport.

"So?" she asked.

Tara's blue eyes had gone comically round with significance. (Her current do was a tightly curled red-blond fluff; the likeness to Little Orphan Annie might or might not have been contrived.) "So I hear he looks like he's suffering from gastric reflux," said Tara. "You know what that means!"

Ariel was flipping through the mail Tara had dropped on her desk. After her conversation with Crowne, she felt queasy herself, and in no mood for gossip. "I have no idea what it means."

"It means he's happy. Haven't you ever noticed that?"

Among the correspondence already opened by Tara and answered over Ariel's signature, one envelope was still sealed. Ariel's name and the studio address were, unusually, handwritten. The script caught Ariel's eye. It was beautifully disciplined, evocative of an era when young people were drilled in the art of penmanship. Having a mind that hoarded irrelevancies and perversely blocked three decades of vital data, Ariel even knew what they'd called the style: the Palmer Method. It had long since dropped from scholastic curricula, so the writer (a woman, Ariel was perhaps prejudiced to decide) was no youngster. There was no return address.

"It says 'Personal and Confidential,'" Tara pointed out. "I don't think it's a letter bomb, but I didn't want to pry. You can open it."

"Thanks," said Ariel, who was already doing so.

"So, anyway," Tara went on with more excitement than was her laid-back wont, "if Valente looks *really* bilious, then he's giddy with joy, and that's gotta mean the award."

"Um," Ariel said. The handwritten letter filled one page. It was signed, simply, *Dorothy*.

"Award, Ariel!" Tara said impatiently. "Sigma Delta. Nondeadline Reporting. Voting was yesterday. You won, do you think?"

"Um," Ariel repeated. She didn't know anyone named Dorothy. Correction: she didn't remember knowing anyone named Dorothy.

"He's heading this way," Tara reported.

The wonder was that this kind of thing didn't happen more often. Hoping she'd missed something—a name, a place, any point of reference to give her a clue—Ariel scanned the baffling letter again. *"You did warn me."* And again. *"The evidence wasn't absolutely conclusive."*

"Bad news?" Tara asked.

Ariel shook her head. Had Henry been around, she'd have the letter in his hands by now, asking if it rang any bells. But Henry was gone, and Henry had been the only person at the studio who knew about her memory loss. The secrecy was often inconvenient; it was also, in Ariel's opinion, necessary.

Advertising her condition in the first frantic days hadn't struck her as bright. Her house had been broken into and ransacked. She'd found somebody's blood on her clothes, and it wasn't hers. Along with the clothes had been a weapon, loaded. Revealing her ignorance of the housebreaker's identity and the object of his search would be tantamount to handing *him* a loaded weapon.

Besides, she'd told herself then, whatever afflicted her was surely a momentary aberration: a short circuit that, if jiggled just right, would reconnect. At any second memories would come trickling or flooding back, filling in the holes, returning her to herself. Meantime, why expose herself as a freak whose mind had quit on her? Why suffer the inevitable pity and skepticism and curious stares?

Now that she was on the air, a publicly recognized figure vulnerable to every stranger with an agenda, discretion was no longer optional; it was imperative.

Tara was whispering, loudly, out of the corner of her mouth. Ariel looked up. "What?" she said. The woman was staring throught the glass walls of Ariel's office, wiggling her eyebrows. Now she was Orphan Annie imitating Groucho Marx. "He looks like he had jalapeños for breakfast and they're repeating on him!" she mouthed.

Ariel covered the letter with spread fingers just as Valente strode in, grasping her other hand and giving it a hearty power pump. "You did it!" he said. "Just got the call. Congratulations."

Ariel thanked him, noticing despite herself that Tara was right. Eyebrows drawn, forehead wrinkled, mouth turned up, Valente's expression was stuck between a smile and a burp. "Second time in the barrel," he crowed, patting the hand he still held, "and you come out clutching gold. Lucite, to be accurate, but it counts."

The story he was referring to had aired three months earlier. It came fully equipped: celebrities, mystery blown up over years of speculation, and—quintessentially *Open File*—sufficient resolution to satisfy the viewer yet leave him wondering. It was Ariel's second on-air appearance. She'd been nearly incapacitated by stage fright, swimming in flop sweat. Although no one knew it, she hadn't altogether dried out yet.

"What's that?" Valente asked, pointing, mildly curious.

"What?" Ariel bluffed. She shouldn't have tried to hide the letter; Valente was known for sharp eyes and a nose that twitched with a lively interest in anything and everything. That's why he was so good at what he did.

"Whatever that is you're trying to keep me from seeing."

He could also read upside down, from across a room, it

was rumored. Ariel glanced down to see the word *murdered* peeping from between her fingers. "Nothing important." She smiled. Valente's eyebrows lifted; mild curiosity was edging toward A Need To Know. "Follow-up on an old story," Ariel amended, "from my deep dark past." She considered showing him the letter and immediately dismissed the idea. She had to have time to think about this. "So deep and dark I barely remember it."

Valente's mouth worked. He sniffed. Having little recourse, he let it go. He patted her captive hand before letting that, too, go. "Well, get your bags packed. The award dinner's next week."

"When and where?"

"The St. Francis," Tara supplied. "Monday night."

"St. Francis?"

"Union Square, Ariel," said Tara. "The Rodeo Drive of the North?"

"Union . . ." Ariel stared. San Francisco?

"Armani." Tara was rhapsodizing. "Neiman Marcus. Gump's. Tiffany."

The envelope was postmarked San Rafael, CA. Marin County. Marin County was just north of the Golden Gate.

"Versace," said Tara. "Escada . . ." She pondered for a second. "Cable cars, et cetera. San Francisco!"

So what? Ariel asked herself. She could hardly go house to house looking for the forgotten Dorothy. The dinner might as well be in Oz; she could go looking for Toto, too. However . . . "I think," she said, "I'll fly up Friday or Saturday. Make it a long weekend."

"Fine. Good," said Valente, whose mind had skipped to Monday night, which was when *The Open File* aired. "You're doing the invasion of privacy story, right? Where are we with it?"

"Just a couple more interviews. We'll be taped and edited before I leave town."

When Valente had exited, Tara gave Ariel a look. "Just a couple more interviews? That aren't firm and that're the crux of the whole story and you've still got—"

"Time," Ariel finished, and returned her attention to the letter. Tara gave it an oblique glance before she, too, left. Ariel didn't notice. She was analyzing the letter feature by feature.

It was dated over a week earlier; either "Dorothy" had been amazingly slow getting it into the mail (or ambivalent) or someone else had been inefficient. The postmark, Ariel saw, was yesterday's date, so neither the post office nor Tara could be blamed.

There was, unhelpfully and as noted, no return address. The greeting was "Dear Ariel," the signature a given name. At one time that would have indicated a personal friend. These days? The letter could have been computer generated. This one, however, was from a real person—who asked help from a woman who, in effect, no longer existed.

Ariel picked up the phone and, checking her Rolodex for Henry's new number, jabbed it in. He was in a meeting. "If it's like most of them," she was told by Henry's secretary, "it won't be breaking up in the foreseeable future." Ariel left a message.

The spelling was accurate, she noted. The punctuation was correct and the grammar impeccable. The writer, as Ariel had already deduced, was well educated. The letter was written with a fountain pen: further confirmation, Ariel felt, that the writer was an older person. (Did anybody name a daughter Dorothy these days?) The ink was blue-black, the paper stock white, heavy, and watermarked. She held it up to the light. Large *L*, small *g*. No common drugstore brand. A quick phone check with a stationer in Brentwood Village filled in the blank: G. Lalo, a French manufacturer sold only in high-end stores. She's got taste and/or money, Ariel observed. The letter was like a living thing in her hand, intimate and urgent. The woman who'd written it was so real Ariel could almost hear her voice as she read.

Dear Ariel:

    I caught your show last night. Excellent! And how fine you're looking! Seeing you was like seeing an old friend, in more ways than one. But that's another story.

    How often I've thought of our conversations and resisted contacting you. I don't think you'll be surprised to hear that. You did warn me. "There is only one way to achieve happiness on this terrestrial ball, and that is to have a clear conscience, or none at all." (I looked up the quote. Who would have thought that Ogden Nash— Ogden Nash?—would haunt me! Sadly, his "Candy Is dandy but liquor Is quicker" is sometimes apt, too.) You had me pegged, my dear; not one day has passed that I haven't felt guilty.

    My husband's gone now. I've run out of excuses and, oh boy! I used them all. The evidence wasn't absolutely conclusive, I told myself, and in any case, it wasn't mine to expose or suppress. I told myself that Sis didn't want to live. I could argue, and have, that my reticence (fence sitting? cowardice?) has actually bene- fited a number of people. Unlikely as it sounds, that's true. The villain of the piece, if you can believe it, Ariel, has become quite the do-gooder. It's an intriguing twist, isn't it? A patron of worthy causes. A philanthropist, no less. Raphael smiles greedily every time the man passes through his doors! I'm unimpressed; I know how he got the money. But, as you pointed out, I have no right to set myself up as judge, no more than he to set himself up as executioner.

    The word is apt. Alone as I am now, I'm scared. I'm a

loose end. Or would loose cannon be more accurate? A
man who's murdered once can't be counted on not to do it
again, can he?
   Ariel, please call me.

It was nearly midnight. The letter lay open, accusing, on the desk beside Ariel's PC. Who was Dorothy? Who was "Sis"? Who was Raphael? And who, pray tell, was *he*, the "executioner"? Ariel rotated her shoulders, trying to dissolve the kinks tied into her trapezius muscles by two solid hours of searching her files.

Many months before, she'd gone through every scrap of paper she'd found in her desk, both at the studio and at home. She'd input everything into her computer: every note, every phone number and address, every name, and every scribble, many of which were, to her, cryptic garbage. Some of the data she'd been able to relate to stories she knew she had produced. A few bits, the ones she could decipher that were still viable, she'd followed through on and used for stories since. They'd been good stories. She wouldn't have attempted to explain it, but she considered them her legacy from B.C. *Before Consciousness,* as she privately labeled it. Ariel Gold's unique twist on the past-life experience.

The wry thought sparked a memory unrelated to her search, a conversation between Laya and herself. Ariel's fingers stilled on the keyboard as she remembered. The subject was reincarnation.

It had been one evening during the past winter, after a small dinner party. The other guests had gone, but Laya had lingered over coffee. Ariel couldn't recall what triggered the conversation. It was more of a debate, really; Laya pro, she undecided. Laya had been quite serious, presenting her arguments earnestly if not, to Ariel, convincingly. Then she'd begun to talk about Jane.

Her intention, Ariel supposed, was to comfort, suggesting that the twin she'd never met wasn't irretrievably gone. When Ariel had stood and, abruptly, begun to clear away the coffee cups, Laya had sighed. "Oh, well," she'd said, "if nothing else, Jane lives on in you." In what sense, Ariel had asked suspiciously; "You mean because we're genetically alike?" "Sure," Laya had said after a beat. "What else could I mean?"

What else indeed? Ariel thought now; I wonder. I wonder what's going on in her mind at this very minute.

She had stopped by the hospital on the way home. It was well after visiting hours, not that Ariel yet qualified as a visitor. The ban still taped to Laya's closed door made that clear. The chair beneath the NO VISITORS sign was empty; the guard, Ariel saw, lounged against the counter at the nurses' station. Dinah, the gruff nurse with the heart of gold, was long gone, by then probably snugly at home, tucking in a bunch of gruff but jolly children. The dimly lighted corridor was quiet except for an intermittent moan from the room next to Laya's. Depressed, Ariel had left.

Now, three even more depressing hours later, she closed down her computer for the night. As far as she could see, not one name or number or place in any file had one blessed connection to the letter she'd received today.

8

"FIRST THING IS," HENRY SAID AS HE SPREAD A LAYER OF STRAW-berry jam over the slab of butter already smothering the tiny tea biscuit, "there's no telling how long ago you had these conversations with Dorothy whoever." He caught an errant drip of jam with his tongue. "What's with these baby biscuits?" he asked before popping the whole over-laden pastry into his mouth.

"It's afternoon tea, Henry," Ariel said. "Genteel. Elegant. You've got jam in your beard."

Three days had passed since she left a message with his secretary. They'd been playing phone tag. Early that afternoon they'd finally connected, and Henry invited her to lunch; she'd been eating a salad at her desk at the time. "Dinner then," he offered. She couldn't. Tonight was Friday night, and she'd be spending a good chunk of it wrapping up her episode before leaving for San Francisco early the next morning. They'd compromised on a late afternoon snack, a tea break in a shop Ariel suggested for no better reason than to watch Henry perch on a spindly chair with a pink napkin on his lap. The letter from Dorothy lay open between them, a safe distance from the food, which Henry eyed suspiciously.

"What is this thing?" He held a small round crustless brown sandwich between thumb and forefinger, gingerly.

"'Pear with cream cheese', the menu said."

He replaced it on the tiered tray. Ariel took it off again, and nibbled. "It's good. Your loss." She swallowed. "But don't you get the feeling from the letter—I do—that the conversations took place not that long ago? I mean, not years ago."

"Obviously, it's been well over one year, since you don't remember her. Look, I know it reads like you talked recently, like it was last month. It may feel that way to her, but you've got to realize something. In our line of work this kind of thing—tragedy, murder, life-shattering experiences—it's everyday stuff. But for the average citizen—"

"Not to me it isn't everyday stuff!"

"Oh? What have your last ten stories been about? What have the last ten you *rejected* as 'too done' been about?"

Henry sipped tea, watching her over the cup rim. "For the average citizen, as I was about to say, very different. Murder's monumental. Biggest and worst thing that's likely to happen in a lifetime. A sister—or somebody familiar enough to be called Sis—dies. Is killed? A friend, or at least a person you know, might be guilty? You're holding some kind of card you feel puts you in jeopardy? Whoa!" he growled, a rumble in his throat. "Then Ariel Gold shows up, strong but sympathetic. Persuasive. It could feel like a connection. You stay in Dorothy's mind, a person she can fall back on if the going gets rough. Her husband's . . ." He glanced at the letter. "'Gone.' Dead? Took off with a bimbo? Whatever, she's all alone. Lonely. Vulnerable. You're way more memorable to her than vice versa." His expression was a shrug. "I mean, even if you could remember, you'd be less likely to remember her than the other way around."

"But I think the connection went both ways," Ariel said. "That's a woman I could talk to right now. A woman I could laugh with, be friends with. I think . . . Henry, you don't have any recollection at all of who she could be and what she's talking about? The death of this 'Sis'?"

"I said no. I have a hunch this was one of your infamous carefully guarded exclusives. We've had this chat. You were not a team player. You did not share. The rest of us at *Open File* didn't have a clue half the time what you had going, not until you were ready with a fait accompli story." He eyeballed the tray and selected a slice of poppyseed cake. "If there was no publicity surrounding the woman's death, if it was considered natural causes and there was no suspicion attached to the 'executioner,' there'd be no reason for me or the public to know anything about it."

"Then how would I have known about it?"

"You're asking me?"

"And why wouldn't I have had some kind of file on it if I was looking into it?"

"Maybe you did once. Maybe it looked like a dead end and you scrapped it. Besides, how could you search your files with no more than you've got to go on? 'He' and 'the man' sure isn't any help. Neither is 'my husband.' 'Sis' may just be what Dorothy called the dead person, a family nickname, maybe, that you wouldn't have used. As for Dorothy herself, if she's really an old lady, you might've called her Mrs. So-and-so no matter how she refers to herself." He scratched at his beard, and his fingers came away sticky. Absentmindedly wiping them on his napkin, he said, "If your notes are anything like mine, it's 'Smith said this' or 'according to Jones.' Without her last name, my darling girl, you're out of luck."

"What about 'Raphael'?"

Henry glanced back at the letter. "'Raphael smiles greedily every time the man passes through his doors' . . ." He made a who-knows face. "She mentions philanthropy. Maybe Raphael runs a mission. Maybe he heads up the local Special Olympics or Greenpeace. Ariel, get real. You can't go there from here."

"I've got to," she said. "Did you read that letter? The woman's scared. She's waiting for a phone call!"

The line runs both ways, Henry didn't bother pointing out. He hadn't known Ariel well pre-amnesia, but he knew the woman she had become very well indeed. From the first day, for reasons about which he could only theorize, she was as different as if she'd molted, shedding a remote, sober persona as strikingly as she had soon shed excess flesh. One defining characteristic, however, remained unchanged: she was as stubborn as a stump. He watched her squash the remains of a scone with the back of her fork, reducing it to flattened crumbs. Her wide mobile mouth was turned down, her

chin thrust out. Henry knew better than to argue with
the set of that chin. "Is San Rafael the same area code as
San Francisco? Did you find any four-one-five numbers
in your PC?"

"Of course. Plenty. I called them. Let's see, I got the De
Young Museum, the Marin Airporter office, a pawnshop . . .
The shop owner, Calvin, his name was, remembered me
from an unrelated story we did a couple of years ago." Ariel
smiled. "He had a crush on me, isn't that sweet? 'Miss Ariel,'
he called me. 'Of course' he remembered me, as if he could
ever forget me, he said."

"Ariel, of course he remembered you. How many times
do you imagine he's been interviewed for TV? How many
media personalities do you think he's met personally? This
is just what I was saying a minute ago. The average—"

"I heard you the first time. Anyway, after half a dozen
calls I got smart and went to the reverse directory. Three
numbers are possibles. Residences with no answer, two of
them, and one with a machine. I left a message."

"Maybe Dorothy will call you."

Ariel nodded halfheartedly.

"Cheer up. You'll head north tomorrow; you'll come up
with something. Congratulations on the Sigma Delta, by
the way."

A phone beeped, and both of them automatically
reached for their phones. It was Ariel's: Sarah Aguilar
returning her call.

"Was that about Laya?" Henry said when she'd disconnected. "I got your message they were going to do a transplant."

"You missed a message. They did it, yesterday afternoon."

"That was fast!"

"Crowne's got connections evidently. He says cornea,
they drop from the sky, like pennies from heaven."

Henry, thinking of where these donor parts and pieces came from, looked squeamish. "And? How'd it go?"

"'As planned,' per Crowne. It's wait and see now."

"So? That's good. What's with the long face?"

"That was the counselor Crowne brought in, Sarah Aguilar. She saw Laya this morning. She's still, quote, less than communicative." Ariel chewed at her lower lip. "Maybe I'm looking at this all wrong, worried for nothing."

"Come again?"

"Maybe Laya's attitude is healthy acceptance; whatever will be will be. Maybe her serenity runs deeper than I imagined."

Having only minutes before suggested that Ariel cheer up, Henry didn't voice his opinion of that rosy view. "Why are you having to guess what she's feeling? Don't tell me you still haven't seen her? It's been what? A week?"

"Ten days," Ariel said wanly. "I'm a washout on that front, too."

That changed shortly after nine-thirty that night.

Ariel approved the last edit on Monday night's episode earlier than she'd expected. She considered stopping on the way home for takeout, but the guilt of teatime calories nagged. No one waited for her at home. Her good friends and near neighbors, Carl and Marguerite Harris, had picked up Jessie hours before. They were to keep the shepherd over the weekend. She was probably ensconced on a doggie guest bed by now, gnawing one of the rawhide bones Marguerite kept exclusively for her (the Harrises' ancient dachshund, Rudy, being long in the tooth but short on teeth).

Impulsively, Ariel turned in the direction of the hospital. She would leave a note for Laya with one of the nurses, saying that she was out of town for the weekend. She would be wasting her time, but that was neither here nor there. If all she could do for Laya, she told herself, was let her know she cared (Ariel refused to use the wretched term "be there for her," even in her thoughts), then that's what she'd do.

The ward was asleep for the night, as it had been on her last visit three nights before. It was so exactly the same, Ariel had the momentary sensation that no time had passed, that she was stuck in this muted, dispiriting, and somehow vigilant corridor. She paused outside Laya's closed door. At least the moaner in the next room was quiet tonight. Resting peacefully, or resting in peace? Ariel shivered.

She plodded to the nurses' station. There was no one behind the counter. A "hello" brought no response. She found a pen and pad, and wrote her note. She was waiting for someone to come back from whatever emergency (Ariel assumed) had taken everybody away when it came to her that one thing was disturbingly different from her last trip here. There was no police guard. She peered up and down the corridor. There was no guard anywhere, and no chair was stationed outside Laya's door. Suddenly, the whole wing seemed not merely muted but eerily quiet. Had the place been evacuated?

Before Ariel could make sense of the situation, the elevator bell dinged just across from where she stood. At last! she thought, relaxing muscles she hadn't realized she'd tensed. She glanced up at the lighted floor number, and waited for the doors to open, hopefully, on the policeman or a nurse.

There was one passenger, a young black man. He wasn't a cop, and he didn't look like a nurse. He wore a T-shirt and jeans: trendy jeans as baggy as if he'd lost a ton of weight or copped them from a person who needed to. Tennis shoes. All that, Ariel took in at a glance. That and one other thing: he looked nervous.

When he caught sight of her, he ducked his head. Eyeglasses slipped down his nose, and he scowled over them at the control panel, as if he'd been delivered to the wrong floor. He punched a button, pushed the glasses back into place, and waited, his eyes on his feet. One foot tapped. His hands flexed at his sides. He looked, Ariel thought, like a gunslinger in the seconds before drawing. Ariel dropped the pen. While she was bending to retrieve it, the elevator doors slid closed again.

In other circumstances, the incident wouldn't have rated a second's thought. Now, like everything else, it seemed odd. The man must have meant to come to this floor; there was no one else aboard to have pushed the button. And, too, Ariel had the feeling she'd seen him before.

She was folding her note, resigned to leaving it on the desk, when the elevator dinged again. This time a nurse hurried out. Her mouth was set in a grim line, the aftermath, perhaps, of whatever scene she'd just left. The line got grimmer when she saw no one manning the desk. "Where's Evelyn?" she asked. "And Rita?" Before Ariel could answer had she known the answer, the nurse said, "Visiting hours are over."

"The police guard who was here," Ariel said, "where is he?"

"Gone." The nurse answered distractedly, peering around for her coworkers. "Who're you?"

"A friend of the patient he was supposed to be guarding," Ariel said. "Gone where?"

"He got a call late this afternoon. Said something about being relieved of duty."

"Relieved of duty?" Ariel repeated. "Why?"

"Maybe the cops are short staffed, too," the nurse said tersely. "You'll have to ask them."

Ariel was handing over her note when, simultaneously,

one nurse emerged from a patient's room down the hall and another, looking abashed, from the rest room. Ariel left. As she neared Laya's room, she looked back to see the three women involved in a heated, whispered discussion. Having made no conscious decision to do so, she paused, did a right face, and slipped into Laya's room.

She stood perfectly still for a moment, her back against the closed door. She was already regretting her impetuousness.

Weak moonlight crept through the slats of the venetian blinds at the window, striping the bed and the cylindrical sheet-shrouded mound that was Laya. She lay on her back, her arms by her sides. One eye was covered by a plastic eye shield, taped to forehead and cheek. Otherwise, her face was featureless darkness against the pillow. The silence in the room was a vacuum. Pity engulfed Ariel in a wave so suffocating that it took her breath. Stealthily, careful to make no sound at all, she opened the door to leave.

"Ariel?"

When Laya spoke, Ariel gulped. She heard herself do it. She sounded like a cartoon character. "I'm sorry," she whispered.

"For what?"

"Were you asleep?"

"I don't think so. Maybe."

"How did you know it was me?"

"I think . . . I must've been dreaming."

"Can I come in?"

Laya shifted her position slightly, laboriously, as if her body had become an unaccustomed burden. "Aren't you already?"

"I guess I am." And now that I am, Ariel thought, what do I say? "How are you feeling?" was too asinine to ask, but that's all she really wanted to know. She tried to recall any item of Sarah Aguilar's advice. She'd already screwed up on *Identify yourself when you come into the room.* How to start? *Let her know when you're leaving* seemed like a good place.

"I called you," Laya said.

"You did? I didn't get a message."

"I dreamed it then. I thought . . . It's still night, isn't it? What time is it?"

"There're no lights on in here," Ariel said, carefully casual. "I can't see my watch."

"If the door's not closed, you'd better close it before you turn one on."

"Then it's okay if I stay a minute?" Ariel pushed the door to, but she left the room dark. It was, somehow, more comfortable that way. "It's ten-thirty," she said. She knew it was around that and didn't suppose five or ten minutes one way or the other made much difference. "I left a note for you. I wanted you to know I wouldn't be around for a couple of days. I'll be back late Monday."

Laya didn't ask for an itinerary.

Ariel tried to dredge up something cheerful to say, something comforting, something at least innocuous. "Why haven't you let anybody in?" she said instead.

"Because I didn't want to see anybody."

Ariel couldn't argue with that for a straight answer. Neither of them reacted to the dreaded *See* word. "Why not?"

"Grieving's not something you can share, Ariel."

"But hope is, and you—"

"And I didn't want to listen to that kind of well-meaning garbage."

It required no effort for Ariel to keep quiet at that point; she couldn't have been more shocked if the bed had spoken. In the silence she heard the purposeful *squish-squish* of rubber-soled shoes in the corridor. They stopped outside the door. There was a faint clink of what sounded like glass against metal. Hypos on a tray? Pills? Vials for blood? Ariel's eyes had adjusted to the dimness. Holding her breath, she watched the doorknob. Absurdly, she felt a twinge of guilt, as if she were about to be caught out, discovered in some breach of regulations far more serious than after-hours visiting. The shoes squished away.

"Thank God!" Laya muttered. "Sometimes, even in the middle of the night, they come in just to futz. 'Here's some fresh ice for you, honey.'" Her mouth was hard. She looked like someone Ariel had never seen before. "They move things around; then I can't find them. I knock things over."

"It's hard to know how to help, Laya; what to do or say."

"Then I've done you a favor by keeping you away, haven't I?"

"I wouldn't put it . . . I'm confused. You do consider me your friend, right? You did call me that night when you needed help."

"No."

"No? The phone rang. You were on it."

"I was trying for O, for the operator. I must've hit redial. Try finding the O when you can't see."

"Redial? But you hadn't called—"

"I did, that afternoon."

That was true. A yoga class was canceled because the gym was being painted. Laya had left a message. "You mean . . ." Illogically, Ariel felt let down. "You got me by accident?"

"So sorry to bother you. Next time I'm in agony I'll be more careful. And, no, it wasn't an accident."

"But you just said—"

"I mean there's no such thing as an accident. You can

believe that or not. I do." Laya's chest rose and fell visibly and rapidly. After long moments it slowed. So softly Ariel had to strain to hear, Laya said, "I'm sorry. I'm not angry at you."

"Who, then?" Ariel nearly blurted, and then she remembered something Dr. Aguilar had warned her about. Disabled people, she'd said, people who feel helpless, often go through periods of irrational self-contempt. Some never learn to accept themselves—or to accept help. "Laya," she said, "you don't have to go through this alone. Why won't you let them contact your sister?"

"Stepsister. Marie has two children and a husband and a job. She hasn't got the time or money to go flying across the country."

"If money's a problem, then let me—"

"No. Thank you, but no. Some people aren't good with . . . sickness. Marie wouldn't be any help."

"Then who? Isn't there anybody else that—"

"Let it go. Please."

Ariel began to pick at a cuticle, realized what she was doing, and stopped herself. She'd had to forfeit that habit when she went on camera. She smiled, hoping Laya could hear it in her voice. "So tell me about your dream."

"What dream?"

"The one you were having when I came in . . . You dreamed you called me, you said. Redial?"

Laya did not smile. "Not that time."

Ariel waited. "Well? What did you call me about?"

Laya averted her face, as if she were sighted and couldn't look Ariel in the eye with whatever she had to say. "I was asking you to do something for me," she said.

"Anything I can," Ariel said seriously.

"No, this is something . . ." Laya moved her legs restlessly. "It was just a dream."

"Then it won't hurt to talk about it."

"It won't help either. The way I feel . . . you wouldn't understand. You couldn't, not unless you'd lost—"

"Temporarily! I'm sure it's only . . ." Ariel caught the tightening of Laya's mouth. "Sorry," she said. "Finish."

"I was going to say, unless you'd lost something essential to you."

Visited, she hoped accurately, by a nudge of insight, Ariel said, "You're not talking about your sight, are you?" And after a moment: "I can understand if you explain."

"Can you?" Laya's mouth worked as she considered the way to begin. Finally, as if a lot were riding on the answer, she asked, "Can you understand what it's like to lose who you are?"

Ariel was startled dumb. Laya didn't know about her, couldn't know. But the question simply, precisely, expressed a conviction Ariel had never shared: that in losing her whole history, she had, in a sense, lost herself.

"Or, I should say," Laya mused, "who you *thought* you were."

Ariel let out her breath. This conversation wasn't about her, and Laya, in any event, didn't seem to require an answer. After a moment the other woman said, "The dark is a good place to think. There's not much else to do."

"Yes?" Ariel prompted.

"I can't live like this."

"Like . . . ?"

"Lying here, hating myself."

"Because you can't see, you mean? That's crazy!"

"Not because I can't see. Because it's my *fault* I can't see."

"Your . . . fault." Ariel swallowed. "Laya, have you talked to Sarah Aguilar at all about these feelings?" She got no reply. "You've got to. I mean it. You can't go on this way."

"You're right. I can't."

Relieved, about to agree enthusiastically, Ariel registered the tone of what she'd just heard. It hadn't been submission. "What are you saying?"

"I'm saying you're right. I won't live like this. You said you'd help me, that you'd do anything you could. Will you?"

"Help . . . ?"

"Yes."

"No!"

"I can't do what I have to do alone."

"Not a chance, lady!" Horror found an outlet in stuttering fury. "I can't believe you give yourself ten days—*ten days!*—and you're ready to give up? And it's not even like there's no hope! This surgery has a chance . . . a good chance of working, and if it doesn't . . . *What's the matter with you!* So maybe life won't be perfect, but there are people who . . . Good lord, you haven't even . . ." Echoes of somebody—Henry, she thought. Sarah Aguilar, too—warning her not to foist her expectations off on her friend, not to endow her with courage she couldn't live up to, were ignored. "You chicken-shit coward!" she burst out.

For a second Laya was still. Then her chest began to heave. She wasn't crying. There was bitterness in her laughter, but it was, definitely, laughter. "You tend, Ariel," she said, "to get just a bit self-righteous sometimes, you know? I am a coward. That's been the problem. What I'm telling you is that I'm through with that, and I need you to help me."

"You're going to have to look elsewhere for your help, Laya."

"You said 'anything.' That you'd do anything."

"Yeah? Well, I draw the line at suicide assistance."

"How do you stand on assault with intent to kill?"

Ariel stared. "That's not funny. Now you listen to me—"

"No. You stop preaching and listen to *me!* I'm trying to

tell you I know who did this to me. If I hadn't been such a 'chickenshit coward,' it would never have happened. He'd have been in jail."

Ariel's jaw dropped. "You know?" she cried. "Who? Why haven't you said—"

"I don't know his name. But what I need from you is to find him."

9

SAN FRANCISCO WAS GORGEOUS. THE CITY COULD BE COLD IN early April. It could be cold at high noon on the fourth of July. Ariel lucked into a perfect slice of spring. A hard rain the day before had left the air crystalline, and Saturday morning's sunshine was a warm blessing. The city pumped with energy. Showed off its unique character. Gloried in its fabled past. Ariel loved it. The first thing she did on entering her hotel room was close the curtains, collapse onto the bed, and take a nap.

Her exhaustion was not from staying late at the hospital the night before; it was from being too wired to sleep after Laya had peremptorily run her out.

"It's a long ugly story," Laya had said, "one I'm not up to tonight. You've got an early flight. Go home." Ariel had pitched a fit. Laya had been adamant. She'd asked if Ariel had a tape recorder with her. "You're a distraction. Lend me the machine. You'll have the details, every one I can remember, when you get back."

Ariel would sooner have eaten razor blades at that point than leave, but then she'd taken a hard look at her friend. There was purposefulness in Laya's expression. She was, at least for the moment, back with the living.

Ariel gave her the palm-sized recorder she always carried and, taking Laya's blunt, strong fingers, demonstrated which buttons did what. She told Laya how to reach her, considered a hug but settled for a pat, and did her the kindness of going away.

She'd called Max Neely from her car. He'd been at home, playing chess with his future stepdaughter. She was winning. He wasn't happy, and he got grouchier when he heard Ariel's question.

"Why did we take the man off the door?" he repeated, his voice rising. "Do you have a clue what it took to keep somebody there as long as we did? Do you have a clue what a budget is? What our manpower situation is? Listen here. We got lucky this week. For some reason—maybe because the Easter bunny's on his way; who knows?—the local citizens took a hiatus from slaughtering each other. Under normal circumstances, I couldn't have kept a man cooling his heels over there for three hours, let alone a week."

"Max, there was not one soul on duty on Laya's floor tonight. No nurse, no cop, no nobody. Any nut off the street could've walked into her room. In fact, I saw one suspicious-acting—"

"A week, Gold. Not a sign of a threat. Not a nut, not a peep."

"Because she had protection maybe? Could there be a cause and effect here?"

"Could it be that the nut who doctored the drops doesn't know your friend from the Queen Mother?" Max sighed, hugely. "Take down this number," he said, and reeled one off. "Private security. You want protection, hire it."

Ariel did. An operative was in place shortly after midnight. Laya need never know there'd been a break in the vigil, or that the man outside her door wasn't courtesy of her own tax dollars. Ariel hoped Laya, at least, had gotten a good night's sleep.

At one in the afternoon Ariel, groggily, stirred. A hot shower cleared the cobwebs. A jolt of caffeine from a corner coffee shop got her into her rental, a convertible, and onto northbound 101. A map fluttered on the seat beside her.

Since she'd made several work-related trips to San Francisco in recent months, it was superficially familiar. Marin County wasn't. After the congested streets of the city, Point Diablo and the windswept headlands beyond the Golden Gate looked barren, the Pacific surf pounding at their feet untamed. As Ariel crossed the bridge, she had a sensation of entering uncharted territory. It was a silly notion. There were hoards of tourists snapping photos from atop the cliffs. And Sausalito lay one exit ahead. Ariel took it.

Winding down Alexander, she could have been in some backwater. Rolling green slopes as empty as a heath swept to the bay far below. Then, with one quick curve of the road, she was face on to a Mediterranean port, or what she imagined one might look like. Houses by the tens of dozens perched one above the other, haphazardly, on vertical, wooded hillsides. Ariel caught the glint of many windows through the trees before the narrowing street doglegged and began its circuitous downgrade. Dead ahead was the bay. It was smooth as a prairie, white sails dotting the shimmering surface. Just before the street plunged into the water, it hung a left. Ariel rubbernecked. It was a postcard. Beyond the bay, beyond the sailboats, like a mirage, rose the skyscrapers of San Francisco. There was Alcatraz, and there the interminable Bay Bridge. She was driving so slowly a parade of cars built up behind her.

Sausalito was quaint as all get-out. And crowded. Ariel edged out a van to snag what appeared to be the only available parking space in the erstwhile fishing village, now artist haven and tourist mecca. The ferry was docking, but drawing her attention more compellingly were the aromas wafting from a nearby restaurant. Definitely hamburgers and frying onions.

She took her cholesterol neat, on a sun-warmed patio with a view of the yacht harbor. Beyond the masts was a peninsula the map said was Belvedere and Tiburon. Across a patch of water called Raccoon Strait lay Angel Island, the entirety of which was a state park. It had been an unusually wet winter; the trees were a deep blue-green, and from this distance the island's surface was moss velvet. Ariel wiped her mouth and stretched like a cat. She couldn't remember the last time she'd felt so relaxed.

She was glad Laya hadn't talked the night before. Whatever help Ariel might be once she knew the facts, she couldn't do one thing without them. For now she was absolved of responsibility. Free. Guiltless. Untroubled by the heavy burden of thinking. As for the letter from Dorothy, the letter that was even now in her purse beside her, it might as well have been stamped "Addressee Unknown" and returned. Four days before, being dispatched practically to Dorothy's doorstep had seemed providential. Now it seemed irrelevant. If any glimmer of a plan for pursuing the woman's identity had been in Ariel's mind, she couldn't recall it.

However, San Rafael was (as B.F. might put it) just up the road a piece. Ariel was soon back on the freeway and heading north.

A quirky neighborhood of houseboats claimed the bay to her right. Mt. Tamalpais loomed on the opposite horizon. As she passed the Corte Madera city limits sign, horses grazed the hills on one side of the freeway. The walls of San Quentin hulked forbiddingly on the other. Ariel sang along with the radio, the combined voices of

Barbra and Celine, fortunately, drowning out hers, and tried to decide how to spend the next day. (A trek through Muir Woods? A city tour?) She very nearly missed the central San Rafael exit.

Although it was the county seat, San Rafael had a nostalgic, distinctly small-town flavor. Ariel found a parking space across from city hall. The street was tree shaded and quiet, staid. The meter still accepted pennies. She walked down D Street to Fourth and was entering the crosswalk when it came to her: this town looked familiar. She stopped in her tracks. *I remember this place,* she thought. *I've been here and I remember it!*

This had happened before. It had come to nothing before. The disappointments didn't diminish the hope that something, sometime, would be the spur that triggered her memory. That stolid old bank building . . . Had she done business there? Was it possible? The café with the antique coffee grinder in the window . . . hadn't she seen that before? Could she have rendezvoused with Dorothy there? She'd definitely seen that card shop sign! No question! It was . . . a chain. With stores in L.A.

Ariel's head cleared. The sensation evaporated. The familiarity, it took her another second to realize, was artificial. She was on Main Street USA, the quintessence of every set from every vintage all-American movie ever made, from every 1950s and 1960s TV series ever rerun. At any moment Jimmy Stewart would whistle past. The Beaver would peddle by on his bike. In actuality, a Jeep Cherokee politely beeped, and Ariel hastened on across the street.

A short walk took her past a Starbucks, and the last vestige of having stepped into a time warp went poof. A long walk confirmed that this trip was a waste of time. Ariel let lost causes go, bought a guidebook, and got down to some serious local sightseeing.

It was a little after five when she approached the site of the Mission San Rafael Arcangel. Built in 1817, it had been the genesis of the Spanish settlement. The original mission (like the poor Coast Miwok Indians who helped build it before being obliterated by the white man and his diseases) was long gone, but the replica constructed more than a century later was imposing. Ariel dutifully read the plaques and, her feet complaining, sat in the little piazza to rest and flip through her guidebook.

One paragraph brought a grin. *American Graffiti*, a classic and a favorite of Ariel's, had been shot on the streets of San Rafael; no wonder the town looked familiar.

She had risen to go on her way when she noticed two men with a dog waiting to cross the street toward her. One man appeared to be instructing the other, who was listening intently, nodding. He wore dark glasses, and the Labrador retriever who led him wore a businesslike leather harness. Either the dog or the man, Ariel decided, were in training. Maybe they both were.

She was so engrossed she didn't hear the doors of the church open behind her. Belatedly, she realized that she was in the path of parishioners leaving mass. Moving aside, she dropped her book; stooping to pick it up, she bumped into an elderly lady. The lessons of the service hadn't taken with granny, who acknowledged Ariel's apology with a sniff. When she'd tottered on, Ariel looked again for the two men with the dog. They were moving away.

"Something else, isn't it?"

Ariel turned to the man who'd spoken. "Excuse me?" she asked.

"The dog," he said. He was an older man, though nowhere near as old as the sourpuss. Also unlike the sourpuss, he was smiling. "The guide dog? I thought that's what you were looking at."

"I was! I've never seen one being trained."

"You're from out of town?"

"How'd you know?"

He nodded toward her guidebook. "That and the fact that most days you can't go far in San Rafael without seeing the dogs. There's a school—" He interrupted himself to greet a young family leaving the church, and to Ariel said, "Enjoy your stay."

Smiling absently, Ariel watched him walk away. Maybe, she found herself thinking, this trip was providentially inspired after all. Or was she being ridiculously premature? She was. Pessimistic even. A jinx. Laya would be fine. She'd never need a cane, let alone a Seeing Eye dog!

The man was too far away to hear when Ariel called out, "Where is the school?" She hurried down the steps to the sidewalk, but he was closing the door to his car. She headed toward her own, keeping her eye out for a phone booth on the way.

The directory listed the Marin Guide Dog Academy, in San Rafael. The address, according to Ariel's map, looked to be no more than a five-minute drive. A phone call netted the unsurprising information that it was too late in the day for a tour of the facility and that she'd have no better luck the next day, Sunday. But there were weekday tours. She had work commitments Monday, but, Ariel assured herself, she could easily free up an hour. Just to do a little spadework: data gathering, something she was good at. It would be interesting. Laya need never know. What could it hurt?

She made an early evening of it and was back in her hotel room by nine. She'd gotten a little sun, she noticed, and it ended where her shirt began. The dress she'd brought for the awards ceremony was strapless; a "farmer's tan" wouldn't make an especially chic accessory. More sunblock tomorrow, she told herself. She pressed

the skin at her cheekbones with her fingertips and then
released it. Maybe a facial? A good night's sleep would fix
things well enough; she could wallow in bed till noon if
she felt like it.

She was reading herself to sleep with the guidebook
when an illustration brought her upright: St. Raphael's, the
church she'd sat in front of for half an hour that afternoon.
She'd noticed that there was a statue—noticed it as she'd
noticed the mission bells and the commemorative mark-
ers—but it was the focal point of the photo. Bronze wings
flared, sandaled feet planted, upraised right hand bran-
dishing a cross, the archangel Raphael was enshrined
directly above the golden chapel doors.

Ariel grabbed Dorothy's letter and found the line:
"Raphael smiles greedily every time the man passes
through his doors!" Could "the man," the unlikely combination of "executioner" and philanthropist, be a parishioner? A church supporter? A frequenter of services? And if
Dorothy knew he was one of St. Raphael's faithful, was it
because she was another? It was a half-baked notion. Ariel
didn't know where to go with it, but it was the only one
she had.

Ariel didn't sleep late the next morning. She didn't trek
through Muir Woods or tour the city. At seven-fifteen she
was back in front of St. Raphael's watching the earliest
mass celebrants arrive. Was "he" one of them? There were
more older women than any other sort of attendee. Could
one of them be Dorothy?

It was foggy. The fog was heavy enough to qualify as
mist. Yesterday's brave foray into spring, Ariel reflected
with a shiver, had obviously been rescinded. She drew her
raincoat close and positioned herself in plain sight. She
made eye contact with anyone whose eye she could catch.
Some smiled and said good morning. Some looked faintly

alarmed. Did they think she was a moocher? Or some kind of anti-religion zealot about to accost and harangue them? No one, man or woman, gave any indication of recognizing her.

When the doors had been closed for a good ten minutes and no latecomers had shown up, Ariel walked to a diner she'd noticed the day before. There would be plenty of time for breakfast; the next mass wasn't until nine.

Except that the crowd was larger and the earlier mist had become rain, the second mass was a repeat of the first. At the ten-thirty service the priest, who must have noticed her lurking about and might have thought her homeless, kindly invited her in. By now she was sodden; she took him up on the invitation.

The service was lovely, but as no generous patron was conveniently singled out for recognition, it was, to Ariel, unhelpful. Blotting her face and lank hair with a handkerchief, she studied the whitewashed adobe walls. There were icons, but no plaques acknowledging benefactors past or present. Each pew did have a brass nameplate affixed to its end, and, later, as the chapel emptied, Ariel studied them one by one. Most common were the names of couples, the "Mr. and Mrs." variety. Among the other inscriptions, there were no Dorothys. No name meant anything to Ariel.

When she approached the priest with what she thought was an offhand manner, and launched into a feeble yarn about a nice woman she'd once met here, a woman named Dorothy whose surname she couldn't remember but whom she'd like to look up, she was asked, solicitously, if she needed help of some kind.

There was to be another mass at noon. It was celebrated in Spanish. Ariel didn't hang around for it.

10

ARIEL LEFT THE RAIN BEHIND IN MARIN, BUT THE FAMOUS native fog was more tenacious. It preceded her into the city, a ghostly blanket so dense it erased the towers of the bridge and swallowed sound. She turned up the car's heater. The windows steamed up to match the weather. She switched to the defogger.

The gray dampness capped off Ariel's mood. The morning had been ill conceived, a silly waste, and she could think of nothing less silly to do next. Walk the streets of San Rafael wearing a sandwich board? Run an ad in the local personals column? *Amnesic TV correspondent seeks Desperate Dorothy.* Lost and Found would be more appropriate. *Memory misplaced. If found, return to . . .* square one. Henry had it right: "You can't go there from here," he'd said. W. C. Fields had it even more right: "If at first you don't succeed, try, try again. Then quit. No use being a damn fool about it."

Ariel was a determined woman; in the opinion of one or two folks she could name, pigheaded. But there was a limit. She wasn't overly concerned with being thought a fool, but she preferred not to actually be one. She hung a left and drove her jaunty convertible into the hotel parking structure. It was quitting time.

The first available space, naturally, was on the roof level. The elevator was for some reason being held on the ground level. Ariel trudged down six flights of windy, open stairwell. Her feet were cold and wet. She could already feel the stinging needles of a hot shower, the embrace of the hotel's thick, warm, dry terry cloth robe.

Hurrying across the porte cochere, she didn't notice the black Cadillac limo in front of the entrance. As she passed it, one of the tinted rear windows was opened a crack, and a voice growled, "About time you showed up, Ariel Gold."

Ariel jumped. She gaped through the inches of open window. "What in the world are you doing here?" she asked blue eyes under frazzled white eyebrows, all she could see of her grandfather.

The window slid noiselessly down. "Came to hear your acceptance speech," B.F. Coulter said. "Even brought my Brownie."

"Your what?"

"My camera, girl. First chance I've had for photo ops, isn't it? Since I missed everything from your christening through your first wedding."

"First?" With a suddenly light heart, Ariel said, "You know something I don't?" She grinned. "Hey, those other times couldn't have been much; I don't recall a thing about them."

"Well, I figured I better get crackin' before we ran out of momentous occasions. How fast can you get packed up?"

"Packed up? To go where?"

"Home with me and our pal Sam here."

Ariel bent to peer into the car's decadent, leather-smelling interior. The driver was a stranger, but the young man occupying the jump seat was Sam Heller, Henry's son. He and B.F. grinned at each other, enjoying what they obviously regarded as a successful ambush. These two, the seventy-seven-year-old and the recently turned fifteen-year-old, had become unlikely companions during the last half year. They were also, Ariel noticed, nearly the same height. B.F.'s six feet and then some, however, was built on imposing proportions. Sam still seemed more limb than trunk.

"Hi," he said. A glass of something fizzy Ariel hoped was

ginger ale occupied one hand. He waggled the other: long, basketball-clutching, octave-spanning fingers. His hands were duplicates of his father's. Henry's ball-playing days were long lost to bad knees. His musical abilities ended with balancing his woofers and tweeters, and, as far as Ariel knew, Sam's mother was no more inclined. Sam's gift for the piano had, apparently, sprung from an errant gene.

"Hi, yourself," Ariel said. She was happy to see the boy. She was happy their mutual regard had survived the vagaries of Henry's and her relationship. She'd worked to make that happen, but it could have gone either way.

"Wait a minute," she said. "Home?" She straightened. Distracted by Sam's presence, the rest of her grandfather's statement only now registered. "What home?"

"You're right. It's not a home; it's a house. *Home*'s one of those realtor words. 'Luxury modern *home* by the bay.' I hate that kind of mealymouthed hype. It's ruinin' the language."

"Thank you for sharing that," Ariel said dryly, "but . . ." She pressed herself against the limo as a car behind B.F.'s pulled out to leave. "An actual answer would be more enlightening."

"I own a house a ways up the highway. Sarge is there now, killin' the fatted calf, fixin' up a celebration dinner for you."

"You won't believe this place, Ariel," Sam put it. "It's got a pool and a Jacuzzi. Killer view!"

"No point payin' for a hotel when we got rooms empty. So go get your grip packed, will you? And make haste about it."

Ordinarily, Ariel would have resisted being ordered about, uprooted from a perfectly comfortable suite (for which the studio, not she, was paying), and dragged off somewhere that was no doubt inconvenient for her appointments the next day, but she didn't argue. She was tired of her own company. She'd seen little of her grandfather and Sarge McManus, his multifaceted companion, lately, and even less of Sam. And she was curious.

Soon, her bags in the trunk, her rental car temporarily abandoned, and her hot shower forgotten, she was once more on her way north. "B.F.," she asked, "exactly how many houses do you own?"

"How many?" the old man said, as if Ariel had asked how many ties he owned. The dubiousness, she suspected, masked pride. It was forgivable in a man born in a shotgun house at the edge of a cotton field lost to boll weevils. The field hadn't even been his own family's to lose. It had belonged to the farmer who supplied the Coulters with the house, fertilizer, and a mule, and who took two-thirds of their crop those years there was a crop. "You need to refine the question," B.F. said. "You talkin' actual residences?"

"As opposed to . . . ?"

"Assets that come and go dependin' how luck runs."

"Luck?"

"Fellow gets a little overextended, gets himself into a game he can't afford . . . that kind of thing."

"The particular house we're going to; it's yours as the result of 'that kind of thing'?"

Sam had been following their conversation closely. "Are you saying you won it, B.F.? Like in a poker game?"

"I won a horse once," B.F. told the boy. "A Tennessee walker. Max Baer, his name was, after the heavyweight champ. A fine stud. Lived to be seventeen, and prolific to his last day."

"B.F.," Ariel attempted to interrupt, "getting back to—"

"Swaybacked as a hammock by then, but still rarin' to go. About kicked the stable down whenever he caught wind of a mare."

"We were discussing the house."

"No, Ariel Gold, *you* were. How I came by it doesn't make for much of a story." B.F. turned back to Sam, made himself more comfortable and, hands clasped across his middle, said, "Now you want to talk about some down and dirty games and hot stakes? *Los Corrientes.* A speedboat, son, sleek as a marlin. Fifty feet, catamaran hull, twin diesels . . . she'd get up to thirty-four knots before you could blink both eyes. I was lucky to walk away from that game with my hide, let alone the free-and-clear title in my pocket.

"This wasn't long after the war, the second war . . ." He caught Sam's look of confusion. "World War Two? You've heard of it? Okay, I was down in Miami at the time, and Cuba, which you may know, is only ninety miles away . . ."

There was no deflecting him, Ariel could see. Like many Southerners, he loved to tell a story, the more convoluted, the better, and he was wound up today. Too wound up? she found herself wondering. And evasive; no question about it. Or was she, as was often the case where her grandfather was concerned, being a worrywart? Uneasily, she listened to his tale, which involved smuggling and alluded to espionage and, for all she knew, was actually true.

When the chauffeur signaled a turn and left the freeway, she noted the exit sign. "Tiburon?" she asked, eyebrows raised.

"Close by," B.F. said. "Belvedere."

"My, my! High toned, aren't we?"

"Oh, it's just a summer cottage. Old, too."

"Hey look, you guys," Sam said, lowering the window. "See? Out in that field there." They could just make out a shape in the fog. "Is that a horse?"

"It's a *statue* of a horse," B.F. corrected. His white hair stirred in the damp breeze coming through the window. "Blackie. And that field's a park: Blackie's Pasture, they call it. Blackie grazed that field for years. The locals put up the statue when the old fellow died."

"How'd you know that?" Ariel asked.

"Funny thing I noticed. Over in Sausalito they've got a statue of a seal in the bay and these two big stone elephants downtown. In Ross it's an iron deer by the city hall. In Muir Woods it's carved wooden bears, and over here they've got a horse."

And in San Rafael, Ariel thought, they've got a saint that smiles at a murderer. "And your point is?" she said.

"I don't know that I had one," B.F. said. "It just struck me as interesting. In the South every town big enough to park a double-wide has at least one two-legged statue with a gun in his hand. Only humans immortalized in this entire county are up at Marin Center, and they do duty for practically every war so far. Big load for two little old statues to carry. Kind of a hardship for the pigeons, too, I imagine, all of 'em havin' to fly to that one spot."

"*Summer cottage?*" Ariel cried when she saw the house.

"That's what they called them." B.F. defended his statement. "Folks from San Francisco used to summer over here. Rode the train over back in those days."

Ariel took in the stained glass window over the door. Ruby red glass spelled out the date: 1901. "Well, you didn't exaggerate," she said; "it's old."

It was Victorian, to be specific, and big, with a broad porch, leaded glass windows and turrets. It was a grande dame, incongruous amidst neighboring villas, ranches, and other far newer houses. The lot was largely level, also exceptional in an area where most were vertical and many houses were cantilevered. This one might have been transplanted from Boston or St. Louis. Except for the view.

Even partially obscured by fog, the view took Ariel's breath.

From the columned front porch she gazed over trees and rooftops down to the bay. Across it, seeming to float on cloudy, silent drifts of gray, Sausalito hung onto the hillsides that swept down to the marinas. They were almost exactly opposite to where Ariel had been the day before. With a telescope, she could probably see the restaurant where she'd had lunch. Even without a telescope, she could see San Francisco.

"What did I tell you?" Sam said at her elbow. "Killer, huh?"

Ariel looked squarely at her grandfather, who'd been watching her reaction. "Killer," she agreed.

"Well, don't say it like an accusation!" B.F. complained.

Ariel laughed lightly, but she still nursed a little nibble of unease. "You're being mighty closemouthed about this house you suddenly pulled out of your hat," she said. "If that fellow in there 'cooking up the fatted calf' weren't a former lawman, I'd be entertaining some dark thoughts."

"You gonna hang around out here all day or you wanna come on in and say hey to the lawman?"

11

ARIEL CAME TO A STOP IN THE LIVING ROOM DOORWAY. "WHO really lives here?" she asked.

The room was fully furnished and appointed. The work had not been done, if Ariel was any judge, by an impersonal decorator. She liked it; she might have done it herself.

"Ain't nobody here but us chickens. Look." B.F. swept

open a set of mahogany pocket doors. The living room and a second, similar room (parlor? drawing room?) had become one grand space. "You like it, I see," he said, too casually. "You want it? Say the word, and it's yours now, not later."

Ariel didn't bat an eye; her grandfather was forever trying to accustom her to the idea that she would be an heiress. She would deal with neither the idea nor the circumstances that would effect the actuality. "You trying to palm off hot goods?" she asked, and wandered away, taking it all in.

Dark period pieces must once have inhabited the formal old rooms; now there were plump sofas, loosely slip-covered in neutral linen, and tables that combined glass with pale porous stone. The big windows were uncurtained. Except for scattered sisal rugs, the honey-colored hardwood floors were bare. The art was bold. Within the context of the house, such a treatment should have been incongruous, but it had been done, to Ariel's thinking, with a sure touch—and maybe a thumb of the nose as well.

A nearly overpowering fragrance drew her into the dining room, where a fat vase of lilacs dominated a deep red, lacquered buffet. The table was set. Ariel counted ten places but didn't ask, assuming she'd get no straighter an answer than she had thus far.

She circled back to where she'd started, a central hallway. The wide staircase had an extra landing, a gallery sort of affair, just big enough to accommodate a string quartet. Ariel was almost surprised to see no musicians ensconced there, tuning up.

"I'll put your stuff in your room," Sam said, but instead of taking the stairs, he went through a door at the end of the hall.

"Where is my room?" Ariel asked B.F.

"We're letting you have the carriage house."

"Lovely," she commented. Two could play at this game.

A telephone rang. "I need to get that," her grandfather said. "Sarge is most likely in the kitchen. Thataway."

Ariel was headed where he'd pointed when she passed a large gilt-framed portrait. She switched on the light above it. The subject was a woman in low-necked satin and a jeweled choker. Her hair was styled in a 1940s upsweep; her dark eyes, at least as the portraitist had seen them, snapped. Ariel glanced toward the sound of her grandfather's voice, a murmur from the living room. Curiouser, she thought, and curiouser. She turned off the light and went through a swinging door into the kitchen.

The counters—and there was a plethora of them— were loaded with enough fruits and vegetables to stock a pushcart, and every burner on the range was taken up with a restaurant-capacity stockpot or saucepan. "So do something!" Sarge McManus ordered the contents of the pot he was stirring.

"What did you have in mind?" Ariel asked him.

"Hey, Ariel," Sarge said, and stuck out his free hand. Assuming he meant her to shake it (Sarge wasn't big on hugging), Ariel proffered her own. He didn't notice. "Thermometer," he said.

"Pardon?"

"That thermometer. Hand it to me?"

Ariel did, smiling to herself. There was something wonderfully grounding about Sarge. The ex-LAPD detective was as solid as he looked, which was on a par with a squat chunk of granite. Granite would be chattier. Sarge didn't as a rule talk much; he acted.

Some years before, he'd decided he owed B.F. a debt. Being at loose ends after his early retirement (the result of a gunshot wound suffered in the line of duty) and a failed venture as a restaurateur (financed by B.F.—part of the debt), he had, from what Ariel could put together, hired himself on in the self-styled position of cook, companion, sometime driver, and full-time bodyguard. He took the last job seriously. Ariel could vouch for it, having once been under his scrutiny herself.

"Need any help?" she asked.

"No, thanks."

"When did you all get here?"

"Last night."

"You flew?"

"Sure."

"In the new Lear?"

"Right."

Ariel picked up an artichoke and tossed it from hand to hand. "You've been busy," she commented.

"Farmers' market. Went early this morning."

"The lilacs from there, too?"

"Yep."

"Nice. Great smell. Like perfume." It struck Ariel that she'd picked up Sarge's shorthand speech cadence. "Soooo," she asked, stretching the word like taffy, "who's coming to dinner?"

"He didn't tell you?"

"He hasn't told me squat about anything, like how he's all of a sudden in possession of this house, for example."

Sarge looked up from taking the temperature of whatever it was he stirred. He rubbed his skull-cropped gray hair for a long moment. "He's had it a while," is all he said.

"Well, what's the big mystery about it? And who's that woman in the portrait out there in—"

"Talk to B.F."

Ariel swallowed her protests; she well knew they'd be wasted. "About B.F.," she said instead, "he seems a little . . . edgy? What's he got on his mind?"

"Ask him."

"Okay, okay. Do I have to ask him about the guest list, too?"

"Now we're cooking!" Sarge muttered to the contents of the pot and, removing the thermometer, began swiftly to add things.

"Sarge?"

"What?"

"Guest list?"

"Acquaintances. People he knows."

"Knows how?"

"You know how. B.F. likes people. They like him, even when they don't know who he is."

"But here, in San Francisco?"

"He's up here some. Pretty regular. Has some interests in the Silicon Valley."

"Oh." Ariel thought about it; the same would hold true, she imagined, vis-à-vis L.A. and the San Fernando Valley or Essen and the Ruhr. When she'd visited her grandfather on Kiawah Island, he'd seemed to be acquainted with everybody in the whole Lowcountry. The top man at Woolf Television, Inc., the conglomerate that owned *The Open File*, was a buddy. (After three years on the job Ariel had yet, to her knowledge, to meet the man.) B.F. had introduced Jane to the owner of her modeling agency; he'd sent Ariel the eminent Dr. Brian Crowne; he'd once, as she'd learned at another of B.F.'s dinner parties, shot the breeze with General George Patton—or so B.F. told the story. Anybody who perceived Southern charm and hospitality as insincere, she thought, hadn't run across B.F. Coulter. "Who?" she asked.

"Who what?"

"Who're the people?"

"Oh, a fellow named Bland—"

"Bland? Ellis Bland? The state senator?"

"Ex–state senator, and his wife—what's her name? Used to be on the stage?"

"Libby Vail. And?"

"Some woman farmer and her . . . date, I guess he is. Local columnist, I think B.F. said she said."

Senator and musical star? Ariel thought. Farmer? Columnist? What a mixed bag of people B.F. knew. Maybe, she reflected, I should ask him if he's come upon a lady named Dorothy in his travels. She watched Sarge fold stiff egg whites into a bowl. "That's eight with us four," she prodded. "Who're the other two?"

"The Blands' son and the son's daughter."

"Interesting assemblage. Good thing I brought a ball gown."

Sarge spared her an impatient glance. "What are you talking about?"

"What to wear."

"Wear clothes. Look, go away, will you? I can't concentrate."

"Great to see you, too. You're looking good. How've you been?"

"Beat it."

Ariel was on her way out when he said, "Oh, yeah, I meant to say. Congratulations."

"For?"

"The award."

"Thanks."

"And, Ariel . . ."

"What?"

"How about moving that vase of lilacs to the living room, will you? Smell's about to do me in."

The carriage house was a cozy domicile all to itself, complete with galley kitchen and a sort of sun porch–sitting room. The latter was furnished with vintage wicker, the cushions covered in a polished Oriental chintz Ariel had seen before. Where puzzled her until she recognized it as a fabric she'd debated buying herself. Only the price had deterred her. Here, constantly exposed to sunlight, it was beginning to fade.

So, too, was a toss pillow on the chaise. HE WHO LAUGHS, LASTS was stitched across it in needlepoint. The message, unaccountably, made Ariel feel sad. She held the pillow against herself and gazed around her. There were a number of ceramic cachepots, all empty. It occurred to Ariel that she'd seen no live plants anywhere in the house. How long, she wondered, had it been since it was inhabited?

She finally got to the hot shower she'd expected to take at the hotel. On a hook in the bathroom she found a thick white robe, not unlike the hotel version she'd also been dreaming about earlier. She was wrapping herself into it when the phone rang.

"Hello?" Ariel answered, expecting someone from the main house, since no one else knew where she was. She hardly knew where she was.

"Yet another Coulter family homestead?" asked a familiar voice.

"Do you have a tail on me?"

"I have a son," replied Henry. "He called to give me the number there, which I told him to do. He mentioned you were in residence. So, is this place, and I quote, 'awesome' as in inspiring wonder? Or as in *totally, dude?*"

"It's not your average summer cottage."

"I was invited to tag along, you know, or maybe you didn't."

"*Mi casa grande est su casa grande.* Hop a shuttle. We're about to party down, I understand. The more the merrier."

"If I'd had a little notice . . ."

"Why should you? I didn't."

"Another time. How's the quest going?"

"The quest? Oh, you mean Dorothy. Dead end. You were right."

"I was thinking . . . the letter came from San Rafael, right? And she mentioned a Raphael? Could we be talking a namesake? I mean, like a place name? A school or a church? A hospital?"

"Been there, but thanks for the thought. If you get any more, let me know, but I think—like it or not—I'm going to have to hope Dorothy tries again. Maybe she'll figure the letter got lost in the mail and write another one, or call. I'm out of ideas."

"Hello? Who is this?"

"You think I like admitting I'm stymied?"

"Makes me kind of sad to hear it. All my idols have clay feet."

"I've got to go. Company's coming, and I'm still in my skivvies." She heard a knock. "And somebody's at the door."

"Under those circumstances, I hope it's somebody you know well." As was his habit, Henry hung up without a good-bye.

B.F. poked his head in. He was dressed already, including a tie, a major sacrifice. "Findin' what you need?" he asked.

"Just like home."

"Good deal."

"Even to the same kind of soap I use at home. The same room spray, too, as a matter of fact. The same toilet paper, I wouldn't be surprised." B.F. stuck a finger between neck and collar and tugged, his expression preoccupied. Ariel waited, but he didn't comment. "Coincidence, I guess," she said.

"I guess." As if he'd developed a slow leak, the old man's face and then his shoulders slumped. He was staring past Ariel. She turned, following his gaze. There was nothing in his line of sight but the needlepoint pillow. The thought came fully formed in that second, and there was no question about it in Ariel's mind. "This house belonged to Jane," she said.

B.F. nodded. "First time I've been in it since she died." Managing to tweak his face into passable neutrality, he said, "Yes'm. It's been closed up. I came to tell you. I was afraid somebody at dinner might've known her, that somebody might say something. I didn't want you taken by surprise."

Abruptly, Ariel sat down. She felt a flash of anger, against what or whom, she couldn't have said. "I don't understand," she said. "Jane lived in Los Angeles."

"Your sister lived a lot of places. She went with me when I traveled—whenever it was possible, I mean— when she was young. After she grew up, modelin' took her all over the globe."

"Presumably, she didn't own houses all over the globe?"

"No," he agreed, suddenly all clipped-voiced business. "Just this one. The house in L.A., the one she lived in with that lowlife womanizing bully she had the poor judgment to marry against my advice and stay with after she knew I was right, was his. McCaulay still occupies it. Jane got this house before she married."

"She lived here then?"

"For a while, a year at the outside. Later on, she and McCaulay used to come up for weekends pretty often, but she had sense enough to keep the house in her name. It was left to her by your great-aunt. Jane put in her will that it was to go to me."

"My great-aunt," Ariel repeated. This was the first she'd heard about one, the first she'd heard about any family beyond the immediate. The woman in the portrait, she thought, the woman with the sharp dark eyes. "This was your sister?"

"Your grandmother's. You needn't look so confused. Your grandmother had a sister, your great-aunt. It's not complicated."

"Her name was . . . ?"

"Claire. Came out from South Carolina in the late thirties. She was a caution, Claire was, a spinster schoolteacher with opinions that didn't suit the time." B.F. had sat down. He rubbed his palms between his knees and chuckled. "Didn't suit anybody that heard them back home, and Claire wasn't shy about holdin' forth."

"A spinster schoolteacher had the wherewithal to buy this house?"

"What she didn't do in the bloom of youth she more than made up for in middle age. Ended up marrying three times, two of 'em rich as czars, and outlived every one, including the last one, who wasn't rich and who, bein' some younger, thought he'd end up with the whole kit and caboodle. Right handsome woman, Claire was, and smart. You, more than Jane did, remind me of her."

Ariel wanted to know about Claire and her sharp eyes and her unsuitable opinions and her three husbands; far more, she wanted to know about Jane. Anything and everything about Jane.

Facts she knew: that, for example, she and her twin were uncannily similar, even to inconsequentialities. Crazy little things, like dropping verbatim quotations at the drop of a conversational hat, and poking fun at themselves with yet another quip. ("I often quote myself. It adds spice to my conversation.") Like wasting time with crossword puzzles and needlepoint. Like being nearsighted, and foolish about animals, and afraid of heights, and putting Worcestershire sauce on grits. She knew that modeling didn't matter to Jane, that she'd wanted to make her marriage work, that she'd wanted a family. She knew that Jane had been pregnant when she died.

Facts weren't what Ariel wanted to know. She wanted to know about the sound of Jane's laugh and whether she cussed when her soufflés fell or cried watching sappy movies. What Ariel ached with were questions that couldn't be answered by anybody alive.

"One thing Jane was like Claire in," B.F. was saying, "was a partiality for this old house. Girl was foolish about it."

Were you, Jane? Ariel stared into space and through space and talked in her head to the sister who wasn't there. *Did you love the mornings? The sun on the bay? Or were you a night person? Did you come alive when the city across the water lights up like a jewel box? Was it you who planted the herb garden I noticed by the back patio? It's running wild now, Jane. Tell me—because I know you didn't choose it—how did you live with that awful pink tile in the bathroom? And that chintz . . . how is it that of all the fabric in the world, you bought the same print I nearly bought, too?* The answers were as irretrievably lost as Ariel's own memories.

"Reckon you better dress," B.F. said, and cupped her head with his big hand, "unless you plan to dine in your housecoat."

Although Sarge had, uncharacteristically, hired help for the evening, a uniformed woman who kept glasses and canapé platters moving as if they were on a well-oiled but invisible assembly line, he couldn't stay away from the kitchen. He was not a party person. His pleasure came from preparation rather than participation, and he kept slipping away, muttering, "'Scuse me a minute."

Ariel wished she could follow him. Try as she might, she was having trouble shaking off her melancholy.

She wondered if any of the guests had ever met Jane. Would the senator and his wife have mixed with her set? (Did Jane *have* a set up here?) The senator's son was the right age to have socialized with Jane and her husband, as was the woman who was introduced as a commercial farmer. Her companion, the columnist, was a decade older, but wouldn't a columnist have been aware of a fairly big-name model owning a house in the area?

Ariel resisted the urge to go from one to another asking; to search out anyone, man, woman, or child, who might have known her sister; to corner the person and clutch him or her by the lapels or any other handhold, and pump for every scrap of information down to the most casual of hellos shared with Jane in passing.

Ariel smiled a party smile, and kept her clutches to herself. She didn't talk about Jane to strangers. Keeping her private life private had, with her growing public recognizability, gone from ingrained habit to hard-core policy. She would not enjoy reading stories in tabloids or slick magazines about the fashion model who was murdered because she was mistaken for her TV news-lady twin.

So far, no one with a column to fill or a talk show to boost had glommed onto the relationship, and that likelihood, Ariel knew, would lessen as time went by. Her face, in important particulars, was not Jane's face. Her name was already better known than Jane's had ever been. The magazines Jane had graced, assuming copies still existed, gathered dust. Memories would fade. Ariel would change. Jane would never be older than thirty-one.

Ariel swam her way out of pensiveness and answered a question about a recent *Open File* segment. A friendly argument ensued. It was quelled by B.F., who cajoled Mrs. Bland (or as theater fans knew her, Libby Vail) into singing her trademark song. Sam, pink in the face, accompanied her on piano. By the time they sat down to dinner, the eclectic gathering was in high gear, and Ariel had begun to enjoy most of her grandfather's guests.

Farmer Meg was a whip-thin, straightforward woman Ariel had liked on sight. It took longer to warm up to her unlikely companion. Rob, a columnist for the *Marin Independent Journal* by trade, author by moonlight, was carefully mussed of blond hair, agile of eyebrow and square of jaw. He even had a dimple. He was a hunk. The looks, Ariel eventually discerned, were deceptive. He was also clever. You could get a paper cut from the wrong side of his tongue.

Ellis Bland was a low-key man with courtly manners, sleepy eyes, and remarkably little to say for a politician. His wife's larger-than-life presence seemed to take up all her space and his as well, but he did listen as enthusiastically as she talked. The same couldn't be said for their son, a passably attractive divorcé. Ariel hoped he hadn't been invited on her account; he kept dropping names that meant nothing to her.

His sixteen-year-old daughter obviously *had* been invited for Sam, who seemed preoccupied less with her than with the flatware, more than he was used to dealing with. Ariel was seated too far away to nudge his leg under the table (and bumping into the divorcé's leg was a mistake she didn't care to make), but she gave Sam a wink and tuned in to the conversation that flowed around her.

Meg was talking about an elderly, reportedly senile woman who'd gone missing from a San Rafael nursing home. It was a story that might get a buried inch or two in the *Los Angeles Times*; it had been front-page news here, and every adult at the table was aware of the details. When the talk turned to a local political race, they all knew the candidates, some personally. It seemed to Ariel that every adult at the table (excepting Sarge, who, again, wasn't *at* the table) knew everybody that everybody else knew.

She was familiar with the demographics—she could come close to citing the numbers—but it hadn't registered until then how comparatively small the Bay Area was. The metropolitan area of San Francisco, she knew, was a tenth the size of Los Angeles. It had roughly one fifth the population. And Marin County had less than a third the number of people of San Francisco. It was, Ariel gathered, a tightly knit community.

Libby was talking to Sam, who'd stopped puzzling over his utensils and seemed interested. Down the table her husband was in low-voiced conversation with B.F., who looked serious. Ariel was about to inquire of her end of the table what anyone might know about the guide dog school when the younger Bland launched into another of his pointless stories.

Rob the columnist wasn't listening. He was, Ariel realized, watching her. With a gleam of interest in his sky blue eyes? Or just one fellow sufferer recognizing another? Conspicuously, he produced a pocket watch. He frowned at it. Shook it. When he murmured, "'Either this man's dead, or my watch has stopped,'" she almost choked on her asparagus.

Just then, Rob pricked his ears in B.F.'s direction. "You knew Mrs. Thibeau?" he asked. He evidently had extraordinary powers of hearing. Ariel hadn't heard a word of the elder Bland and B.F.'s conversation, and she didn't know who Mrs. Thibeau was, but she was grateful for any change of subject, even to (she presumed from the use of the past tense) a deceased person.

"For many years," B.F. said.

"We were making plans to ride to the service together tomorrow, Libby," Bland told his wife, who nodded somberly. "I can still hardly believe it," she said. "And so soon after her husband! But that's the way it often happens, isn't it?"

"With old people, sure," Rob agreed, "but she was no more than, what? Sixty?"

"Sixty-six," B.F. said under his breath. He blinked, cast his gaze around the table in a disoriented way, as if he'd been lost on some overgrown trail of memory, and smiled a big smile that Ariel could tell was a reach. "Meg," he said a shade too loudly, "you haven't said a word about your gleaning project."

Throughout the account of a plan in which disadvantaged city kids picked or dug or otherwise reaped vegetables left after commercial harvesting and then donated to food banks, Ariel kept one eye on her grandfather. Apparently, her award was only one reason for his trip to San Francisco, and the memories in this house weren't the only ones that had him unsettled. Who, she wondered, was Mrs. Thibeau?

12

THE QUESTION WAS TO BE LEFT HANGING.

The dinner guests lingered. Their reluctance to leave was a compliment, but their host was wearing an increasingly fixed smile by the time they did. The old man's eyes were open, his expression beatific. Ariel wasn't deceived; for all practical purposes, B.F. had left the building.

When at last she closed the door on Bland *fils*, who had lagged, oblivious to social signals to the bitter end, promising with a wink to call her (God forbid, Ariel thought), Sarge went to check out how the hired help had left the kitchen, probably a white glove inspection, and Sam retired, probably to fall asleep with his Walkman clamped to his head. Ariel and B.F. were left to turn out lights and lock doors. When they realized that, independently, they'd both paused at front windows to take one last look at the view, each chuckled.

"Shangri-La," Ariel said.

It was deeply quiet. A waning moon could be glimpsed

behind fast-moving, smoke-colored clouds. The lights across the bay shimmered as if they were filtered through tears.

"Or Xanadu or Brigadoon," she murmured. "Fabulous, anyway."

"Weren't those places," B.F. asked, "where folks never grew older?"

"I think. One or two of them, anyway."

"Then this ain't them. Oh, they give age a run for its money here . . . aerobics, liposuction, antioxidants, wishful thinkin'. But you do get old, and you do die. Here like everywhere."

"Heartening."

"A mood, I guess."

"'Americans think death is optional.'"

"I hope that's one of your quotations. If it's an idea you want to chew the fat about, I'm not up to it."

"Rob said it. He's writing a book about dead people."

"What?"

"Never mind that. Who was Mrs. Thibeau?"

B.F. took in a lungful of air, scratched his white mane lustily on the exhale, and left the window. "Just an old friend," he said.

"That you'd known 'for many years.'"

"And hadn't seen for I don't know how many of 'em, not that it's any of your business, so don't go thinkin' I'm fixin' to bust into lamentations, okay?"

"Uh-huh," Ariel said. "Your accent's getting thicker."

"What the devil is that supposed to signify?"

"Diversion. If I were Henry, my little radar blip would be starting to hum."

"Ah, yes, Henry."

"Ah, yes, Henry?"

"He'd've had a good time if he'd been here this evening. I invited him along, but he had 'other plans,' he said."

"That's too bad."

"Didn't call his plans by name," B.F. said sotto voce, as if he were mulling over a problem mildly puzzling to him.

"The name, I think, is *Newsfront*."

"You right sure about that?" B.F. had leaned over the last lamp, and the light caught the raising of one single bushy white eyebrow just before he clicked the switch.

"Is there some point to this?" Ariel asked. "If there is, I'm missing it."

"You know, Ariel Gold, if I had raised you, you'd have better manners. What you're *missing* is exactly the point. You've done nothing but work for months now. You got any private life at all?"

"Apparently not."

"Do tell," B.F. murmured with a smile he hid. "Mrs. Thibeau," he unexpectedly relented and said, "is—was—a lovely lady I used to see. At that time she was Miss—not Ms., you understand; it was too many years ago for that . . ." He headed for the stairs, Ariel trailing. "It ever strike you that Southerners were sayin' 'miz' long before everybody else? Of course, we always used it to distinguish ladies who didn't mind folks knowin' such an irrelevant thing about them as their marital status. I kind of like the idea of marriage havin' relevance myself, but then I'm an old man and, no doubt, clouded in my thinkin'."

By now, Ariel had more or less given up any hope of actual information.

"Miss Mayes, she was at the time," B.F. reminisced. "Thirty years ago, I'd venture to say. She was what we called then a 'career woman.' High up in the retail fashion field, and not a bit interested in domestic bliss, or not at any rate with me. A widower with a granddaughter to raise? She declined the honor." B.F.'s smile seemed cheerful enough. "Her loss," he said, "in my opinion. Well, sleep tight."

He stopped with his hand on the newel post. "Oh," he said, "sorry about subjectin' you to young Bland."

Ariel grinned. "He is well named."

"Umm," B.F. agreed. The old wood creaked with his weight as he started up the stairs. "Reckon meddlin' in other folks' love life is a thing we'd all do better to steer clear of."

The next day was a race. Ariel had two interviews in the city, one an immediate and hot prospect for an *Open File* segment, the other a wild goose chase, before returning to San Rafael, nearly late for her two o'clock tour of the Marin Guide Dog Academy.

The grounds were beautifully laid out and landscaped. They could have been the campus of a college except for the signs warning motorists to slow for dogs in training, and a distant cacophony of yelps and barks from what Ariel assumed were kennels.

In the administration building she gave her name to a receptionist, and sat down to wait for the tour guide. Portraits of harnessed dogs adorned the walls: German shepherds and Labrador and golden retrievers, the former breed in noble profile, the latter two smiling broadly. Two live dogs, one a shepherd that resembled Jessie and the other a yellow Lab of advanced years, lay behind the receptionist's desk, heads resting identically on forepaws.

The lobby was a hive of comings and goings, the receptionist a veritable juggler. While Ariel watched, she directed visitors and signed for a UPS delivery, all the while efficiently answering and dispatching phone calls through a headset. Several minutes had passed before it became apparent that the woman was blind.

"Sorry to keep you waiting!" the tour guide called out as she approached Ariel at a trot. Shaking hands, avoiding Ariel's eyes, she gave her name and said, "Well, so you are *that* Ariel Gold."

"Am I the whole tour group?" Ariel asked.

"You were, yes, but . . . this is awkward now that you're here, and I apologize, but it would be better if you would come back at another time."

Ariel frowned her puzzlement.

"The person you want is our PR director, Frank Trout," the guide said. "Unfortunately, he's not in this afternoon."

"I don't understand, Ms. . . . I didn't catch your name?"

"Bess. Mr. Trout is the one who liaises with the press, you see, and when you called about visiting, the receptionist didn't recognize that you were, you know, press. I really am sorry."

How long, Ariel wondered, before I get used to this?

As a producer, her name and face had meant nothing. People only heard the name of the program. Sometimes they were intrigued; sometimes they were intimidated. More often than not, however, mention of *The Open File* had been an entrée. But from her first on-air appearance, Ariel had seen a dramatic change. When she turned up unexpectedly, people tended to be taken aback, even awed, as if her mere presence were an ambush.

"Well, Bess," Ariel said, and smiled, "this is a strictly personal visit. I'm not press today, just an interested civilian."

"I'm afraid—" the woman began uncomfortably. "It's policy. Mr. Trout okays or handles all press contact. It does make sense. I'm a new volunteer, still learning. I wouldn't want to get some fact wrong that—" She broke off as the elderly yellow Lab lumbered over from the receptionist's station. He sat down beside her, looking up expectantly, as if presenting himself for an introduction. "Hadley," Bess scolded gently, "you're supposed to be on a down-stay!"

Hadley recognized reprieve when he heard it; he opened his mouth and panted contentedly.

"Spoiled rotten," Bess grumbled, obviously much relieved by the interruption. "Hadley's a retired guide dog," she explained.

"I didn't know they got put out to pasture." Ariel knelt to stroke the graying muzzle, and Hadley, blissful, closed his eyes.

"Oh, working dogs have to be in peak condition. They've got to have excellent vision and hearing to do their jobs. If they're arthritic, which this old man is, it gets too hard on them."

"What becomes of them?"

"The owner has first option on keeping the dog as a pet. If that's impossible, then the person or family that raised the dog can get him back, and if *that* can't happen, the school places him. We have a waiting list. I was on it, and Hadley's mine now."

"Lucky boy!" Ariel told the dog. "How long do they work?" she asked Bess, who had relaxed, now that she no longer had to be the bad guy.

"Average, I think, is about seven years. Depends on the animal, of course."

"Do you use all breeds?"

"Just shepherds, Goldens, and Labs. All purebreds. Oh, except, now they're starting to breed Lab-golden mixes, too. You should see the puppies!" Bess bit her lip, and looked miserable again. "When you come back, you will. I'm really sorry I can't—"

"You breed them here?" Ariel interrupted smoothly, and off went the enthusiastic Bess again. When Ariel left the lobby half an hour later, she hadn't seen the facility (which had never been a priority), but she knew as much about it as the tour guide did.

She paused beside her little rental convertible, looking over the grounds, and woolgathering—wondering whether what she'd learned would ever be needed, hoping that Laya's progress would make the trip a waste of time— when her eye was caught by one particular structure.

It was at the far edge of the complex. Among the functional, contemporary buildings, this one stood out like an ornate wedding cake set against loaf bread. It was wood shingled, three stories, white with a froth of gingerbread trim, turrets, and atop the multigabled roof, at least four lightning rods. Pre–World War One, Ariel guessed. An incongruous wing had been added to one side, an insult to the original, imposing architecture. Imposing, she mused, and a bit forbidding. It would be at home on the cover of a gothic romance. Behind the big old building would be thunderous clouds and jagged lightning. In the foreground would be a cloaked and hooded damsel, fleeing into the storm. She'd be glancing over her shoulder, eyes wide with horror, her cloak parting just enough to expose cleavage.

Ariel heard frenzied barking. Right on cue, she thought: the hound of the Baskervilles! She grinned. The afternoon in real time was bright and sunny. The campus was peaceful. Flowers bloomed. The most threatening thing to be seen was the barker, a half-grown golden retriever, leggy, bursting with pent-up energy, and dying to run. He passed within a few yards of Ariel, dragging the laughing, frowning woman on the other end of his leash.

Ariel glanced back at the odd, old building. One thing nobody can say about you, she told herself as she climbed into her car, is that you lack imagination.

13

"HOW WAS THE FOGGY CITY?" LAYA ASKED.

"As advertised," Ariel replied.

"And your acceptance speech? How did that go?"

"Fast." The questions were idle. Small talk. Laya's mind, Ariel could see, was clearly elsewhere. So was Ariel's.

She'd gotten in very late the night before, but she'd been up with the sun and at Laya's bedside shortly thereafter. She itched to get hold of the tape recorder she'd left four nights ago, but she mentally sat on her hands. She couldn't read her friend's mood. There was an edginess that was uncharacteristic of Laya.

"A fast acceptance speech?" Laya asked. She smiled, or, more accurately, the muscles around her mouth quivered. "No weeping? No kissing the statuette?"

"It's not a statuette; it's a chunk of Lucite, which I'd look pretty silly smooching with. Although, according to B.F., that's about what my social life's reduced to."

The ghost of a smile had already faded. As absent was the note of resolve on which their last visit had ended. If the tape recorder hadn't been in plain sight (Ariel had spied it right away on the nightstand) the conversation of that visit might never have taken place. Laya seemed to have forgotten her claim that she knew who'd blinded her. She seemed to have forgotten Ariel's presence, or lost interest in it. Her fingers crept to the shield that still covered her eye.

"What's the matter?" Ariel asked anxiously. "Is anything wrong?"

"Good thing your interview questions are smarter than that," Laya said, "or you wouldn't be winning awards."

"I was just . . ." Ariel swallowed her retort. Adjusting to this new, mercurial Laya was challenging. "Good point," she said. "About the tape—"

"They're dismissing me."

"*Dismissing* you?"

"That's what I said. There's nothing more they can do here for the time being. Nothing to do now but wait."

Ariel shouldn't have been surprised; if she'd thought about it, she'd have realized they wouldn't keep Laya hospitalized indefinitely. She hadn't thought about it. It came to her that Laya was probably having trouble focusing on anything else. Worrying herself sick about it, in all likelihood.

"It seems chemical burns are different from other kinds of injury," Laya went on, her voice flat, "so we probably won't have to wait long, Crowne said. We should know pretty quickly whether the graft takes. Just weeks, probably. If it ulcerates, if it starts to scar . . . 'opacifying,' they call it, then—"

Ariel cringed at the image. "Where will you go? I mean—"

"Sarah Aguilar was here. She knows of a place. A sort of convalescent home, run by a nonprofit foundation."

"Are you comfortable with that?"

"I'll be fine."

She didn't look fine. She looked scared. Ariel thought fast, flipping through possibilities. Every positive one would require money. Pleasant and nurturing accommodations didn't come cheap. Caregivers didn't come cheap. She knew Laya well enough not to play Lady Bountiful. "When?" she asked.

"Anytime. As soon as Dr. Aguilar can make the arrangements."

Ariel regretted that she had no proper guest room to offer. At some unremembered time in the past, two bedrooms in her house had been incorporated into one. The alteration made for a wonderfully luxurious master bedroom, but it precluded invitations to friends. From what she knew about her solitary former life, that hadn't been a consideration. It occurred to her that up until now in her *present* life, it hadn't been all that much of a consideration. It was something she might want to give some thought to when she had a free minute or two. "I have a sofa bed in my study," she said.

"What?"

"It's comfortable. Not the Ritz, but comfortable, and private. There's a guest bath. You're welcome."

"We'll be roomies, is that what you're suggesting?" Laya gave a bad imitation of a chuckle.

"Is tomorrow okay to pick you up?"

"Don't be silly."

"Too soon? The next day, then?"

"No day."

"Give me one good reason why not."

"I can give you ten. Let's start with I'm not a charity case."

"No, you're not. You're a friend."

"I can't move in with you!"

"Sure you can. I'll hardly notice you. I'm gone all day, and . . . I see the problem. We'll get somebody to come in during the day. We'll work it out."

They proceeded to argue long enough to make Ariel late for an appointment. About the money the "somebody" would cost. About the inconvenience to Ariel. About her rashness in making the offer, rashness Laya contended she'd regret. She refused to be adopted, Laya said, like some stray. Some *helpless* stray. "Do you know the first thing about coping with a blind person?" she challenged.

"I'll learn," Ariel countered; "we'll both learn. We're not talking about forever. We're talking weeks. That's what you said."

Laya revealed a stubborn streak heretofore unsuspected. She was, however, out of her league. "Tell me you prefer some convalescent home," Ariel demanded. "Strangers. Hospital smells. Bad food, I'll bet. Scratchy sheets. Just tell me that's what you would really prefer, and I'll say '*vaya con Dios*,' and visit when I can."

The other woman swallowed, and turned her face away.

"That's it!" Ariel exclaimed. "You're coming. Excuse me a minute." She plucked her cell phone from her pocket and rescheduled the appointment she was late for. "So," she said when she'd disconnected. "Tomorrow . . . what time?"

"I can't do it."

"You can."

"There's something you don't know," Laya said in a voice too small for such a big woman.

Ariel's stomach thudded with shame. She'd been behaving as if nothing had changed, she realized, as if Laya were up to a debate, as if she were still a match for Ariel's own healthy strength. "Something about the man you believe did this to you?" she asked.

"No," Laya whispered, "it's Jessie."

"Jessie?" Relief, unfortunately, made Ariel laugh. "What's Jessie got to do with anything? Are you allergic to dogs?"

"Not allergic."

"Then what?"

"I'm afraid of them."

"You're joking!"

Laya held out her arm, angling it so that the tender underside was visible. Beginning just below the elbow's crease and running about four inches toward the wrist was a scar. From its irregular appearance, Ariel guessed that the wound hadn't been stitched properly, if at all. "The dog belonged to people down the block," Laya said. "Big old teddy bear–looking mutt. Never had a minute's trouble with him before, so they said. He'd always 'loved kids.'"

"That kind of thing happens," Ariel conceded. "But that was one particular dog, and it must have been a long time ago."

"True. I was three. I remember every second." Laya

licked dry lips. "Amazing but true. His teeth . . . I can still
see his teeth. In my arm. He was shaking me like a rag
doll."

"That's bad. It's awful! But—"

"They couldn't make him let go."

"But, Laya—"

"You think I don't know this is a phobia? *Just* a phobia?
That it's irrational? You think I haven't worked on it for
years? You think I don't know—compared to my real
problems—this is *stupid?* That doesn't make the fear less
real."

Ariel knew a thing or two about irrational fears herself.
High places—reading about high places, even thinking
about high places—made her toes curl. But dogs? She
could hardly conceive of it. Oh, unfamiliar, unleashed
Rottweilers appearing out of nowhere, okay; feral dogs in
packs, sure. But *Jessie?* Ariel was thankful she hadn't mentioned her visit to the guide dog school. "Hey," she comforted, "don't be so hard on yourself. Anybody who went
through what you did—who's going through what you
are—is entitled to a qualm or two."

"A qualm? I'm terrified!" Without warning a tear
slipped from beneath the eye shield, and then another.
Even the night of the injury, Laya hadn't wept. She'd cried
out. She'd moaned. But Ariel had never heard or seen the
woman succumb to tears. Of course, until this horror happened, she'd never seen the woman victimized. Or blind,
or helpless. "Don't!" she begged, feeling as if she might
join in. "That can't be good for your eye?"

Laya rubbed at her cheek with the back of her hand. "I
am scared," she said. She reached toward the nightstand,
fumbling to open the drawer. She felt for and found a cassette tape, which she waved in the air. "I'm scared of this!
Of *him!*"

Ariel glanced at the recorder, wondering abstractedly

why Laya had removed the tape. She clasped her hands together to keep from reaching for it. "Do you want to talk about that?" she meant to ask but didn't get a chance to.

"But I was scared before this thing happened to me," Laya interrupted. "That fear, that *spinelessness*, is why it *did* happen. I deserve it! You'd see if you heard this. Every second in this black, bottomless hell is my fault. I have to live with that."

"What some crazy did to you is not your—"

"And that doesn't scratch the surface of what I'm scared of. I'm scared to leave this bed. I'm scared to leave this room. I'm scared of everything, do you hear what I'm saying? Including dogs, including Jessie."

Ariel latched onto the last sentence; the rest was too much to deal with. "Okay," she said. "Okay, I can see she might look intimidating to somebody who doesn't know her. But you do. You've been around her. You've been to my house . . ."

"You've invited me who knows how many times. I went exactly twice. I kept the length of the room between your dog and me. I had trouble forming a coherent sentence. And that was when I could see her!"

It was true that Laya had been quiet. Ariel had thought she was being her cool, inscrutable self. "But Jessie's gentle as can be," she said. "You know that. She's trained. She's—"

"She's *big*, Ariel! I'm afraid. Every sound I can't identify. Everything I can't see. Odors. Smoke. I have a horror of fire. I dream about it. I smell smoke. I feel the heat, and I'm trapped. I can't find a door. There're no windows. No doors. No one hears me screaming because I can't make a sound." Laya stopped, breathing through her mouth. Her fingers curled and uncurled. She swallowed convulsively before she said, "You know what I'm the most afraid of? The thing I'm most afraid of is being alone."

"I understand, but you're not—"

"No, you don't. You think I'm talking about other people? Not having friends or family to count on? You mean well, Ariel, but you do not understand."

"Then explain it so I can."

"My God, would you *quit!* It's that . . . I tried to tell you the other day. I don't have *me* anymore!"

"Go on."

"I can't. I don't know how. I'm not good with words."

"Oh, yeah?" It was true that Laya wasn't a big talker. She'd said more today and revealed far more about herself than Ariel had ever known her to. But in one situation she'd always been eloquent. "In class," Ariel said, "at the end when we're into relaxation? The things you say then are like poetry."

Laya's mouth twisted. "Your enlightened teacher! So evolved, so in the now." Her voice took on a lulling, hypnotic quality as she said, "'Let your thoughts come, and let your thoughts go. Let them drift away on a gentle wind. Focus on that spot in the forehead center, the third eye . . .'" Laya's voice went flat. "Too bad that third eye's mystical," she said. "I could use it now." She made an effort to laugh. "Preaching all these years about primal joy . . . about inner peace. About banishing fear, and banishing the fear of fear. What a fraud!"

It seemed that hours passed before, more calmly, she said, "Before now, solitude held no threat. I was never less alone than when I was alone, do you see? I had me."

Ariel nodded, caught herself, and said, "Yes."

"I spent years achieving that. Seeing myself as I am. Learning to be at peace in myself. I knew who I was. But my sense of self was a lie. The person I thought I was doesn't exist. There's just this . . . hollow darkness."

Ariel kept quiet. She couldn't understand the process Laya had been through, but she could understand the vacuum. She was engulfed by a surge of memory: the earliest days of her memory loss, days of panic, of lonely desolation. Surely that wasn't so different from what Laya was feeling now.

"I told you," Laya eventually said, "that I couldn't explain it. You can't understand."

Ariel didn't doubt what needed to be said, just whether she was the one to say it. But she was the only one here. Groping for the words, determined not to sugarcoat them, she said, "You've got reason to be scared. Real fears. Legitimate fears, and I don't only mean this . . . man, whoever he is. Dealing with a world you can't see? Not knowing if the transplant will work? If it doesn't, you'll have to adjust to a different future than you expected to have. And you *will* have to find a way to forgive yourself for whatever it is you think you've done or . . . or . . . betrayed."

Ariel paused, distracted by the word. She found herself remembering the quote from Dorothy's letter. "There is only one way to achieve happiness on this terrestrial ball, and that is to have a clear conscience, or none at all." She didn't think Ogden Nash would make the same impression on Laya as he had on Dorothy. "I can't make guarantees about those things. Nobody can. You'll deal with them or you won't. If you'll let me help, I will. There's just one thing I can absolutely guarantee: my dog will not harm you."

"Forget it."

"This is one fear, Laya, that you can face down. You've got to. If you don't, you might as well pack it in. You won't heal. Fear will undercut you, and fast or slow, sooner or later, it will destroy you."

Laya didn't reply.

"It's step one," Ariel said quietly, "and all the odds are in your favor. A win-win situation."

Laya lay stiffly. Her chest rose and fell, fast, as if she'd been running. After a while she took a deep breath. Her breathing slowed. It was some time, though, before she spoke. "Easy for you to say."

"Actually, it was hard, which is why I've probably said it all wrong, but I've never been more sure about anything in my life."

"Is that right? I'll tell you what, Ariel . . ." Laya felt around the sheets. The cassette she'd dropped earlier was in plain sight near her hip, but Ariel held still and let her find it for herself. "I'd changed my mind," Laya said, "about letting you have this, but here . . . Do you want it?"

Ariel's curiosity had gotten her in over her head before. "Of course I want it," she said, reaching.

"One thing first. What's on here is said in confidence."

"Okay," Ariel agreed.

"You break trust, and—"

"I said okay."

Laya hesitated long enough to make Ariel fear she'd changed her mind again. "You listen to it," Laya finally said. "Then you come back and tell me you still want me in your house. I'll go. I'll *face down* your dog. I'll *face down* all my bogeymen. I'll be the all-time champion blind woman." She put the small plastic rectangle into Ariel's hand. "But listen to the tape first."

14

"WHAT I'M ASKING YOU TO DO, ARIEL, IS PROBABLY IMPOSSI-BLE."

Despite the disclaimer, Laya's taped voice was strong, a one-eighty from her mood of that morning. Ariel had to remind herself that this had probably been taped days

before, when the emotional roller coaster Laya was riding
had been on an upswing, when she'd been feeling res-
olute. Even then, however, she'd been realistic.

It was late evening now, and Ariel was in Laya's apartment, directed here to retrieve a folder of newspaper clip-
pings. She'd found it just where Laya had said it would be.
It was thin. There were only two articles inside, both
brief. The one from the African-American–owned weekly,
the *Sentinel*, was only a line or two longer than the one
from the *Times*. Ariel was surprised there'd been any cov-
erage at all; in fact, she couldn't understand why there had
been. Assaults, even grievous assaults, in the crime-
scourged South Central district of L.A. didn't normally
rate ink. A night *without* an assault would rate a special edition.

She lay on her friend's living room sofa. The file and
the recorder rested on her stomach. She turned the single
lamp in the room low, the better to concentrate on the
contents of the tape, some of which she'd already listened
to. She'd played snatches during every free moment of
what had developed into a three-alarm afternoon. Now,
she intended to hear it through, start to finish. Pressing
Stop and Rewind, she spoke in unison with the opening
statement: "'What I'm asking you to do, Ariel, is probably
impossible.'" Ariel hit Pause. *Probably* impossible? Laya
understated, as she herself had later come to realize; finding the man she believed had blinded her was a lost cause.
However . . .

Ariel sighed hugely. Letting her forgotten friend
Dorothy fall through the cracks still rankled, but she'd
(mostly) accepted that. There had been no further communication from the woman; she had little choice. As to
Laya, she had no choice; if there was anything she could
do, she would. She'd give it her best shot.

When she'd again pressed Play, she set the recorder on

the coffee table, and got to her feet. She began to pace, listening, alert for anything helpful she could have missed before.

"It would've been tough," Laya's voice continued, "when I could see. Now, how I could begin to identify him is beyond me, but I have to . . ." Ariel heard a small growl of dissatisfaction and Laya muttering to herself, "Start over, girl. Start at the start.

"This was a week, no, five nights before . . . before the eyedrops. The Friday before. It must've been around nine. I was leaving Martine's. Martine Brown, I'm talking about. She runs . . . I guess you'd call it a settlement house. It's an informal kind of thing for teenage girls. Strictly volunteer, pro bono, but she's got good connections. Women come there and hold classes. A CPA, beauty operators, a chef— like that. A neighborhood artist who's getting a name . . . It's on Adams, a big yellow house in the twenty-one hundred block. I teach yoga Friday nights.

"I'd stayed a few minutes after class to have a Coke or whatever with Martine, so when I left, all my girls had gone already. Martine wanted to walk me to my car because—well, you know what that area's like, and I'd had to park down the block quite a ways. If I'd taken her up on her offer, if she'd been with me when . . ." There was a sibilance on the tape, a sharp hiss of impatience. "No ifs. I know better than to start with the ifs! Okay . . ." Laya drew breath and let it out before she continued.

As she had that morning, Ariel remarked Laya's unaccustomed talkativeness. She was aware that losing one sense may sharpen others, but she'd never heard of blindness whetting the tongue. Perhaps being unable to see other people made Laya feel, in some strange way, invisible herself, disembodied and free. Talking, then, to an inanimate object over which she had total control must have been doubly liberating. Or, perhaps it was only that she had held in her story too long; her words flowed like water through a ruptured dam, rushing and snagging on impatient self-censorship and breaking through again.

"I'd just passed what's left of this store," Laya was saying. "A little Asian mom-and-pop that got torched during the riots . . . you'll see it if you go over there. I was at the alley that runs by the store. That was when I heard it. The sounds. It was something like, I don't know . . . Yes, I do. It was how a melon would sound if you smashed it with a lead pipe. Then there was this . . . this *oof!*, like how a person would sound if you smashed him in the stomach with a lead pipe. And grunts, like somebody working hard.

"I made a racket, I remember. My foot bumped a bottle or something. It got quiet. I could hear loud breathing. And moaning. I could hear somebody moaning. I walked . . . I went to where I could see into the alley. I mean, I could see shapes in the dark. They were about halfway down, about . . . maybe twenty feet from me. Three of them. Three men. One was holding another one. Like from the back is what I'm saying, by his arms. The third man was in front of the . . . the victim. Closest to me. Facing me. He stood there a minute, watching me. He didn't say a word. Then he turned back around—like I wasn't even there! Or he didn't care if I was . . . that I saw. And he raised this thing in his hand, this tool, and he brought it down . . . hard, on that man's shoulder. I heard it break! My God, the bone . . . !

"It was a tire iron. I read that later in the paper."

Ariel had scrunched into the sofa, slumped against the armrest, totally focused on Laya's voice, which filled the small, dimly lit room. Any unexpected noise just then would have been startling; the crash at the front door nearly launched her into orbit. Bolt upright, she cocked her head and listened.

She heard another, smaller crash, and then a voice. A

deep, bass mutter. That she could hear it clearly enough to make out the angry curse did not instill confidence in the solidity of the door. The door she wasn't dead sure she'd locked. The door that was probably hollow core. Anything stronger than a swift kick would shatter it. A tire iron, for example. A tire iron would reduce it to kindling. Ariel made herself move toward it. The lock was in place. The guard chain was not. She slipped it home.

Laya's apartment was in a nice enough area; it was not in a security building. There was no common entry hall, no doorman, no buzzer to control admittance. Exterior iron steps led from ground-level apartments to the open landing of the second level, Laya's, then to the third and topmost level. Anyone could come and go. Whoever had come hadn't gone; Ariel could hear him outside the door.

The peephole revealed nothing but a fish-eyed distortion of the concrete block wall across the landing. Pressing her ear against the door, Ariel heard a soft thump, from below, from the vicinity of her feet. She frowned her confusion. Seconds passed. What seemed like minutes passed. Laya's strained voice continued unheeded in the background. The block wall remained unobstructed. Then Ariel distinctly heard the sound of someone moving *away* from the door. Still, she could see no one outside. Was the man a midget?

There was no handy weapon near the door. No baseball bat. No umbrella. Not even a fly swatter. Aware that she was being foolhardy but unable to stand it a second longer, she braced herself, turned the lock, and eased open the door till it met the chain's resistance. No one was there. Nothing happened. She looked down to see pot shards and dirt. She could, just, see the prickly edge of a cactus in the debris. Fear ebbed as anger surged. The brave little garden outside Laya's door was, apparently, history. It had been in decent shape, she'd been glad to notice, when she arrived. Guilty to notice. She'd forgotten all about the plants.

She angled her eye to the right. One still-upright palm partially obscured her view, but a slice of steps going on to the third floor was visible. A man's head entered her line of sight, and then his body. He appeared to be crawling up the steps.

"Eight," he said, "and . . . seven." Laboriously, he made another step, where, rump wavering, he paused. "Seven and counting," he said. He sang tunelessly for a moment. His head dropped back as he squinted upward, toward the possibly unattainable summit. "'Why?' you ask," Ariel heard him say. "I'll tell you why," she thought he said. The words were slurred. "'Because it's there.'" He sounded pleased with himself. "Onward!" he said clearly, and almost lost a step.

Relief made Ariel sponge-kneed. Leaning her forehead against the door, she started to ease it closed. Then something on the concrete floor beyond the threshold caught her eye. She unfastened the chain. Plunk in the middle of scattered dirt and broken pottery was a bottle. In the bottom was a scant quarter inch of wine, and poked into the neck was a twenty-dollar bill.

She peered up at the happy drunk, who by now had scaled the pinnacle and was pulling himself upright with the help of the iron banister. Pay as you go, she thought; cash on the barrelhead.

After the comic relief, returning to the tape, to real menace, was tough. Ariel rewound it until she'd found her place.

". . . he raised this thing in his hand, this tool," Laya, mechanically, repeated, "and he brought it down . . . hard, on that man's shoulder. I heard it break! My God, the bone . . . !

"It was a tire iron. I read that later in the paper.

"I think I yelled. I can't swear it. He said something to his buddy, and then he laughed. He laughed! He was tossing the tire iron from one hand to the other, like you'd do a ball. To show off what good hands you've got? He never took his eyes off me. Those few seconds seemed like they went on forever, like everything was in slow motion. And then he started toward me.

"I was closer to my car than I was to Martine's, so that's where I ran. I could hear him behind me. I thought I did. I didn't look back. When I'd got the car started, when I was moving, I did look back. I didn't see him. He's getting his car, I thought, to come after me, or . . . he's gone back." Ariel heard what was clearly a swallow. "To finish what he started."

There was a rustle then, as of sheets, and a clatter some distance from the recorder. Laya reaching for a tissue? No, water; Ariel could hear ice clinking. She wondered if Laya found the glass where it belonged or if one of the nurses, "helpfully" tidying, had moved it. The tape turned nearly silently for a few seconds.

"Where I grew up," Laya eventually said, and she had a rein on her voice, "was no Sunday school picnic, let me tell you. People wonder—you know?—how they'll react if they ever come face-to-face with real danger? If their . . . well, their *courage* were tested? Not this kid! I knew. When push came to shove, I shoved back.

"You hear the stories about witnesses to street violence. The ones who pull down their shades and don't get involved? They don't see nothing, they don't hear nothing, they don't do nothing. Even after years of yoga—you know, *kshama*, forbearance, tolerance—I still had contempt for people like that. I couldn't help it. Couldn't imagine that kind of callousness. If I saw a fellow human being victimized, I wouldn't think twice! I'd *do* something."

The recorder had been turned off then, for how long Ariel had no way of knowing. "What a mouth I've got on me tonight," Laya said when she came back. "I meant to give you the facts, not my life story. And I don't have to explain what I mean, anyway, do I? You know what I'm talking about. It's the kind of thing you think you know about yourself, deep down, as sure as you know anything. I would no more be a coward, I believed, than I'd be a thief.

"I've thought about that night . . . every minute, over and over. I've rewritten every second. I see me screaming bloody murder and running for help. I rush to a phone and call nine-one-one." Ariel heard a weak laugh. "I use my police whistle. Yep. Had one in my bag the whole time. Then . . ." Laya exhaled. Her voice was different when she said, "There's this other fantasy I have.

"*Ahimsa*. You know what that means? Do no harm. Nonviolence. Basic yogic principle. Well, in this other scenario I get in my car and drive straight through that alley, gunning it like a bat out of hell. I sit on the horn. Blast away loud enough to wake the dead. I wish to God I had! Aimed at that evil bastard and pinned him to the wall! Let *him* see what pain felt like. Yeah, right.

"I couldn't get out of there fast enough!

"I drove . . . I don't know how far, just trying to put distance between me and them, before I got my brain working. I *was* thinking on some level. I understood . . . I grasped that what I'd seen wasn't somebody killing somebody. One blow with that tire iron, aimed right, would've done that. What I'd seen was punishment. Inflicting pain. And the one handing it out liked what he was doing.

"When I did stop at a phone, finally, it was dead. It was blocks before I saw another one. I didn't have to get out to see the receiver was missing. I was frantic by then! Why would I expect a phone in that war zone to work? How long had I been gone? How many more times had that guy been pounded? How many more bones broken? What I should've done was obvious. It didn't hit me till then: Martine's house! Why hadn't I driven there to start with?

"By the time I went back, a police car was already there. Blocking the alley. Lights flashing. Cops yelling. I kept driving. Leave it to them, I told myself. There's nothing you can do. They're used to that kind of hell. Trained for it. Of course, by the time they got there it was too late to *apprehend* the *perpetrators*, as they say on TV. They were long gone. And as for the victim, he was trashed. Mush for brains. James Price, his name is. I read it in the paper the next day. He was in a coma. Still was, the last time I called the hospital *anonymously* to check.

"So there you have it, Ariel. Pretty sorry tale, isn't it? I guess somebody else saw, too, or heard. Somebody with the guts to report it. I was off the hook. Nobody would ever have to know I was there. Nobody, that is, but me. And him.

"I saw him, Ariel. Not the man holding Price; him I didn't see except as a shape. I've got no sense of him at all. I don't think of him at all, not even now. But the other one . . . when he looked at me . . . when I thought he was coming after me, he stepped into what light there was. I did see him then, and he had to know it.

"What he did not know is I wouldn't talk. I didn't get a good enough look. I didn't! I couldn't describe him or pick him out of a lineup. I couldn't say what he wore. How old he was . . . How tall, or if he was little or big.

"I came up with every reason in the world not to talk— even to blaming the victim. I know him—know of him. He's no good. A dirtbag." Laya laughed, bitterly. "See? That's the kind of argument I give myself for keeping quiet. But nobody deserves what I saw being done to James Price.

"This was likely a gang thing. In L.A.? What're the odds it's anything else! And we know what happens to witnesses. You read about *good citizens* who have the guts to talk. If they're lucky, it stops at threats, not just to them. Their families. Maybe just a beating. If they're unlucky, they're the latest AK-47 victims. A few get away. All that happens to them is they move someplace else and spend the rest of their lives looking behind them.

"But this guy—Mr. X—couldn't know, could he, that I wouldn't be a good citizen. Too spineless. But he saw me, and he saw my car . . ."

There was a momentary lull, and Ariel imagined that Laya might have been picturing that car. A VW bug she'd bought used, misused by a host of former owners, and treated only marginally better by Laya, to whom automobiles held no interest as long as they started and rolled. It was painted the color of an egg yolk, visible from distant galaxies. The vanity plate, a gift arranged by a student of hers who'd died of AIDS, read: N THE NOW. If "Mr. X" saw that car and that plate, Laya might as well have left her card.

"He found me, Ariel," Laya said then, "and he found the one way short of killing me to make sure I couldn't point the finger at him."

The recorder had definitely been turned off at that point. Ariel had a hunch it had been for the night. She took a break, too, to clean up the mess outside Laya's door and salvage what could be salvaged of the plants, but mostly to gain distance from the ugliness of what she'd thus far heard. Laya, she figured, had felt the same need.

As she swept up pot shards, Ariel found herself wondering, inevitably, how she would have reacted that night in that place. She pictured the scene. She could actually feel her muscles tighten, ready to . . . do what exactly? She would like to believe she'd have coped better than Laya.

Of course she'd like to believe it. Anybody would *like* to believe they wouldn't freeze. Wouldn't panic. Wouldn't run. Might even be heroic. The truth was, she didn't know what she'd have done that particular night in those particular circumstances. No one, man or woman, could know until they were faced with two feet of solid iron in the hands of an animal who enjoys breaking bones. Breaking a skull.

Ariel went back to the tape. Laya's voice was businesslike, entirely different, as if the bright light of day had brought her a colder perspective.

"I listened to this during the night. I'm not giving it to you. I can't stomach the thought of anybody hearing it. There's no point. I couldn't have identified Mr. X even when I could see. If I couldn't then, I sure can't now. All I could tell the cops or you is that he was black. Doesn't exactly pin him down, does it? Before you ask—no, I didn't hear his voice. So you can forget that whole thing about helping find him. Stupid idea. Can't be done.

"I almost erased the tape. What I decided to do instead is hang on to it. Put it somewhere safe. If anything else happens to me, you'll find it, and you'll know why . . . whatever happens happened. Who knows? Maybe then, put together with new evidence, this long song and dance will actually be some help.

"You think I'm being paranoid? Don't.

"You know I sometimes have a way of sensing things. Knowing things, shall we say. I don't talk about it because it makes people uncomfortable. It makes *you* uncomfortable, doesn't it? But it's true, and you know it's true. Believe me when I tell you, Ariel, this isn't over. There's something coming at me, something bad, and all I can figure is that he's not through with me yet."

15

ARIEL SAT FOR QUITE A LITTLE WHILE THINKING OVER WHAT she'd heard. Eventually, she roused herself and made a quick reconnaissance of the apartment. Her intention was to make sure, belatedly, that everything was as it should be—perishables cleaned out of the refrigerator and garbage taken out and windows closed, all the things she should have come over and checked long before now—but she found herself lingering in the bedroom doorway, staring at the spot where she'd found Laya nearly two weeks before, reliving the ghastliness of that middle-of-the-night call and all that followed.

Maybe it was suggestibility, but she had a strong feeling Laya was right: this thing wasn't over.

It was not within her power, Ariel realized, to conceive of such a man as Laya described. Not in any real, dimensional way. She could not make real the kind of individual who could torture a fellow human, could slaughter inch by inch, bone by broken bone. What came to mind was stereotype: the maniacal leer of some cartoon villain, some cinematic Nazi hissing venom. But a man who could inflict excruciating pain, not in the throes of rage or fear or madness, but coldly, and with pleasure? No.

She closed her eyes. She tried to put herself into a mind that would enjoy not only the physical sight and sounds and stink of suffering, but that could also thrill to the *image* of suffering. He existed. A blind woman with eyes that might never heal, with a soul that might never heal, was proof of it.

He had sowed the seeds of destruction, and then, at a

distance, at his leisure, he had envisioned a woman going about her life, feeling safe in her own home—not thinking about safety one way or the other; it would be the furthest thing from her mind—engaged in an act as ordinary as reaching for a small plastic bottle in her medicine cabinet.

Ariel's eyelids fluttered. She felt her heart accelerate, the blood pumping into her fingertips. In that instant, with a clarity that was electric, she connected. She was there, when it happened.

Through someone's eyes, she could see the woman, bathed in the white glare of the bathroom light. The woman is opening the little bottle, humming along with the saxophone on the radio and thinking of changing the station because of the static. She glances into the mirror, noticing a line in her face that she thinks is new, but not caring overmuch. Her eyes feel gritty from staying up too late. She sees the redness of the veins, anticipates how soothing the eyedrops will feel. And then she tilts her head back and squeezes the bottle, blinking, one quick squirt and then another, shutting her eyes to keep the liquid from leaking, and she gasps, and she cries out, and the universe has gone horribly wrong, and she claws at her eyes and her cheeks in disbelief and panic, and, finally, in agony.

Ariel's skin crawled. It leapt. Her eyes flew open, and she shook herself, shuddering the image away. She was shaken. She was, literally, shaking. Cold sweat was drying on her skin. Her hands were clenched into fists. She forced them open, staring at the nails. She knew as surely as if she'd been in this room that night: what she'd just seen was what had taken place.

It had been too real. A vision? An emanation? From what source? Did Laya's eerie repertoire include telepathy? Did traces of the abilities she claimed linger here among her things like a vapor? Some sort of psychic afterglow?

"Swamp gas!" Ariel said aloud, and snorted at her foolishness. What she'd seen, what she'd *imagined*, had come neither from Laya's mind nor from that of the person who'd victimized her. He, Mr. X, was probably just a thug. A punk "banger." His mental voyeurism was the product of her own fevered brain. Laya was probably right. His objective was to make sure she couldn't identify him, period. He'd doctored the bottle, and assumed he'd get the desired result. If . . .

If the man in the alley and the man who blinded Laya were one and the same.

Would a thug who got off on suffering deny himself the pleasure of seeing Laya's agony up close? Would he go to the trouble of doctoring eyedrops—hardly a surefire solution to neutralizing a witness—when he could ring Laya's doorbell, confront her face-to-face, and toss acid into her eyes? Was it the face-to-face part that deterred him? Why didn't he just shoot her dead? Ariel suddenly thought of Mr. X's cohort. She kept forgetting about Mr. Y. If X favored the hands-on approach, what about Y? The kind of slime who'd hold a man while he was beaten senseless was as deadly as his partner. Was he more devious? More cowardly? Ariel's mind reeled with questions.

And speculation's not going to answer them, she told herself. It was time to go. But first, briskly, she made herself complete her original mission: to check the place out. It wasn't a big apartment, and Laya was a tidy lady, and it didn't take long.

When she'd selected some clothes for Laya and locked the door behind her, she took the stairs to one of the ground-level apartments. She had called earlier, and was expected. Lugging a carrier to her car with her cargo making unhappy noises inside it, Ariel went home. It would be interesting, she thought, to see what Jessie would make of Arthur the cat.

• • •

"What time can I pick you up?" Ariel asked Laya over the phone. It was nine the next morning, and Ariel had already been at her desk for two hours. She scanned the mail Tara had left. (No hand-addressed envelope, no San Rafael postmark, no follow-up from Dorothy. It was reflex by now; Ariel was hardly aware she was doing it.) "It's best for me early afternoon," she said into the phone, and began flipping through message slips. One caught her eye. The call was from the 415 area, from a Rob Millen. Who? she thought, and then saw that he'd helpfully identified himself: "Meg's friend from the dinner party." Hmm, she thought. Maybe she'd seen a gleam of interest after all. Whatever. She was just relieved the call was from Rob the columnist rather than Bland the bore. "Say twelve-thirty?" she said to Laya. "I picked up some clothes at your place. I'll bring—"

"Did you listen to the tape?"

"You thought I wouldn't get around to it for a while?"

"And?"

"And you're being way too hard on yourself. Merciless. You weren't perfect? The yogic ideal? The quintessence of self-sacrificing fortitude? So you won't be canonized this month."

Very quietly, Laya said, "I was afraid I couldn't make you understand."

"I understand that you found yourself in a situation that would've had anybody sane heading for the hills and changing his drawers when he got there."

"Anybody? What about you, Ariel?"

"I'm sane," Ariel said.

"Yeah? What if everybody was 'sane'? What would it be like in this city if everybody who saw another person in trouble cut and ran? Think about it. What if everybody behaved like me?" When Ariel didn't immediately answer,

Laya said, "Do something for me, will you? Call the hospital—Martin Luther King—and find out how James Price is."

Ariel didn't volunteer the information that she already had called. "I can do that," she hedged.

"Oh, God, let him be all right!" Laya prayed. "If I'd intervened, if I'd done the *minimum*—called for help right away—"

"The police might have gotten there a minute or two faster. Or not."

"I should've—"

"Should've what? Cut yourself some slack, Laya. The man you saw in that alley is a monster. Look what he did to you. Isn't that bad enough? If you'd interfered in any way that night, you'd almost certainly be dead."

"I'm surprised."

"At?"

"Your not challenging whether it was the same man. The man in the alley. The man who blinded me. I figured you'd be skeptical about that."

"We'll proceed on the assumption they're the same."

"Oh, Ariel! *Proceed*? Proceed where?"

"We'll talk about that later. Can you get sprung by twelve-thirty?"

Ariel had, in fact, been as skeptical as Laya expected until only an hour before. Her skepticism had diminished considerably after she'd called around the hospitals and found no patient named James Price, and had then called a friend at the *Times*, who consulted her computer and located a follow-up story Laya had missed. Ariel saw no reason to mention that story to Laya now or later.

It was as brief as the two Laya had clipped. It reported that James Price, twenty-one, a resident of Los Angeles, had died from injuries received during a brutal March twenty-seventh assault in an alley in the 2100 block of

Adams Boulevard. "The assailant or assailants," the story said, "remain unidentified."

The story ran in the morning edition of the paper on March thirty-first. In the pre-dawn darkness of the following morning Laya had been blinded.

16

A CRISIS ERUPTED AT *THE OPEN FILE* AT PRECISELY HIGH NOON. The legal department suddenly decided to renege on okays for Ariel's next segment, and within minutes her office was awash with dark suits, hot tempers, and convoluted adverbs no one but a lawyer would consider using. When Ariel actually heard "hereinbelow" spoken aloud, she broke. Everyone was shouting, no one was listening, and she was due to pick up Laya. She stuck two fingers between her lips and whistled. It worked with Jessie, and it worked with this crew, all of whom stopped dead, looking appalled.

The issue was less than a tempest in a teapot; it was a tempest in a thimble, easily fixed, as someone finally pointed out, by cutting one question in an interview. It wasn't even a pivotal question.

Ariel was twenty minutes late to the hospital. Laya was waiting. Stiff backed, she was perched on the side of the bed, her purse on her lap and a plastic bag parked at her feet, which dangled. She cocked her head when Ariel burst breathlessly into the room, clutching Laya's clothes and babbling apologies. Laya's shoulders relaxed marginally, but her hold on her purse tightened, as if she thought it might be snatched away. Her mouth tightened as well. Ariel's own mouth snapped shut. She experienced an instant of disorientation so strong she almost apologized again, for having gotten the wrong room; she could hardly recognize the woman she'd always known for her tranquility, her utter self-possession.

Laya was already dressed, in a garment unlike anything Ariel had ever seen her wear. The pastel dress had small pearl buttons, and delicate cutwork on the collar. It looked old-fashioned and virginal, and in it, Ariel fancied, Laya looked like an anxious mail-order bride awaiting collection at the depot.

The dark glasses not quite hiding eye shields made for a jarring note.

"They're getting another wheelchair," Ariel said. "There was a mix-up, and the one they'd ordered got taken away." Laya nodded. Light glinted off the glasses. "Because I was late, I guess," Ariel added, and forced down a repetition of her apology. "We've got a really pretty day out there," she said, "nice and sunny." Laya turned her face toward the window, as if to check whether Ariel might be misrepresenting the weather. Her mouth turned up. A patently polite smile. The disappointed mail-order bride being agreeable, Ariel thought, making the best of a bad bargain.

"So, are you all set?" she asked, and was nauseated by her chirpiness. "I sound like I'm trying to sell you something."

"Ariel . . ."

"What?"

"Tell me one thing."

"If I can."

"What color is this outfit I've got on?"

"It's pretty. Where'd you get it?"

"One of the nurses."

"Gave it to you?"

"She said it was an 'incentive purchase' that didn't

work, when she was in Weight Watchers. It was giving her the guilts hanging in her closet, she said."

"Sounds like Dinah."

"What color is it?"

"Kind of lemony. Or maybe citron."

"Crap!" Laya sighed. "I look like a fruit bowl."

Ariel burst out laughing. "You look nice. You don't look much like yourself, but you do look nice."

The easing of tension didn't last. There was a last-minute glitch with a release form; the nurse steering the requisite wheelchair shouldn't have been issued a license for it; and when they emerged through the hospital's front doors, Laya looked as if she were being wheeled to the edge of a precipice. She stumbled getting from chair to car, and when she was securely belted inside, she was breathing as heavily as if she'd been sprinting.

She looked more anxious with every mile Ariel drove.

"I'll be working at home this afternoon," Ariel said with a glance at her passenger, "so you won't be left to Jessie's mercy." There was no discernible reaction. "And, hey, I made up a gumbo for dinner," she went on to say. "It's slow-cooking as we speak." Correction: as *I* speak. As I babble. "Strictly vegetarian," she said aloud, "I promise." That got the barest suggestion of a negative head shake. "Laya? What . . . ?"

"See?" Laya said grimly. "I was right. It's starting already."

"What is?"

"You're having to take time off, working at home, and . . . where *will* you work? You're being run out of your own study! And feeling uptight about your own dog. And changing your eating habits. Call Sarah Aguilar. She can still make arrangements for me."

"Laya! Would you please—"

"Call her, Ariel. This is not going to work."

Without warning, Ariel changed lanes, squealed to the curb, and hit the brakes, startling Laya as well as the man in front of whose house she'd stopped. He clutched his leaf blower, a painfully loud machine, and stared. Ariel waggled her fingers in greeting, as though they were expected guests, and smiled, and then ignored the man entirely. "You're right!" she said. "It's not!"

"Fine," Laya agreed.

"Let me finish." Ariel raised her voice to be heard over the noise of the machine as well as a sanitation department truck that rumbled by just then. "It's not going to work with you acting like the poor little match girl."

"The what?"

"You heard me! I said poor little—"

"I did not hear you. What's that awful noise?"

"MATCH GIRL!" Ariel shouted.

"Where are we?"

"In front of some man's house."

"What man? What's that racket?"

It abated as the homeowner, watching them over his shoulder, moved away. Ariel took advantage of the comparative quiet to say, "Listen to me! I wouldn't have invited you if I didn't want you! We won't be joined at the hip! If at any time I'm inconvenienced, it won't kill me! But I will not keep walking on eggs around you!"

"Could we please go?" Laya said, her teeth clenched.

"No. We're going to get this settled," Ariel said. "Come with me or don't, that's up to you, but stop with the attitude."

A junker vibrating with rap cruised past. "All right!" Laya exclaimed, her voice rising. "I'll come. Let's go."

The leaf blower man was making his way back, looking suspicious of their continued presence in front of his home. He came toward them, his chin jutting, his leaf blower held in front of him like a weapon. (Yard rage?

Ariel thought.) She waved bye-bye, put the car into gear, and nearly sideswiped a car she hadn't seen. When, horn blaring, it was safely past, she pulled swiftly away. "God help me!" she thought she heard Laya mumble into her chest. She appeared to be praying.

"I'm sorry," Ariel said, "and that's the last time I'm going to say that to you. I'll probably be a crummy host-ess, and, no doubt, I'll break every rule in the book as regards coexistence with a visually impaired person, so I'll just make one big blanket apology now and get it over with. Forgive me?"

"For what?"

"Yelling. Jumping on you. Whatever. All past and future sins."

Laya waved a dismissive hand. "What attitude?" she eventually said.

"You're kidding, right?"

"No."

"Anger I can handle. Self-reproach bears discussion. As for self-pity, well, you've got a right, but there's got to be a quota." Half-facetiously, Ariel said, "Tell you what. Let's agree on a signal. Anytime I see you going down for the third time, I'll say . . ." She thought of the Hindu word with which Laya concluded her classes, palms pressed prayer-like to her chest. "*Namaste?*" Like "aloha," she'd been told, it served as both hello and good-bye. It had always had a benevolent sound to Ariel, like a blessing. She glanced at her passenger. Laya's expression was stricken. It dawned on Ariel that being reminded of classes she no longer taught wasn't likely to snatch the woman from the depths of despondency. "Sorry," she said, and nearly missed the last turn onto her street, "bad idea."

"You apologized again," Laya said.

Her skin felt clammy when Ariel took her arm to guide her up the walkway to the house. "Two steps," she said, and without mishap, Laya took them to the porch. Ariel glanced through the window. Jessie was there. Having recognized the sound of Ariel's car, she was stretching luxuriously, preparing to greet her mistress. Ariel gave the shepherd a signal, a swift downward sweep of her hand, and Jessie immediately dropped to her belly.

"Okay," Ariel told Laya, "Jess is in the living room. She's lying down, and she'll stay until I say otherwise. If you want me to, though, I'll put her in the kitchen or someplace till you get oriented. Why don't you wait here, and I'll do that?"

Laya gave her head a quick shake, and put her hand out, memory, no doubt, telling her that the door was just ahead.

"Another couple of feet," Ariel said. "Okay, here we are." She inserted her key, glancing again through the window. Jessie lay quietly, panting with anticipation. Ariel tried to see her—to perceive her—as Laya did. Jessie watched curiously. "Are you sure you don't want me to shut her in another room?"

"She can't live shut in another room."

Ariel's mouth, oddly, was dry. She felt uneasy, as though it were she who was meeting a test, almost as though they really were about to confront danger. "Everything will be fine," she encouraged; "you'll see."

As she reacquainted her guest with the layout of the entry ("Step down here, remember?") and the living room ("Footstool at two o'clock, and oh! I forgot; new table since you were here."), Jessie lay calm and observant, taking in the activity. Nothing moved but her tail, which thumped once. Ariel could almost believe that, beyond scenting fear, the dog comprehended the situation.

The two women had made it as far as the dining room when the phone rang.

"The machine'll pick it up," Ariel said.

"No." Laya firmly disengaged her arm. "Go ahead."

The nearest extension was back in the living room. The caller was Ariel's grandfather.

"I've got something I think might interest you," he said.

"Oh? What?" Ariel was watching Laya. She stood as rock still as a monument in a park.

"It's no big thing," B.F. said, "it may not be anything at all. But I know you're always trying to dig up whatever you can about your past, so when I recalled—"

"B.F., where are you?" Ariel cut in. "I'm going to have to call you back. I'm kind of in the middle of something."

Jessie, as if to question when she might be allowed to move, made a small sound in her throat.

Laya jumped. Her hands out in front of her, she bolted—if one could be said to bolt when one's feet are scuttling in baby steps—toward the kitchen.

"You can't call me back," B.F. was saying. "I'll be—"

"Whoa, Laya!" Ariel called out. "Just a second!" And to her grandfather, she said, "Hold the phone!" Before the words left her mouth, she saw that Jessie had taken to her feet and was heading for Laya. Ariel, almost more astonished than dismayed, ran in pursuit. Jessie had planted herself directly in the blind woman's path. Ears erect, muzzle lifted, the dog was mere inches from the lemon-colored skirt. Laya was rigid. Her hands were plastered against her chest, as if to keep them from ravening jaws. "Oh, God!" she was whispering. "Oh, God! Oh, God! I hear her! Where is she?"

Ariel took in the situation at a glance. "It's okay," she soothed, and moved to Laya. "You're fine. You're okay." She put her arm around Laya's waist. The woman was vibrating with fear. "Good girl, Jessie!" Ariel said quietly. "Sit." Jessie did.

Laya took a step backward. Her voice was an octave higher than usual and rising when she said, "*Good*? You said the dog wouldn't move! You said she wouldn't, not until—"

"Let me tell you what happened, okay?" Ariel interrupted. "I'm sorry to admit it, but there's a mop and bucket right square in the way. You would've tripped over them in four more steps." She moved the offending objects. "You could've hit your head on the table. Maybe sprained something." She smiled. "Your dignity at the least."

"Where is . . . What's the dog . . . What was she trying—"

"Roadblock. She stationed herself between you and the bucket."

"Are you trying to tell me that . . ." Laya licked her lips. Her shoulders sagged. Querulously, she said, "What's a mop and bucket doing out in the middle of the floor!"

"My cleaning lady was here this morning. She tends to get in a hurry when she's finishing up. One time she left the kitchen garbage on the dining room table."

"You need a new cleaning lady."

"She has her virtues. She's crazy about Jessie."

After a moment Laya asked, "You're saying the dog knew? That I couldn't see? How? How could she know?"

Ariel peered at Jessie. Jessie cocked her head. "Laya," Ariel said, "it beats me!"

"What's she doing now?"

"Sitting there looking at us. She knows we're talking about her. I don't suppose you'd consider petting her?"

"Not a chance."

"Later, then. Right now I've got a surprise for you."

"No more surprises. Please!"

"You'll like this one."

Arthur the cat was ensconced on the sofa bed Ariel had made up for Laya, looking affronted to have been cooped up in one small room all morning long. When Ariel opened the door, he voiced his objection, loudly. Laya's face dissolved. "Oh!" she cried, and immediately began to feel her way toward the sound.

"Four unobstructed feet straight ahead," Ariel said and watched her friend locate the bed, bumping it with her shin.

"Probably it would've been okay," Ariel explained, "to let him have the run of the house. He and Jess didn't exactly smooch when I brought him in last night, but neither one seemed particularly bothered by the other. No hissing or baring of teeth. Still, I didn't want to take a chance leaving them together unchaperoned."

"Arthur grew up with dogs before I got him," Laya said into his pumpkin-colored fur. "No phobias."

The cat suffered cuddling for all of three seconds before, with a warning comment, he escaped to groom his ruffled coat.

Ariel picked up the litter box. "Let me move this someplace airier, and I'll help you get settled," she said.

It was ten minutes longer before Ariel remembered her grandfather. She hastened to the telephone, but, unsurprisingly, he'd long since hung up. There was no answer at his home number. She wouldn't be able to call him back, he'd been trying to warn her, "because he'd be" . . . Be what? Ariel hadn't a clue.

17

As if time-out had been called, there was no discussion that day or night about the man Laya had seen beating James Price or, to Ariel's relief, about Price himself. There was, in fact, very little discussion of any subject. After the outpouring on the tape and in the hospital the day before, Laya seemed deflated, as if all the words she had so painfully hoarded had been spent.

She napped a good part of the afternoon away. Shortly after a dinner spent with one ear cocked toward the room in which Jessie slept, she retired again, exhausted by what seemed to Ariel minimal activity for a woman who, not two weeks before, breathed effortlessly after an hour of steady and strenuous sun salutations, a total-body workout that would have had Ariel calling for oxygen, assuming she could have accomplished it at all. Normally, Laya's idea of relaxation was the *shirshasana*, known to the Western world as a headstand. She often meditated in the posture, she'd told a disbelieving Ariel, who could focus on nothing while upside down except keeping her balance. Laya had been in better physical condition than 90 percent of the population of a city more health conscious than 90 percent of their fellow countrymen. Getting dressed and riding seven miles in a car had worn her out.

It was a lesson to Ariel. Laya's body was no less fit than it had been two weeks before. What today had made clear was the toll taken on the spirit.

One other thing had become abundantly clear to Ariel as well: the responsibility she had blithely taken on. She didn't regret her offer. Impetuous as it may have been, she couldn't have done otherwise and felt right. But she had not thought it through. Was doing the right thing doing right by Laya? Ariel hadn't until today fully comprehended Laya's helplessness. She tried to recall every nuance of Sarah Aguilar's advice, and wished desperately for a rule book. There had been more than one moment when she was in total agreement that the arrangement couldn't work. There had been one brief, craven moment when, if Ariel could have dreamed up a graceful way to do it, she'd have reneged on the spot.

She went to bed early herself, intending to read. The magazines stacked on her bedside table seemed to click like a clock. If you want to stay on top, Ariel was well aware, you work at it. You watch the competition, and you read. Reviews. Crime. Scandal. Politics. Human interest. Periodicals of every sort. You keep abreast, you don't miss an issue, you don't miss an article; you scan, you note new trends, new concerns, a new angle. Tonight, she tented her fingers on her chest and ignored the guilts.

She lay staring into space, listening to subtle night sounds. A neighbor's wind chimes noticing a breeze. The restless settling of the house. Jessie's tags clinking as she adjusted herself on her bed. She was restless, too, with a second animal and an unfamiliar person in the house.

The coming days, or weeks, Ariel mused, would be a challenge. Not knowing what the future held was the problem. Whether Laya would be able to see. If the graft took, how good would her one good eye be? It would be different if they knew. It would be different if they knew she would be permanently blind. Ariel squirmed to think it, but it was true. Action could be taken. There would be social service caseworkers to render help, disability compensation to look into, orientation and mobility specialists to consult, all sorts of aids to investigate. Items as simple as a cane, as sophisticated as a computer with a voice synthesizer, as utilitarian as a scale that gives you the bad news out loud. Unlikely as it seemed now, a guide dog. But who'd want to learn to cope with being blind if there was a chance they could see again? Nobody. So Laya would live in limbo, marking time in the dark, unable to do anything more useful than hope. And me? Ariel asked herself. What can I do? What could anybody do about the man responsible?

She'd been in touch with Max Neely several times over the past days. She'd called the station house for an update only that afternoon. Max was out on another case, his partner told her, one that had a chance of going somewhere. The investigation into Laya's assault was going nowhere at a pretty brisk clip.

It had been determined that what the eyedrop bottle contained was unalloyed hydrofluoric acid; what it did not contain was Zap-O, the rust-dissolving fluid bought at the store where Laya shopped and later found in the Dumpster.

The loss of that clue compromised an entire scenario: that the perpetrator obtained the Zap-O that same night in that same store with the intention of substituting it for Laya's drops. That the deed was done while her groceries were left unattended. That a discussion overheard between Laya and the druggist gave rise to a plan to blind her. In short, that Laya was singled out as a victim.

Store register tapes were requisitioned and checked. (The most recent purchase of Zap-O, incidentally, was days prior to Laya's visit, by an employee; ignoring the corrosive product's warnings, he'd used it on a fender of his car. The fender bore evidence.) All employees were questioned. All customers identified by check or plastic to have been shopping at the same time as Laya were questioned. None knew her personally. None had any ascertainable reason to wish her ill. None saw anyone behaving suspiciously.

Laya's acquaintances had been questioned. Her students and her students' families and the owners and employees of the various places where she taught had been questioned. The few possibilities that arose had been checked out; they led nowhere.

Max Neely never had believed there was a connection between Laya and her assailant. Now, he, the LAPD, and federal officialdom were operating under the assumption that she was the random victim of an unknown (and, quite possibly, untraceable) person who could be states away. Who might have a grudge against the company that manufactured the eyedrops, or against the world at large.

But the authorities didn't know about the attack Laya witnessed only days before she was herself attacked. About the man who saw her watching, and who, Laya contended, saw her car and her license plate, and either traced her down or followed her, and did his best to make sure she wouldn't be able to identify him or anything or anyone else by sight again.

Ariel had doubts about that contention when she heard it; she still did. However, things had changed. The crime Laya witnessed was no longer assault; it was murder. It became murder immediately before her blinding. The timing kicked up the validity level quite a few notches. And the man who killed James Price was out there somewhere. The same man who called the hospital and asked if Laya would be able to see again? Who, when asked his name, hung up?

"A man who's murdered once can't be counted on not to do it again, can he?"

For a second Ariel couldn't remember where she'd heard that. Then it came: she hadn't heard it; she'd read it, in Dorothy's letter. The question, sent from four hundred miles away, a week past, and in regard to an unrelated situation, was uncomfortably apt.

Ariel may have given insufficient consideration to other aspects of this caretaking arrangement, but she had not discounted the aspect of risk.

Like the average Angeleno, her home was equipped with an alarm system. She'd dismissed the rent-a-cop as of that morning, but her neighborhood subscribed to a private patrol service. Her dog was attack trained. And she had a gun. She was proficient in its use, and she knew from grim experience that she would use it if there were no alternative. Ariel was satisfied that Laya was as safe here as she'd been in the hospital, safer by far than in her own home, and safer, too, than in a convalescent facility with strangers free to wander in and out at will.

Of course, if the authorities were right in their assessment, there was no threat. The damage had been done. Laya was as safe as anyone can be in a world where twisted, hate-filled people plant poison on the market shelf. And even if the authorities were wrong, even if Laya had been singled out by her "Mr. X" or by anyone else, the fact was that two weeks had passed without further incident. If he had wanted to hurt her again, he would have made a move by now. If he had wanted her dead, he would have killed her to start with. He had wanted her blind; she was. As long as she stayed that way, it seemed reasonable to believe, she would be left alone.

Ariel reached to switch off the light. She stopped, struck by a new thought: what if the man who'd beaten Price to death had already been caught? (The *men*, she reminded herself; influenced by Laya, she tended to focus only on the one who'd delivered the blows, who'd seen Laya and coldly stared her down.) The odds were against the crime being so quickly solved, but it was possible. Price might have regained consciousness before he died and named his assailants. Whoever placed the 911 call that brought the squad car might have seen their faces. The men—the man—might be behind bars. Both gruesome affairs might be as good as resolved. *If* Price's killer and Laya's assailant were the same man. *If* he could be tied to both crimes.

A gang member? Some punk meting out instant street justice? Laya's assumption wasn't unreasonable. It was L.A. County's dubious honor to lead the nation in gang violence, some estimates putting the number of gangs at more than seven hundred, the armies of hard-core "affiliates" at a hundred thousand. Gang killings accounted for nearly half the county's homicides, and half the victims, Ariel knew, were innocent bystanders. Like Laya?

Another thing Ariel knew: she wasn't suicidal. If this was a gang thing, it would not be she who'd bring the culprit to justice. There'd be snow on the streets of South Central L.A. before she'd go poking her little white fixed nose into gang politics. She'd told Laya that she'd been smart to react as she had: to run far and fast, to leave the carnage to the cops. She'd take her own advice.

It was imperative that she tell Laya's story to Max. No, it was imperative that she convince Laya to tell Max her story—and tomorrow. She turned off the light. Turning off her mind was another matter. Tomorrow, she reminded herself, would be an interesting day in more ways than one. It would see the launching of an experiment that was pure inspiration or sure debacle. There would be, she thought, no in-between.

It had been B.F.'s idea. He'd come up with it over breakfast Monday morning in Marin County, a passing suggestion for future reference. He'd had no more notion than did Ariel that the suggestion would be taken up that very week.

"You reckon Hattie could be any help to Laya?" he'd wondered.

Hattie Best was B.F.'s live-in housekeeper. Housekeeper, plural. She was nominally responsible for them all, but she kept mainly to the original two, residences in Florida and South Carolina, cottoning neither to "up north," which encompassed everything on the wrong side of the Mason-Dixon, nor to "yonder," which began somewhere around the Alabama line and extended to the Pacific.

Ariel had been told Hattie's history, what portion of it was known to tell. She had been employed as a young woman by Margaret Coulter, B.F.'s wife and Ariel's grand-mother. At that lady's demise thirty-odd years ago, Hattie stayed on with the widower, disregarding a number of other job offers and gossip as well. The family, whether they'd liked it or not, had been adopted.

They were a sadly dwindled family. The Coulters' only child, Suzanne, was by then estranged and unfind-able, having eloped with a man who, in B.F.'s opinion, was as useless as a boil. Margaret's death, in B.F.'s further opinion, stemmed more from heartbreak than heart dis-ease. B.F.'s heart was in no great shape either. Whatever pain Hattie felt, she kept to herself. She humored him when she could bring herself to do it, and lambasted him when she couldn't. She was unsentimental. She was "about as agreeable," B.F. had said, "as a dose of salts." And, evidently, as therapeutic. If one could be browbeaten back to health, he figured he had been.

And then, out of the blue, the son-in-law showed up (slunk up, as Ariel heard the story, when he was sure B.F. wasn't around to pound him into powder), and dropped two bombshells: the news of Suzanne's death, and Jane.

When the infant was dropped into her astounded grand-father's lap, Hattie offered her own, literally. She reared Jane. If they'd known of Ariel's existence, Hattie would have reared her as well.

The thought was intriguing, as was B.F.'s suggestion on Monday morning. "Hattie?" Ariel had repeated dubiously. "Help how?"

"Woman's rattlin' around that old house on Kiawah all by herself," B.F. had mused. "Said she needed to spring clean, but I spec she's not doin' anything more useful than agitatin' her kin thereabouts."

What, Ariel had asked, did he have in mind? He hadn't known, really; he was just thinking out loud. "Laya lives by herself, isn't that right?" he'd said. "Might be she could use somebody—till she gets on her feet, I mean—to cook up a little something from time to time. Run errands. Tidy up."

"She'll need a whole lot more than that," Ariel had countered, "if this transplant doesn't work out."

B.F. hadn't argued. "Keep the offer in mind," he'd told Ariel, "should the need arise." Hattie's salary wouldn't be a factor, he'd pointed out; it was already paid. And as he had no immediate plans to travel south, she was underworked, and being underworked made her irritable. "She's got nobody handy to boss around," he'd said; "that makes her mean."

The very quality one desires in a caregiver, Ariel thought now. She plumped her pillow and turned onto her side, willing herself to give up worry about an arrangement already set in motion. She couldn't be with Laya during the day. Somebody had to be. Hattie, after rumination, had agreed to be the somebody. She would bunk at B.F.'s condo, which was less than ten minutes away. She would see to Laya's needs while Ariel was at work and would sit evenings if necessary. Ariel had complete confidence in her ability to cope with any situation, even crisis. It wasn't her competence that worried Ariel. She closed her eyes, letting her mind drift to the events of a little more than a year ago and her introduction to Hattie.

Her grandfather (she smiled remembering) had taken to Ariel from the day he met her, the same day he'd learned of Jane's death. He considered her then and now a gift of Providence. He'd trusted the timing. He'd trusted that once again, the loss of one loved one could be made bearable by the gain of another.

The other members of his ménage had been less sanguine.

Sarge McManus was the first hurdle. Cynicism was

bred into his bones, and a career with the LAPD had
honed it. But Sarge was objective. Once he'd thoroughly
checked Ariel out, he'd given her the benefit of the doubt.
Hattie had not.

Ariel was a stranger, her "ways" strange, her motives
suspect, her "foreign" California accent issuing from a
mouth that might look (Hattie conceded) "a little" like
Jane's, to somebody *wanting* to be fooled. Particularly galling
were Ariel's personal quirks, the tastes and habits and ges-
tures that were too hauntingly familiar. No one who hadn't
known "her girl" could possibly know about those. That
Ariel did know made her not less suspect but more; such
familiarity had to be guile. It was plain to see: there was a
fortune in the offing, and this woman was after it. She was
an imposter. She must not be allowed to take Jane's place.

Ariel tried not to mind. She had a theory: Hattie had
known the truth in her heart. Ariel's presence was a cruel
reminder of all that was lost, her worst sin being that she
was alive and Jane was dead.

The breakthrough, if it could be called that, had come
one night last summer on Kiawah Island. The two
women had found themselves in a situation where they
were forced to cooperate to stay alive. That experience
instilled in Ariel a healthy respect for her erstwhile oppo-
nent. It knocked out a big chunk of Hattie's reserves. If
the sword wasn't beaten into a plowshare, it was
sheathed, and if no word of apology or acknowledgment
had as yet been spoken, Ariel made do. Taciturnity beat a
sharp tongue; with Hattie, it amounted to warm and
fuzzy.

Ariel turned again, yawning into the pillow, gradually
relaxing. She heard the murmur of a car on the street only
subliminally, unaware that it triggered her last clear
thought: Hattie's arrival. B.F. had "arranged transport." It
should cause a stir in the neighborhood, Ariel imagined

dozily. Picturing Laya's caregiver being delivered in a chauffeured car, she fell asleep smiling.

Ariel stiffened, semi-awake in the dark, confused as to why. What had she heard? A thump? Had she dreamed it? Jessie's head was up. Her ears were erect, assessing the need for action. So it was no dream. But the dog hadn't moved. Why? Through her fog, Ariel remembered Laya: there was another person in the house.

She sat up. The cobwebs of sleep began to clear. The burglar alarm hadn't gone off, so everything was fine. Or was it? The shepherd had gotten to her feet. But, Ariel realized, she could be reacting to the alarm she sensed in her mistress. What they'd heard was almost certainly Laya. Ariel frowned, remembering the thump. It must have been a big thump to wake her. Laya falling? Hadn't she better go and check on her? She pulled back the bedcovers.

But what if it wasn't Laya? She wasn't just any house guest; she was the victim of a malicious attack. And this wasn't just any night; it was the victim's first night unguarded. And she, Ariel, was responsible. She put her feet on the floor. Feeling for her slippers, she strained to separate ordinary sounds—a subtle plumbing belch, the whir of the clock, her own pulse—from any that didn't belong. That, definitely, was the click of a door closing. But that? Was that a muffled cry?

Ariel got up and put on her robe. So you're overreacting, she told herself. So you'll be embarrassed. You'll have egg on your face. There're worse things. She slid open the drawer of her bedside table. Her fingers touching cold metal reality, she hesitated. She took out the gun. Lots worse things.

The bedroom door creaked when she eased it open. Though it was no louder than a sigh, it seemed like a shriek. Ariel felt something at her thigh and looked down. Jessie was beside her. The hallway was dark. It would be;

Laya wouldn't turn on a light. It appeared to be empty. A floorboard complained when she started down the uncarpeted hall. Jessie's nails clicked like castanets. Ariel looked into what was now the guest room. The bed was rumpled and uninhabited. The desk chair was square in the middle of the room. A stack of papers that had been on the desk was now scattered on the floor. Ariel went in. When Arthur pounced from a bookcase onto the bed, she nearly stopped breathing. Jessie barked.

"Quiet!" Ariel hissed, and, with a last, uneasy look at the disorder, crept from the room. The door to the guest bath was closed. She reached for the knob, and stopped, torn. She listened to utter silence for a long moment before she called Laya's name.

"Yes?" came from behind the door. Definitely Laya's voice.

"Are you all right?" Ariel asked.

"I'm fine."

Ariel stood uncertainly. "You sure?"

"I'm fine, Ariel."

"Okay." There was no excuse for invading the privacy of the bathroom. None. The toilet was flushed. Ariel heard the benign sound of water running. The gun in her hand suddenly felt not only heavy but ridiculous. She went back to bed.

18

AT SEVEN SHARP THE NEXT MORNING AN UNREMARKABLE SMALL blue rental car rolled to the curb in front of Ariel's house. Through the window, she saw the driver alternately peering at the numbered curbstone and then at something in her hand. Apparently satisfied that she'd reached her destination, Hattie Best emerged. She'd never been to Ariel's, and she paused for a moment, giving the place the once-over. She frowned. Ariel frowned. She found herself mentally reviewing the state of the house and yard. She caught herself. Next thing, she'd be rushing out to do some quick weeding.

At dinner the night before Laya had asked Ariel to tell her about Hattie. "Gray haired," Ariel had said. "Bony. In her early seventies, I suppose, but she's—I don't know—ageless. Salt of the earth in a kind of, er . . . salty way. No nonsense."

"Black or white?" Laya had asked. "Or what?"

"Black." Ariel had tried to see Hattie dispassionately, to be Laya's eyes. "Lighter than you, kind of the color of a penny, with a sharp nose. I've wondered if she might be part Native American, but I don't know. I don't know anything about her origins." Anxious not to prejudice or dismay Laya, she had added, carefully, "She may seem brusque, but don't let that put you off. It's just her way."

This morning Ariel took her own advice. When she'd put Jessie on a down-stay, she briskly opened the door and called good morning. Hattie nodded. She reached back into the car to retrieve an enormous black patent leather handbag, and marched up the walk. "Hydrangea gets too much sun where you got it planted," she said by way of greeting. "Gonna fry come summer."

"I thought B.F.'s driver was bringing you," Ariel said.

"You thought wrong," Hattie said.

"Thanks for doing this," Ariel said.

"That's a mighty big dog," Hattie said.

"Jessie," Ariel said.

"Stays in the house, does it?"

"She's an indoor dog. Is that what you're asking?"

"Something wrong with her?"

"Wrong? No. Why?"

"Why's she just layin' there?"

"I told her to. Does it bother you? Having her inside?"

"Don't bother me as long as I don't have to clean up after her. She gets up when you say to?"

"Jessie," Ariel said, "release."

The shepherd went to Hattie and sat down at a polite distance, looking up in silent communication.

"She let me pet her?"

Ariel was surprised, but kept her voice neutral. "She's hoping you will."

Hattie did. "Humph," she commented directly to the dog.

"I'm afraid Jessie does bother my friend," Ariel said. "Laya's trying hard, but she's afraid of dogs."

Hattie lowered her voice and said, "One thing. You said this blind woman . . . Laya?"

"Right."

"What was her last name again?"

"She just goes by Laya."

"'Goes by'? That's not her real name?"

"I doubt it's her given name. She chose it, I imagine." This, Ariel thought, was going to be worse than she'd dreamed. "What 'one thing' was it you wanted to know? Or was that it?"

"You said they operated on one eye. What's the story on the other one?"

"An operation wouldn't help."

Hattie slowly shook her head and made a *tsk*-ing sound. "Well, come on," she said, "and introduce us. No point standin' here."

They found Laya at the kitchen table. There was a bruise on her temple, Ariel noticed (the bump heard in the night?), but her dark glasses were intact and in place. Her hands were clasped in her lap, as if she were waiting to be

called into the dentist's office. Introductions were politely
acknowledged, and then both women, Hattie clutching
her giant purse, and Laya clutching her fingers, turned
expectantly to Ariel, who in a burst of inanity, said,
"Well!" She looked from her teacher, her formerly confident guru, to the woman who, but for a quirk of fate
would have reared her, and had begun to treat her as if she
had. Now, it seemed, Ariel was den mother. "Hattie," she
said, "let me show you around."

"I can find my way," said Hattie. "You go on and do
what you need to do." She dropped her purse on the
counter, popped the lid off the flour canister to check its
contents, and began opening cabinets. "You got any lard?"
she asked.

"I don't think so. I mean, no."

Hattie found a can of shortening. "You like biscuits?"
she said a little too loudly in Laya's direction.

"I love biscuits," Laya answered equally loudly.

Hattie paused, mouth pursed, and gave her a long look.
Then, at normal volume, she said, "Too much to hope
there's any buttermilk either, I reckon, but we'll manage."
Over her shoulder, to Ariel, she said, "You plan to stay or
go?"

"Go," Ariel said, "but I've got a call to make first." After
which, she planned to talk to Laya.

The call was to Max Neely. He listened to her question
and, un-Max-like, sounding harried, asked none of his
own. He'd check the third precinct, he said, and get back
to her in five. Ariel used the time to try B.F. He wasn't
answering, still; she hadn't been able to reach him since
he'd hung up on her. She picked through message slips
brought home the day before. She was, finally, about to
return the call from Rob the columnist when the phone
rang.

The man or men who'd beaten James Price to death,

Max told her, talking fast, "remain, as they say, at large,"
and large, he added, was the number of people who
would have been happy to have done the deed, or so he
gathered. Laya, too, Ariel remembered, had alluded to
Price being a less than savory character: a "dirtbag," she'd
said on the tape. How come, Ariel asked Max, Price was
such an unpopular man? How come, Max asked Ariel, she
wanted to know about Price? Possibility of a story, Ariel
said vaguely. Max *was* busy; he didn't pursue it. She got
the name of the detective assigned to the case, asked if
there were any new developments in Laya's, and was told
"Get real."

From Eddie Rials, the detective working on the Price
homicide, Ariel got nothing but attitude. He was not a fan
of the media. He was highly suspicious of why a nation-
ally syndicated TV newsmagazine would be interested in
an unpublicized, unexceptional killing. He was not at liberty to discuss the dead man's character, his connection
(or lack of connection) to a gang, or the details of his
assault. The police were "following a number of leads,"
and "if you people have information pertinent to the
case," he challenged, "you'd best say." Ariel agreed; she
simply wasn't in a position to comply.

It was a short conversation, and unsatisfactory. The sub-
sequent conversation with Laya was more unsatisfactory,
and worrisome. It began with the question Ariel had been
dreading: had she called the hospital to ask about James
Price? Ariel hardly hesitated. Laya was too fragile yet to be
hit with bad news. She was profoundly glad the other
woman couldn't see her face when she said, "No change in
the last few days." It wasn't a lie; it was worse than a lie.
Ariel regretted it when she realized that Price's death was
her most convincing argument, and she'd just thrown it
away. "It's time for you to talk, Laya," she said firmly. "Past
time."

Laya had not changed her mind. A search for her assailant was a fool's mission. If it were not so obviously futile, it would be just as obviously dangerous. She was in no condition to fight thugs or gang-bangers or whatever. She would have no part of it.

"*I* don't want any part of it either!" Ariel cried. "You think I'm suggesting we form a posse? What I'm saying is you need to talk to the cops!"

And say? Laya wanted to know. "I saw two men. One was in the dark. I couldn't see him. The other was in bad light. He was African-American. I don't know him. End of statement."

"What do you know about Price?" Ariel asked.

"Nothing the cops don't know."

"How do you know what they do and don't know?"

"It's in his record."

"He's got a record? For . . . ?"

"Attempted rape that I'm aware of. The time he was charged wasn't the first time it happened."

"How do you know?"

Laya shrugged. "I heard."

Ariel changed tack. "The man you could see; was he tall?"

"Average."

"Thin? Heavy?"

"Average."

"Was his hair long or short?"

"Average."

"Laya!" Ariel paused to marshal her arguments. Admittedly, Laya, in her mulishness, had a point. Why should she put herself on the line? She couldn't describe or identify either assailant. The victim was no innocent. He was (even if Laya didn't know it) beyond help. There was no proof that the attack was connected to what was done to Laya. If it wasn't connected, if Price's killers didn't know the identity of the witness, then coming forward was mad. Coming forward *belatedly* wasn't too smart either. For all Ariel knew, Laya might be opening herself up to some kind of legal charge. Failure to report a crime? Obstruction? At the least, she'd be exposing herself to hassle. At worst, she'd be exposing herself to danger. To her way of thinking, she'd be exposing her shame. If there were arguments to marshal, they didn't occur to Ariel.

What followed was one of those moments of such perfect misunderstanding that in other circumstances it would have been comical. As Ariel had begun to say, "I can see your point," Laya cut her off. "Yes," she agreed. "*You* can see. I can't!"

"What she said then, verbatim, is: 'And as long as I can't see, I'm safe,'" Ariel worriedly reported to Sarah Aguilar, whom she called the minute she reached her office.

"Did you ask her what she meant?" Dr. Aguilar said.

"She didn't give me a chance to," Ariel replied. Forbidding Ariel to talk to Max or anyone about what she'd revealed in confidence, saying she intended to leave well enough alone and be left alone, Laya had groped her way out of the room so hurriedly and clumsily that she'd bumped a table and overturned a vase of flowers. "So," Ariel asked the psychologist, "what do you think? Does it sound as scary to you as it did to me?" (Admittedly, Ariel had entertained the thought herself that if Laya was blinded to neutralize her as a witness, she was now rendered harmless; ergo, safe. But her own thinking, Ariel told herself, was deductive reasoning; Laya's was unhealthy, as in: as long as I'm blind, as long as I'm mute, as long as I denounce everything I believe in, and shrink away to nothing, I'm safe.) "Can she mean she doesn't *want* to see?"

"I don't know in what context she made the state-ment," Sarah Aguilar said. "It sounds as though she believes somebody's after her. Does she?"

Ariel hesitated. Gag order or not, she needed help with this new direction Laya's thoughts seemed to be taking. "Let's say," she hedged, "for argument's sake, that some-body *is* after her."

"I thought she said she didn't know of anyone with rea-son to harm her?"

"That doesn't mean *he* doesn't know *her*. She could have been targeted by a sicko just the same as she could have been the random victim of a sicko, right?"

"Could have been? Sure. Was? I don't know the details of the police investigation, so I can't answer that. It's no great leap, though, that someone who's been attacked as she was, indirectly and uncontrollably, would feel vulnera-ble."

"Hey, Dr. Aguilar, call me crazy, but being blind makes her a heck of a lot more vulnerable! Could she possibly—"

"See her blindness as security? As insurance against a further assault? Irrational but . . ." Dr. Aguilar hmmm-ed thoughtfully. "You and I talked about the stages of grief, didn't we? Bargaining and so on? Could be bargaining, I suppose; i.e., I've been hurt enough, fate, move on to another victim. Or . . . it could be some other thing entirely. I've got a patient in five minutes, Ariel, and," she said dryly, "I'm not Doctor Ruth. I can't, without knowing your friend far better than I do, extrapolate what she's feeling or why."

"What I was going to ask was, could she possibly will herself not to get better?"

"Of course she could," Dr. Aguilar answered promptly. "You don't need me to tell you that!"

"Yeah." Ariel couldn't have explained why she'd asked a question to which she knew the answer, or what she'd expected from a woman with whom she'd been forbidden to share the facts.

"The mind," the psychologist went on, "can play a pivotal role in recovery from physical trauma for anyone. And your friend? With her yogic mind-body-spirit connection . . . ? If she's capable of transporting herself or whatever she'd done when she was admitted to emergency, then she is one strong-willed lady."

"Was," Ariel amended glumly. "*Was* strong willed." She ignored the buzzing of her phone, and signaled "later" to one of the show's researchers who just then stuck his head in her door. "Laya was 'on the Path,'" she reflected aloud, and then laughed a little to hear herself say it. "Sounds cuckoo, doesn't it, if you're not into the spiritual aspects of yoga. Now she doesn't even practice."

"That's hardly surprising, is it? Under the circumstances?"

"You mean because she's blind? Even if she can't do the postures—and there's absolutely no reason she couldn't—there's still meditation, and deep breathing . . . What do they call it? *Pranayama*, and—"

"She was viciously assaulted *just two weeks ago.* Ariel, give the woman a break!"

"Dr. Aguilar—"

"Sarah."

"What I'm trying to say is, Laya's not just different from the person she was, she's the opposite. If you could have known her . . ." Ariel stared, unseeing, at the undulating screen saver image on her monitor. "This is a woman," she said, "who was incredibly self-possessed. Positive and open-minded. Confident. She had a stillness about her that was about as near serenity as mortals get. You couldn't be around her without feeling it. It was the essence of who she was." Was she describing Laya as she'd been, Ariel couldn't help wondering, or as she'd perceived her to be? "She embraced life, Sarah; now she hides from it." Fumbling for a better way to say it, failing, Ariel cleared her throat. "Oh, well," she said. "'The bigger they are, the harder they fall,' I guess. Well, look, I'm wasting your time and my money. Send me a bill—"

"I really don't have but a minute and I'm not about to practice secondhand therapy, but I will tell you a very short story. Your friend makes me think of a young woman I once knew."

"Oh?"

"She was a postulant."

"Pardon?"

"A nun-to-be. You know, a penguin." Ariel didn't know if she was meant to laugh; she hadn't thought of the psychologist as being much of a jokester. "Back to my parable. This girl had always known she'd be a nun, like she knew the sun would come up in the morning; like she knew water was wet. Then she lost her sight."

"Yes?"

"You take away the core of a person, Ariel; it leaves a big hole."

"I don't think I understand what you're telling me."

"She lost faith, dear. Faith fled; despair filled the hole. Think of, oh . . . a musician going deaf. Or an artist whose hands are crippled by arthritis. Think of anyone who loses what defines them."

"But Laya's eyesight isn't what defined—"

"No. I'd say she's lost her inner harmony, the peace of her mind. Her. . . I don't know the proper yogic term. Her unity with the universal spirit or whatever." Dr. Aguilar stopped abruptly. "Maybe I'll get myself one of those quick-fix call-in shows after all."

"You should," Ariel said. "You're right on."

"Really? If you think about it, I was merely following your lead. Your friend's the one who has the missing piece."

"Missing piece?"

"The why. Why has she lost her certainties? What's corroding them? This atrocity was done *to* Laya. Anger would be a usual reaction. Blind, you should pardon the pun, *rage* would be. For the average bear, directing that rage inward, self-hate, is not an unusual reaction. But Laya's not the average bear. She's devoted herself to self-awareness. To a rare degree, you imply, she had achieved it. Yet she's turning this tragedy on herself. Why?"

Ariel, who wasn't allowed to supply the missing piece, *pieces*—guilt, self-disgust, penance—asked instead, "What happened to the postulant? Did she ever regain her faith?"

Sarah Aguilar chuckled. "Oh, she's safely back in the fold."

"And did she become a nun?"

"She changed fields, and her patient's waiting. She'll send you a bill."

19

THE REST OF THAT THURSDAY AND THE NEXT TWO DAYS GAVE Ariel a profound appreciation for jugglers: specifically, people who juggle family life and a career.

The first ball went into the air midmorning when Ariel was called to Chris Valente's office. Just outside it was a blackboard on which were listed approved stories and those still pending. One of the latter, a child's controversial disappearance, had languished under Pending for months, stalled for want of viable leads.

The Open File was aptly named: open to interpretation, open to investigation, open to the possibility of resolution. Stories without even a whiff of resolution turned viewers off. So far, the legal staff contended, any whiffs in this story were actionable.

A call had come in, Ariel's boss told her, from a former neighbor of the missing child's family. She sounded legitimate. She was, belatedly, inclined to talk. It wasn't Ariel's story, but the correspondent who'd been on it was trapped in a quarantine situation in Mexico. Valente pointed to Ariel. "Go!" he said.

As she rushed home to pack for an overnighter to Philadelphia, she was working out the logistics of who'd do what with which of her own stories in her absence. That was no big deal; unplanned trips were not uncommon in Ariel's life. Normally, however, she had no worries on the home front beyond making arrangements for her dog. Jessie was the least of her concerns today.

What if Hattie and Laya weren't getting along? Ariel fretted as she drove. Would Hattie be willing to stay overnight? Would she brave the freeway (not her favorite thing) to take Laya to her apartment to pack a suitcase? Laya had to have clothes. And where, Ariel tried to remember, was her spare house key? Did her neighbor still have it from the San Francisco trip? Should Jessie go back to Marguerite's in deference to Laya's anxieties? But wouldn't it be better, security-wise, for her to stay at the house?

Security! Not until then did Ariel remember that she hadn't set the alarm when she left home that morning. She hadn't told Hattie to set the alarm. She hadn't told Hattie *how* to set the alarm, or even that it existed.

She began a mental list of all Hattie needed to be told. Numbers: cell phone, Dr. Crowne, the vet, the neighborhood patrol. What else? Not to run the dishwasher unless the disposal's empty; it would overflow. To leave the side gate open for the gardener tomorrow; to remember to lock it after. And . . . where to find stuff: garbage bags, emergency candles, toilet tissue, flashlight . . . (Wait. Back up to tissue. Was she out?) Her cell phone rang.

"Return to base," Tara Castanara told her. "Mission aborted."

"*What?*" Ariel almost but didn't yell. What was going on? she wanted to know. Tara couldn't tell her. "Ours not to question why," she said mildly.

"Yours may not be, but mine is!" Ariel said. She'd noticed in her assistant of late a tendency toward spouting quotations. She'd found it flattering; "Imitation is the sincerest of. . . " et cetera. At the moment, she knew why people often rolled their eyes when she herself so spouted. "And it's not 'question' why," she muttered as she considered a U-turn, "it's 'reason.' I'd like one."

"What?" Tara asked.

"The quote is, 'Theirs not to *reason* why.' Tennyson, 'The Charge of the Light Brigade.' 'Theirs not to make reply/Theirs not to reason why/Theirs but to do and die.' Somebody's going to if they don't stop screwing around with my life." Ariel decided against the U-turn. She was closer to home than to the studio; she might as well go see what was on for lunch.

"Will you call everybody we canceled," she instructed. "See what you can reschedule. Especially Shaw," she said, naming a U.S. congressman she'd courted on the phone for what seemed like a lifetime. He was in town for one day only. "Please, Tara, get Shaw back! Beg if you have to. Call me if you can't get through to him."

Tara didn't require the instructions; she knew what to do without being told. "Yes, memsahib," said she. "I live to serve."

"Don't start!" said Ariel. "Forget today's lunch date. It's too late. I'm three blocks from home. I'll grab a bite there."

"Then I'll toss this message."

"What message?"

"The one somebody calling from your house left."

Ariel pressed down on the accelerator. "Who? Who called?" Hattie to say she'd changed her mind? To say Laya'd had an accident? To say Jessie had eaten Arthur the cat?

"No name," Tara said, "but it's your home number."

"What was the message?"

"Call home."

The house hadn't burned down, Ariel saw when she got there. There was no evidence of accident or mayhem in the living room, she saw as she trotted through it; no blood or flying fur. There was no person or animal anywhere to be seen in the house, she discovered when she hurried from one room to another.

Hattie's car . . . ? Had it been parked out front? Surely Hattie hadn't piled everyone in for a trip. Laya and Jessie crammed into the same confined space? Never! But where was Jessie? The dog always greeted her. Concern began to spike toward genuine alarm.

Laya's bed was neatly made, the guest bath empty. Ariel headed for the kitchen. "Hattie?" she called. "Laya?" Soup of some kind simmered on the stove. In the utter quiet of the deserted house it struck Ariel as ominous. "Anybody?" she said.

The door to the back patio opened. "Would you hush yelling?" Hattie whispered. "She's taking a nap."

Ariel backed into one of her new antique kitchen chairs, sitting heavily. It creaked. She sagged. "Napping where?" she asked. "Where *were* you? Where is everybody?"

Hattie closed the door quietly behind her. "Never knew you to be so high-strung," she said, and went to the stove to stir the soup. "What's got into you?"

"You left a message at the studio."

"That's right. I said 'call.' I didn't say 'come.'"

Ariel got up and looked out the window. Laya lay on one of the chaise lounges. Earphones were clamped on her head, and she held what looked like a transistor radio on her chest. Arthur was curled beside her, his eyes on the window. "Where's Jessie?" Ariel asked.

"In the yard last I noticed," Hattie replied.

Just then Ariel caught sight of the shepherd. She lay in a patch of sun in the far corner of the yard. All four paws waved in the air as she wriggled, scratching her back.

"Hattie," Ariel said, "what's wrong? Why did you call me?"

Dipping a ladle into the pot, Hattie spooned up liquid, peering at it critically. "You're out of toilet paper," she said, and blew steam from the spoon. "I called to say stop and get some."

"Toilet paper?" Ariel asked dumbly.

Hattie sipped soup, smacked her lips, and commented, "Not worth a flip without a ham bone." She dropped the ladle into dishwater. "Yes, toilet paper," she said. "Comes in handy now they don't put out the Sears 'n' Roebuck catalog anymore." She smiled at her little joke. "I'd've gone and got it myself, and a ham hock, too, but I didn't know where the store was. I need to know that and a lot more unless you want me on the phone to you every minute."

Ariel nodded. She would draw a map. She would draw up a list. She poured herself water, and after draining it, said, "Forget the ham. Something else I should've told you; Laya's a vegetarian."

"Tell that to the hen that's for supper."

"What?"

"You had it in the freezer. I'm defrostin' it. I asked her if chicken and dumplings was okay with her. She said fine."

"'Fine'?" Ariel stared, and then waved a limp hand. "Fine. Maybe she's not vegetarian anymore. I can't keep up with her." She glanced outside. Laya hadn't moved. "How is she, do you think?"

"No change so you'd notice in the last five hours." Hattie followed Ariel's glance, the lines that scored her thin face deepening. She opened the refrigerator and began examining the contents of the vegetable drawers. Her voice was muffled when she said, "Don't have a great deal to say, does she?"

"Not usually, no." There was a pillow under Laya's head, Ariel observed, and the afghan from the living room was tucked around her legs. On a table near to hand was an empty plate and a tall glass with a lemon slice straddling the rim. My, my! Ariel thought; and she'd feared Hattie would be disobliging? She stole a look behind her. The old woman's head was still buried in the refrigerator; her bony rump poked out from behind the door. Who was this kindly stranger, and where was the real Hattie? Ariel returned her wondering gaze to the scene outside. A book lay open on the other chaise, she noticed. Had Hattie read Laya to sleep?

"What's this thing?" Hattie held out a daikon, somewhat past its prime.

"Garbage." Ariel took it and tossed it.

"What was it before it was garbage?"

"A Chinese radish. Has Laya been okay with Jessie being out there? So nearby, I mean?"

"Dog pretty much steers clear. Keepin' her distance from the cat, I spec. You want some soup?"

"Sure, thanks. She's sleeping too much. Laya, I mean. That's all she seems to do."

"Then she needs it."

"It's like . . . she used to have this light, you know?"

"This what?"

"It was a sort of inner glow. It's gone out." Ariel sighed. "Looks like you're taking good care of her."

Hattie looked as if she'd been caught in some embarrassing misconduct. "Woman's grieved," she said. "Won't hurt to spoil her a little." Spooning soup, she changed the subject. "You got phone calls. I wrote 'em down on a paper there someplace. B.F. was one."

"B.F. called?"

"Nothing important, he said tell you."

"Where is he anyway? I've been trying to—"

"Started out to talk about some woman—curious name—some friend of his, but then—"

"Woman friend?" Ariel, all ears, paused in her search for the paper.

"—never mind, he said; he'd tell you later."

The paper on which the messages were written proved to be an invitation to a dinner Ariel was supposed to have attended the evening before, and had forgotten entirely. "Damn!" she muttered.

Hattie pursed her lips.

"Oh, well," Ariel said, and turned the invitation over. "So B.F. didn't say where I could reach—"

The phone rang. Tara had rescheduled what she could, she told Ariel. Congressman Shaw had already filled Ariel's time slot, but if she could get to his hotel immediately, he would meet with her.

Ariel took the soup in a thermos and ate it on the way.

At five o'clock that afternoon she called home to say she might be a little late. At 6:10 she was packing her briefcase with homework when she came upon the invitation to the dinner she'd missed. She took the time to make a quick call of apology, reading Hattie's cryptic phone messages as she did.

Henry No number, Hattie had written. And *Thorpes gone 1 WK mail?* Ariel interpreted the first to mean Henry had called and left no number, and the second that her neighbors, who were leaving on vacation, were reminding her to hold their mail. The last message was inscrutable. *B.F. found old nole.* Hattie had crossed that out and written: *B.F. home soon Will call.*

Ariel hung up the phone, said "Nole?" and tossed the card. She was zipping her briefcase when Tara tore in with the news that the next Monday night's wrapped-up segment had just come unwrapped.

At nine Ariel arrived home to find Laya and Hattie standing side by side in the living room. Erect and immobile, their eyes closed, they looked as if they were waiting to be beamed up.

"She calls it 'mountain,'" Hattie told Ariel in the kitchen a few minutes later. "Your dinner's in the oven."

"Mountain pose," Ariel said, and took out the foil-wrapped plate. "*Tadasana.* Thanks. Sorry to be so late."

"I asked her to show me something from yoga, but I can't say I see much to it," Hattie said. "You stand in one spot and do nothing. What's the good of that?"

"I know what you mean," Ariel agreed, wisely deciding not to explain something she wasn't sure she understood herself. She was too relieved that Hattie wasn't upset by being kept so late, that Laya was doing something besides vegetating, that Laya and Jessie and Arthur were still in the same house together and nobody was hyperventilating or drawing blood.

The next day, Friday, events escalated.

The canceled trip to Philadelphia was uncanceled. Hattie agreed to stay overnight, and, after studying an L.A. map as carefully as if she were plotting a course to Alpha Centauri, she agreed to drive Laya to her apartment for clothes. Marguerite would take Jessie. Ariel reclaimed her extra house key and turned it over to Hattie, who was subjected to a crash course acquainting her with the locks and the alarm system and major and minor appliances and household supplies. She was given all pertinent phone numbers, and a hand-drawn map whereon were located the nearest grocery and pharmacy and hospital.

Feeling frayed, Ariel left for the City of Brotherly Love, where she conducted interviews with people who seemed unacquainted with the sentiment. She spent thirty hours away, a disproportionate number of them working; they were restful by comparison to those immediately preceding her trip. She returned late Saturday night to find what appeared to be every light in and outside her house ablaze. The neighborhood security patrol was parked out front.

20

"WHAT?" SHE CRIED, STREAKING INTO THE HOUSE. "WHAT'S HAPpened?"

Hattie was planted in the middle of the living room, feet squared, arms folded. Laya sat on the sofa, her cat on her lap. Lamplight glinted off the lens of her dark glasses when she lifted her chin. It trembled just noticeably. Ariel could hear rustling sounds through an open window, as of someone moving about in the shrubbery, and the faint erratic crackle of a walkie-talkie. "Who's that?" she asked. "Is that the security man?"

Her eyes on Laya, Hattie nodded.

"Well, you two, please! What's going on?"

"Somebody was out there," Laya said.

"You . . ." *Saw somebody*, Ariel almost asked. "You heard somebody?"

"Yes."

"In our yard?" Ariel asked, dropping her purse and overnight case on the floor, and going to the window. She could see the beam of a flashlight, skating the surface of her eugenia hedge. "The only way anybody could get in," she said, "is to scale the fence or break the lock on the gate. Or . . ." She turned to Hattie. "The gardener was here yesterday. Did you lock the gate after—"

"I locked it," Hattie said.

Ariel peered again through the window, but she saw only bushes, stirring gently in an almost imperceptible breeze. The flashlight beam disappeared. "What did you hear?" she asked Laya.

"Somebody moving around."

"Hattie, did you see—"

"Hattie was in the kitchen," Laya interrupted. "She didn't hear or see anything."

"Are you sure it was in our yard? Could it have been on the other side of the fence?"

"No," Laya answered. Her fingers, Ariel noticed, were pressing against her temple, against the bone of the eye socket, as if she were finding it hard to concentrate.

"There's nobody home next door," Ariel said. "They're off camping." And, she only then remembered, she was supposed to be picking up their mail, which, for some reason, made her think of Henry. She grimaced. He'd called the same day her neighbors had; she hadn't called back. She heard footsteps coming from the rear of the house just before a male voice called out "Hello."

"We're in here," Ariel called back.

The neighborhood security man was outfitted much like his official brothers, including the holstered gun at his hip. He didn't look old enough to be trusted with it. "All clear outside," he said, and then he noticed Ariel. Coloring slightly—all but shifting his feet like a schoolboy—he nodded. When she introduced herself, he said, "Yes, ma'am, I know. Enjoy your show." He cleared his throat before making more or less the same observation she had.

"Gate's locked tight. Only way in as far as I can see would be over the fence." His hat shifted forward as he scratched at the back of his scalp, assessing the situation. "Not all that high. Nothing to keep somebody *from* climbing over if he was in real good physical condition, or had something to climb up on. Except . . . he'd have had to do that from one of your neighbors' yards."

"The people to the west are away," Ariel told him. "Mr. . . . ?"

"Todd McCutcheon. Yes, ma'am, the Thorpes. For the week, I believe. Well, I'd better go check out their premises." With a "Be right back," he left to do that.

The three women waited in silence, hearing an occasional muffled sound from beyond the fence, thumps and radio static. Ariel began to pace. Hattie straightened a picture, then flicked a mote of dust from the frame. The silence stretched. Laya twitched like a marionette when Arthur, for no discernible reason, made an abrupt exit from her lap. Ariel had the sudden sensation that they were all actors who'd been abandoned onstage without a script.

Hattie broke the tension. "'Premises,' he says."

Laya turned to her. "What was that?"

"He's gonna go poke around in the yard next door. Why couldn't he just say so?" She sat tiredly, shaking her head. "Kid playing cops and robbers." After another endless moment, she asked Ariel, "Did you eat yet?"

Before Ariel could answer, there was a polite tap on the door, and McCutcheon was back. "Nobody over there now," the young security man said. "Can't tell if anybody was, but . . ."

"But?" Ariel asked.

"I was going to say the padlock's hanging on the hasp of their gate, undone, you know, so anybody could go in. And the flower bed there by the fence does have some prints.

Relatively fresh and a pretty good size. A man's, more than likely." He noticed Ariel's expression and the slight, negative shake of her head. "Ms. Gold?"

"I'm thinking . . . the Thorpes use the same gardener I do." Ariel turned to Hattie. "His crew was around yesterday afternoon?"

Hattie nodded.

"I expect the Thorpes left the gate unlocked so they could get in. The prints . . ." Ariel gave a small shrug. "Could be theirs."

Abruptly, McCutcheon asked, "You still have your dog?"

"Yes," Ariel began, "but she's not . . . How did you know I have a dog?"

"Big purebred shepherd, right? Well trained? I see you out walking her. You introduced me to her one day, remember? Right after you first got her. Must be a year, year and a half ago now."

"Oh, sure. Of course." Ariel wondered if the day would come when she was entirely comfortable hearing about things she'd done of which she had no recall whatever. She smiled. "You've got some memory. I thought you'd cleverly deduced that I had a dog."

"Wouldn't be all that clever, since there's a half-chewed rawhide bone in your backyard, and a pooper-scooper. So, tell me; when you ladies heard the noise, how did the dog react?"

"Jessie wasn't here."

"That's too bad." McCutcheon did the head-scratching thing before he said, "You know . . . there's a surprising lot of wildlife in this area. Any chance what you heard might've been an animal? A possum, maybe? Or a raccoon? Raccoons can get pretty bold—"

"It wasn't a raccoon," Laya said.

"Yes, ma'am." McCutcheon nodded. "Well, I'm on all

night, and I'll be making extra passes by. You hear anything, give a shout."

When the door had closed behind him, and Hattie had gone to collect her belongings, Laya said, "He doesn't think anybody was out there; you know that. He thinks I imagined what I . . . heard."

Ariel caught the almost imperceptible pause, and wondered about it. She also noticed that Laya's fingertips had again strayed to her right eye. "Perhaps," she said, "but he seems like . . . Laya, is your eye bothering you?"

"It's just . . . uncomfortable."

"Uncomfortable? Let me look at it."

"It's all right."

"Then let Hattie look at it. She's pretty smart about—"

"I did hear something, you know. And what's-his-name, McCutcheon, doesn't believe me."

Ariel agreed; the man doubted that there'd been anybody lurking around. "It isn't likely," she said carefully, "that whoever did this to you would still be keeping up with you. Do you think? Following you? How would he know where you—"

"Ariel, you came to the hospital often. Daily. I know that. Maybe he does, too. You're a newswoman. Am I talking to you? he's got to wonder. Telling you what I saw? Who I saw? Are you working on an exclusive that'll air anytime? How's he going to know you were there as a friend?"

"But Laya, *now*? Two weeks after—"

"There were cops at the hospital, right? I was protected. I've only been here three days, right? So it took him that long to find out where you live. Or it's taken you that long to persuade me to talk, or to check out what I've told you, or to fit the story into your schedule, or . . . how do I know what's in his mind? You think a person who'll do what he did thinks like you and me?"

"I think . . . I'm having trouble seeing a person who'd poison medication—the kind of person who favors sneaky, anonymous evil—as having the nerve to show up here. Lurking around in the bushes where he could be—"

"How about the kind of person who deliberately beats a man to death? Can you see him having the nerve to show up?"

"Did you say . . . to death?" Ariel asked.

"Yes," Laya confirmed. "I know about James Price. I've called the Medical Center several times. Today I finally got somebody who'd 'give out that information.'"

Ariel opened her mouth and, not knowing what to say, closed it.

"Why," Laya asked, "would you lie to me about him? Why didn't you tell me he died?"

"I thought you had enough to worry about," Ariel said.

"And now I've got something else to worry about," Laya said softly. "Trust between you and me."

There were probably any number of mollifying things to be said, but Ariel couldn't think what they were. She reached for her purse. "Tell Hattie I'll be back in a few minutes," she said. "I'm going to get Jessie."

Jessie slumbered the night away on her own bed, peacefully. The same could not be said of Ariel. She was awake until late, scanning a magazine on her propped-up knees, pausing occasionally to scribble a note on a steno pad beside her. If she listened carefully, she could make out the sound of the patrol car on its slow and frequent rounds. McCutcheon might be skeptical, but he was as good as his word.

Ariel's jottings were unrelated to her reading matter, to which she was giving only half her mind. They were questions and arguments she intended to put to Laya. The confrontation would be businesslike, just as if it were an interview for an *Open File* segment. It would take place come morning; it could probably take place then and there. Ariel sensed that her guest, closed behind the study door, was as restive as she.

"Ow!" she said five hours later when she turned over onto the ring binder of the notepad. The magazine had slipped to the floor. Sunlight, inexplicably, streamed into the room. She grumbled a sigh, suffering the dig of metal under her hip, tempting sleep back with her stillness. It was Sunday, early Sunday, she knew as one does, vaguely, informed by some little inner gyro that functions even when one is only half conscious. There was no need to rush, nowhere to go, nothing to do that couldn't wait until . . .

Her eyes snapped open when she heard the front door being unlocked. Her glance flew to Jessie, whose ears twitched, but without alarm. The shepherd yawned, rose, and, luxuriously, stretched her body into a perfect yoga posture: appropriately, *adho mukha shvanasana*, downward facing dog. Ariel beat her to the living room.

Hattie hadn't been expected at all that morning, but there she was, and dressed up, too, in navy dotted Swiss with a snowy white collar. Her face was screwed into a mask of effort as she punched buttons, disarming the alarm system. "What this country's come to is beyond me," she was muttering. "Like livin' in a jailhouse!"

"Good morning," Ariel said quietly and froggily. She cleared her throat. "What are you doing here?"

"Y'all all right?" Hattie whispered back.

"We're good. You're supposed to be having the day off."

"Get out of there!" Hattie ordered Jessie, who was sniffing the heavy-looking plastic grocery bag that hung on her arm. "It's my day," she said. "I reckon I can do whatever I want to with it." She frowned ferociously. It

took Ariel a moment to recognize that what she was seeing wasn't displeasure but uncertainty. It wasn't an emotion she'd had much occasion to connect to Hattie.
"What's in the bag?" she asked.

"Ham. A Smithfield, and pole beans and yams."

"Yams?"

"And lemons for a pie. You don't like yams?"

"I like yams fine."

"You forgot, didn't you? You hadn't even thought about
it."

"Hattie . . . thought about what?"

"It's Easter," Hattie said. "You got something you want
to do, go on and do it. I'll fix for her." She tromped toward
the kitchen, tossing over her shoulder, "Or if you don't,
there'll be plenty."

About seven different things occurred to Ariel at
approximately the same instant. That Hattie was right;
she'd blanked on the date and pretty nearly on the sea-
son. She'd virtually ignored a whole month of spring
already. That holidays during her known year had too
often been spent alone, slipping by unnoticed because
she was working, which was, in effect, what she'd
planned for this morning. As for all the holidays of all
the years before . . . if there had been happy celebrations
within a group she could call family (and she suspected
otherwise) she wouldn't recall them anyway, so why
cry over spilt memories? She had a group now: if not
precisely family, then people she cared about, living
under her roof. It didn't feel like a loss of privacy. It felt
good.

She heard the sound of the kettle being filled, and one
further insight came to her: Hattie was a woman whose
hours were too often empty of usefulness. She trailed into
the kitchen. "How many yams have you got there?" she
asked.

"Three," Hattie said, tying on an apron. "You want more, go get 'em."

Ariel got three more. By one o'clock she, Laya, and Hattie were sitting down to lunch with Henry Heller as well as the eminent playwright Marguerite Lambert, and the former actor Herbert DeForest, more cozily known as Marguerite and Carl Harris, Ariel's neighbors, friends, and sometime dog sitters.

The Harrises had arrived bearing a basket of elegantly painted eggs. Henry brought a decent wine and what, from the looks of it, must have been the last potted Easter lily in any store in town. The latter he presented with a flourish to Laya. She accepted in kind, sniffing at the plant's heavy scent, and pretending to cough.

Ariel breathed easier. She'd had qualms about the impromptu party, even though none of these people was a stranger to Laya. She'd had qualms about socializing on the heels of last night's disagreement. But if Laya's amiability toward her was a polite pretense, and if her playfulness with Henry had been a little forced, she had at least made the effort. And if, having made the effort, she then fell quiet, that had always been her wont. She didn't appear to require worrying about.

Even Hattie broke down and relaxed. She had actually set a place for herself at the table, and occasionally occupied it. She was seen to take a modest sip of wine. Ariel would have been no more astonished had she yodeled. Hattie and Sarge were two of a kind when it came to socializing. Their bottoms would hardly make contact with a seat before they remembered some necessary chore, and sought escape.

Neither the Harrises nor Henry had ever met Hattie. Henry, however, had heard about her. He had always been bemused by the fact that Ariel was heir to a way of life that involved family retainers. Aside from a cleaning lady who operated in his absence and left terse notes about depleted cleaning products, he'd had no truck with domestics. He couldn't seem to decide how to behave toward this one. Seated nearest her, he kept popping up when she did, and holding out her chair when she'd return with a refilled bowl, or some condiment she'd remembered. After two or three such, to Hattie, disconcerting episodes, she stayed rooted to her chair, her expression not unlike the cat pursued by Pepe Le Pew.

B.F. made it in time for dessert. The reason for his recent inaccessibility was more exotic than usual.

"You ever been in a submarine?" he asked, pointing his fork at Carl Harris, and then canvassing the table at large. "No? Well, I just got back!" He looked tanned, or windburned, and was nearly frothing with enthusiasm, the slice of lemon icebox pie in front of him forgotten. "Docked this morning," he announced.

While he described the "fantastic" experience, arranged by "a retired admiral friend of mine," Ariel shuddered. She could think of nowhere, with the possible exception of a caved-in coal mine, she'd rather not be than under thousands of tons of water in a tin tube that, for her money, might as well be a coffin. Just imagining it made her claustrophobic.

She stole a look at Laya, whose own phobia (a fear of dogs was cynophobia, Ariel knew, because she'd looked it up) seemed to have abated. Jessie, it was true, posed no threat at the moment, as she was elsewhere, probably scouting for crumbs. It was also true, as Hattie had remarked, that the dog seemed to steer clear of Laya. Ariel didn't think it had anything to do with Arthur; other than the occasional obligatory sniff, the two animals hardly gave each other the time of day. Ariel believed, foolishly or not, that Jessie sensed Laya's fear and had the grace to keep her distance.

"How were you able to call the other day?" Ariel asked her grandfather. "Friday, was it? If you were playing Captain Nemo?"

"You do surface from time to time, Ariel Gold," B.F. answered, and was about to launch into a dissertation on that subject when Ariel headed him off, leaning close to his ear to say, "I tried to call you back *many* times. What on earth is a 'nole,' by the way?"

"A what?"

"Was the sub on maneuvers?" Carl asked him, and as the conversational theme seemed stuck on underwater travel, Ariel left them to it. She was making a fresh pot of coffee when Hattie came into the kitchen bearing the last of the meal's remains and, after getting back into her apron, began to scrape out serving dishes.

"Tend to your company," she told Ariel. "I'll see to that."

"Everything was great, Hattie," Ariel said, and went ahead with what she was doing.

"Country ham would've been better," grumbled Hattie, who wasn't much on accepting compliments.

With a furtive glance toward the dining room, Ariel said, "I didn't get a chance to talk with you alone last night."

"Talk to me about what?"

"About what happened."

"You know as much as I do."

"You didn't hear anything at all?"

"Don't mean there was nothing to hear."

"I didn't say there wasn't. Did she call out to you when she heard . . . whatever?"

"No."

"Well, what did she do?"

Hattie took her time deciding how—or perhaps whether—to respond. She attacked a Pyrex dish vigorously, digging at a baked-on chunk of yam and burnt sugar. Then, keeping her eyes glued to the chore until the glass squeaked protest, and speaking quickly, as if she were divulging something of an embarrassing personal nature, she said, "I'd finished up here, and I went to see did she need anything. She was sittin' straight as a poker, lookin' at the window. I don't mean she could see. You know what I mean. Her face was aimed that way. She was listenin' hard, like the dog would if it heard a wrong kind of noise. She had chill bumps on her arms. I asked her what was the matter, and she said, 'He's out there.' Who? I asked her, and she put her finger up against her mouth, and I hushed and listened. After a minute she says, 'You hear?'"

Ariel was spellbound, as much by Hattie's communicativeness as by what was being communicated. If that's what one taste of the grape would do for the woman, Ariel vowed to keep it flowing. She forgot the coffee and the guests she'd been preparing it for. "And?" she prodded, as Hattie appeared to have run out of story.

"And nothin'. I didn't hear one thing but . . ." Hattie blinked rapidly. "I know when people can't see, their ears get pretty sharp. I turned out the light, and went and looked out the window. There wasn't anybody out there, I told her. She went to shakin' her head, slow. 'Oh, but there was,' she says, real low and real sure." Hattie's voice dropped, too, as if in imitation. "'I felt him.'"

"You what?"

"I'm tellin' you what *she* said. 'I felt him.' Then she let go that stiffness in herself, like the starch had gone out of her, and she says, 'He'll be back.'"

"Are you telling me she never actually heard anything? That she just *felt* that someone was outside?"

"No, that is not what I'm telling you. That is not what I said." Hattie sniffed, took time to pull a handkerchief from her pocket, and dabbed at her nostrils. "Just because she might've had a bad feeling come over her didn't mean she didn't hear something, too. She could've. One don't undo the other."

What an unlikely alliance, Ariel thought to herself: the one woman who believes she can see with her mind, and the other who believes only what her two eyes tell her, and that with a grain of salt. "What has Laya said to you?" she asked.

"Said about what?"

"About what happened to her."

"She's not a big one to talk about herself. She don't bring that up, period."

"What *does* she talk about to you?"

"You mighty full of questions."

"I'm interested. 'Curiosity is one of the permanent and certain characteristics of a vigorous mind.'"

"And nosiness is a sign of poor rearing." Hattie squeezed out the scouring pad thoroughly, taking her time, before she said, "Sometimes we talk about my girl."

"I see," Ariel said. Jane. The unlikely alliance was beginning to make sense.

"Nothing big, just . . ." Hattie's eyes had lit on some distant thing outside the window, but her hands, by rote, continued to work. Absently, she rubbed at one spot on a frying pan, the smallest of strokes, creating a short but shiny path. The pan slipped and banged against the sink. Hattie focused. "Just everyday things," she said. "And she talks about you." She gave Ariel a curious look. "She don't know about you, does she?"

"Know what about me?"

"About you not remembering things."

"No."

"You don't trust her?"

"It's not that." Ariel gestured toward the dining room.

"The Harrises don't know. No one I work with knows. The only reason you know is because B.F. told you."

"How come you don't talk about it?"

"Because . . ." Part of the answer, it seemed to Ariel, was too obvious to have to explain, and too "biggety" sounding to explain to Hattie. *Because,* she thought, *my grandfather's a wealthy man, and I'm in TV, and those two facts make me vulnerable like I don't even want to think about, to fraud and exploitation and cheap hoopla, too. Stupid checkout stand headlines are as sure as a slip of anyone's tongue, even a friend's.*

"Well, why don't you?" Hattie prodded. "You ashamed of it?"

"Am I . . . ?" Ariel was caught short by Hattie's insight. It was, admittedly and secretly, true. She felt like an emotional cripple, or, worse, a joke: a character in search of a soap opera. "Why would I be ashamed?" she protested. "'It' isn't something I brought on myself. I don't talk about 'it' because . . ." *I'd just as soon not be the object of morbid curiosity, or pity, or—your own reaction, Hattie, if you recall—outright disbelief. Even senile people have flashes of clarity. Even the slowest-witted know the names and faces of their friends. I couldn't recognize the woman I grew up believing was my mother, Hattie, or the man whose last name I carry—not his face, not his voice, not the feel of his hands on me, not how I felt when he died. I don't talk about "it," Hattie, because what's the point? I can't make anybody understand what it's like to look back at nothing. What I knew and did and felt is stored somewhere, waiting to be collected, but I don't know where to go to find it. I don't talk about "it," Hattie, because whining's not something I admire.* "I don't talk about it," Ariel said aloud, "because it's my own business."

"Any chance of more coffee?" Henry asked from the doorway.

While Ariel was filling his cup, he said, "Laya's not looking so hot, is she?"

"No?" Ariel asked.

"Dropped some weight," Henry observed. "Too much."

Ariel realized that it was true. Having seen her friend on a daily basis—and having been more attuned to other, more profound changes—she hadn't noticed. Preferring not to have one more thing to fret about, she said, "You expected what she's going through to improve her looks? You called me the other day."

"I did? Oh, yeah, I did. It's so long ago I forgot."

"Sorry. I've been crazed."

"I had an idea for you."

"About what?"

"Your mysterious friend Dorothy. I assume you're still interested in tracking her down?"

21

"DOROTHY DIDN'T ACTUALLY SAY IN THE LETTER THAT HER husband died," Ariel pointed out. "She said he was 'gone.' For all I know he's gone to join the circus or gone to Margaritaville or—"

"Gone to glory," Henry said, "in which case there's an obituary."

"Which helps me how? I don't know his name."

"The wife of the deceased," Henry said, "is listed by her first name."

The Harrises had left to attend an Easter egg hunt for their grand-godchildren (a term of their own devising); Hattie, Laya, and B.F., respectively, were watching, listening to, and napping through *Quo Vadis* on TV; and Henry was suggesting to Ariel one possible way to find Dorothy.

He shrugged. "It's worth a try."

Ariel went to her computer. In a matter of minutes she had the *San Francisco Chronicle*'s Web site, and a few seconds after that, she said, "Current week's death notices only."

"How about the Marin paper?"

Another minute passed. "Their archives aren't on-line."

"They've got internal archives," Henry said. "Make a phone call. Somebody up there punches a Search key."

"I met one of their columnists." Ariel was already dialing 415 information. "I owe him a call, in fact." She didn't mention the gleam of interest she may have seen in his baby blues. "The number, please," she said, "for the *Independent Journal*."

When the phone was answered, Ariel said, "Rob . . ." and blanked. She'd met him only a week before. He'd sat next to her at the table. Talked to her about the book he was writing. He'd made her laugh. He may have ogled her. He'd left his name when he called. *Rob the columnist* was all she could think of. What had she done with the message slip? She must start paying attention during introductions, and she must *always* return phone calls. "Excuse it," she said, and hung up.

B.F., roused from "resting his eyes," thought for a minute and groggily guessed a last name: "Miller?"

Ariel hurried back to her study and pressed redial. Henry, who'd stopped to slice himself another piece of pie, trailed.

Rob Millen (not Miller), she was told, worked from home, and "we can't give out that number." She left her own. The person who handled obits, she was predictably told, wasn't working on Easter Sunday, "but I'll ring the department in case somebody's around."

Somebody was. A very junior trainee, from the sound of her: eager and, fortunately for Ariel's purpose, open-minded.

"Let's see if I'm getting this right," the girl, Kristen by name, said. "What you're saying is you want me to search our obit archives for the given name Dorothy?"

"Please."

"And she would be the deceased person's wife?"

"Right."

"But you don't know the deceased person's last name?"

"No."

"And when would this man have died?"

Ariel didn't tell Kristen that she wasn't sure the man *had* died. She had the letter in front of her; it was dated nearly three weeks earlier, the thirtieth of March. "Last month," Ariel answered, and then no less briskly, "Or the month before."

"And this Dorothy, she'd be, like, listed in 'survived by'?"

"Right again. Do you have time to check it out for me?"

"I've got all the time in the world. It's dead here. Practically everybody's off but me, and I'm bored silly."

"Would you still have the obits from February and March saved?" Ariel asked.

"I'm guessing yes," Kristen said, "but I'll tell you in a minute. Okay, I'm retrieving the file."

Ariel nodded to Henry, and covering the receiver with her hand, said, "Why didn't I think of this?"

"Don't get too optimistic," Henry cautioned.

"Super sleuth Ariel! Wasting precious time—"

"Got it," Kristen reported. "Let's look at January."

"So you'll be a little late making the call," Henry said. "How bad can that be?"

Ariel crossed her fingers. "Be dead, husband!" she muttered.

"Not too popular a name, Dorothy," Kristen said. She'd hardly finished the statement before she said, "Oh, wait! Here we go!"

Ariel grabbed a pencil. "Read it?"

"Deceased was an Anthony Jenkins, survived by . . . Never mind."

"What?"

"You said wife, right? This Dorothy's the mother. That's it for January. In February I've got . . . a whole bunch of dead people."

Ariel tapped her pencil.

"Hey!"

"You found her?"

"Oh, no. I just recognized the name of a high school teacher of mine. I didn't know he died."

"I'm sorry."

"It's okay. He was really old, even back when he taught me."

"Which was?"

"Tenth grade. Five years ago. I'm in March now, and . . . okay, okay! Got one in the first week!"

Seeing Ariel's excitement, Henry leaned forward. "What?"

Ariel waved him quiet and began to write. Almost immediately, she stopped, a peculiar expression on her face. "Spell the last name?" she said.

"What?" Henry asked. "What's the matter?"

"That's the only Dorothy in March?" Ariel said. And then, "I see. I really appreciate your . . . Kristen, do April, will you?"

"Why April?" Henry asked. "She wrote you the end of March. He was already dead if he is dead."

Ariel was paying him no attention. She'd covered her free ear with her palm, listening intently. "Yes, I'm here," she finally said. "It is sad, yes. 'But that's the way it often happens.'" (Who was it she'd heard say that? She couldn't at the moment recollect.) "I don't suppose you could fax those to me?"

When she'd given Kristen her number, she thanked her again, and hung up.

"Did she find it or not?" Henry asked. "What's sad?"

Ariel rapped the knuckles of one fist against the other, and rocked back in her chair. Several seconds passed before she looked up at Henry.

"Uh-oh," he said when he saw her face.

The fax machine twittered, and paper began to inch laboriously through.

"'How bad can it be?'" Ariel said quietly. "Isn't that what you asked? How bad can it be that I was 'a little late' calling my old friend Dorothy?" She waited until the fax dropped into the tray. "I'd say," she told Henry as she handed it over, "as bad as it gets."

Frowning, he skimmed. Kristen had efficiently circled the obituary for the husband, "survived by his loving wife, Dorothy." He'd been a practicing physician, a GP, as well as coauthor of a medical textbook, former county coroner, veteran, and Mason. It was a lengthy tribute, perhaps written by a family member, maybe by Dorothy herself. Nothing jumped out as warranting Ariel's reaction.

A second fax fell into the tray, and Henry picked it up. His eyebrows climbed. "How did you know to check April?" he asked.

Ariel seemed not to have heard the question. "Isn't that something? I was right there the day they buried her."

"Which you didn't know—not at the time—so how did you know today?"

"Well, sir, I'll tell you." Ariel rubbed at her forehead, massaging a spot over one eye as if she felt a pain there. "Dorothy *Thibeau* was an old flame of B.F.'s."

"What?"

"I'm not lying. About thirty years ago that old gentleman in the living room proposed to my friend Dorothy. My deceased friend Dorothy. She turned him down."

"And . . . what? They were still in touch? I'm not—"

"He hadn't seen her in years, he told me. They went their separate ways, and she eventually married . . . what was his name?"

Henry glanced at the first obit. "Dr. Raymond Thibeau."

"Right, and they lived happily ever after until he died last month of . . . whatever it was he died of."

"Liver cancer."

"And she died . . . five weeks later? 'But that's the way it often happens.' It was Senator Bland's wife who said that."

"Senator Bland's . . . Ellis Bland? What's he got to do—"

"That *is* the way it often happens. It's true. I've read statistics. Couples are together for years . . . one dies, the other loses heart, loses the will to live, and *pffft!* However . . ." Ariel laughed a little. "I don't think that's what happened in this case. I mean, it must have been only one day, maybe two days after I got her letter begging me to call *because she was scared!* She was scared, and she needed help. But, of course, I didn't call because I didn't remember who she was."

"And that's your fault?"

"No! Certainly not! I can't help it if I'm brain damaged."

"You are not brain damaged."

"If I'd called—"

"She'd still be dead. You're not a miracle worker. You're not a doctor. She died of heart disease; it says so right here."

Ariel took the obituary from his hand, and read it again, wanting badly to be convinced, wanting badly to let herself off the hook. "Still, though . . . she must have been hurt when I didn't call. She thought we were friends. We'd talked a lot obviously. We were simpatico. Look at that letter. She wrote the way people do who've struck a chord with somebody, so even years later they just pick up where they left off like no time has—"

"Ariel."

"What?"

"Shut up."

Ariel's jaw dropped.

"What you're doing to yourself is stupid. You can't help it that you didn't remember the woman. You tried your best. You knocked yourself out to find out who she was, and—"

"And while I was knocking myself out, running around San Rafael, she was dead a few miles away. She died thinking I didn't care that she was in trouble. "

"Are you finished?"

"I guess." Ariel shook her head. "This sucks," she said.

"Yeah, it does. It's also still not making much sense to me. If B.F. told you a week ago that he knew this woman, why were you still in the dark?"

"He never called her by her first name. I didn't know her last name." Ariel's eyes widened as a thought struck. "Don't you think it's amazing? That Dorothy and I met . . . whenever we did? An old girlfriend of B.F.'s? What are the odds? It's like some kind of—I don't know—cosmic joke!"

"Oh, good God, would you get a grip! Your grandfather's met one hell of a lot of people in nearly eighty years of living, a lot of that living in the same state *you've* been in for thirty-three years. It doesn't exactly qualify for *Ripley's Believe It or Not* that you once ran into somebody he knew. What are the odds you *wouldn't* ever run into somebody he knew?"

Ariel had the grace to look sheepish. After a minute she said, "So I get carried away." After another minute she said, "Actually, I meet people who know him or know of him all the time. He's not exactly a low-profile sort."

"And he's right in there on the sofa. What I suggest is you get him in here. See if he can tell you about whatever it was that had Dorothy Thibeau so scared."

22

B.F. WASN'T NEARLY AS SHOCKED BY HER NEWS AS ARIEL HAD expected. Told that she had once met his old sweetheart, all he said was, "So it *was* you. Small world."

"What was me?" Ariel asked, bewildered. "What are you talking about?"

It was then that B.F. came to attention. "How do you know you met her? It was two years ago. You haven't started to get your memory back?"

Ariel shook her head. "What do you mean, it *was* me? And how do you know it was two years ago?"

"You remember I called you the other day, and you were too busy to talk to me?"

"I wasn't too busy! Laya was about to fall over a . . . Never mind. Yes, I remember. You said something about my past and having something that might interest me that might not be anything."

"I don't believe I uttered anything quite that senseless."

"Really? When you called back and talked to Hattie, you said something about a 'nole.' I looked it up. There's no such word."

Abruptly, B.F. went to the door and shouted, "Hattie!"

"Oh, B.F., forget it," Ariel said. "Get back to what you were saying!"

Hattie came at a trot, alarmed, clutching a towel from the guest bath, where, apparently, she'd been occupied. "What the devil you yellin' down the hall for?" she exclaimed. "You like to give me a heart attack!"

"I want you to clear something up."

"Your leg broke?" Fuming, Hattie said. "I'll tell you

what's the truth, mister, you do that again, your leg better be broke! You better be at death's door."

Henry was fascinated. B.F. was determined. "Listen to me," he said, "when I called Thursday and spoke to you, what did I say?"

"You don't know? Have you turned simple?"

"Seems there's some confusion about it."

"Didn't say enough to get confused about." Hattie refolded the towel neatly. "You asked how was I gettin' along over here, and how was Laya, and so on."

"And then I started to tell you something else, remember? But my time ran out, and I had to get off the phone?"

Hattie thought for a second. "Something about some note?"

"Ah, a *note*," B.F. said. "N-o-*t*-e."

With an exasperated look at them all, Hattie said, "I'm missin' my movie," and left.

"What note?" Ariel asked.

B.F. took a sip of the coffee he'd brought in with him, settled into a chair, and said, "Dorothy Thibeau was on my mind last week, as you can imagine. A whole lot of people I know have gone on to their reward, some, I spec, surprised by what it turned out to be." He gave a snort of mild amusement. "But Dorothy was a dozen years younger than me. When your younger friends and acquaintances go, it's . . . disquieting."

Ariel folded her arms and waited. B.F. would tell a thing his way or not at all.

"I got to thinkin' about her, like I said, rememberin' our courtship—brief but, if I may say so, memorable—and I suppose I sank into something of a sentimental mood." B.F. set his coffee aside and, tenting his fingers on his belly, said, "Dorothy wrote me a few fine letters back then, back when people took the time to write. I got a notion to reread them."

Ariel couldn't stand it. "And?" she put in.

"And nothing. I looked, but I couldn't find them. Probably threw 'em out twenty years ago. Too bad. They were right interesting epistles. The things I did come across, though, in that box of old stuff! Birth announcements for folks that have babies of their own now. Jane's report cards. Your *mother's* report cards.

"And . . . I did come across two or three stray communications from Dorothy. Christmas cards. An invitation to her and her husband's silver anniversary. Some bash it must've been. I didn't go."

Ariel had begun to nibble at her cuticle. Henry slapped her hand away from her mouth.

"She included a note—you know, could I believe twenty-five years already and she hoped I'd make it and so forth—and a picture. You might be interested in that," B.F. said, as if the idea had just occurred to him, and reached into his pocket.

The envelope was professionally addressed, hand-lettered in a flourish of calligraphy. The postmark was two years earlier. The invitation was engraved. The note folded inside was written on a smaller version of the stationery used for Ariel's letter, and the handwriting was Dorothy's, by now as familiar to Ariel as her own.

"'My dear *Biff*'?" she read.

"Dorothy's pet name for me," B.F. explained. "It's what she always called me."

Ariel thought about it for a second and decided to leave it alone. She started to read silently before she remembered Henry. "'My dear Biff,'" she began again, aloud. "'Twenty-five years? God bless us one and all! Speaking of time, the enclosed was taken the last time you graced us with your presence, so long ago I think I was still naturally blond. I dug it out solely to convince you it's been too long. Do come! Jane is. I saw her—'"

Ariel felt a sharp kick of surprise in her belly. "Dorothy knew Jane?" she asked her grandfather.

"Sure. I told you . . . didn't I tell you? Takin' on the task of raisin' Jane—that it wasn't for her—was one reason Dorothy spurned my suit. Regretfully and, as it turned out, fortunately."

"Yes, but I didn't realize . . ."

"Dorothy was a good deal more comfortable as Jane's pal than she'd've been as her stepgrandmama."

One sentence in Dorothy's letter to Ariel made sense to her now. *Seeing you,* Dorothy had written after watching Ariel on TV, *was like seeing an old friend.* "What I wonder," Ariel said aloud to herself, "is whether she—what's that?" Something had slipped from the envelope into her lap and then onto the floor. It was a photo, a black-and-white glossy. She retrieved it and momentarily forgot the note altogether. "When was this taken?" she asked.

"About eight, nine years ago. The last time I saw Dorothy."

It had been snapped at some formal event, the three subjects dressed to the nines. It was the sort of shot one sees in society columns.

B.F. was not quite as full in the face as now, and his hair was more gray than white, but he was relatively, and reassuringly, unchanged by the years since. Jane's face was partially obscured by his, against which her cheek was resting. Her distinctive wide mouth was stretched in an all-out grin. Even then, which must have been early on in her modeling career, the arch of her neck was elegant. She looked, to Ariel, piercingly young.

Ariel tapped the photo, the woman on B.F.'s other side. "Is this . . . ?" He nodded.

Ariel hadn't been aware until then that she'd been carrying a vague image of her "friend" in her mind. Dorothy Thibeau was as different from that image as Princess

Grace from Mother Hubbard. She was a mature, classic beauty. Her fair hair was severely styled, sleeked back from a wide, still smooth forehead. Her well-shaped brows arched over eyes so dark they looked black, and her lips were slightly open. She had been caught, Ariel guessed, on the verge of speaking.

Henry had leaned over Ariel's shoulder. "Wow!" he said.

"She was fun, too," B.F. commented.

"She looks younger than I thought she'd be," Ariel said.

"She *was* younger then. We all were." B.F. squinted. "You want to tell me now how it is that you were thinkin' about her a'tall?"

Ariel shook her head. "In a minute," she said, still studying the lovely face.

"She would have been . . ." B.F. did the simple math. "She'd have been around fifty-seven, fifty-eight then."

She hadn't looked it. There was, it was true, a little extra flesh under the jaw, a discernible fold to the eyelids: the pull of gravity that gets stronger with age. This woman evidently hadn't been overly concerned; she'd done nothing to fix the evidence.

"You said she was in the fashion business when you were seeing her?" Ariel asked.

"Fashion director for what used to be the premier specialty store in San Francisco. Carriage trade. Store's gobbled up now, like most of the independents."

Ariel took one last look at the three carefree faces and went back to the note.

"'Do come!'" she read. "'Jane is. I ran into her the other day in the Emporium tearoom. We had a stimulating chat about *Doppelgangers*. She has one, I told her; a reporter, I think the woman is, with a TV news show. Jane was intrigued.'"

Ariel shot her grandfather a look. *Jane knew about me?*

she thought in disbelief. *Was it me? It had to be!* She needed to absorb the implications of that; she needed far more to keep reading. Nearly tripping over the words, she read: "'I exaggerated about the likeness; for one thing, this TV person likes her vittles'"—Ariel straightened her shoulders—"'likes her vittles a bit overmuch. You might say she was Jane's "double" in more ways than one. It made for a fun conversation. We've missed too many of those, my old friend. We've got a lot of catching up to do. Mark the date; the champagne's on ice.'"

The close was discreet. "Fondly," Dorothy had signed.

Ariel looked at her grandfather, whose thoughts, she could tell, had traveled to some other time and place. Her own thoughts were racing too fast to catch hold of. Jane had been told about her! As a conversational gambit, yes, a passing fribble of gossip, but she had been told. Had she pursued it? Had she sought the "TV reporter" out? *Did we meet?* No! B.F. would've known. But Jane had been "intrigued" . . .

"I don't recall," B.F. said, "why I couldn't go to the party. I wish I had. I don't remember RSVPing." His forehead creased. "I did, surely. Why, that might've been my last communication—"

Henry made a small murmuring sound in his throat.

"Hmmm?" B.F. asked.

"Now I know where she gets it," Henry said.

"Where who gets what?"

"Where your granddaughter gets her bent for schmaltz."

He didn't even get a rise out of Ariel, who was rereading the note, but B.F. laughed. "And her liking for vittles?" he asked. "Henry, you're right. Of course I answered the invitation, or had my secretary do it. My manners are better than my memory."

"Why didn't you say anything about this before?" Ariel

asked. "You've had this all this time. You knew about me!"

Henry covered his eyes and groaned. B.F. was kinder. "Honey," he said, "I didn't know you were on the planet. I read in a note over two years ago that a friend saw a woman who reminded her of Jane. So what? I didn't remember it two minutes after I read it."

"I wish—"

"Well, don't we all? But you run into people who resemble other people every day of your life. Listen, I once had a woman mistake me for somebody else, an old boyfriend or a boss who'd pinched her fanny or who knows what. She walked right up to me and slapped my face. Then she took a closer look, said 'Excuse me, I thought you were somebody else,' and walked away."

Ariel managed a fleeting smile. "Dorothy wrote that Jane was intrigued when she told her."

"I'd guess Jane was bein' sociable. It was idle . . . It was Dorothy Thibeau bein' chatty. Castin' bread upon the conversational waters. That was Dorothy."

Ariel knew she was being unreasonable. That there might have been contact between Jane and herself was a fantasy that was hard to let go. Knowing there never would be was harder.

"Tell me if I'm out of line," Henry said to B.F., "but I'm curious. You said it turned out to be fortunate your—how'd you put it?—your suit got spurned? Why's that?"

"Well, sir, Dorothy was . . ." B.F. thumped the arm of his chair thoughtfully, choosing his words, and then he opened his hand as he might to release a butterfly. "Effervescent. You know who she reminded me of? Auntie Mame. She had great style, great joie de vivre. She . . ." Suddenly inspired, he said, "Jane came up with a quote that described her perfectly. She was as bad as you," he said to Ariel, "for confounded quotes. It went something like: 'Some people are born to lift heavy weights . . .'"

"'Some are born to juggle golden balls,'" Ariel finished. "Max Beerbohm. He also said 'Of all the objects of hatred, a woman once loved is the most hateful.'"

"Hogwash in this case. To answer your question, Henry, time proved I wasn't so much in love with Dorothy as charmed by her. I'd guess she ran into that pretty often. For all her flightiness, though, Dorothy wasn't without sense. Charm doesn't have much day-in, day-out stayin' power, and she knew it."

"But she did marry," Ariel argued, "and she stayed married for twenty-five years."

"We'll have to believe Ray Thibeau was more than merely charmed, and I hope she felt the same. Must have. Her love of livin' left her, looks like, when he did." Abruptly, he checked his wristwatch. "It's five o'clock somewhere in the world," he said briskly. "Pour me something sustainin', Ariel Gold, and then sit down here and tell me how you found out you met Dorothy."

Even fortified by the premium bourbon Ariel kept as his private reserve, B.F. seemed hard hit by her letter from Dorothy. It would have been kinder, she worried, watching his face as he read, to have described the contents. She could have; she knew every word by heart. The bit about catching *The Open File*, about how seeing her was like seeing an old friend . . . Ariel sighed, the rest of the letter running through her mind.

> How often I've thought of our conversations and resisted contacting you. I don't think you'll be surprised to hear that. You did warn me. "There is only one way to achieve happiness on this terrestrial ball, and that is to have a clear conscience, or none at all." (I looked up the quote. Who would have thought that Ogden Nash— Ogden Nash?—would haunt me! Sadly, his "Candy Is

*dandy but liquor Is quicker" is sometimes apt, too.) You
had me pegged, my dear; not one day has passed that I
haven't felt guilty.*

*My husband's gone now. I've run out of excuses and,
oh boy! I used them all. The evidence wasn't absolutely
conclusive, I told myself, and in any case, it wasn't mine
to expose or suppress. I told myself that Sis didn't want to
live. I could argue, and have, that my reticence (fence sitting? cowardice?) has actually benefited a number of people. Unlikely as it sounds, that's true. The villain of the
piece, if you can believe it, Ariel, has become quite the do-
gooder. It's an intriguing twist, isn't it? A patron of worthy
causes. A philanthropist, no less. Raphael smiles greedily
every time the man passes through his doors! I'm unimpressed; I know how he got the money. But, as you
pointed out, I have no right to set myself up as judge, no
more than he to set himself up as executioner.*

*The word is apt. Alone as I am now, I'm scared. I'm a
loose end. Or would loose cannon be more accurate? A
man who's murdered once can't be counted on not to do it
again, can he?*

Ariel, please call me.

When he reached the last request, undisguised as it was
by any attempt at clever, self-deprecating banter—need
laid bare—B.F. slapped the paper against his thigh, raised
his eyes to the ceiling, and held the attitude. "You poor
child," he eventually murmured. Ariel thought he was
talking about Dorothy, and then realized he meant her.
"You just got this out of the blue?" he asked. "Not knowing who she was or what . . . *Do* you have any idea what
this is about?"

"No, sir. All I know is what you just read, what you
told us, and what it said in her obituary, which was precious little."

B.F. looked at the one-name signature on the letter. "Has my mind quit on me altogether," he asked, "or did I miss something?"

Ariel explained how she'd finally connected the letter writer to a last name. "I'd tried everything I could think of. If it hadn't been for Henry, I still wouldn't know who she was."

"Hurray for Henry," said Henry, who'd been intermittently scribbling on a scrap of paper.

"Reckon," B.F. said, "who this 'Sis' was?"

"I was hoping you'd know," Ariel said.

"I know it wasn't a blood sister. She didn't have one. Don't know any Raphael either."

"Henry and I had the idea she might mean the archangel."

B.F. stared.

"There's a statue of him, of Raphael, at the mission in San Rafael."

"A statue?"

"It's above the door of the church. We thought that if this man she's talking about was a parishioner, then—"

"B.F.," Henry said, looking up from the notes he'd been making, "was Mrs. Thibeau Catholic?"

"Why?"

"I'd just like to resolve Raphael, eliminate him as an actual person to be concerned with. Stands to reason someone who went to that church, who saw the statue often, would be more likely to think of it and refer to it."

"Oh," B.F. said. "Well, I don't know what Dorothy was. Her funeral was what you might call ecumenical. She wasn't, that I recall, noticeably spiritual."

"But she was fanciful," Henry said. "A woman who'd find it amusing to personify a statue? I'm wondering . . . how fanciful?"

"How do you mean?"

"Is there a chance your lady friend was imagining a threat?"

The old man gave it thought. "Hard to say," he decided. Quite seriously, the soft edges of his enunciation subtly honed, he said, "I don't know that I could claim to know Dorothy, truly know her, even thirty years ago. Was all that gaiety camouflage, or was there nothing *to* camouflage? Was what you saw all there was? I haven't laid eyes on her in a decade. Probably got a sympathy card when Jane died. I don't recall. But I hadn't talked to her, even on the phone, in . . . Good Lord. A year or two? Has to be that or more, since she obviously didn't know who Ariel was to me."

"You're not telling us what you think," Henry persisted.

"Dorothy was given to taking the rosy view: avoiding trouble, including, when she could manage it, the trouble of thinking. But you look at this . . ." B.F. jabbed the letter. "The introspection? The rationalization she recognizes and admits to? You could say that if she'd gotten to the point where she was afraid—"

"Then she had reason to be?"

"Maybe, maybe not. Dorothy wasn't averse to a little dramatization."

Ariel eyed her grandfather curiously. She'd never known him to be so noncommittal. "You're still not telling us what you think," she pointed out.

"I think it's academic."

Ariel's jaw dropped. "What do you mean, academic?"

"I mean, Ariel Gold, that the lady is unavailable to decode her letter. She's also beyond the reach of mortal harm, and there's no reason to think she was helped to get there."

"I can't believe . . . The fact that I got that letter just a few days before she died doesn't bother you a little?"

"You got it when?"

"That same week. Wednesday or . . ." Ariel reconstructed. "It was Tuesday. It was mailed the day before, on Monday."

"The week she died?"

Ariel nodded.

"And you've been tormenting yourself? Picturing a frightened woman mailing off this desperate plea, sitting by the phone during her last days, wondering why you didn't call?"

"You wouldn't have done the same?"

"Ariel, it didn't happen."

"You're not saying she didn't write that? It's the same handwriting as your note. The same style, the same *voice*—"

"I'm not saying she didn't write it; I'm saying she didn't mail it."

"B.F., there it is!"

"Dorothy was in the hospital all that last week, I was told. Better than a week, in intensive care. She wasn't writing any letters, let alone going out to mail them."

"But how did—"

B.F. glanced at the paper in his hand, and did a little calculation of his own. "You didn't wonder that the letter was dated over a week earlier?"

"Of course I did. I figured she was ambivalent about asking for help, that maybe she was afraid she was exaggerating the . . . I didn't know her, but she didn't sound like a whiner."

"You're right about that anyway. Honey, she died of heart failure. Complications of pneumonitis. A virus. I know because I asked. She wasn't in great physical shape when it hit her, from what I understand, so—"

"Not in great shape? How do you know?"

"One or two comments I heard at the service. Opinion was, Thibeau's death took her hard. She was despondent.

Not eating, not sleeping. Not taking proper care of herself. Not *being* herself."

"Who said?"

"Different ones."

"Worried?" Henry speculated. "Afraid?"

"I can't say she was; I can't say she wasn't. I wasn't there. I can say, however, that what she died of was heart failure."

"Heart failure!" Ariel scoffed. "Everybody who ever died, died of heart failure. Was there an autopsy?"

"Not to my knowledge." B.F. rose from his chair, and stuffing his hands into his pockets, began to prowl the room. "I don't know why there would be."

"She wrote the letter," Ariel said, "and then she got sick."

"You don't know that it was cause and effect." Henry stated the obvious. "Sounds like she was sickly already."

"Whatever the timing, she wrote it, and she wrote it to me."

"This is a superfluous question," B.F. said, "but you're going to pursue this, aren't you?"

Henry rolled his eyes. The other two didn't notice. Ariel didn't bother to answer. "Who mailed it?" she wondered aloud.

"Who and why?" Henry said, consulting the paper on which he'd been making notes. "When did Dorothy get sick? And did she talk to anybody about her fears? Who was Sis? More to the point, who was Sis's husband or significant other or heir? What evidence wasn't conclusive? What didn't she have a clear conscience about—"

Ariel held up her hands. "*I* know the questions! I need to talk to her friends. B.F. . . ." She twisted to see her grandfather, who appeared to be studying the spines of the books on her shelves. "Who should I call?" He didn't respond. "B.F.? I said—"

"I heard you." He slid a book from its niche, fanned through the pages, and then replaced it. "Libby Vail, I suppose."

"Mrs. Senator Bland?" Henry asked. "You said something about her a while ago, Ariel. What's she got to do with—"

"I met her at B.F.'s dinner party," Ariel told him. "She and Dorothy were close?" she asked B.F.

"They ran in the same crowd."

"Meantime," Henry put in, "you can do some easy research closer to home."

"Like?" Ariel asked.

He made a little gimme gesture. "Let's see B.F.'s note." He scanned it, mumbling to himself, "... 'stimulating chat about *Doppelgängers*. She has one' ... Okay, right here," Henry said, and read, "'a reporter, I think the woman is, with a TV news show.' Doesn't sound like you were bosom friends at that point, does it?"

Ariel popped up to read over his shoulder. "Yeah," she said, "but just because she didn't get that I was a producer doesn't mean much. Most people don't understand—"

"And then here." Henry pointed. "She refers to you as 'this TV person.'"

"Okay. So?" Ariel draped her forearms over Henry's shoulders.

"Let's assume for the sake of argument that she knew little about you except that you were in the news business. She saw you, maybe, with a mike or a cameraman. Which suggests—"

"I was working on a story."

"And since you've got a general time frame"—Henry glanced at the date on the invitation—"February four, two years ago—"

"I can pinpoint which story it was. Way to go, Henry!"

Ariel cried, and gave him a spontaneous head-to-head hug. She felt his shoulders stiffen, and, very casually, she removed herself, turning to include her grandfather in the moment. He was no longer in the room. Neither she nor Henry had noticed when he'd left.

23

HENRY AND ARIEL'S SURMISE WAS CORRECT: ARIEL HAD BEEN IN San Francisco during December two-plus years before. Finding out which story had taken her there was a piece of cake. Problem was, that particular story had nothing to do with Dorothy Thibeau or her husband. It was unrelated to the death of someone named Sis; no death, homicide or otherwise, entered into it at all.

"Remember the pawnshop piece?" Ariel asked Henry, calling from her office the next morning.

"Pawnshop . . . ?" Henry repeated vaguely.

"The one about all the unredeemed stuff these different brokers had collected? The bloodstained set of scalpels, remember? And the champagne cooler from the *Titanic*, and the derringer—"

"*Oy vay!*"

"You do remember it."

"I'd like to forget it."

"Well, I *had*, obviously, so I took a look at it. 'Pawn Ticket to Nowhere.' Not your brand of news, was it?"

"It wasn't news. It barely qualified as fluff. Chloe's story, wasn't it?" he said, naming the correspondent whom Ariel replaced.

"And I produced. I saw not one thing that in any way, shape, or form could be connected to Dorothy."

"Not the derringer?" Henry suggested facetiously. "What was the inscription again?"

"'Till death do us part, Love, Emily.' The derringer was hocked in 1908, in Tulsa, which was one of five different cities I did interviews in, I found out, all within two days. I went to Opelika, Alabama, for Pete's sake! I must have been in San Francisco for a total of three hours, Henry. When did Dorothy see me, and where? When and how did we meet? When did we talk?"

"That was your only San Francisco trip around that time?"

"Only one I found any expense reports for, and I checked for months both ways. I could have gone on my own time, I suppose."

"Wouldn't surprise me. Might be you caught some local story while you were passing through town, and went back to check it out. Wouldn't be the first time you ever chased off on your own hook."

"Yeah, yeah, I've heard all your Lone Ranger stories. It must have been fun, having the old me as your underling."

"Having the new you was," Henry said.

Ariel did a double take. Henry did not refer to their past relationship. He certainly didn't indulge in double entendre about it. When he went on in a perfectly ordinary tone of voice, she decided she'd misinterpreted. She also entirely missed what it was he said next. "Pardon?" she asked.

"Local stories," he repeated. "I said, have you checked to see what was going on there at the time?"

"I've got one of the researchers on it."

"Oh? This is going to be an *Open File* piece?"

"Maybe."

"Well, it does qualify as open. You call Libby Vail yet?"

"First thing. She's away. She and her husband are touring Italy, but they'll be back at the end of the week."

"Um." Henry's attention had drifted. "Ariel, pawn-shop."

"Pawnshop . . . what?" Ariel asked.

"That day we had tea you mentioned a San Francisco pawnshop owner. You'd called all the four-one-five numbers in your files, remember? You talked to some guy you said had a crush on you."

"Right. Calvin Soo. I just saw him on the tape, in fact."

"Soo?"

"He was one of the collectors I interviewed, the one with the *Titanic* champagne cooler. What about him?"

"That pawnshop is where you were while you were in San Francisco on that trip. From what you say about your schedule, you were in and out of the city too fast to be much of anyplace but there. Maybe that's where you met Dorothy."

"*Dorothy*? Hocking her valuables? Did you see the invitation to that anniversary bash? Did you see the clothes she was wearing in that photo? She was married to a doctor, Henry. She had bucks."

"Maybe she also had a gambling problem, or she was having an affair with Mr. Soo."

Ariel laughed.

"What's funny? He had a thing for you, you said. Maybe he's a romantic."

"If you could see Soo . . ." Ariel heard a weak groan, and laughed again. "Sorry," she said, "I couldn't resist saying it. If you could see him, you'd know how funny that is. He's huge, Henry!"

"Big people don't have romances?"

"I'm talking sumo. Wheeze-when-he-breathes big. Soo in the throes of passion?" Ariel grinned, shivering. "I don't want to think about it!"

"Hey, the 'old you' wasn't exactly a sylph, my dear."

It took Ariel a second to process what she'd heard. Her

grin dissolved. "Well," she said, stung—very nearly stunned. Unkindness wasn't a trait she'd ever encountered in Henry.

"Ariel," he said. "I shouldn't have said that. I don't know why I did."

Ariel thought she did know; she recognized unresolved anger when she heard it. "Henry," she began, "do you have something you'd like to—"

"You're probably right," he interrupted, determinedly brisk, "about Dorothy. It's unlikely she frequented pawn-shops."

Ariel tried to get back into focus. "No . . . let's look at this. I wish I could remember the neighborhood where the shop's located."

"Because?"

"I'm wondering, could there be offices in the same block? Her lawyer, say, or dentist? Or restaurants—a deli she liked?"

"Or her car broke down and she was looking to use the phone?"

"I think I'll give old Calvin Soo a call." Hearing the sound of a throat being delicately cleared, Ariel looked up to see Tara Castanera at her office door. "Hey," Ariel said to her, "I've got your former boss on the line. You want to . . ." It was only then that she noticed Tara's agitation. "Henry, can you hold a second?" she said, and, to Tara, "What?"

"Your, uh, housekeeper," Ariel's assistant said, "or what-ever . . . ? She just called from a Dr. Crowne's office. She asked could you come there. *Now*, she said."

Ariel was in her van and on the way before the sensible thought presented itself: she'd jumped the gun. Crowne's office was no more than ten minutes from the studio; still, she should have called before riding off to the rescue.

She'd asked Tara exactly what Hattie had said. "'Ask Ariel can she come here . . . now!'" Tara repeated with the same dire emphasis. "She sounded stressed," was all she could add.

It was probably an "emergency" of the out-of-toilet-paper variety, Ariel assured herself; some inconsequential thing. Maybe Hattie, who prayed under her breath when driving in L.A. traffic, had dinged a fender on the way to Crowne's office.

But why were they *at* Crowne's office?

Laya had admitted the night before last that her eye felt "uncomfortable." Had she said anything yesterday? Ariel tried to think whether she'd seen that telltale massaging of the eye socket. She had, now that she thought of it. And as soon as she and Henry had emerged from her former study, now Laya's bedroom, Laya had gone in and closed the door. She'd retired for the night at seven-thirty, while it was still light out. Ariel had paid little attention. She'd been too full of plans about Dorothy Thibeau.

Those plans and any Ariel had for the rest of that Monday would be put on hold. After talking to Crowne, she was more concerned about Laya, who seemed determined to put her life on hold.

Hattie and Laya had taxied to the doctor's office, Ariel learned, shortly after she'd left home that morning. Laya had asked Hattie, please, to call Crowne and tell him she needed to see him.

Ariel drove them home. It was a heavily silent trip. Laya faced the passenger window, as if watching the passing landscape. Hattie heaved an occasional ponderous sigh from the backseat. Ariel spent the time trying to reason out what Crowne had told her.

The transplant hadn't taken. The new cornea was turning cloudy, the eye drying and losing its normal gleam.

There were any number of reasons, Crowne explained, why transplants may not be successful; sometimes there was no reason. He recommended a second try. Laya declined.

"It's not an unexpected reaction," Crowne told Ariel in private. "In her mind this is a devastating setback. The thought of trying again, maybe failing again . . . And that could happen; there are no guarantees. It's tough."

It would take time to find another donor, he went on to say. He would be looking for the healthiest cells, a cornea with the optimum chance of success. By then, Laya would have had time to adjust. "She'll see things in a different light then," he said.

Ariel wasn't so sure. Waiting at a stop light, she glanced over at her passenger. Laya didn't seem devastated. Even if her equanimity was just for show, it was astounding. "Do you need to stop for anything before we go home?" Ariel asked her.

"No, thank you," Laya replied.

The light changed, and Ariel drove a block or so before she asked, "Do you have any vision at all?"

"I did."

"You did?" Laya had never let on, and Ariel had assumed . . . One of these days, she told herself, she would learn not to make assumptions about Laya. "You could actually see?" she asked.

"Mist." Laya's lip curved, and, under her breath, she said something that sounded like, "Rose colored."

"Are you in any pain?" Ariel asked.

"He gave me drops."

"Drops," Ariel repeated. She felt her skin creep. How the woman could bring herself to put drops of any kind into her eyes was beyond her. How Laya could restrain herself from leaping at any possibility of seeing again was beyond imagining.

When they'd reached the house and Ariel had the van safely parked, she asked the question, "Will you tell me why not?"

"Why not . . . ?"

"Dr. Crowne says there's a chance a second transplant might work. Why not try again?"

"I can't afford it."

"You can't . . . you can't *not* afford it! Money's not an issue."

"No? I suspect I've already been a charity case . . ." Laya let the statement dangle like bait. When Ariel said nothing, she reached the obvious conclusion. "You know how I feel, about charity *and* about being 'protected' from the facts." She opened the door. "However," she said, "I wasn't talking about money."

She got out and, without mishap, made her way to the porch, where she waited to be let in. Ariel and Hattie exchanged grim looks before they followed. Once inside, Laya started immediately for her room. She'd become more surefooted, Ariel, even in her distraction, noticed; more confident in her movements. "Laya," she said, "if it isn't money you can't afford, then what is it?"

"What is it." Laya made a statement of it, mulling it over, as though it were a philosophical puzzle. "Hope," she said. "It can kill you. I've decided to live."

"'To live' . . ." Again, Ariel looked to Hattie. What was she missing here? Hattie was squinting at Laya, equally lost.

"I won't go through it again," Laya said, "the agony of hope." She walked to the nearest window. She must have been counting the steps because she stopped within inches of it, and as if she were commenting on what lay beyond it, said, "Things look a little clearer today, *don't they*? That's how it goes when you suffer hope. I'm sure the light's brighter today, you tell yourself. The edges sharper. Every day you wake up and open your eyes—or in my case, the only eye that counts—and you convince yourself it's true.

"You learn to sneak up on hope, cut around behind it, so as not to tempt it to trick you. You look at things obliquely. That's a light. I see it. Or is it real? Is it some flare happening inside my own eye? That swirl of movement . . . I couldn't see that yesterday! It's curtains, stirring in the breeze. And you reach to touch them, and there's nothing there. Shadows."

She touched her fingertips to the windowpane. "And then comes that heart-stopping moment when you're absolutely sure you're not fooling yourself. There *is* a difference this time. You're starting down the steps, and you can tell. Your depth perception's back! You trust it, and you take a step, and the next thing you know, you're on your knees, and your tongue's bleeding where you've bitten it. And you know it wasn't different at all. It was never one iota different. It was wishful thinking." Her voice dropped, and her fingers stilled. "What does it mean, you ask yourself, that my eye's burning? Does that soreness mean it's healing—or scarring? Is it starting to ulcerate? To turn into dry, useless skin? Are the cells dying? Is that cornea as dead as the poor soul it came from?"

Laya's hand dropped to her side, and she faced the other two women. "I was never an ideal transplant," she said. "I haven't gotten better. Not for money, not even your money, Ariel, or your grandfather's or whoever's it was, am I going through that again."

"And I actually believed," Ariel said, aghast at her own stupidity, "that you weren't upset when Crowne broke the news."

"I wasn't. I knew already. And I know another transplant would go the same way."

"Child." Hattie spoke up. "How could you know? You can be strong a while longer. If there's a chance—"

"And when the second transplant doesn't work," Laya said, "will we go on to all the miraculous alternatives? Do you know they're using amniotic membranes from placentas now? Should we try that? There's even a prosthesis of some kind. Can you believe it? It's made out of plastic. It doesn't *work* too often, but let's go for it! Some vision-impaired people, people with retinitis pigmentosa, get themselves stung by bees, hoards of bees! Surely there's some 'natural' magic like that for me, too? Let's give snake handling a shot."

"You don't fool me," Ariel said. "You're shattered. You'd have to be superhuman not to be. You need to give yourself some time."

"I intend to. Time doing, not waiting. I know when to let go. I'm getting on with my life *as it is*."

"You can't give up this easily."

"*Easily?*" Laya held on to her composure. She swallowed; she even managed a smile, albeit a strained one. "Please," she said.

"I want you to ask yourself something," Ariel blurted.

"What?"

When Ariel hesitated, Laya tilted her head, as if she might have missed the question, and said, "Well?"

"You don't have to answer me," Ariel said, "but ask yourself."

"Ariel, what?"

"Is this a rational, healthy decision, or could it be that you're punishing yourself?"

Hattie, Ariel noticed from the corner of her eye, reacted to that with a questioning frown.

"Punishing yourself for James Price," Ariel said. Such a thing hadn't occurred to her until now, so, certainly, she hadn't thought it through. To her surprise, Laya seemed to.

After what appeared to be serious consideration, she said, "Ariel, you've been the best friend a person could ask for. I'll be indebted to you as long as I live. With all due respect, though, this is a really bad time for amateur analysis." Touching the nearest chair, to orient herself, Ariel knew, Laya added, "This also isn't your decision to make." And then she started out of the room.

To her back, Ariel said, "What do you intend to do now?"

"I intend to look into training."

"And then what?"

"And then I'll decide what. I believe I can still teach."

"How can I help?"

That stopped Laya. Her hands, which had been rigid at her sides, relaxed. One sought and found the wall, which she seemed, just then, to need for support. "Thank you," she said.

24

LAYA HADN'T BEEN TALKING IDLY WHEN SHE SAID SHE INTENDED to get on with her life. That same day she placed an ad to sell her car and bicycle. Declining Ariel's help, working through the information operator, she began inquiries regarding Social Security assistance. Then she made an appointment with an orientation and mobility instructor from the state Commission for the Blind.

Passing the room that had been her study, Ariel stopped, blatantly eavesdropping on Laya's end of that last conversation: a question about access to talking books, tentative probes about talking computers and some sort of terminal that, it would seem, connected to the Internet.

Ariel was torn. Whether this was dealing heroically with a disability or embracing it, she couldn't decide. But, as had been pointed out, it wasn't her decision to make.

Later, when she went to the kitchen to brew a pot of tea, she found Hattie hunched over the table, shelling pecans. Laya was out of earshot, not napping as would have been the case on any previous day but sitting on the floor of her room, tucked into lotus position, apparently oblivious to Arthur on her lap. Hattie glanced up, cracking a nut with such vehemence that it shattered. "You got to do something," she demanded. "This ain't right."

"What?" Ariel asked.

"What she's doin'."

"I meant, what is it you think I can do?"

Hattie shook her head. "I reckoned it was the shock. What the doctor said knocked the wind out of her. She'd be bad off for a while, then she'd see sense. But uh-uh. No ma'am. She's climbin' down into a black hole and pullin' the dirt in over her."

Ariel couldn't say she disagreed. "She's more herself," she offered, "than she's been since she lost her sight."

"I wouldn't know about that. I didn't know her before she lost her sight."

"Steady, focused . . . For the first time, she's got a direction to go in."

"Yeah," Hattie muttered. "Backward."

Except, Ariel thought, the inner glow she'd once tried to describe to Hattie was back. "She's meditating again," she said.

"Meditating won't fix her eye." Hattie ran a fingernail through the ridge of a pecan, gouging out dusty red residue. "She can't know that another operation wouldn't work. She's got no crystal ball. She's not God."

"Neither," said Ariel, "am I. And I'm not her mother.

She's going to do what she's going to do. I've got no say in it."

Hattie shelled another half dozen pecans, the meats cleanly excised and intact. Ariel poured tea and sat down. Head down, her eyes on the mug, she said, "She may not have a crystal ball, but she does have a way of . . . knowing things." Surprisingly, Hattie didn't argue. "Sensing things," Ariel added, "even before they happen." Still no argument. "Of course," Ariel proceeded to argue with herself, "I do think, to a degree, it's that she sees . . . she saw more than the average person. She's far more observant than most people. She listens. *Actively*, I mean. She hears. But that only explains so much. It doesn't explain how she can—"

"Some folks got the gift," Hattie interrupted as offhandedly as if she were referring to a light hand with bread dough. "You don't have to convince me."

Ariel realized her mouth was ajar. "You believe in second sight?"

"My granny had it. Ran our lives by what her voices told her, and some of the time she was right. But"—she pointed the nutcracker at Ariel and waved it for emphasis—"nobody's right a hundred percent of the time. Was, they'd run the world."

Ariel couldn't say she disagreed.

"Now," Hattie said, sweeping her nut meats into a plastic container and sealing it with a firm pop, "what was that about her wantin' to punish herself? Who's James Price?"

"If Laya hasn't told you about it, then I can't."

"What's that mean?"

"It's something she told me in confidence."

Hattie squinted and then blinked a time or two, giving that a mental once-over. She stowed the pecans in the refrigerator. "Whatever it is," she said, "does she deserve punishment for it?"

"No." Hearing how stonewallish she sounded, Ariel relented. Hattie wasn't a spy. "It's nothing she did," Ariel said; "it's something she had the misfortune to see."

"See as in . . . ?" Hattie made woo-woo motions with her fingers.

Ariel grinned. "As in the same way you and I do it."

Hattie's eyes widened as a thought struck. "This . . . what she saw don't have to do with her bein' blinded?"

"Hattie, you're going to have to ask Laya—"

"And what she heard on the outside night before last, was that . . . ? Is somebody after her? Somebody out to do worse?"

Ariel didn't believe Laya had heard anything outside, nothing more menacing, at any rate, than a skunk or a possum. She didn't know who was responsible for the acid, but she didn't for a minute believe that person had cooled his heels for nearly three weeks and then decided to have another go. On the other hand, she did *not* have second sight. "In my opinion," she said cautiously, and that's as far as she got before Hattie muttered, "Lord almighty!"

Ariel felt her heart thump. Hattie wasn't given to exclamation, particularly to expressions which were, to her way of thinking, dangerously close to swearing.

"Those calls," Hattie said.

"Calls?" Ariel asked. "Phone calls?"

Hattie abruptly sat back down, rubbing her lower lip, hard.

"Calls from who?" Ariel asked. "Whom?"

"I don't know. A man. The first day I was here some man called up to talk to her."

"To Laya?"

"Yes, to Laya. Who do you think?"

"He didn't give his name? Well, what did he . . . ? Wait a minute. Called *here*? For *Laya*?" Who knew Laya was here? Ariel did a quick run-through. Sarah Aguilar and Dr.

Crowne and . . . someone from the hospital? The people there knew she'd picked Laya up, but not where they were going. The security guy? McCutcheon? He didn't know until Saturday. Hattie was talking about . . . it would've been Thursday. Laya's first full day here. Ariel could think of no one outside her closest friends and B.F. to whom she'd mentioned her house guest. But who might Laya have spoken to? Even if she'd called only one friend, who might that friend have called? It was pointless speculation without questioning Laya. "What did he want?" she asked.

"To talk to her." Hattie shrugged. "She was takin' a nap, I told him. He said how was she. I said fine, who could I say called. Just a friend, he said, fast like—you know how I mean—like no big deal, and that he'd call later on. That was that."

The conversation sounded familiar to Ariel. Why? Then she had it. The police guard at the hospital. What calls had come in, he'd reported, had been "kosher," except for one. The caller had asked about Laya's condition. He'd asked if she'd be able to see again. *Shy type,* the guard had said. *When I asked his name, he hung up.*

"Why," Ariel asked Hattie, "didn't you . . ." Mention this before? she'd been about to ask. The question would be an insult, and the answer was obvious. For all Hattie had known at the time, Laya had friends by the score, all aware of her whereabouts, all calling on a daily basis for a progress report. "You told Laya about the call?" she asked.

"Sure I did. After a while she brought it up again. Did he say anything else? That kind of thing. I thought then she was just curious, you know, about what friend it might be. Now, I'm not so . . . Listen here," Hattie blurted. "Was she blinded on purpose? I thought . . . I took it some crazy person did it." Her hand made a vague sweep of the air. "Some stranger up to meanness."

"Hattie, you said 'calls.'"

"I said what?"

"Calls plural. More than one. How many more?"

"One. Would've been two days later this one called."

Which made it the day Laya had—or hadn't—heard an intruder in the yard. "'This one'?" Ariel repeated. "A different man or the same one?"

"It didn't dawn on me it could be the same one till now."

"But was it the same sort of—"

"What he claimed was, he was from some office, a government office it sounded like. I can't say now what he called it, and if he gave his name, I didn't get it." Hattie looked as if she didn't know whether to fume or wring her hands. "If I'd've known . . . If you'd've told me . . ."

"I know." With hindsight, Ariel agreed entirely. If there was a chance that a threat existed, however remote, Hattie had a right to know. She should have been put on her guard. Not only would it have been the right thing to do, it would have been the smart thing to do; Hattie had a pretty accurate B.S. detector. "So did Laya talk to this second—"

"She was in the tub, so I said could I get his number? Then he said . . ." Hattie squeezed her eyes shut, thinking back. "He'd got her name, he said, to 'follow up on.' Would she be needing any counseling or special services? And how they were free from the government, and . . ." Hattie clearly didn't relish telling this. She squared her bony shoulders. "I said, well, I'll get her to call you, but I believe she might want to wait a while on that. Because she's had this operation, and she might be just fine." She looked steadily at Ariel. "That was the wrong thing to say, wasn't it?"

Instinctively or deductively, Hattie had cut straight to

the heart of the matter. "Maybe not," Ariel said. "He might've been just what he claimed." *Except where did he get this number?*

"Maybe so. Only that was a Saturday. I remember thinkin' what kind of government office stays open on Saturday? But it was just a idle thought." Hattie shook her head uncertainly. "It was a black man both times. I think so, anyway. Out here, it's harder to tell."

"You have a reason to believe they could be the same man? Like any similarity in speech? Some kind of accent? Or a way of—"

"Polite, both of 'em. Neither one talked street talk or anything like that. The second one, for sure . . . well, they both sounded educated."

Ariel absorbed that with some relief. Alley toughs were more likely to hold blades or automatic weapons than degrees.

"Fast talkers," Hattie said. "They both were fast talkers. Anxious like."

"People out here might just sound brusque to you, though; do you think? The pace is different. You're used to—"

"What's the most obvious thing, of course . . ." Hattie tapped her forefinger against the table, her nail clicking decisively. "They both hung up without leavin' their name or their number."

"You said you didn't remember if the second man gave his name."

"If he said it, he didn't *leave* it. There's a difference. And I know he didn't leave no way to get back to him. They neither one of 'em did."

"You ought to be a private eye," Ariel told Hattie. She sipped at her lukewarm tea. "What did the second caller say when you told him about the operation?"

"Just, his office hadn't had that information. He'd make

note of it. They'd be 'following up on her progress,' he said."

"'Following up on her . . .'" Ariel frowned. Did that sound bureaucratic or ominous? "And what did Laya say about the call?"

"Didn't seem to take notice of it any more than I did. You can't tell with her sometimes, though."

Ariel saw the next thought register in the other woman's hooded, dark eyes. "You said she told you whatever it was in secret," Hattie said, her voice rising. "You don't mean to tell me the police don't know about it?"

Ariel lifted a hand in a shrug. "She wouldn't be happy with me if she knew I'd discussed it with you."

"You ain't told me diddly-squat, but I'll tell *you* something. You're the one's not goin' to be happy if something else happens to her because you kept shut! Why would you go along with such a thing? I thought you had better sense!"

"Yeah? You've seen how much luck I have changing Laya's mind about anything."

"Well . . ." Hattie huffed out a breath. "Can't argue that. You might as well spit in the fire."

"And, I have to say, she does have her reasons. They're not altogether . . . unreasonable."

"These phone calls . . . you think they're something to worry about? What you gonna do about 'em?"

"I'm going to ask her who she's told that she was staying here. If either one of those calls can be explained, I'll only worry half as much. If neither can, I don't know what to do."

"I've got a thought," Hattie said, her expression suggesting she was in the throes of having it as she spoke. "I take her someplace else for a while. Back home."

"Get her out of town?" Ariel thought about it. "Not a

bad idea," she said. "It gives me what might be an even better one."

The phone calls could not be explained.

Ariel wasn't especially surprised to learn that Laya hadn't told anyone where she was staying. She wasn't a gregarious person under ordinary circumstances; since she'd lost her sight, she'd cocooned herself, barring admittance to her room at the hospital; informing no one, not even her stepsister, where she was going from there; calling no one—friend, teacher, or student—during the five days she'd been at Ariel's.

"Just out of curiosity," Ariel asked her, "why didn't you tell me about the phone calls?" When Laya didn't answer, Ariel, surprising even herself, blew. "Is this some kind of fatalistic thing?" she asked, angrier by the second. "Some kind of death wish? Making sure you stay blind isn't enough for you? You've got to die, too?"

"I have no desire to die," Laya answered, calmly, Ariel would have said if she hadn't heard the huskiness in her voice. "I told you; I mean to live. But wallowing in terror isn't living."

"That's not an answer," Ariel said.

"I'm taking your advice. Face my fears, remember? Face them down, you said, or they'd destroy me."

"I was talking about getting over your fear of Jessie! I wasn't suggesting you wait around like a target while some twisted lowlife comes after you!"

"Be quiet, please, and listen. I'm not claiming I can shed my fear like so much excess baggage. Like a . . . a snake molting or whatever. But I'm trying. I'm working on it. I've lived in the same house with the dog for five days. I don't stop breathing every time I sense her nearby anymore. I touched her the other night, did I tell you that? It was by accident, but I did actually—"

"I'm glad. That's swell. Could we get back to the subject?"

"I faced that . . ." Laya's voice clutched. She cleared her throat and began again. "I faced the knowledge that the graft bombed, that I would stay blind, permanently. Don't interrupt! You don't have to tell me what you think, that that's an arbitrary decision on my part. Some kind of misguided . . ." She waved her hand, casting for the word. "Superstition. It isn't. *I know what the outcome of another operation would be!* The point is, I faced it, and I didn't panic. I didn't go into a decline. I'll tell you what else. I faced the fact that I have to accept help. I'm no good at that, but I spent an hour today asking for it, from strangers. I'm facing the fact, Ariel, and it is a fact, that I can't outrun . . . what's coming."

Ariel dropped her face into her hands, shaking her head in utter frustration.

"I don't know when," Laya went on, "or even . . ." She faltered, momentarily unsure of herself. "Or even where it's coming from, but it's coming. I can't evade it. I might as well deal with it."

"It?" Ariel echoed. "What—you want to tell me?—what is this *it?*"

"I don't know," Laya admitted, nearly inaudibly. "It has to do . . . with fire."

"Fire. Terrific. Good to have advance notice." Ariel was being bitchy; she knew it. "Should I increase the insurance on my house?" Unable to stop herself, she said, "This fire, this *it* came to you in a vision or what?"

Nothing from Laya.

"A dream, I'll bet. It was, wasn't it?"

Again, nothing from Laya. She looked, however, more preoccupied than defensive.

"Do you have any idea," Ariel said flatly, "how you sound?" She did stop herself from saying how *asinine* you sound.

"Supper's in fifteen minutes," Hattie said from the doorway. She hadn't gone back to B.F.'s condo when she normally would have. She showed no sign she planned to leave at all. Ariel wasn't sure but what she might bed down on the sofa, guarding her chick like a militant mother hen.

"Then I've got time for a shower," Ariel said, and stomped out.

As the hot water pounded her, gushing—ecologically irresponsibly, possibly illegally—from a doctored showerhead, she remembered an incident from a couple of months before. Laya had shown up at class looking preoccupied. Afterward, Ariel had asked what was up. "A dream," Laya had said, "about Jules."

"Jules?" Ariel had vaguely recalled a quiet middle-aged woman who'd drifted away from the class not long after she herself had begun. "So, what'd you dream?" She'd grinned indulgently, expecting to hear the nonsensical stuff of which dreams are usually patched together. That one had been as cryptic as most. Laya could describe only one fragment with clarity. Her former student had been leaning against a tree, her back pressed against the trunk. Her forehead had been slick with sweat. "She had on a sleeveless T-shirt," Laya recalled, "and trunks."

"In February?" Ariel joked. "She should've been shivering, not sweating."

"And running shoes."

"And?" Ariel asked. "What'd she do? What happened?"

Nothing, Laya admitted. "It was just . . ." She shook her head, unable to say what bothered her. "I hadn't thought about Jules in months, and . . . it was such a sharp image."

Within days they heard that the woman had suffered a heart attack. It hadn't been fatal; the prognosis, they heard through the grapevine, was good. She'd been jogging, it seems, when the attack had occurred. Another jogger discovered her crumpled under a tree.

That sort of incident was not unprecedented.

Ariel turned off the water, giving an extra hard twist to the cold knob. It needed a new washer or something; it had for months.

Over dinner, she announced that she needed to do some in-depth digging on a story in the San Francisco area. "Kind of a semipersonal thing," she said. She'd bring it up at tomorrow's story meeting (if there was one; sometimes there wasn't sufficient staff in town for a quorum). She might have to memo Chris Valente. If he didn't go for the idea, she'd take time off; she was owed time, big time. She hadn't taken a vacation since . . . She couldn't remember taking a vacation. (Had she ever? She doubted it.) Nor would this be one. She'd be setting her mind at rest about Dorothy, and she'd be getting Laya the hell out of Dodge. Two birds, et cetera. She thought it was a brilliant idea. She didn't delude herself that it would be an easy sell, with Valente or with Laya. As to her other, still nebulous plan of coaxing Laya out to the guide dog school . . . "I'd be gone a few days," she said. "A week maybe."

A movement from Hattie caught her eye. The old woman had suddenly grown two inches taller in her seat. She was looking at Ariel as if she'd spied a rat scuttling from a sinking ship.

"B.F. has a house in Marin County," Ariel said meaningfully. "A nice big house."

"The one used to be Jane's?" Hattie asked.

Nodding, Ariel said, "There's plenty of room, a separate carriage house even." In the nick of time she thought better of extolling the view. Laya, she saw, had lowered her head, concentrating on capturing peas on her fork; Ariel couldn't see her expression. "I thought we could all three go up," she continued. "Drive up. Take the animals. Have you ever been there, Hattie?"

The old woman was shaking her head, perilously close

to smiling. It made her face look odd. "Jane used to send me postcards. Great old big trees?"

"Redwoods," Ariel supplied. Hattie knew that, there was not a doubt in her mind, as well as she did.

"Right," Hattie agreed, "redwoods. And the crooked street. And—what is it again? That tower?"

"Coit."

"Uh-huh. And the bridge and all."

Laya abruptly gave up on the peas. She laid the fork on her plate, too near the edge. It fell off. "Why?" she asked.

"Why what? Why am I going?" Ariel laid down her own silverware. "I said. Business."

"That's not what I was . . ." Laya pressed her lips together. She already knew the answer anyway. Ariel took a swallow of water, readying the arguments and rebuttals she'd rehearsed. If necessary, she'd plead. She nearly choked when Laya said, "Okay." There was, Ariel would swear to it, relief in her voice. "Great!" Ariel said. "Hattie? How about you?"

"I always wondered," Hattie said, "why do they call it the 'Golden' Gate Bridge? Looks red to me."

25

BY THE END OF THE FOLLOWING DAY, ARIEL'S "BRILLIANT" IDEA was fizzling like a soggy firecracker. Chris Valente, lacking facts Ariel wasn't prepared to supply, "couldn't see" the Thibeau story. Dr. Crowne, convinced Laya would change her mind about a second surgery, insisted she stay available during the critical wait for a donor. And Ariel couldn't get hold of B.F. Getting his okay to use the house wasn't really necessary, but getting the key was. Even Jessie thwarted her plans. The shepherd developed a sudden digestive indisposition. She would not, for the time being, make an ideal travel companion within the confines of a van. And then Laya, maddeningly, began to have second thoughts about leaving town. Ariel, aggravated, began to have thoughts about strangulation. "Last night you agreed going was a good idea," she said.

"I made a good start with the O&M instructor today," Laya said, folding up her new white cane. "Orientation and—"

"You can get oriented and mobilized later," Ariel said.

"I want to go look at a talking computer. I really—"

"They have talking computers in San Francisco." Ariel gave her friend a penetrating look. "What's going on?"

"Running away again," Laya said, "won't change the inevitable."

Ariel rolled her eyes; they were back to the incredible, inevitable It! "'The better part of valor,'" she quoted, "'is discretion.'"

"You know," Laya said irritably, "I never have understood what that means."

"Okay, you want simple? How's this? A smart woman—" Just then the phone rang. Laya visibly tensed. Ariel caught the reaction. "A smart woman," she repeated as she lifted the receiver, "is 'one who in a perilous emergency thinks with her legs.'"

"Come again?" queried her grandfather.

"Just philosophizing," Ariel said. And improvising, she didn't say; she'd improved on the quote for her purposes. "I'm planning a little trip to Northern California. Hattie and Laya and I." Her glare at the blind woman went unappreciated. Laya couldn't have seen it even if she hadn't been leaving the room. "May I have the Belvedere house for a week or so?"

"You can have it in perpetuity; I told you that." He gave

her the name of the property manager, told her where a spare key was hidden, and asked what she was up to.

Ariel braced herself. Judging by his cool, very nearly indifferent attitude when last she'd seen him, he wouldn't favor her answer. "Dorothy," she said. "I want to know what happened."

"Good."

"Good? I got the impression . . . Could I ask you something? What was with you Sunday about Dorothy?"

"With me?"

"Yes, with you! You weren't yourself. You've had me worried." That last wasn't, strictly speaking, true. Ariel had until now expunged his reaction and any implications thereof from conscious thought. That the steely old man might lose his edge, that the day would ever come when he began the slide into dispassion or (God forbid) worse, didn't bear thinking about. "I was raising some pretty obvious questions, but you didn't want to hear it."

"You're right," B.F. confirmed. "I didn't."

"You just said it was good that—"

"You wait till you're old enough to know more dead people than live people, Ariel Gold. You'll understand."

"What's that got to do with—"

"It's one thing if they go naturally," he went on, "that's sad enough. When it's voluntary, by their own hand or will, it's awful. But when they're victims of their fellow man . . . well, I've seen too much of that over the years. I've seen it one time too many."

There was no question in Ariel's mind that Jane was foremost in his.

"So, yes, ma'am," B.F. said, "your suspicions were nothing I cared to hear. Made me feel sick."

His voice—tired, deflated—made Ariel ill, with fear. It made her brusque. "This isn't you," she said. "Why aren't you angry? Why aren't you seething at the possibility of . . . Dorothy was your friend! For one brief shining moment a dear friend. And you don't want to hear there might be something wrong about her death?"

In the poignant silence that followed her outburst, Ariel thought about what she'd just said. "Well," she muttered, "that couldn't have been a dumber question."

"I don't see how," B.F. agreed.

"You want me to leave this alone?"

"Would you if I asked you to?"

Ariel hesitated. "I could be wrong that anything *was* wrong."

"I hope you are. Bein' as how I'm over my weak spell, however, let's find out for sure. I reckon you called Libby Vail?"

"Out of the country till the end of the week. I left another message for Rob Millen, too, but it seems he's taken a leave of absence to finish his book. The one he mentioned at your dinner? He's 'in the field' researching. What do you know about him?"

"The columnist? Nothing. Meg brought him. What do you think he can tell you?"

"Anything he can and will about Dorothy and/or her husband."

"So what you're sayin' is you don't know any more now than you did two days ago?"

"I believe I know where she and I met. I was in San Francisco December two years ago, five weeks before your note was written. This morning I called the place where we were shooting."

Calvin Soo, the pawnshop owner, hadn't hidden his nearly shivering delight over Ariel's second call within as many weeks. She'd heard the alarming, bellows-like wheeze of the fat man's breathing when he said, "I knew I'd be hearing from you again."

"Why's that?" Ariel had asked.

"Oh, Miss Ariel, don't kid a kidder! You phone me up out of the blue the other day—after two years! And you're *verrry* mysterious. 'Just updating your Rolodex,' you say, 'touching base with old sources.' No offense, but hah! This lady's too smart, I think to myself; too big a wheel to be doing donkey work. She's got people, assistants, for that. So . . ."

Ariel wondered how smart Soo'd think her if he knew the truth about that first call: she'd had no clue who'd answer the phone.

"So, something's up!" He'd giggled as if he'd been goosed, cleared his throat, and, in a deliberately deeper voice, said, "Another story, am I right?"

"Right, Mr. Soo," Ariel had said, "and there's an off chance you can help."

He had.

"A hockshop?" B.F. asked now. "You're tellin' me you met Dorothy Thibeau in a *hockshop*?"

"Looks like it."

"No way!"

"He had a customer by that name, Soo said. It's not a common one." Ariel let that sink in. "I described her. He remembered her, B.F.; she wasn't his typical trade." After a silence Ariel interpreted as unconvinced, she said, "You think it's coincidence she was known at the one place in the city I know I went?"

"Keep going," B.F. said.

"She pawned a bunch of silver, sterling, Soo said, not plate, and jewelry. He's a little foggy as to whether it was the day we were there, but he does remember when she redeemed what he still held. It was January, the next month, about the time you got an invitation to an expensive party. Oh! In case you're still not convinced we're talking about the same woman, he itemized—"

"You're saying," B.F. interrupted, his words clipped,

"that Dorothy had been strapped for money, but something changed, and she no longer was. I get it, but, frankly, I don't believe it. This isn't fun. Get to the point, will you please?"

Ariel mentally, forcefully, kicked herself. She realized that while she was intrigued by every scrap she could glean about Dorothy, what B.F. was hearing was sad gossip about a friend in difficulties. What Ariel had been about to relate would've made him sadder still. Soo had volunteered a description of the jewelry. The brooch Dorothy wore in B.F.'s photo, or one like it, was among the pieces. All the jewelry, by the time she'd been in a position to redeem it, was long gone. "The point is," Ariel said, "she could easily have been in the shop the same day I was."

"There must be hockshops in Marin. Why the city? Why drive so far from . . . ? Okay, that's obvious." B.F. exhaled unhappily. "Hell! What difference does it make where you met her anyway!"

"It's more than I knew before, which was nothing." After two weeks of head-banging helplessness, being able to put together pieces that made up a real person and a real part of her own past felt to Ariel like a breakthrough. She'd been stoked after talking to Soo. Immediately, she'd quizzed the cameraman who, according to the credits, had been on the shoot, asking if he recalled seeing her talk to a woman who fit Dorothy's description. He'd looked at Ariel like she was a brick shy of a load, and asked why he'd remember some woman she talked to two years before if she didn't. She'd be checking with other crew members and with the correspondent whose story it had been. It was a start. "Don't you think her financial situation is germane?" she asked her grandfather.

"To her death? It occurs to me that—"

"She was being blackmailed?"

"—you've been reading too many thrillers." B.F. snorted. "A crime under every bush!"

Ariel found herself grinning. She'd been worried that the old man was sinking into apathy? "Then you tell me," she challenged, "why the wife of a prominent doctor, a society matron, was reduced to pawning her valuables. Bad luck in the stock market?"

B.F. laughed, a good strong chortle. "Dorothy? Trading options and futures? Hardly."

"Okay. You knew her. You tell me why."

"It's all speculation without more information than you currently have. Raymond Thibeau's credit rating might tell us something. I'll look into it."

"You can . . . ?" Ariel caught herself. "Of course you can. How well off," she asked, "would you have judged the Thibeaus to be?"

"Comfortable." After a minute's thought: "It wasn't my impression they were wealthy."

"I had the idea they were."

"Based on?"

Ariel considered it. The expensive stationery Dorothy used? The confident, sophisticated look she had in the photo? The fact that her husband was in medicine? "Assumption, I guess." The truth was, she still knew little about this woman. "Everybody at your dinner party knew them, as if they were A-list. Society. Moneyed."

"If Dorothy had been into money, she'd've jumped at the chance to marry me, wouldn't she?"

"Still, if they were 'comfortable,' why . . ." The sour tone of what he'd said registered then. "I thought," Ariel said, "it was the child-raising issue that got in the way of your romance?"

"You ever hear of hiring a nanny? Jane wasn't the obstacle. Dorothy turned me down. She married Thibeau."

It was the first glimmer Ariel had seen of the hurt of

that rejection. The wound, to his pride or his heart or both, might be long healed and scarred over, but Ariel had a sudden conviction it hadn't been superficial.

"At any rate," B.F. said, once again businesslike, "Dorothy had no head for money. I don't mean she was unclear on the concept, she just wasn't particularly interested."

"How could she have been a successful retail 'career woman'?"

"She was good enough at what she did to get away with attitude, I'd guess. 'I don't do decimals,' she used to say. 'I do bon ton.' Style, that was her forte."

"Hmmm," Ariel sagely commented. Many a woman of Dorothy's generation who protested she couldn't (simply *couldn't!*) balance a checkbook could, in fact, have balanced the budget of a good-sized city.

"Dorothy was good-looking and fun to be with," B.F. was saying. "Interesting. Always. Suppose she must've worked at it, but—" He paused and, as if it had only then occurred to him, added, "Thibeau was, too, actually."

"'Too' what? Good-looking?"

"Interesting. Fun." Grudgingly: "Not bad-looking."

"Tell me about him."

"I saw Ray Thibeau a grand total of twice that I recall, maybe three times. I don't think I qualify as his biographer."

"Talk to me."

"Medium sized. Slim. Dapper, you could say. Dressed well. I met him socially," B.F. protested, "across dinner tables."

"You're a good judge of character. What was he like?"

"Glib. A social . . . what's the male equivalent of a social butterfly? But then . . ." B.F. gathered his thoughts. "Here's a thing I noticed. He didn't only talk—didn't only entertain—he listened. Maybe it was just good manners, but he made people feel like they had something to say worth listenin' to. Even boring people. I don't know that he was especially smart," he finished, "not a world-beater, but he was pleasant. I liked him."

Ariel imagined that he hadn't wanted to.

"I don't see," he grumbled, "how any of this is relevant."

"What made you think he wasn't smart?"

"I wasn't talkin' about brains so much as drive. You called him a 'prominent' doctor. Not to sound like sour grapes, but he wasn't. His *daddy* was. Made a big name for himself. Ray followed in his footsteps, I surmised, not from ambition or a passion for medicine but because it was expected. Path of least resistance."

"And yet, according to his obituary, he was still practicing when he died. How old would he have been?"

"Old enough to retire. Maybe he eventually developed a passion after all."

"Or maybe he was in no financial position to quit."

B.F. grunted in disgust. "I feel like a gossip. No, worse! A ghoul. Ray's not the one you think was . . . whatever; Dorothy is."

"Hmm," Ariel said. "What was it again that *he* died of?"

"God bless America! There you go again—evil hidin' behind every bush! People die, Ariel Gold!"

The Call Waiting beep signaled. Saying "Hold a second, will you?" Ariel switched lines and said hello. She said it twice, to silence. There was someone on the line. Ariel could feel the presence. Her finger was poised to disconnect when she heard, was pretty sure she heard, a faint cry—a child? someone in pain? the echo of her own imagination? The line went dead. For no reason Ariel could have justified, the skin across her shoulder blades quivered. *Evil hiding behind every bush?* Nuisance calls happen, Ariel Gold, she told herself, and flashed back to her grandfather. He despised Call Waiting. He'd hung up.

26

Shortly after first light two days later, a Thursday, Ariel shoved the last bag into the back of her van, made certain no dog appendages had strayed too near the rear hatch door, and slammed it shut. It was going to be a glory of an April day, a good day for long-distance driving.

"All aboard that's coming aboard!" she called out. "Let's roll 'em out!" She laughed at herself. She sounded demented, a cross between a riverboat captain and a wagon train master, but then she was only technically awake, and light-headed. She stretched, every joint and vertebra cracking gratefully. She'd had four hours' sleep, less the night before. Monday's segment was in the can, and she, for a long weekend at least, was as free as the morning's unusually clear air.

Hattie emerged from the house looking preoccupied, hesitating before she pulled the door closed behind her. "She out here or where?" she asked, peering at the van.

"Laya's in the car. Set the alarm and let's go before she changes her mind again."

"The cat?"

"Arthur's in the carrier. Jessie's in her accustomed place between the front seats. Cooler's packed. Coffee's in the thermos."

"You cancel the paper?"

"Check," Ariel said.

"Got the mail held?"

"Check."

"Call the security people?"

"I did. Check, check, and double check."

Hattie pulled the door to and tested the knob. The phone picked then to ring, a feeble but insistent twitter muffled by the thick stucco walls of the house. Hattie looked to Ariel, who said, "A pox on it. We are no longer subject to its tyranny."

"Are you fit to drive?" Hattie inquired. "You sound drunk."

Ariel laughed. "With freedom. I feel like school just let out. First day of summer vacation." The phone's ringing stopped as abruptly as if the cord had been cut when the answering machine took charge. "I'll pick up messages later, when we've gone too far to turn back," Ariel said. "Climb in. You're riding shotgun."

Laya was in the middle seat, her head resting against the window. She appeared to be finishing her interrupted sleep. Out of consideration the other two women spoke little, and that quietly, until well after they were humming up the bleak, dun-colored monotony of I-5.

"Parched out there," Hattie commented in a murmur. "Ugly."

"Fast," Ariel explained. "Six and a half hours' driving time."

Hattie glanced back at Laya. "Reckon we ought to wake her up?"

"Why?" She reached for the cell phone. "Let's see who called this morning."

"Nuh-uh!" Hattie said. "No, ma'am! Drive or talk on that thing, one or the other."

"I'd be listening, not talking."

"You gonna get the number with your ear, too? People drive sorry enough with both hands on the wheel."

It was an opinion Ariel shared. "Okay," she said. "You do it." She handed the instrument to Hattie, who studied it with a mixture of distrust and interest before punching in the numbers Ariel called out. Suddenly, the old woman made a strangled coughing noise. It took Ariel a second to recognize it as a laugh. She couldn't remember if she'd ever heard Hattie laugh before. "What?" she asked, smiling in reflexive anticipation of the joke.

"It came to me," Hattie said, "what if they'd invented these things before push buttons, back when you still had to dial."

Ariel frowned. "I'm not—"

"Folks would be wreckin' their cars right and left." Picturing that mayhem apparently tickled Hattie; she cough-laughed again. "Start over," she said. "I lost track."

The caller had been Rob Millen. Thanks for returning his and sorry to be so long returning hers, he'd said, and Hattie relayed, but he just got the message. "'What is it you need?' he says." He was currently on leave and "'crunched for time'" winding up his . . . "'opus'?" Hattie looked at Ariel, who nodded. "Says . . ." Hattie listened and repeated, "'We'll play' . . . *heck*," she edited, "'connecting' if you don't get right back to him." She wrote down a number. "If you miss him, 'leave specifics about' . . ." Again, Hattie looked to Ariel for clarification. "T-bo?"

"Push that button there to disconnect," Ariel instructed. "Thibeau." She spelled it out. "It's a name."

"I've heard it somewhere." Hattie muttered the word under her breath, wrapping her tongue around the unfamiliar feel of it. "That's the name B.F. said on the phone the other day, all that about a note or whatever he was carryin' on about Easter Sunday."

"Right. Dorothy Thibeau—she was an old friend of B.F.'s, an old girlfriend—and her husband—"

"Dorothy? You don't mean that woman he courted? What was her name? Mayes? Dorothy Mayes?"

"That was her maiden name, yes. She married a man named Raymond Thibeau. You knew her?"

"It had to be twenty-five, thirty years ago B.F. had her to the house. Jane was little. Oh, I remember her, all right!"

"Because?"

"B.F. Coulter don't propose marriage every day of the week! What you want to know about her for?"

"She died."

"Died? Is that right? When? Wonder why B.F. didn't say anything to me about it."

"Why would he?"

"I know why he didn't. He thought I didn't like her."

"Why not?"

"What'd she die of?"

"That's what I'm wanting to know. Why didn't you like her?"

"I didn't say I didn't; I said he thought I didn't."

"This conversation . . . ," Ariel said, and gave her head a quick shake. "Okay, why did he *think* you didn't like her?"

"She was all right. I can't say she wasn't friendly and all, but—not to low-rate the dead—she just wasn't the right one to raise my girl, and I told B.F. so."

I'll bet you did, Ariel thought, stealing a glance at her grim-mouthed passenger, and would have whomever he'd "courted."

"So why," Hattie asked, "are you askin' this Millen fellow what she died of? Is he a doctor?"

"He's a newspaper writer in Marin County. He knew both the Thibeaus. Dorothy Thibeau is the story I'm going north to work on."

"B.F. asked you to look into it?"

"No. I met the woman myself, but, unfortunately . . ." Ariel gave Hattie a meaningful look, and lowered her voice. "It was two years ago when I did, so . . ." Getting a blank look, she repeated, "*Two* years ago?" She tapped her head with a forefinger.

"Oh!" The time frame sank in. "You mean before . . . you know?"

"You got it. Before *'you know.'* I'll tell you about it later."

"Why not tell us now?" came a quiet voice from behind them.

Both women started. "Oh, hello!" Ariel said. "You're awake."

"I would be if somebody would be nice enough to pour me some coffee," said Laya. While Hattie located the thermos and poured, Laya said again, "Tell us, Ariel."

"Oh," Ariel said dismissively, "it's a complicated story."

"We must have a few hours' drive yet." Laya took the Styrofoam cup Hattie handed her, testing the coffee level with her finger. "Nothing but time on our hands."

There was something about Laya's voice that caught Ariel's attention, a studied casualness. Had it come from someone else, she might have read it as baiting. "What it's time for," Ariel said, "is a break." She slipped into the exit lane, where a sign advised that a roadside park lay ahead. "I need to call Rob Millen," she said.

Laya waited until they were parked and Ariel was trying to clip a leash onto an impatient Jessie before she said, "We just don't seem to be able to get this trust thing down, do we, Ariel?"

"What are you talking about?" Ariel asked.

"I'm assuming 'you know' is a reference to your memory loss. That's what I'm talking about, but I guess you're not ready to."

Ariel fumbled the catch and dropped the leash. Jessie snuffled at her hand inquiringly.

"You need to make your call." Laya was full of surprises today. "And it sounds like Jessie needs out," she said. "You want Hattie and me to walk her?"

She even asked for—or agreed to take—the leash, Ariel was amazed to observe, as the two women strolled away.

Ariel watched them as she dialed. Jessie, having been confined for a long period, then brought to unfamiliar terrain rife with tantalizing new smells, and given her lead with no direction to heel, would normally be zigzagging to sniff every clod of turf and blade of grass, and superimposing her own unique scent over it all. The shepherd walked sedately to the designated pet area.

The women had made their own pit stops, and after traveling several silent (and, in Ariel's case, thoughtful) miles north, she said, "It wasn't a lack of trust, Laya."

"Good," Laya said from beside her.

Hattie, when she'd returned to the van, had discreetly slipped into the middle seat. Pulling a skein of navy blue yarn, crochet needles, and an unidentifiable woolly item from her bottomless black purse, she'd begun clicking away. She appeared to be wholly immersed in making the item larger if no more identifiable.

"Handicaps," Laya murmured, "aren't easy to accept. To talk about. Ask me "

"I'd appreciate it," Ariel said, "if you wouldn't talk about this one to anybody."

Laya's chin dipped, her lip curled, and her posture improved, considerably. "Gossip that I am," she said dryly.

"Okay, sorry. I guess you understand why—"

"Ariel, I get the picture. I understand."

"Well, I don't. How'd you know? How long have you known?"

"From the first . . . in a sense."

Ariel shot her a disbelieving look. "How?"

"I said." Laya smiled gently. "I sensed it."

"That's impos—" Ariel tactfully rephrased. "I find it hard to accept that you took one look and *divined* a loss of memory."

"You want a more conventional explanation?" Laya appeared to choose her words carefully. "Let's just say, I felt, talking with you that first day, that you were not . . . whole." She didn't appear content with that, but she let it go. "Of course . . ." Another quick smile came and went. "I'd have to have been blind not to notice you'd been hurt physically. The cast on your hand. A limp. Slight but there." She paused. "You'd been in an accident?"

Ariel gave a sideways bob of the head that could mean yes, no, or maybe. What it signified didn't matter, since the other woman couldn't see it. "I imagine," Laya said, "it was diagnosed as traumatic amnesia?" And then: "I've always wondered if that was the same 'accident' that killed Jane."

The van swerved. Hattie's needles stopped. Into the silence she muttered something that sounded like "Lord help!"

"That," Ariel said, "is neither here nor there." This thing was getting out of hand. "Could we go back to the memory—"

"Okay. For one thing, you were supposed to be a professional producer. An experienced investigative reporter. You were so nervous you could hardly turn on your tape recorder. You interviewed me as if you were making up how to do it as you went along."

Ariel remembered the day vividly. She was interviewing Jane's friends and acquaintances, working from a list B.F. had supplied. It was the first time she'd worked as an amnesic, in effect, her first day on the job. She'd thought she carried it off pretty smoothly. "None of that even begins to explain how you could—"

"I guess not," Laya agreed. She chuckled deep in her throat. "I'll try to come up with something better. Meantime, tell us about B.F.'s old flame. Dorothy, is it? What is it about her death that's concerning you?"

With a last, dissatisfied glance at the blind woman, Ariel began from the beginning.

Hattie's needles resumed clicking. Arthur scratched irritably at the litter box in his carrier. Jessie eased herself up, backed from her spot between the front seats, and padded to the rear window. She made herself comfortable there, panting, peering out as though she were watching an absorbing drama on TV. They'd stopped again, for an early picnic lunch, by the time Ariel was concluding the tale.

"From what B.F. could find out," she said, "the Thibeaus lived not lavishly but comfortably. A cruise now and then, country club membership, entertaining—what you'd expect with an upper-middle-class doctor and his wife. Then, two and a half years ago, their finances went through a rocky spell. They got a second mortgage on their house. They hadn't been big savers, nor especially savvy investors. They started cashing in. Hefty withdrawals—"

"How would a person find out such about somebody else's business?" Hattie demanded.

"Do you really want to know?"

"No, I sure don't. All I can say is I'm feelin' better and better about my mattress."

Ariel laughed. Hattie didn't.

"You're not serious?" Ariel asked.

"Just get on with it," Hattie said.

"Where was I? Oh, there were these withdrawals, and, on top of that, not much coming in. That went on for about four months, give or take. Then in January—"

"When you met Dorothy?" Hattie asked.

Ariel nodded. "Not long after. She called Soo about redeeming her things, there was a deposit into their account. Twenty-five thousand. Cash then, cash every month from then on: five thousand, first of the month like clockwork, for a year."

"Dollars?" Laya asked.

"Eighty-five thousand. Not a fortune but—"

"It's not?" Laya asked. "What planet do you live on?"

"Payoff money," Hattie said decisively.

"I thought about blackmail, too," Ariel said, "the other way around, when I found out Dorothy was pawning things. B.F. said I read too many thrillers."

"Maybe B.F. don't read enough," Hattie said. "So this pawnshop . . . you feel sure that's where you met her?"

"Oh, yeah. I talked to the soundman from the shoot and showed him Dorothy's picture. He remembered her all right. He hit on her."

"He what?" Laya cried, waking Jessie, who lay under the table.

Ariel nodded, laughing. "Stan's a geezer. In fact, he's retired since then, but he still fancies himself something of a Lothario. Said 'madame' declined politely. He can't say which city we were taping in when he cast lustful eyes upon her, but it was definitely that story, the pawnshop one. She stood out like a sore thumb, or, as he put it, like a 'duchess in a soup kitchen.'"

"She *was* right swanky," Hattie said. "Dressed like somebody in a magazine."

"Well, that was her business, after all."

"Magazines?"

"Fashion."

"I didn't recall what her job was, just that she was high up in it. I was thinkin' it was something else . . ."

"Nope. Retail fashion."

". . . something to do with . . . no, now I remember. She was sayin' what she had *wanted* to be."

"Saying when? What do you mean?"

"It was when B.F. had her to the house that one time. She come in to where I had on the TV, the news, and she said, 'See that?'—meanin' this reporter on the show, woman out in front of the White House. What was her name?"

"I don't know who you . . . In the sixties? There weren't all that many women reporters, not network. Pauline Frederick?"

"Could be. Anyway—"

"Nancy Dickerson?"

"Makes no difference. What she said was, she'd wanted to do that when she was younger. Couldn't get anybody to take her serious, she said, not even at local stations."

"Interesting," Ariel murmured, and to her it was, as was everything to do with Dorothy. But the recollection wasn't really to the point. "At any rate—"

"You wondered," Hattie interrupted, "how you and her got to talkin'? What got you together? I bet that was it."

Ariel thought it through. Was it something as innocuous as Dorothy's nostalgia, her failed hopes for a career in TV journalism that drew her to me? That and the resemblance to Jane? She could see it having happened that way. "You look a bit like a young friend of mine," Dorothy might have said. "A model," she might have thrown in, to flatter a less than chic and trim woman who was, however, in "the biz." "So what are you people shooting?" she'd naturally ask. And, reminiscing: "I wanted to be a broadcast journalist back in the Dark Ages." Ariel imagined she would have laughed a little then. "But I was ahead of my time. Things were different in my day." Entirely plausible, but then what? How, Ariel puzzled, would we have gone from an idle chat about equal opportunity to a discussion of murder?

"Earth to Ariel!" Laya waved her hand in the general direction of Ariel's face.

"Hattie," Ariel said, "you could be right. But when did we talk again? That's what I want to know. And where? And—the big question—who were we talking about? Who was 'Sis'?"

The researcher Ariel had assigned to check out Bay Area stories during that time frame had come up dry on Sis. No victim, accident or homicide, had been referred to by that name in any paper. The name Thibeau was also absent from the news.

"Did you get that newspaperman you called?" Laya asked.

Ariel nodded. "He wants to know why I'm asking about the Thibeaus. He's a feature writer, not hard news, but did he sound cagey! He's not ready to give out information to TV. Not for free."

"Does he have any information?"

"He thinks he 'might just be able to help.' I told him Dorothy had been a friend, that my interest was purely personal."

"That sounds fishy even to me. He bought that?"

"He did when I asked about the book he's writing." Ariel began to pack away the lunch remains. "I suggested that, when the time comes, he have a press kit sent to my attention at *The Open File*."

"You're bad," Laya said mildly.

"No, he's good. I checked out his column." Ariel laughed.

"What's funny?" Laya asked.

"Goes to show you. I've been thinking ever since he called last week that he was interested in irresistible me. The gentleman's interest, I do believe, lies in promoting his book. Which is fine by me. It's about the old San Francisco Columbarium, and it sounds deliciously morbid. Could be a good segment for the show."

"What's a columbarium?" Hattie asked.

"A vault, for cremains."

"What are . . ." Hattie's nose wrinkled, as if she'd smelled out the meaning. "Never mind. What kind of help you think he can be?"

Ariel shrugged. "Rob Millen isn't only a good writer, he's also smart, he's observant, and, unlike me, he's well connected locally. If anybody can come up with anything, I think he's my man. He'll get back to me at B.F.'s."

27

THEY REACHED THE HOUSE IN BELVEDERE MIDAFTERNOON. THE sun was still bright on the water far below, the view as perfect as Ariel recalled. A knockout floral arrangement greeted her on the front porch. It was from Rob Millen.

"That man moves fast!" Hattie exclaimed. "You sure it's his book he's pushin'?"

The flowers weren't all that was waiting. B.F. had obviously called the property management company. In the house were a fruit basket, an extra key, and their business card. From the dustless surfaces, Ariel deduced that they'd even hustled in a cleaning crew.

Late that evening she made herself comfortable with a stack of newspapers beside her, intending to do a little work before turning in. She was back in the carriage house, assigned there by Hattie, who'd declared it too isolated for Laya. Ariel propped her feet on the old wicker chaise, and adjusted a lamp for better light. She took the top newspaper from her stack, but after a moment she lowered it to her lap.

Indulging herself (testing herself), she let her gaze roam the room her sister had furnished. An antique bamboo table that (Ariel imagined) had been left to Jane by the feisty great-aunt. The Oriental chintz she'd window-shopped and Jane had bought. The pillow with Jane's needlepoint adage: HE WHO LAUGHS, LASTS.

"Ha-ha," Ariel said out loud, and then did laugh. Secretly, she'd been afraid that returning to Jane's house might be a melancholy thing. To her relief, she didn't feel at all moony. She felt welcomed. She heard a scratching at the door, and got up to admit Jessie, who'd been checking out the fence line. "All secure for the night?" Ariel asked the dog, and plopped back onto the chaise.

This trip had been smart in every respect; she was sure of it.

For the first time she had real hope that she'd find out what she needed to know about Dorothy. Rob Millen would come up with something. Or Libby Vail would supply some vital nugget of information. She'd introduce Ariel to others who "ran in the same crowd" as Dorothy, and they'd know still more. Sooner or later—sooner, Ariel had a feeling—she would lay that obligation to rest.

And, Ariel knew, she'd been right to drag Laya along. For a few days they could all lay low and breathe easy, safely out of reach of nuisance phone calls and anything, nuisance or menace, Laya might have to fear. *"There's something coming at me, something bad."* Laya's words flashed across her mind. *"I can't outrun what's coming."* The premonition seemed melodramatic at the moment. The "something" seemed not four hundred miles, but a world away.

There'd been a sort of holiday ease at dinner that evening, and Laya had been as unbuttoned as Ariel had ever seen her. When Hattie joked about Jessie averting her eyes from Arthur ("Look at her! Makes out like if she can't see the bloomin' cat, he's not there"), Laya had come back with, "Why're you laughing? It's a proven fact. What you can't see can't bother you. Look at me," she'd said, palms up. "Total serenity!"

Ariel took advantage of the mellow mood, and, as offhandedly as if it were the most inconsequential of topics, brought up the idea of a Seeing Eye dog: a neutral, amazing-what-those-critters-can-do kind of observation. "You know," she'd said to Laya, "there's a training school here. We could take a look at it." A week before, Laya would have freaked. Tonight, she'd conspicuously averted her face from Ariel, and said, "Jessie's right! It works."

Ariel considered the reaction a thumbs-up. Tomorrow they would tour the school. Then maybe they'd walk the beach or take the ferry into the city. She hoped to see Libby Vail in the afternoon, but the morning was theirs to kill.

Ariel made herself comfortable on the chaise, snapped open the *New York Times*, and began to scan. She had it down to a relatively fine science; she could dispatch, if not digest, the average *Times* page, and make effective, if cryptic, notes in four minutes.

After the New York and Washington papers, the locals went faster, but she was losing concentration by the time she got to the *Los Angeles Times*. A news-in-brief Metro story rated no more than a glance.

"Neighborhood Activist Slain" read the headline. "71-year-old Carrie Murphy brutally beaten" was all Ariel took in of the lead. Gruesome, she would have thought if she'd spared a thought before moving on to an equally chilling article about the number of high-risk sex offenders currently on parole in the state.

Despite the masochistic bedtime reading, Ariel caught herself in an ear-stopping yawn. She put the paper aside. Nicely dozy and pleased with the day, she would, she was sure, sleep like the dead.

Had she read to the end of the neighborhood activist story, it's doubtful she would have slept at all. That the Murphy woman resided in L.A.'s Crenshaw district would have raised no flag. Nor would her address; Ariel wouldn't know that the house backed up to the alley in which James Price was assaulted. What would have put her heart into overload and sent her racing for a map of L.A. was a quote from the victim's daughter.

"Momma died because she wouldn't put up with what goes on around here," 52-year-old Letitia Murphy Bond tearfully told reporters. "Gangs and crack dealers and all. She wasn't afraid to make enemies." Ms. Bond pointed toward an alley behind her mother's house. "Right there," she said, "just a few weeks ago she looked out her window and saw a man being beat up. She didn't only call the police, she worked with them. You see what I'm saying?" Ms. Bond asked. "That's the kind of woman she was."

Ariel called the Marin Guide Dog Academy first thing the next morning. When the public relations director understood that her interest was not professional, that she was calling on behalf of a blind friend, he offered to show them around personally.

Laya was strapped into the van before being informed of the first stop on their itinerary. She began immediately to unhook the seat belt. "Chicken," Ariel jeered. "Ariel!" Hattie snapped. Laya hesitated with her hands on the buckle.

"What happened," Ariel asked, "to the 'world champion blind lady'? To 'getting on with your life'?"

"Ariel," Laya said.

"You want to be independent? With a dog you can be."

"Ariel," Laya said.

"Think about it! You can get around by yourself. You can go back to teaching. You can do—"

"Ariel!" Laya shouted. "I'll go! I'll go anywhere and do anything if you'll lay off the speechmaking!"

• • •

Frank Trout was a good PR man because he had a passion for his product. "Not a dime," he told the three
women as they walked the facility's manicured lawn, "do
we get from tax dollars. We're supported entirely by private donations. Have been since 'forty-two, when we
were established for war veterans."

Ariel had been asking the questions because Laya was
acting as if she were not only blind but mute. "How much
does a dog cost?" Ariel asked. She knew the answer from
her previous visit. She was anticipating an obstacle Laya
would raise if she ever decided to regain the use of her
vocal chords.

"If you mean how much to train dog and student, it's
between sixteen and seventeen thousand. If you mean
how much does it cost the student, it's zero. No charge for
the dog or for the training we do in residence, or," he said,
"for transportation here, or equipment, or follow-up services, for the student and the dog."

"Wow!" Ariel crowed at Laya as she took her arm.

Laya used Jessie's trick; she averted her face.

"Do most blind people use a dog?" Ariel then asked.
That was a question to which she did not know the
answer; she shouldn't have asked it.

"No," Trout said. "Only about two percent."

Laya faced Ariel, and smiled broadly.

"For a number of different reasons," Trout went on.
"Some people aren't physically capable of handling a
dog."

Ariel squeezed the arm of the woman she'd seen do a
hundred rapid-fire push-ups without raising a sweat.

"Some *legally* blind people can function with a cane,"
Trout said, "and there are, of course, people who're frightened of dogs."

Laya tensed slightly in Ariel's grasp.

"Although," Trout added, "I have to say I've never

known one who didn't get over that if they made up their
mind to."

After they toured a dormitory, as well maintained and
modern as the rest of the campus, Ariel noticed again the
one exception: the incongruous wooden dinosaur of a
structure she'd fantasized about on her first visit.

"What's that old building?" she asked Trout, pointing.
"The gingerbready one way over there?"

"'The Manse,' you mean?" The PR man chuckled.
"That's our latest addition, and completely remodeled and
adapted inside. It was a gift from one of our supporters."

"Quite a gift!" Ariel said. "What's it used for?"

"A second dorm. We're able to take nearly twice the
number of students since we were fortunate enough to get
that."

Trout led on, to the kennels. As he and every employee
and volunteer knew, they were the highlight of the tour.
The nursery especially. No one was immune to the puppies. Even Hattie cracked a smile, bending to tease a shy
male with a worried expression.

"That," Trout said, consulting a card affixed to the pen,
"is either Chan or Cody or Checker. The females are
Chablis and Cay and Cara. All the pups in each litter are
given names beginning with the same letter, and no two
working dogs can have the same name. You wouldn't
believe what we go through to come up with new ones!"

There were many pens. Ariel had never seen so many
pups. The current crop was heavy on yellow Labs, fur
balls that tumbled over one another, gnawing with sharp
puppy teeth on their litter mates. As alike at this age as if
they'd been cloned, they'd soon exhibit distinguishing
characteristics that would make one right for one partner,
one right for another, and some unsuited to the calling.

"What becomes of the ones that flunk?" Hattie wondered.

"The 'Career Change' dogs," Trout said. "We've got a waiting list you wouldn't believe for those guys. Sometimes, the hitch is nothing more than that they're too sensitive. Like they can't tolerate loud noise or they balk at a grate or—"

"A grate?" Hattie asked.

"In the sidewalk," Trout said, "you know. Some dogs are afraid to cross a grate, but from time to time you do encounter one. You might have to cross over it to get where you want to go."

"How much of that was a setup?" Laya asked.

She and Ariel were walking along the shoreline at Rodeo Beach, west of the Golden Gate. The sky had begun to cloud over, and the waves grumbled, slapping peevishly against the sand. Hattie had elected to sit on a hunk of driftwood and contemplate the horizon. Ariel could see her in the distance. She looked totally absorbed.

"No setup," Ariel said. "Too bad Jessie's not here. She'd love this."

"None of it was? Not the bit about people with a dog phobia?"

"No."

"Not the bit about how many of the graduates go on with their careers as lawyers and stockbrokers and writers?"

"Nope."

"And teachers?"

Laya stumbled, steadying herself with her cane. When she was moving again, Ariel said, "You're a good teacher."

"Yes, I was," Laya said. "I am."

28

"*BUON GIORNO!*" LIBBY VAIL GREETED ARIEL. THE SEMIRETIRED musical theater star and wife of ex-senator Ellis Bland and friend of Dorothy Thibeau laughed. "I hope you're impressed with that because it's about the extent of my repertoire."

She and her husband had gotten home from Italy in the wee hours of the morning, but Ariel had been invited to come on over "whenever." When she arrived at the Bland home at two o'clock, the lady was swimming vigorous laps in the pool.

"Pull up a chaise, *cara mia*," she said as she emerged dripping, inadvertently, on Ariel. "Oops! Sorry." She handed over a towel. "Let's get out of these wet clothes and into a dry martini!"

Ariel laughed. "It's a mite early for me."

"Well, it's eleven at night in Italy," said her hostess, who then made wet footprints to an outdoor bar.

When they were settled with their various refreshments, Ariel got right down to business. "This isn't altogether a social call," she said. "You were a friend of Dorothy Thibeau's, weren't you?"

"Dorothy?" Libby nodded, surprised. "And Ray—Dr. Thibeau—too. Why?"

"And Sis?"

"Who?"

"Another friend of Dorothy's. A woman who was called Sis?"

"Can't say I know her. Tell me, how's B.F.? We had a great time at dinner the other night!"

"The truth is," Ariel vamped, "Dorothy's death has him down."

"Oh?" Libby made a sympathetic face. "I'm sorry to hear that."

"I don't know if you're aware, but the two of them were once very close."

"I kind of got that impression. When he rode with Ellis and me to the funeral? Listen, Ariel, you tell B.F. from me that he really ought not to be too awfully sad. Dorothy . . . well, she was a very unhappy woman after Ray died. They were so close. Real sweethearts, like—oh, I don't know—Ronnie and Nancy."

"Ronnie and . . . ? Oh," Ariel said. "*That* Ronnie and Nancy. When you say she was 'unhappy' after Mr. Thibeau—"

"Truth be told, she wasn't the same since the first time he got sick."

"And that was when?"

Libby sipped her drink, tapped her toothpick-speared olive against the glass, and said, "Oh, gosh, Ariel . . . a year and a half ago? At least that."

"Could it have been closer to two and a half years?" Ariel asked on a hunch.

"I won't say it wasn't. They didn't think he was going to make it then, I heard. Dorothy was about as bad off as Ray, from worry. Then they went off to a clinic—I forget which one, the best they could find—and he got better."

The best they could find, Ariel thought, might explain the hefty withdrawals from their bank account. "How do you mean, Dorothy 'wasn't the same' since then?"

"What *do* I mean?" Libby asked herself, thinking it over. "Like I say, she'd worried herself to a frazzle. Even after he got better she wasn't herself. Nervy. Hovering over Ray . . ." Libby wiggled her glass. "Maybe drank a bit more than was good for her?"

It was true, Ariel knew; Dorothy had admitted it in her letter.

"She tried, bless her, to act gay as ever—they even threw a party, I remember, for their anniversary—but you could see it was an act. Forced, you know? It was like she was waiting for the other shoe to drop."

"And when her husband did get sick again? When he died?"

"I tell you what, I was shocked when I saw her at his funeral. She looked so drawn! And that was one of the last times I did see her. She virtually stopped going out. Well, we're only talking about a few weeks, aren't we, before poor Dorothy died, too?"

"Were you surprised by her death?"

"Floored! I hadn't thought she was that bad off! I thought she was just grieving. She went downhill fast, I guess."

"Did you find the suddenness at all . . . questionable?"

"Questionable?" Libby said, startled. "Good lord, no! You're kidding, aren't you? You're *not* kidding! Ariel, this isn't a social call, you said . . ." As if she'd developed a chill (or suddenly felt underdressed), she reached for her beach robe. "Are you here in a *professional* capacity?"

"No, no. I'm just curious because I . . . knew Dorothy myself, actually. Slightly. I got a letter from her, after she died."

Libby's eyes grew big.

"My grandfather told me she was too ill to have mailed it herself, so, naturally, I wondered—"

"Wondered?"

"Who mailed it."

"Oh. Of course you would. I can tell you that."

Ariel felt a thump of excitement clear to her stomach.

"It would have to be Alice Manning," Libby said. "Do you know Alice? She's a friend of ours, closer to Dorothy, truth be told, than I was and sort of a, um . . . take charge sort of person? Type A? She jumped right in when Dorothy went into the hospital. Handled the nitty-gritty like taking in the paper, watering plants, calling people. All that stuff. Keeping vigil? Everybody needs a friend like that. Sad to say, I'm not it."

"What makes you so sure she mailed my letter?"

"Tell you what! Let's ask her." Libby picked up a portable and dialed. Ariel listened to a brief one-sided conversation before Libby said, point-blank, "Alice, sweetie, when you were being so good taking care of Dorothy, did you by chance mail any letters for her?" Libby cut her eyes toward Ariel. "I guessed as much," she said. "You were an angel." To Ariel, she said, "You want to see her?" Ariel nodded. "Alice," Libby said, "what are you doing now? Uh-huh, but the benefit's hours away. Are you tied up this minute?"

In short order Ariel was on her way to nearby Corte Madera and her impromptu appointment with Alice Manning. Thirty minutes later she was driving home, digesting what she'd been told by both women.

The mystery of the mailing of the letter was solved. Alice had taken over her friend's affairs with the zeal of an officious aide-de-camp, from laundering her nightgowns when she fell ill to choosing the outfit in which she was soon buried. It was she who apprised minister and attorney and accountant of Dorothy's illness, she who liaised between Dorothy's physician and her friends. And it was she who, keeping an eye on Dorothy's house, noticed a stack of overdue library books and unmailed correspondence, and returned the former, and posted the latter.

Unfortunately, Alice could add little of substance to Libby Vail's account of the period preceding Dorothy's death. Oddly, since she was Dorothy's closest friend, she knew of no one within their circle of acquaintances whom she'd ever heard called Sis.

"What made you think this person was a friend of Dorothy's?" she'd asked Ariel.

"Because Dorothy used her nickname," Ariel replied. And, she thought, because she had sufficient access to the woman's private life to have evidence (if not "absolutely conclusive" evidence) about her cause of death, and because she knew enough about the woman's state of mind to believe she'd lost interest in living.

"Ms. Gold," Alice said, as if she'd caught the last of Ariel's thought, "she died, you said. This 'Sis'?"

"My guess is a couple of years ago."

Thoughtfully, Alice said, "Dorothy volunteered . . ."

"For . . . ?"

"She did volunteer work. Charity work. Not in recent times, but back before Ray got sick. She and I sat on committees together and so on, but she was involved in other things, too, where I'm sure she would meet any number of people I'd have no idea of."

"Yes?"

"For one thing, she was a Pink Lady." Catching Ariel's baffled expression, Alice said, "She visited hospital patients. You know. Read to them, spread cheer. Dorothy was good at it. Sometimes one just holds their hand and listens. But what I was thinking is, caregivers tend to be informal dealing with sick people. Calling them by their first names as if they were children. I happen to think that sort of familiarity's patronizing, but she—"

"So you're suggesting Sis may not have been an actual friend, but a sick person Dorothy got to know."

"If the woman died," Alice Manning had said, "she probably wasn't healthy, right?"

As theories went, Ariel mused as she drove, it hung together rather loosely, but it did fit the known facts. It was unlikely that Sis had been a close friend, or Dorothy's friends Libby and Alice would have known her, too, or at least heard of her. If Sis hadn't wanted to live, as Dorothy believed (or tried to persuade herself), it was entirely possible that it was because she was sick, perhaps terminally. And the timing was right. Dorothy gave up her charity work when her own husband fell ill, which was, Ariel now knew, roughly the time she and Dorothy met and talked.

Putting together what she'd been told, first by B.F. and then by Libby and Alice, Ariel felt she was finally getting to know the woman she had forgotten.

Dorothy Thibeau had been a sociable and effervescent woman, who had once enjoyed a very nice life. She was devoted to her husband, and he to her. They were comfortably off. She was free to volunteer her time and, all credit to her, she did. Handsome and well liked by all who knew them, the couple lived well, and not cautiously, as if their lives were charmed, as if there were no tomorrow. The wife was blasé about money, the husband no financier. And then the unthinkable happened. Ray Thibeau was diagnosed with cancer. He must have gone from doctor to doctor to get a second opinion, a different opinion. Dorothy worried nearly to collapse, not just about her husband's health as her friends supposed, but about money. The two, presumably, had also been cavalier about insurance, and professional courtesy would have been extended only so far. The bills mounted. The savings shrank. The house was mortgaged. In desperation, Dorothy snuck off to the city where her friends wouldn't see, and pawned whatever would bring the most. And Ray, in desperation . . . did what?

Where had the windfall come from?

What had one or the other Thibeau done to obtain the money that paid for the best clinic? That began to flow into their bank account on a monthly, cash, basis? That allowed Dorothy to redeem what was left of her belongings, and to plan the celebration she must have feared would mark their last anniversary together?

Was it drug money? Doctors dispensed drugs.

A horn blew behind Ariel. She realized she'd been driving at a crawl. Lost in thought, she'd forgotten she was behind the wheel. And where was her mind? She was so caught up in patching Dorothy together from her friends' memories, she'd lost track of what she'd known from the beginning. Go back to the letter, she told herself.

You know, if her friends don't, that it wasn't only concern for her husband that changed Dorothy. That made her "nervy" and caused her to drink "a bit more than was good for her." She was "waiting for the other shoe to drop" because, as she'd written, her conscience was bothering her. And because she was afraid.

The money was a payoff. A bribe, hush money or blackmail. And whatever was done to get it had been done by Ray. It wasn't drugs he sold; it was silence about the evidence that wasn't "absolutely conclusive," that hadn't been Dorothy's "to expose or suppress." What kind of marketable evidence was a doctor likely to have?

A man who's murdered once can't be counted on not to do it again.

The money had come from the nameless *he.* The "executioner." The philanthropist. And the evidence would have implicated him in murder. Thibeau hadn't been only a doctor, Ariel only then remembered from his obituary; at some point he'd been a coroner.

29

ARIEL ARRIVED HOME WITH HER MIND RACING. THE HOSPITAL IN which Dorothy volunteered, Alice had said, was Marin General. Was it possible to find out which patients she might have visited? The time frame was vague: winter of two and a half years ago. Ariel had no idea how a Pink Lady worked. Were they assigned certain rooms? Certain floors? Did they wander the hospital at will?

Ariel parked the van. It would be easy enough to get one fact: exactly when Dr. Raymond Thibeau had been Marin County coroner. But once she had that, how to learn what cases had been investigated through his office?

She might be looking at a lot of calls, a lot of time expended, all based on conjecture. That Dorothy's volunteer work was part of the equation. That Ray's position as coroner entered in. But wouldn't it be something, Ariel thought as she climbed the steps to the front porch, if she turned up one patient with whom Dorothy had become friendly, who died in the winter of two and a half years ago, whose death had warranted investigation, and—connect the last dot—if the investigation occurred during Ray Thibeau's tenure in office? Just one name!

The front door opened. "You look like a cat eatin' briars," Hattie observed.

"I love it when the puzzle starts to come together!" Ariel said. "I'd forgotten how much . . . I look like what?"

"Happy."

"It's Dorothy. The pieces are starting to fit, Hattie. You find that piece of blue sky that fits against that piece of red kite, you know? And then—"

"She means to stay up here," Hattie said.

It took Ariel a second to process. "Laya, you mean? Is staying . . . where, exactly?"

"Right here, if it's okay with B.F." Hattie came out, and pulled the door closed behind her. "I said I reckoned it would be."

"Well, sure, but why?"

"Says she's goin' to the school if they'll let her in."

"You're joking! Why, that's . . . But, how can she? I mean how can she now? It takes time to get in. Applying. She has to apply. And interviews—"

"She set one up for Monday."

"For Monday." Ariel couldn't get her mind around the speed with which Laya was taking charge of her future. "You don't look too thrilled about it," she noticed and said.

Hattie went to the porch rail and put both hands on it. She took a good long look at all there was to see before she said, "That's as pretty as anything I ever saw in my life. It's a waste that nobody stays here to enjoy it."

Ariel glanced at the view, but then she turned back to Hattie.

"Here's what I think," the old woman eventually said. "The dog idea's fine for a person that's got no chance to see. She does. Might be a chance in a thousand. Might be a million. Don't matter. If there's any chance, she's wrong to pass it up."

"Did you tell her that?"

Hattie looked at Ariel. "Ariel Gold," she said, sounding remarkably like her employer of nearly forty years, "I met that woman a week ago. What right have I got to tell her what to do?"

"What did you say to her?"

"That I'd stay while she talked to the school people."

Ariel nodded.

"Oh! While I think of it," Hattie said. "You got a call

from that newspaper man. Said to ask you if you felt like a party."

"You wouldn't lie to me?" Ariel asked Rob that same night as they drove to San Rafael. She looked over at him and resisted the impulse to stare. She'd remembered that he was good-looking; she hadn't remembered how drop-*dead* good-looking. He wasn't a kid, and he hadn't been worked on, not by a plastic man. Ariel would swear to it. This was genes. He'd been engineered by some celestial studio makeup artist. *"We put these aging lines here by the eyes and the mouth, for maturity. Character. We don't fool with the lips. They're good as is. Let's do one dimple there in the cheek, and add a little silver to the hair, at the temples. Just dust the blond with silver."*

Oblivious, perhaps, to her thoughts, he grinned. "Lie?" he asked. "About what?"

"You guarantee this affair's not *haute* dress?" Ariel hadn't packed for serious partying. The slim, wine-colored jersey tunic she wore was what fashion ads would call (dubiously, in Ariel's opinion) "day into evening." At least it fit; a year before she would have looked like a bratwurst in it.

"I only lie about *reee-ly big* things," Rob assured her, doing Ed Sullivan. "You look swell."

He looked like he'd just strolled out of *GQ*. His wardrobe was big budget. Custom tailored. His car was a new Lexus, an interesting vehicle, Ariel thought, for a local columnist. Maybe he'd gotten a hefty book advance? "Besides," he was saying, "you're going to this shindig to see, right? Not to be seen."

"I already have seen one person who'll be there," Ariel told him. "You know Alice Manning?" The party was the same benefit to which she would be going. According to Rob, there would be a number of people attending who'd known both the Thibeaus.

"No grass growing under your feet. Who else have you talked to?"

"Just Libby Vail."

"Learn anything?"

Ariel wasn't sure how to play this. Rob Millen's antennae were practically waving in the air. She figured he wouldn't leave her side for one second that evening. The last thing she wanted was to have him muddy her waters, but she could use him. He also could use her and, she was sure, fully intended to. She seesawed her hand. "How's the book coming?" she asked. "It sounds fascinating." She'd never known a new author who wouldn't be diverted by that opening.

"Woof!" Rob said.

"Pardon me?"

"When you throw the dog a bone, you don't want to hit him between the eyes with it."

Ariel frown-smiled, as if at a loss.

"Whatever can you mean? said the lady." Rob laughed. "I've seen that butter-wouldn't-melt-in-my-mouth tactic on your show."

He was, Ariel reminded herself, no dumb blond.

"Now, you've got to know," he said, "that there's no way I'm not curious why you're asking about the Thibeaus, and as delighted as I'd be if *Open File* did a segment on my book, I won't lay down and die to get it. So what I suggest is, we make a deal."

Ariel nearly grunted. In a pig's eye.

"You tell me what's prompting the questions, I do two things. I introduce you to people who might be able to answer them, and I tell you an interesting anecdote about the good doctor Thibeau."

"I'm perfectly capable of introducing myself," Ariel said.

"Not if you're not at the party."

"You're going to take your toys and go home?" Ariel was beginning, perversely, to enjoy this. "I have a car. I know where the party is."

"And I have the invitation that'll get you in." Rob wiggled his eyebrows like a man about to whip open his raincoat and shout "Surprise!" He had very flexible eyebrows. "Your turn," he said.

Ariel mentally sarcastically congratulated herself on picking a resource with a hyperactive curiosity. Or was this more than curiosity? She thought it over. Why was a feature writer so bent on worming information out of her? What did he plan to do with it? Scoop her in his column? So what if he did? Getting a story had never been her priority. Getting to the truth was. "What about this 'anecdote'?" she asked.

"Did I mention that no one but me knows it?"

"Tell me."

"Uh-uh!" he said. "You go first."

"Dorothy Thibeau sent me a letter saying she was frightened of someone. A man. Before I could react to it, she was dead."

Rob Millen stared.

"Hey!" Ariel said. "You want to watch where you're driving?"

"What man?" he asked.

"I don't know."

"What's that supposed to mean?"

"What part of 'I don't know' don't you grasp?"

"But . . . why you? Why would she write *you*?"

"We were friends."

"So you said on the phone."

"I did. It's true."

"Like it's true that your interest in her is a 'purely personal matter'? If you were such friends, why didn't you say a word that night at dinner when we were talking about her?"

"I'm a good listener."

"Why didn't you bother to go to her funeral?"

"I was tied up."

"Why wouldn't you know who she was afraid of?"

"Because she didn't tell me that."

"Come on! She thought his name wasn't important?"

She thought I'd remember it! Ariel screamed only in her mind. "Why would I make up that she sent me a letter?" she said. "I only lie about 'reee-ly big' things."

"Why was she afraid of this unnamed man?"

"Because," Ariel said, and turned square on to face him, "she believed he was a killer. And *I* believe it's your turn."

He drove a long block before he gave the appearance, at least, of conceding. "Wait'll I get parked." They'd arrived at the Falkirk Center by then, where the dinner was being held. Finding a parking space took a while, and, evidently, concentration. He didn't say a word during the process. It struck Ariel that he was selectively editing his story as she'd done hers, slipping a detail or two up his sleeve for future negotiation. They finally left the car several blocks away. While they walked back, he talked.

"This was about two years ago. I was doing this column, tub thumping about structural repairs for Marin Center . . . You know it's a Frank Lloyd Wright building? Okay, I happened to be out there researching, and I ran into Thibeau. He was on his way into his office. You knew he was coroner his last few years?"

Ariel nodded. "I didn't know the time frame."

"I knew him casually, enough for small talk, which we made. He mentioned some article he wanted to show me, so I went to his office with him. While I was there, he got a call."

"From?"

"The name?" Snidely one-upping, Rob said, "He didn't tell me."

"Cute," Ariel said. "Go on."

"He didn't look too chipper before the call—I'd heard he wasn't well—but he looked worse a few seconds into it. It was bad news, or he wasn't happy to hear who was calling. He got pinch-faced. He said something like, 'I don't want to hear about that.'"

"Maybe it was about his health. A bad report from his doctor."

"If it was his doctor, he should've gotten a new one. He did not like the character he was talking to. He hung up on him, or her. That was not a Thibeau I'd ever seen. He was an amiable man."

"Who knows?" Ariel said. "Could've been something as ordinary as an associate who fouled up, or a neighbor complaining about a noisy party." Except, Ariel thought, the Thibeaus weren't doing any partying around that time; they were too busy trying to stay afloat and, in his case, trying to stay alive through chemo or radiation or whatever he'd had done. "It is interesting, though," she admitted.

"The one other thing he said was more interesting." Rob had timed the end of his account for maximum impact. He opened the door of the Falkirk Center, and as he ushered Ariel in, he said, "Just before Thibeau hung up, he said, 'You're getting damned good value for your investment. I suggest you remember that.'"

30

TRUE TO HIS WORD, ROB MILLEN INTRODUCED ARIEL TO A number of people who had known Dorothy or Raymond or both, well or socially or to recognize. As she'd anticipated, he glued himself to her side. That, it quickly became apparent, was a good thing. Ariel was sure she'd caught a fleeting dubiousness in one or two faces when she was introduced, a hint of stiffness. She was, as she'd feared, underdressed for the occasion, and she assumed that was the reason.

"Or is it because I'm a reporter?" she asked Rob.

"It's where you're from," he explained, amused. "Gomorrah."

"Huh?"

"There's been an influx of L.A. refugees the last few years, sullying the Promised Land with their crude and ostentatious ways. Never fear, I'll vouch for you and translate the local tongue."

During the cocktail hour the two of them worked the room like campaigners. They smiled and pressed the flesh, engaged and deftly moved on. Wedging the Thibeau name into conversation took ingenuity. It was more trouble than it was worth. Other than one or two comments that confirmed earlier reports or impressions, Ariel learned nothing of consequence.

Unbeknownst to her companion, however, she had a second item on her agenda. A benefit dinner, she reasoned, would provide optimum opportunity to meet "the philanthropist." For all she knew, she had. He could have been the chairperson of the Literacy Campaign or the

Volunteer Council or the local Special Olympics. Ariel met
them all. Everybody in the joint was a paragon of community virtue. Some volunteered. Some merely wrote checks.
All, it seemed, served.

At one point, when they'd retreated from the fray, Ariel
said, "Mighty lot of movers and shakers you've got here,
pal!" She scanned the room. "'Charity edifieth.'"

"It whats?" Rob said.

"'Knowledge puffeth up, but charity edifieth.'"

"Yeah, well, I didn't get edified, did you?"

Ariel shook her head. "I see your lady farmer friend
from B.F.'s dinner party over there. Meg?"

"Talking tomatoes and turnips, I expect."

"Am I correct in assuming you two aren't an item?"

"Buddies," Rob said. "I've helped out with her gleaning
project."

Ariel was surprised. "You do good works, too?"

"Just call me Mister Mover and Shaker," Rob said. His
laugh set his dimple into action.

Realizing she was staring at it, Ariel turned back to the
room. "Who's that man in the dark suit and striped tie?"
she asked.

"Which man in the dark suit and striped tie? Who's *not*
in a dark suit and striped tie?"

Ariel pointed with her glass. "That one."

Rob spotted him. "The gray-haired guy?"

"Which guy's *not* gray-haired? But yes, him."

"Name's Barnes. Why?"

"Why does he look vaguely familiar?"

The small mystery was solved when the gray-haired
man, whose name was Charles Barnes, asked what Ariel
thought about the guide dog school.

"So that's where I've seen you," Ariel said. "Do you
work there?"

"I volunteer there," he said.

"Well, of *course* you do," Ariel said before she could stop herself. Hurriedly, she went on to mention that her friend was hoping to be trained, "But I hear there's a waiting list."

"Umm?" Charles Barnes said. "She's applied?" He listened politely as Ariel told him about the upcoming interview. She was talking about Laya's failed graft when dinner was announced.

Ariel was seated between a man she hadn't met and Rob. The man said hi and returned to conversation with the person on his other side. Rob was being flirted with by the woman next to him. The entrée was prime rib. Ariel's, unappealingly, was still oozing its lifeblood. "'Charity suffereth long,'" she said under her breath.

Rob caught it. He turned back and grinned, flashing his dimple. He couldn't help it, Ariel decided; it was a reflex.

"Sad thing about your blind friend," he said. "Tell me more."

Ariel shrugged. "Not a lot more to tell."

"Okay," Rob said agreeably, "then tell me what Dorothy Thibeau really said in her letter."

"What makes you think there's anything more to tell?"

"Common sense?"

"It was a short letter. Vague." *Why would she bother with names and facts I supposedly knew?* "I gave you the salient points."

"'Dear Ariel,'" Rob extemporized, "'I'm scared of this anonymous man I think killed somebody. Love, Dorothy.'"

Ariel's mouth twitched. The letter may as well have read that way for all the help it was. "She did not tell me the alleged killer's name, Rob. I swear it on my Sigma Delta award."

"What about the alleged victim's name?"

"Victim?"

"Kill? Victim? You don't see the correlation there?"

"What I said is Dorothy *believed he was a killer*. That might not mean he'd killed, but that he had the potential to kill."

"Semantics. I know who the victim was anyway."

Ariel sloshed the water she'd been about to drink. "You do?"

"Sis."

"You said you didn't know her!" Ariel had asked on the phone the day before, casually, if he happened to know a woman who went by that name; that's all she'd said. "How could you possibly . . ." She stopped. She'd blown it. "You were guessing. You didn't know."

Rob smiled. "I do now. You may as well tell me the rest."

"There is no rest! Look, she thought I'd call her, that we'd be talking right away. Presumably, she would've filled me in then. The letter got delayed until it was too late."

"Why didn't she call you to start with?"

Ariel had wondered about that more than once. "I wouldn't be surprised if she tried," she replied honestly. "Calls to the on-air people are routinely screened. If I wasn't there to say yea or nay to taking it, she would've been told to write me in care of *Open File*, which is what she did."

"Your *friend* didn't have your home number? Or your address?"

"No, Rob," Ariel said. "Unfortunately, she didn't."

Ariel came home to find Laya alone in the dark living room, pajamaed and stretched out on the sofa, the stereo turned low. Jessie lay some yards away from her, keeping watch. Ariel wondered if Laya knew the dog was in the room.

"Hello," Laya said quietly.

"How'd you know it was me?"

"Jessie thumped her tail."

"Oh. Why are you listening to Mario Lanza?"

"Hattie put it on. You'd be doing me a kindness to change it."

"She told me about your decision to try for a dog. Gutsy."

"Onward and upward."

"And awayward, from L.A. and creepy callers. That's a bonus."

Laya crossed her arms over her chest, her body language subtle but articulate.

"Ah!" Ariel said. "Even four hundred miles away, your thumbs still prick."

"Pardon?"

"'By the pricking of my thumbs, something wicked this way comes.'"

"Not funny."

"The dreaded *Inevitable!*" Ariel quavered witchily, and tickled Laya's outstretched bare foot. She got a kick for her trouble and a grudging smile. "Did you have a good time?" Laya asked.

"I didn't go to frolic."

"Okay then, did you *do* any good?"

Ariel turned on a lamp, sat down, and took off her shoes. "The brilliant sleuth did not uncover the answers she seeks."

"She will." Through a stifled yawn Laya said, "Your date seemed nice."

"I wouldn't call it a date, but, yeah, the people we met tonight were partial to him, especially the women."

"Hattie said he was 'right good-looking.'"

"He stops traffic."

"Well, unless it's to hijack cars, why do you make that sound like a crime?"

"Did I?" Ariel got back up to look through the CDs. "No crime. He's just not my type."

"Because of?"

Ariel stared at the CD in her hand. She turned and stared at Laya. "Sexism?"

"He's a sexist?"

"Not him! Me! I'm a piggette."

"You are not."

"Well, what then? It's like I can't get past the face."

"To . . . ?"

"I'm like a man who can't believe a pretty woman can have smarts, too. He keeps catching me off guard."

"He's got smarts?"

"He was smart enough not to try to charm information out of me. He pumped away like he was drilling for oil."

Laya snickered. "You two must have made quite a couple."

During breakfast the next morning someone from the admissions department at the school called. Would she be available, Laya was asked, to begin the interview process today rather than Monday?

Plans for ferrying into San Francisco were scrapped, and Ariel drove Laya to the campus. After she was delivered, Ariel, as always fascinated by the process, stopped to watch a dog in training. So had the PR director, Frank Trout. He appeared to be explaining what was going on to a group of wide-eyed grade school children and their teacher. The trainer was holding the dog at a curb; there seemed to be some failure of communication between the two.

"The problem's the slope," said a quiet voice from behind her.

Ariel turned to see the gray-haired man from last night's dinner. "Mr. Barnes, good morning," she said, relieved to remember his name. "The slope?"

"It's Charles, please. Don't make me feel even older than I am." His eyes crinkled when he smiled. "The curb's sloped for wheelchair access."

"Yes, I see that."

"Easy enough to teach a dog to stop at a regular curb, see, but when there's no clear step down, they take a while to get that it *is* a curb."

"Ah!" Ariel said. "You volunteer, you said. As a trainer?"

"Nothing nearly that important." They both watched the dog for a minute. "I saw you inside," he said. "Was that your friend with you? The one you were telling me about?"

Ariel nodded. Here was a rare breed: a man who actually paid attention during party small talk. "She got a call asking if she could get started interviewing today. Out of the blue!"

"I don't suppose . . ."

"Yes?"

"Do you have time for a cup of coffee?"

Ariel didn't see why not.

"Have a seat, will you?" He pointed to a bench beside a mock pear tree. "I'll be right back."

Ariel did as he asked. She was surprised when a few minutes later he returned with a metal lunch box in hand. It was the utilitarian, curved top variety commonly carried by workmen. He looked like a workman, she thought, or an outdoorsman. His skin was sun-weathered. He looked about sixty to her, but it might be the aging effect of all those rays; he might be younger.

"Here we are," he said cheerfully, and seating himself with the box between them, he took out a scarred thermos and two plastic mugs. "Colombian," he said. "Leaded."

Ariel saw that a sandwich and what looked like Oreos remained in the box, and carrot sticks. It was the sort of lunch moms packed for kids, or wives for husbands. "Does your wife volunteer here, too?" she asked as she took the mug. The coffee smelled fine.

"Don't have one of those," Charles Barnes said in his quiet, rather diffident way.

He was dressed very casually, Ariel noted, even for a Saturday. In fact, he verged on looking down at the heels. His shirt was a much-washed plaid flannel. His khaki pants were sharply creased—somebody had done them justice with an iron—but they, too, looked as if they'd been with him for a while. What, Ariel couldn't help wondering, had this man been doing at last night's dinner? She had a fair idea what the plates had gone for.

Maybe Barnes was one of those good-hearted people who had a mail route their whole working lives, or were sales clerks or meter readers, and, considering themselves blessed, devoted their later years to those they considered less blessed. She read about them occasionally. She'd even pitched a segment on one: a school lunchroom worker who, astonishingly, accumulated over a hundred thousand dollars and gave it all to Habitat for Humanity.

Or maybe he was a self-made zillionaire, an eccentric who never forgot tighter times and went on pinching every penny. The type existed. Her own grandfather occasionally surprised Ariel with some holdover thrifty tic. "What do you do, Charles?" she asked.

"Retired. A few years now," he said. "I was in construction."

Hauling I beams or running the show? Ariel wondered. "Oh?" she asked.

"You know what I'd really like?" Barnes said. "I wish you'd tell me about what *you* do. It's got to be fascinating."

He was in earnest. He reminded Ariel of the kids she'd seen with the PR director, wide-eyed and all ears, and she didn't exactly say no to answering his eager questions. She was still new enough at what she did—in her own mind anyway—to love talking about it, so she did, at length.

"Are you up here to be with your friend," he eventually asked, "or are you working?"

"In my business," she said, laughing, "you're always working, or you're liable to find yourself *out* of work." Which reminded her that he was one person she hadn't gotten around to probing the previous night about the Thibeaus.

As if hearing an echo of her thought, he said, "You're doing a story about our late coroner?" He caught her look. "I overheard you talking with somebody about him at the dinner."

"Depends," said Ariel conversationally. "Is there a story?"

Charles stared into his cup, blinking several times in rapid succession, as if giving serious consideration to his answer. "Probably," he said.

Ariel swallowed. "Probably . . . ?"

"Generally speaking, every man's life has the seed of one."

Ariel hid her disappointment. This was to be a philosophical discussion, apparently.

"Have to be careful about what sprouts, though, don't you think? Without knowing all the circumstances."

Or was it philosophical? "Did you know Dr. Thibeau?"

He nodded, then qualified the nod with a shrug. "Knew of him," he said. "Did you?"

"I never met him, no. Knew what of him?"

"You mean, do I know anything unsavory?"

"Well, no, not unsavory, necessarily."

"'Necessarily'?" Charles smiled. "He was, as far as I ever heard, well regarded."

A long moment passed. Ariel waited, receptively. A receptive silence often got her some pretty unlooked-for reactions. It did this time. "How long have you known Millen?" Charles asked.

"Rob? Two weeks."

"Umm," remarked Charles Barnes.

"Does 'umm' mean something I should worry about?"

"Let's just say Millen hasn't always behaved with . . . scruples. Look . . ." Charles rubbed the back of his neck, as if he were massaging out every word against his better judgment. "A fellow I know once told Millen something he meant to be off-the-record. Millen used it in his column. Didn't say where he got it, but it was one of those situations that didn't leave much room for doubt."

"Your friend made it clear it was off the record?"

"It was understood, my friend said."

Ariel grimaced her skepticism. "I'd have to believe Rob's smart enough not to renege on that sort of agreement, not if he wants to keep making a living."

"Oh, I don't think Millen's got a lot to worry about on that score, but you're right. I shouldn't have repeated the story, having just one side of the picture."

Ariel narrowed her eyes. "Was that an object lesson?"

"I've got dogs to walk," Charles said with a glance at his watch. He stood up. "To answer your question, I didn't make the story up."

"Then thanks for the warning," Ariel said. She smiled. "Lucky I ran into you."

"You believe in luck?" Charles snapped the lid closed on his lunch box. "I don't. Not in luck or coincidence. Everything happens, I think, according to a plan. Things happen for a reason."

After lunch Sunday Ariel left to drive south, alone except for Jessie and the cat carrier, from which she heard nothing more stimulating than an occasional scratching.

Laya would be having a second interview at the school the next day. Hattie was, as promised, staying with her. Ariel had to go back to work.

The drive was long and boring. More than once she questioned her sanity in making a thirteen-hour round-trip over one weekend. "But," she told Jessie, "I didn't expect to be doing the second leg solo, did I?" Jessie didn't argue, though she looked a little hurt to hear that Ariel considered herself unaccompanied.

"And," Ariel said, "Laya's going for a dog." That alone had been worth the trip. "If she's dead set on getting on with her life as is, she might as well do it right, right?"

And, although she didn't mention it to the shepherd—she'd hardly verbalized it to herself—Ariel had expected to stay longer. She'd had the half-baked idea she'd be calling the studio to announce that she had a hot story working. Leads that demanded immediate follow-up. She'd be needing a crew to fly up any minute. Hadn't happened.

If it was even possible to learn about the Pink Lady patients, Ariel could do it as well from L.A. as in person. Meantime, Rob—for better or worse—was on the scene, and far more involved than she'd originally intended.

Miraculously, the big time crunch on his Columbarium book seemed to have gone away. Although she couldn't figure just why, he wanted in on every aspect of the investigative research. Was he tired of being a columnist? Looking for a career-making scoop?

Or did he smell a second book deal in the making?

Oh . . . my . . . lord! He was after a book. The more Ariel thought about it, the more she was convinced it was true. A true-crime coup. She could see the jacket copy.

Dorothy Thibeau is the widow of a prominent physician. She's socially elite, she's still elegant at sixty-six—and she's in fear of her life, terrified of a man she claims has killed before, a man she has reason to believe will kill again. Then, suddenly, the lady is dead. A cruel twist of fate—or murder?

Ariel snorted. She'd missed her calling.

The seeds for tragedy had been planted two years earlier, Rob would write. *I was there when the late Doctor Raymond Thibeau took the phone call that . . .* blah, blah, blah. It would be a TV movie of the week. *Had Thibeau made a deal with the devil—and left his wife the lethal legacy?* With Rob's looks, he could even play himself: iron-jawed investigative reporter.

Screw him, Ariel thought. His journalistic scruples or lack thereof didn't concern her; whether he would stonewall her did.

She mulled. She wished she'd thought of the book possibility—and heard Charles Barnes's little story—before rather than after talking to Rob. She hadn't shared every detail, but there was little he couldn't deduce from what she had said.

She'd blabbed her theory that Sis was a hospital patient whose death had occurred and been reviewed by the coroner's office in the winter of two years before. "When I overheard the phone call," Rob had said. He'd jumped on it with both feet. He'd check out coroner reports, he said, for three months before and three after the call. He would also search the archives at his paper for mention of any coroner's investigation that had been challenged, or impacted a criminal case, or otherwise rated ink.

Ariel hadn't given him the financial data—the Thibeau's straitened circumstances or the cash deposits—or Dorothy's comment about suppressed evidence, but if he didn't assume Ariel suspected a bribe, he wasn't half as smart as she knew he was.

Another thing she'd kept back—but this was something he had no way of knowing or inferring—was the one clue she had about the nameless man they sought: that he was heavy into charity. It wasn't much of an ace in the hole.

The last hour of the drive home seemed to take three, and dark had fallen by the time Ariel reached her empty house. She'd seldom felt lonely in it. Tonight she did.

31

LAYA CALLED THE FOLLOWING NIGHT WITH THE GOOD BUT, TO Ariel, amazing news that she would begin training immediately.

"There's a new class starting," she reported, "twenty-eight days. They had a last-minute dropout."

"But I thought there'd be more preliminaries?" Ariel said. "Seeing where you live and whatever."

"I have to move in any case, to a ground-level apartment. We'll work that out." Laya sounded giddy. "But the evaluations they put you through, Ariel! They're like tests."

"And you aced them. Good for you!"

"They give you this harness, no dog, just a harness, and then . . ."

On she went. Ariel was happy to let her.

"One orientation and mobility guy," Laya said, "told me he's never seen anybody more in touch with her body 'and the world around her.' Twenty years of yoga, girl! *And* angels guiding my feet!"

The whole thing seemed like a miracle of timing to Ariel, or maybe, as Laya said, angels had intervened.

Hattie saw Laya settled in at the school, and then flew back to L.A. to pack a box of clothes to ship north.

"Never seen a woman so determined," she told Ariel. "This trainer with a dog stopped next to her? She stuck her hand right out so the dog could sniff it. I thought she was going to faint and fall down, but she did it."

The next day Ariel was scheduled for a quick, three-city trip culminating in Sacramento. She decided to make it four cities. When she'd wrapped her interview at the capitol, she rented a car and drove the hour or so to San Francisco, arriving there early on a cool, overcast Friday afternoon.

It was May Day, one month to the day since Laya was blinded. If the police were no closer now than then to knowing why or by whom the tragedy had been inflicted, at least she had come through it. By dint of will, and in an incredibly short time, she was pulling herself out of the slough. True, during her latest call she'd no longer sounded so excited—she'd sounded subdued—but growing emotional scar tissue would be an ongoing process. A little bolstering couldn't hurt. That, however, was not why Ariel had detoured back through the Bay Area.

It was also one month, nearly to the day, since Dorothy had written her letter. That Ariel had made so few inroads into decoding it was why she was back, and on her way to Marin Hospital.

Thus far, she'd hit a wall in regard to Dorothy's volunteer activities, but one nurse, a woman named Johnson, had sounded promising over the phone. ("Dr. Thibeau's wife? Sure! She was coming in when I got back from maternity leave. She gave me these sweet little booties for Emily—that's my baby girl.") And Nurse Johnson was a devoted *Open File* fan. An in. Ariel had a gut feeling that if she could talk to her face-to-face, she'd get somewhere.

She did.

"Mrs. Thibeau was something else," Ms. Johnson told

Ariel. "Here's this chic lady—she always looked like a million—and you'd think: another do-gooder. No, ma'am.
She really *was* good with patients. Comfortable with
them. Even the terminals."

"Terminals?" Ariel's heart bumped.

"Yeah. We used to give her their names? Kind of nudge
her their way? She'd go in . . . be in with them a little
while, and we'd hear them talking . . . laughing even!" The
nurse shook her head in admiration. "That's one lady I
hated to see quit."

Ms. Johnson couldn't remember any specific patients,
terminal or otherwise, with whom Dorothy had visited,
and she didn't recall ever having a patient called Sis by anyone. She did know that Pink Ladies who worked her floor
worked only one other floor as well: maternity. And she
knew the time span in question. ("Emily's two and a half
now, and I don't think Mrs. Thibeau was around but about
four or five months all told.") She accessed the records for
the two floors for a six-month period. No maternity
patients had expired. There'd been a number of deaths on
her own floor. She printed out the names for Ariel. ("Don't
suppose that violates anybody's rights. They're dead. It's
public record.")

Ariel deleted obviously male patients and called Rob.
He was surprised to hear she was back in town so soon,
but as available as if he had no book in progress and nothing to do but play detective. He suggested they meet near
the hospital, at a café in Ross.

An hour later, over coffee and muffins, they were com-
paring Ariel's list with the one Rob had compiled at the
coroner's office. They found not one but four matches.
During Dorothy's stint the deaths of four third-floor
Marin General female patients had required a coroner's
ruling as to cause of death; one required autopsy. Ariel
nearly choked on her muffin. "Yes!" she exclaimed.

"No," Rob said. "That one, Thompson, came in at two
A.M., and died at six-thirty the same morning 'due to or as
a consequence of drug overdose.' I don't imagine Mrs.
Thibeau volunteered graveyard shift?"

"What about her?" Ariel asked, pointing. "Lorine
Culligan?"

"Brought in comatose. Died three weeks later without
regaining consciousness. And the Watanabe woman's out;
she spoke no English."

Neither of the first three women could have held a discussion of any kind with Dorothy Thibeau.

Ariel read the bad news about the fourth woman herself: Elizabeth Lyons, ninety-four, succumbed to infective
endocarditis; as if she hadn't had enough grief, she'd also
been a victim of advanced senile dementia. Sis, according
to Dorothy, "didn't want to live." Mrs. Lyons may have
felt the same, but it was unlikely that she was capable of
expressing a coherent opinion about it.

"You'd think with four we could get a strike," Ariel
moaned. "In fact, why so many? The druggie I can understand, but why would the deaths of these other three be
investigated?"

Rob, with newfound knowledge resulting from his
research, proceeded to enlighten. Unlike Ariel, he seemed
to be enjoying the exercise. "Keep in mind, what we're
talking about isn't autopsy—the county only does about
three hundred of those a year—but *investigation*. Review.
Which might consist of a phone call and an immediate ruling. Formality, basically."

"Still, I'm surprised—"

"Don't be. California's big on investigation. Probably
leads the nation. We're talking any death from communica-
ble disease, for instance. State law. Hepatitis C, tuberculosis,
endocarditis like the Lyons woman, AIDS . . . Which brings
me to Marin. You've got a false population situation. Any

AIDS victim in the state prison system gets sent to San Quentin, so that increases . . ." Catching Ariel's expression, Rob said, "Round numbers. Fifteen to eighteen hundred people die in the county annually. Eleven to thirteen hundred get reviewed by the coroner." He shrugged. "You asked."

"And I can't tell you how sorry I am that I did," Ariel said.

"I'm assuming you *won't* be sorry to hear what I've got to tell you about Mrs. Thibeau."

"What about her?"

"I talked to her doctor."

"Oh," Ariel said. She didn't much like the news; she'd planned to handle that interview herself. "What did he say?"

"Tell me, what's the bottom line for you in all this?"

"What are you talking about?"

"Since the lady was your friend, I'm assuming your preference would be that no harm came to her, right? You would *prefer* that she died a natural death?"

"Prefer?" Ariel felt her hackles rising. "Well, now, there is no upside, is there? Either way she's dead. But of course I'd *prefer* that she wasn't murdered. Why would you even ask that?"

"Just making sure you're not going to mind losing a story."

"The only thing I'd mind is if somebody got away with killing her. This doctor . . . what did he say?"

"She. Marian Scopes. We're not talking some hack here. She's a well-respected internist. She says her patient died of pneumonitis. Acute respiratory failure due to severe bilateral pneumonitis, if you want to get technical. That's what it says on the death certificate, she told me in terms no way uncertain, and that was the cause of death. She was not pleased to be second-guessed."

"Too bad for her." Ariel heard herself, and was not

pleased with the childish, knee-jerk response. What *was* the bottom line for her in this? Why this compelling (obsessive?) need to delve into a death no one else seemed to regard as anything but sad?

It wasn't that she coveted a story; she didn't give a rip about the story. So what was it? Some kind of mental drill? A righteous game of Clue?

The letter wasn't an adequate reason. Dorothy must have written it in some dark moment and put it aside, in time thinking better of mailing it. She had not sought Ariel's help. She had not waited, frightened and in vain, for a response. She had been otherwise occupied when Alice Manning helpfully dropped that envelope among several (probably bill payments) into a post office box. Otherwise occupied? Right. She'd been busy dying.

True, the timing of her death seemed questionable. Was it? Dorothy hadn't been a young woman; she'd been nearer seventy than sixty, beaten down by worry for her husband, and by grief at his death. Her resistance was low. She'd gotten sick. She'd been diagnosed by a competent professional.

Okay, fine, Ariel thought; one fact remained: the dead woman had been her friend.

No. That might be a fact, but it wasn't true. Whatever conversations had taken place between herself and Dorothy Thibeau two years before, whatever meeting of the minds might have occurred or bond forged, they were not friends. Ariel did not know the woman. If she didn't remember her, she didn't know her. Simple as that. Dorothy was a stranger.

"Ariel?" Rob said.

Ariel, please call me. The last line of the letter, mailed by Dorothy or not, wouldn't go away. She might have been a stranger to me, Ariel thought, but I wasn't a stranger to her. She considered me her friend.

"Hello?" Rob poked her arm.

"*What?*"

"Let's make sure we're on the same page, okay?" His eyes on Ariel, Rob took a swig of coffee. When he'd set the cup down, he said, "You haven't laid it out, but clearly you think Mrs. Thibeau was eliminated because she knew too much. And what she was supposed to know is that her husband fixed an autopsy ruling, right? You're assuming he took money to misrepresent findings or to keep quiet about some incriminating item of evidence or whatever."

"So?"

"One thing I'm wondering is how much thought you've given to that assumption. Thibeau wasn't a forensic pathologist, you know. He was an elected official. He, personally, didn't perform autopsies. He contracted them out. How could he have covered up what some lab might've discovered?"

Ariel had, in fact, given that question considerable thought. The considerable thought hadn't thus far produced an answer.

"Another thing I ask myself," Rob said, "is why you'd think she, Mrs. Thibeau, and not her husband would be seen as the threat. Or do you think he was done in, too?" As if they were sharing a joke, he said, "First the elusive Sis, then Thibeau, then the missus? Wow! Serial killer!"

When Ariel made no response to the banter, he said, "Sorry. Not funny." He did look contrite. Even contrition, Ariel couldn't help noticing, looked good on that face. He sighed. "Okay, let's speculate—I suppose you already have—that the payoff wasn't a one-time transaction. It was ongoing. Say when Thibeau died, his wife meant to pick up where he left off, and the bad guy was tired of being bled. But come on, kiddo, two-plus years later? Why would he wait two years to bump off the Thibeaus? And how did he contrive to make them sick?"

Ariel looked away. At that moment the whole scenario she'd constructed fact by painstaking fact, guess by educated guess, seemed less substantial than a fable. Actually, it seemed pathetic.

"My friend," Rob said, "it don't float. Those people got sick, and they died."

People die. As an argument it was irrefutable. Her grandfather, Ariel recalled, used it. Then he got over his "weak spell." His last word on the subject was, "Let's find out for sure."

"No crime," Rob said. "No story. You're absolved of responsibility."

Ariel's ears pricked. No *story?* "I'm curious," she said. "If you're so sure I'm out in left field . . . Thibeau couldn't have put the fix on a coroner's report, Dorothy imagined Sis *and* her killer *and* the threat to herself, Dr. Scopes or whatever her name is couldn't make a diagnostic mistake—she walks on water, I guess—why were you willing—no, *anxious*—to check into this at all?"

He smiled. "You're curious? Me, too. We're two of a kind in that respect. I had time to give it some serious thought, though. Clearheaded thought."

Ariel considered slapping him silly.

"No offense," Rob said, "but maybe you're too close to the situation to be objective."

"Doubtless," Ariel bit out. "And after all this thought, you're sure it's a nonstarter. No harm, no foul. 'No crime, no story.' So why did we go through that routine with the hospital and coroner's records a while ago?"

"Because I want you to be sure, too."

"Really? Why?"

"Because she was your friend. Why do you think?"

What I think, pal, Ariel said to herself, is you want me gone. "Tell you what," she said. "I'll do what you did. I'll give it some *clear*headed thought."

32

IF ARIEL HAD COUNTED ON A VISIT WITH LAYA TO COUNTERACT her joyless meeting with Rob Millen, she was in for a let-down.

It was a little after four when she arrived at the school. Assuming that her friend would still be busy—in a class or involved with a trainer—she checked in at the desk.

"She's in her room resting," the receptionist told her after making a phone call. "Hasn't been feeling up to snuff, they said."

Laya's room, Ariel learned, was in the "new" dorm, the school's most recent addition. She parked beside the imposing old structure—the Manse, as the PR director Frank Trout fondly referred to it—and, despite some concern over Laya, found herself grinning. It had been over-cast all afternoon. Now a great cumulonimbus cloud had stolen in. Ominous and dark, it loomed behind the white gingerbread bulk of the building as if it had been ordered by special effects. *Last night I dreamt I went to Manderley again*, Ariel refrained from saying out loud.

Inside, she saw what Trout meant about the dorm having been remodeled and adapted to be user-friendly. Handrails had been fitted to the walls of the long hallway. It was wide and unobstructed, all doors safely closed. The floors were a dull finish so as not to reflect light into the eye; there were no rugs to become tricky obstacles. When Ariel looked into the common room, she saw that the furniture was pushed against the walls; nothing lurked to attack an unsuspecting shin. The corners of tables were rounded.

From phone to vending machines, Braille labels were

affixed to everything. Beside them were regular labels in
large print. Like the room numbers, which were three-
dimensional and oversized, they were in consideration,
Ariel guessed, of students with residual vision. The doors
were painted in bright primary colors, probably for the
same reason.

The building's interior retained little of the exterior's
nostalgic character, but it was immaculate and practical.

Laya didn't answer her knock. When Ariel called out, a
moment passed before she heard a faint "Come in."

"It's me—Ariel," she said. "I hear you're under the
weather."

Laya lay on the made-up bed with a sweater over her.
"I'm all right," she said. She didn't look it. "Where'd you
come from?"

"Sacramento and points east. I came to invite you out
for dinner."

Laya groaned.

"What's the matter?" Ariel asked, alarmed.

"The thought of eating. Thanks anyway."

"Your stomach's upset?"

Laya interrupted herself mid-nod, scrambling from the
bed, and hurriedly feeling her way to the adjoining bathroom. The sounds Ariel heard from behind the closed door
made her feel distinctly nauseated herself. She looked
around. It was a small but efficient room. One single bed,
one upholstered chair, a desk with a phone. Braille numbers.
Again, no rugs. On the floor beneath the built-in vanity was
an empty metal bowl, waiting to hold water for the dog that
would eventually move in. There was a hook screwed into
the wall above the bowl, a tie-down, Ariel supposed. Sliding
glass doors led to a small patio with a white resin chair, and
beyond that was a grassy plot. She heard water running,
and, shortly, Laya emerged looking as if she'd been run over.
"Flu?" Ariel asked.

Laya sat, cradling her belly. "It comes and goes."

"Something you ate?"

"Maybe."

"Or nerves?"

"Nerves?"

"About the training? The dogs?"

"Haven't had much contact with them so far, but . . ." Just then, oddly, as if she'd forgotten whatever she'd been about to say, Laya lifted her face. Her head swiveled, a small slow arc. Maybe it was the conversation they were having, but she made Ariel think of a dog scenting the air.

"What are you doing?" Ariel asked.

"It's just . . . Is it cold in here to you?"

"No. Look, I'll go and let you rest. I'll come by tomorrow. Is there anything I can do? Anything I can bring you?" Laya seemed not to hear. "Hey, Laya?" Ariel asked.

Laya turned to her. If the woman were sighted, one would have said she stared blankly. "Sorry," she said after a moment. "What did you say?" Ariel repeated the questions.

"Thanks, no."

Ariel hesitated at the door. "Should you see a doctor?"

"There's one here. I saw her already." Laya was curling back into a fetal position. "Go in peace but go away."

The group of students Ariel saw on arriving at the school the next morning included Laya. They worked on a grassy expanse at some distance. Ariel watched. The trainer seemed to have assumed the role of the dog. A nervous-looking woman had hold of his harness. Ariel heard her yell "Sit" loudly enough to make every dog in the county drop to its rear.

She'd come back later, Ariel decided, or call. She was returning to her rental car when she saw Charles Barnes get out of a well-broken-in truck.

"Morning, Charles!" she called out.

"Well, hello!" His weathered face creased in a smile. "Have you moved up here permanently?"

"What? And give up L.A. smog? Never trust air you can't see, I always say." She waited while he approached, his lunch box and a sturdy leather leash in hand. "We've got to stop meeting like this," she said. "Every time I come out, here you are."

"It's Saturday morning. I volunteer Saturday mornings. Some people go to gyms. The dogs work me out."

There was a small awkward moment, the kind that can happen when two people feel amiable, but have little groundwork yet for conversation. "Well, I'm—" said Ariel. "I see your friend is—" said Charles. Ariel laughed. "Can I go with you while you exercise the dogs?"

The first one he was assigned was a young yellow Lab. Charles hooked on the lead. The dog had plans to travel. Three dogs later Ariel was panting, and glad to sit down. They settled on the same bench as the week before, and, again, Charles shared his good coffee. "How long have you been doing this?" Ariel asked.

"A few months. How long have you been doing what you do? Investigative reporting, I mean."

Thinking about yesterday's dead ends, Ariel's mood slipped. She found herself growing irritated all over again. "Too long or not long enough, I'm not sure which."

Charles eyed her over his cup. "Work's not going well?"

"It's been suggested that I might be deficient in the perspective department. That in regard to a particular . . . investigation, I'm 'too close to the situation to be objective.'"

"This investigation—I'm gathering because you're here—it's local?"

Ariel nodded.

"Not Dr. Thibeau?"

"Mr. Barnes?" a female voice called.

The woman was on her way into the administration building. She was white-haired, solidly built, in her mid-sixties. Her shirt bore the school logo. She shielded her eyes with the flat of her hand, squinting against the sun. "I thought that was you," she said. "How're you doing?"

Charles smiled and waved.

"A girlfriend?" Ariel teased. The woman had looked at least ten years older than Charles.

He turned sunburn pink. "Just an acquaintance."

"I bet lots of female acquaintances wouldn't mind being more."

"That one's husband might mind. Where were we?"

"Where I remembered your advice about discretion."

"I gave you advice about discretion?"

"About knowing the facts before you start spouting off."

Charles laughed. "Good girl! So, tell me about your friend. How's she adjusting?"

"Sorry to say she's had a bug or something. But she must be better today. She's out with the other new recruits."

"Maybe just tired? Training's strenuous work in every respect, including physically."

"Could be. Laya's not all the way back yet."

"Back?"

"From the trauma of losing her sight. Normally, she's in prime physical shape. She's a yoga teacher."

"Yoga? I thought that was more a religious thing. Metaphysical or whatever."

"There's nothing metaphysical about being able to maintain a handstand for ten minutes. She can. But, yoga aside . . ." More for shock value than for any good reason, Ariel said, "The lady does have a certain . . . knack, shall we say?"

"How's that?"

"Her talents do not *exclude* the mystical."

"She reads tea leaves or something?"

"Or something, yes. Don't laugh. I'm serious, actually."
A little ashamed of making chitchat at her friend's
expense, Ariel said, "Laya's what you might call a sensitive."

Charles's eyebrows rose, and then came together. "I'd
be willing to, but I don't know what that is."

"She's very attuned to . . ." What? Ariel asked herself.
How to do Laya's ability justice without making her
sound like a cuckoo, or a witch? "She has a way of knowing things," she told Charles as she'd told Hattie. "Things
she has no explainable way of knowing. She senses them
or feels them. Dreams them sometimes."

"Like, she can tell the future?"

"And see the past."

"I can do that," Charles said. "It's not second sight, it's
hindsight."

Ariel shrugged good-naturedly. "'Skepticism,' somebody said, 'is a hedge against vulnerability.'"

"You believe in this?" Charles abruptly asked.

"I've seen it."

"How?"

"Does she do it? I don't know."

"No, I mean you've seen it how? What, specifically,
happened?"

Ariel thought for a minute. Now that she'd touted
Laya's prescience, she felt compelled to trot out a persuasive example. There wasn't a plethora to choose from;
Laya didn't pop out revelations like toast from a toaster. "I
did this *Open File,*" she said. "A woman's killed, her body
dumped by the highway. Her car, a Jag, is found racked
up in a town about sixty miles away. Her husband's
nowhere to be found, but his blood's on the car seat—"

"I saw the show," Charles interrupted. "The husband eventually turned up."

"Nearly a year later, right."

"He told a convincing story."

"I didn't believe it."

"That was obvious," Charles said. "Hope you don't mind my saying so, but you went after him like it was a personal vendetta."

It had been. The man claimed they'd been carjacked. He'd been struck on the head, he said, and everything after that was a blank. Ariel was convinced, by personal experience more than the pending insurance claim, that he was a fraud. She was mad as hell that he'd use amnesia; his kind stole credibility from anyone unfortunate enough to genuinely suffer the illness.

"You remember," she said, "how, supposedly, he'd wandered around all that time, taking odd jobs, never knowing what had happened or who he was? He'd only then regained his memory?"

Charles nodded. "He looked sincere. I felt bad for him, I remember."

"Yeah? Well, what you don't know and what we didn't know when we did the show is that just two months after the murder, he spent a night in a mission on the other side of the country. That night he slipped up. He used his real name, the name he supposedly didn't remember until months later."

"What's this got to do with your friend? You're not going to tell me she saw that in a burning bush or some such thing?"

"The day after the show aired, Laya and I had lunch. The segment was still on my mind. There had to be something—I just knew it—that the cops and my people had missed. She could see I was nutso. I told her why. 'This man,' she asked me at one point, 'did you say his name was Jackson?' It was Bertulucci, I told her, and raved on.

"Unbeknownst to me, the man who ran the mission had seen the show and recognized Bertulucci. He'd called the police."

"And? I don't get what—"

"The man who ran the mission was named Jackson."

Charles opened his mouth, and then closed it. It was taking him a moment to assimilate the information. To credit it. "Did you ask her where she came up with the name?"

"Sure I did! She said it 'just came to her.'"

Frowning, Charles turned toward the knoll where Laya and the other students worked with the trainer.

"I know!" Ariel laughed. "Believe me, I argued coincidence, too, then and other times. I don't fight it anymore. Who knows? Maybe we're all born with the same ability. Some of us just forget how to pay attention to it."

Charles didn't look convinced. In fact, he seemed lost in troubled contemplation. Perhaps, Ariel thought, he was one of those people who don't like having their certainties upset. Then she saw that what he was looking at was his lunch pail. "Would you like to share a sandwich?" he asked. "It's turkey."

He wasn't disturbed about her story at all, Ariel concluded; he was ready to eat, and didn't want to be impolite.

"Hey," she said, "why don't you save it? If Laya's up to it, I'm going to take her to lunch. I'd like it if you'd come, too."

They ended up eating à deux.

"Sorry your friend didn't feel like coming along," Charles said over soup in a café he'd recommended. He blew steam from his spoon. "You're worried about her, aren't you?"

Ariel nodded. "She felt okay while they were working," she said, "but when she went to her room to wash up, she started feeling dizzy." Ariel crumbled a cracker into her soup, which had obviously been made with canned vegetables. It was inexpensive, though. She wondered again if Charles was an eccentric miser.

"Shouldn't she see a doctor?" he asked.

"She did. The staff doctor examined her thoroughly. Couldn't find any problem."

"But you're still worried."

"That maybe her being here isn't such a great idea after all, and it's because of me she is here. I sort of talked her into—no, that's not true. Laya doesn't get talked into anything she doesn't want to do. But it was my idea."

"And it was a good one. If she weren't here, I wouldn't be having the chance to get to know you."

Ariel smiled. "Except what if she's not ready for this? People who go through what she has can take months just to *begin* to adjust. To work through all the emotional stuff, the anger and grief and so on." And the unresolved fear, she fretted, mentally replaying what had occurred when she'd gone to Laya's room.

Laya had declined lunch. She'd hardly acknowledged the invitation. "Is there somebody outside there?" she'd asked, gesturing toward the patio doors of her room. Ariel saw a gardener clipping a hedge, and said so. "What does he look like?" Laya had wanted to know. When she'd heard that he was a thin, white-haired man in a coverall, she'd been visibly relieved; still she'd asked Ariel to close the draperies.

"I'm thinking," Ariel said aloud, "what if she's moving too fast? Denial, you know? If the scab forms before the wound is healed, so to speak, the wound can fester." Ariel remembered that they were eating. Or he was. "Sorry."

"What makes you believe she's not ready? The stomachache?"

"Do you realize," Ariel asked, "that I bend your ear right off your head every time I see you? You never get a chance to say boo."

"Boo."

Ariel grinned. What was it, she asked herself, about her and older men? She'd felt some of the same sort of affinity with B.F. the first time she met him. Of course, Charles was nothing whatever like B.F. He was as reticent as B.F. was boisterous, as retiring as B.F. was aggressive. He was probably twenty years younger. He was also a good twenty years older than she. Right in the middle between her and her grandfather, just about old enough to be her . . . Soup splattered as Ariel dropped her spoon.

"What makes you believe she's not ready?" Charles repeated.

Ariel wet a paper napkin in the water glass and dabbed at a spot on her shirt. "It's just . . . she's acting kind of funny."

"Oh?" Charles finished his soup.

"She reminds me of how she was right after she lost her sight," Ariel said. "Not that severe—she was totally closed off then—but . . ." She thought about it. "Detached. When I was with her yesterday evening? She drifted off. Just for a minute. Same thing a while ago, like I wasn't there. She started . . . I know this sounds strange, but I was talking to her, and she started humming."

Charles set down his milk glass, staring. "She started what?"

"Humming."

"You mean like when you're preoccupied? You might hum a little snatch of tune?"

Ariel shook her head. "I mean like when you're all by yourself, and it was no tune I ever heard. It only lasted a few seconds, but I'll swear she didn't even realize she'd done it."

... receive one message of conversation for because they were jealous of a colleague or superior. Unlike, or just plain eager to gossip, there were, ironically, a lot of people who, when it came to sharing certain answers and frustrations, and with little more than token questions or ...

33

AS LONG AS SHE WAS IN THE BAY AREA AND OF NO USE TO Laya, who wanted only to sleep off her grippe, Ariel was determined to make hay on the Thibeau front. Ready to ride at the drop of any suggestion of new information, she started making calls.

Who knew, she asked herself, what Marian Scopes, Dorothy's "well-respected" internist, had really said to Rob? Ariel wouldn't know anytime soon; Scopes was not on call that weekend. "The doctor," she was informed by a phlegmatic answering service (or a recording; Ariel wouldn't swear she was talking to an actual person) "is away on vacation. Do you have an emergency?"

She ground her teeth, left a message, and called the coroner's office. Amazingly, she did find a clerk at work. He'd been employed for two weeks. "Thibeau?" he asked. "There's no one here by that name." Perhaps she could call back on Monday?

Her fingers tapping against the phone, Ariel thought over her next move. As far as she knew, Rob hadn't talked to Ray Thibeau's doctor, and, while she'd never felt that Thibeau's death had been anything but natural, she figured a few questions couldn't hurt. Alice Manning supplied the oncologist's name. He practiced in San Francisco. When he returned her call two hours later, he'd just come out of surgery. He was tired, grumpy, and suspicious.

Some people were astonishingly forthcoming when *Open File* staff came calling. Intimidated, or flattered to be consulted, or titillated to be in on something important, or craving the release of confession (or because they were jealous of a colleague or carrying a grudge or just plain prone to gossip; there were as many reasons as there were human frailties), they would volunteer answers and gratuitous information with little more than token questions of their own. Ariel never failed to be amazed by it. Thibeau's doctor wasn't one of those people.

"What exactly do you want to know, Ms. Gold?" he asked.

"According to Raymond Thibeau's obituary," Ariel said, "he died of liver cancer?"

"I didn't read the obituary, and he was not under my care at the time."

"But he had been diagnosed by you two years before?"

"And his medical records were subsequently forwarded to Johns Hopkins, where he was treated. I suggest you call there."

"Can you give me the name of his doctor there?"

"It's in my files. I'm not in my office."

"Did you and Doctor Thibeau, by any chance, have any relationship beyond the professional? Were you acquainted—"

"I was once seated next to him at the opera. He fell asleep. Which one of those shows did you say you're with?"

"*The Open File*. Just bear with one last question? During the time you were his physician of record, did he say anything to indicate he might be in any kind of personal difficulty?" Anticipating his response, Ariel added, "Other than his medical problem?"

"Ms. Gold, in my opinion programs such as yours are a boil on the arse of civilization. I don't read tabloids, I don't watch them, and I certainly don't contribute to them. Good day."

"My show is not a tabloid," Ariel said to dead air.

A call to a woman who cleaned house for Dorothy, and to a neighbor, and to her hairdresser (all of whose names Ariel had also gotten from Alice) were less contentious but no more productive. When you hit a wall, Ariel advised herself, stop banging your head against it. She showered, changed, and went out to dinner with a photojournalist she knew who'd relocated to San Francisco.

There were two messages waiting when she got back to B.F.'s house at eleven.

The first was from Hattie, who was sitting Ariel's own house, and who, Ariel imagined, remembered the days when long-distance calls were a big deal. She sounded as if she'd been reading from notes she'd made beforehand, and the entire message came in under six seconds. "The dog's fine. The cat's fine. I called to talk to Laya. She sounds funny. What's the matter with her? I gave a detective named Neely the number there at the house."

The second was from Max Neely. "You asked about an assault homicide a while back? James Price? Heard something you might be interested in. You'll owe me. How about you bring me back a case of Sonoma white. Anything expensive. Oh! If you don't get this tonight, don't call tomorrow. I'll be off, and I'll be asleep."

Ariel found him at his desk.

"Why was it you were asking about Price?" was the first thing he asked.

"Just fishing for a story," Ariel said, "that didn't pan out." She thought she sounded offhand.

"Yeah, sure," Max said. "One of eight million stories in the Naked City."

"What?" asked Ariel, who'd still been in diapers when that particular TV series had last aired.

"You know something about this Price that's interesting enough to make the tube?" Max wanted to know. "Because I sure don't. You could put his face on just about any bum's sheet you want to pull. Only thing he had going for him I know of was his uncle."

"What uncle?" Ariel asked.

"Who you didn't know about, obviously, so what's the deal?"

"What uncle?" Ariel repeated.

"Billy Williams. Used to be assemblyman. Crooked as they come, not that that was any impediment to his political career. He was greatly admired even after he went away for misuse of city funds."

"That could explain why the story made the *Times*," Ariel deduced aloud.

"What story? What are you talking about?"

"Price being related to a somebody. That wasn't mentioned in the paper, but I guess it's why his beating got picked up at all. It was hardly newsworthy otherwise."

"I believe you just made my point."

"Max, upfront: I can't tell you anything that will help you guys make whoever killed Price."

"Can't or won't?"

"Can't." Even Laya couldn't help, Ariel thought, and she was there when it happened. "I haven't even discussed this thing with anybody since . . . what was his name? The cop on the case whose name you gave me?"

"Eddie Rials."

"Right, him. And that was two weeks ago. See? I had the mistaken idea, just for a minute or two, there might be a story, but I've moved on."

"Okay. Since you're so uninterested, sorry I bothered you."

Max listened to thwarted silence for a few seconds before he laughed, and said, "Okay, I was playing ball this afternoon with some of the guys. Rials was one of them. He got to talking about a job he's on, an old woman done in her kitchen. Her house, Gold, backed up to the alley where Price got taken apart. Bedroom window over-looked it."

He waited, letting Ariel connect the dots. "She saw the beating? She was a witness?"

"She's the one who called in. That endangered species known as a good citizen."

And now she was dead? Ariel went weak in the knees. How could she have let herself grow lax about the fact that someone deliberately blinded Laya? Had beaten James Price to death? Had called her own home not once but several times? Had the telephone number and, maybe, the address. Might have been there, lurking outside.

Thank God Laya was four hundred miles away from Los Angeles!

"You still there?" Max asked.

Could she be traced here? Was there any way?

"You want to hear the rest of this or not?"

"Please," Ariel murmured.

"Yeah, okay, this old lady was a tiger, Rials said, a self-appointed, one-woman neighborhood watch. When she called about Price? She stayed glued to the window, God love her! Described the action like a play-by-play."

"The men who did it, did she describe them?"

"What makes you think there was more than one?"

"I just assumed, I guess? Price was beaten so badly . . ."

"With a tire iron. Put one person, even a little bitty person, on the business end of a tire iron, and that's all she wrote."

"Max! Could she describe him or them or not?"

"Them. Two. One big, one medium, both black. The big guy was bald as an egg, she said; more likely a shave-head. He was behind the iron. Medium was holding the victim, and not doing too good a job of it. Too busy yelling at Big."

"Yelling what?"

"Witness couldn't hear. Price got loose or fell. Dropped like a stone. Medium knelt down—"

"To help Price?"

"Probably to go through his pockets. When they heard the sirens, they took off in different directions. Medium passed under the old lady's window. He was early twenties, close-cropped hair, dressed interchangeably with every other punk on the streets. She looked at the mug books. He was definitely not there, she said, which, in itself, tends to set him apart from the norm."

"How about a sketch? Did she work with an artist?"

"Yeah, but she couldn't make up her mind. Rials said they ended up with Mr. Generic."

"What about the other one?"

"Big Baldy she got less of a look at, but she put him at older. She did give them a few maybes from the books. They were hauled in for a lineup. She said no cigar, but, she said, she thought she'd recognize him if she saw him again."

"Oh, Max! Do they think that's what happened? She saw him—saw them—and . . ."

"Not much doubt about it. Rials came on late the night she was killed, and saw she'd left a message he should call her. By then—this was hours later, I guess—she was history."

"When did this happen?"

"The end of last week, I think? About a week ago."

"How was she . . . ?"

"Same as Price. Bludgeoned to death."

In the first minutes after she hung up from talking to Max, Ariel was numb. Then frenetic. She couldn't get the image of the valiant old woman out of her mind. She paced. She pictured Carrie Murphy—that had been her name, Max said—pictured her seeing the two men on the street, or in a store, or by her doorstep. Hanging out. Catching the old woman looking at them, the look too piercing, lasting a few seconds too long.

She sounded like a sharp cookie, but she'd been in her seventies, Max said. She must have given her recognition away. Maybe she'd been foolhardy enough to say something. Maybe they knew her reputation in the neighborhood, and knew where she lived, and put two and two together. Or they'd left town after the assault on Price, and only then returned, and only then heard about Mrs. Murphy's cooperation with the police, her statement that she'd recognize the assailants if she saw them again.

Maybe, maybe, maybe. There was no maybe about the poor old woman being dead, and no coincidence.

For an hour longer, Ariel sat curled on a sofa in the living room. The carriage house where her bed and her things were seemed like a long and vulnerable journey away. The house felt strange to her, and very large and empty.

More than once she picked up the phone to call Max back. She debated calling Hattie to tell her to get out of the house. Put the animals in a kennel or in the car, and either way, leave. Drive north. Drive anywhere.

It was one in the morning by then.

"This thing doesn't make sense," Ariel said aloud. She'd said it before, several times. It had been a solid month since Laya's blinding. A month since Price died. Punks capable of that fatal assault and of maiming Laya wouldn't kick back and wait to see what she might do. If they knew where to find her, they wouldn't make the occasional polite phone call just for the fun of it. Punks capable of killing one witness would have no compunction about killing two. So they didn't know where Laya had been, and they didn't know where she was now.

Ariel plumped the sofa cushions, turned off the lights

inside, and turned on the ones outside. She peered through the glass pane of the back door. After thoroughly scrutinizing every shadow on the path between house and carriage house (silly or not, she did it), she made the short trip uneventfully.

She was brushing her teeth when a thought occurred. Laya had been face-to-face with her "Mr. X," with Max's "Big." How could she have failed to notice that he was hairless? Even if she hadn't absorbed his size or his age, surely a gleaming bald skull would've made some impression?

Shows what sheer terror can do, she concluded.

Carrie Murphy was not a subject Ariel had any intention of broaching with Laya. But when she saw her the next morning, sitting on the lawn outside her room, absorbing the spring sunshine and looking normal (and feeling somewhat better, she reported), Ariel reconsidered. The victims were stacking up. Two people were dead now. True, Laya had been nearly destroyed by guilt over one. On the other hand, she'd made her feelings about being protected, about being lied to by omission, all too plain.

Mrs. Murphy hadn't gotten as good a look at X's face as Laya had. Even if Laya didn't register what she saw, she saw. What if she could remember? What if she could help? The decision, based on all the facts, should be hers. If she could do anything to make things right with herself, Ariel mentally argued, to redeem her shattered image of herself, wouldn't that help her to heal? Wouldn't that be the only way she ever would?

She was still vacillating when Laya yawned, apologizing. "I didn't get a lot of sleep last night," she said.

"Your stomach?" Ariel asked, willing to be distracted.

"Not so much that . . ." Laya picked absently at the

grass. Her attention seemed to have drifted, and Ariel feared she was going into another of those odd reveries. "I had this feeling," Laya said. "Oppression, like the walls were closing in on me."

"Your room *is* smallish," Ariel said.

"The size of the room wasn't the problem."

"At least you have it to yourself. I toured the other dorm; they're two to a room in there."

Laya smiled a little. "I can't see if the room's small or not, you know. Anyway, it must have been nearly dawn when I finally gave up and went to the lounge. I was listening to TV when, next thing I knew, I was sleeping like a baby. I had a dream . . ."

"Oh, no!"

Laya laughed, grimly. "Don't worry, nothing spooky. I've been having some bad ones lately, but this was just an ordinary dream. I was teaching again, working, and, you know, I don't even know if I could see? That didn't seem to enter in. Isn't that strange? But I felt . . . I was me again. At peace. It was good." She sniffed at a blade of grass she'd plucked. "Too bad it was a dream."

Ariel decided to take that as a sign. "Laya," she began tentatively, "remember you said you couldn't describe Mr. X?"

Laya turned sharply, obviously jarred by the question.

"If you could," Ariel went on, "if there were a way to recall what you saw, what you don't consciously remember, would you?"

"What are you talking about?" Laya asked.

"Hypnosis." When Laya stiffened, Ariel said, "Not that it always works. I tried it, in fact, last year, and got nowhere, but it's possible that—"

"Why are you bringing this up?"

"I don't necessarily mean it's anything you'd want to do this minute. But sometime? What I'm thinking is maybe you've skipped a step. Patched the surface without repairing the underlying—"

"Oh, please! No platitudes. Or is that one of your quotes? Do let's hear an inspirational quote!"

"I'm trying to cut down."

If Laya was amused, she didn't let on.

"Snarky," Ariel said. "It was just a thought." Here's another one, she said to herself: you can't go home while those two men are running loose. Abruptly, she asked, "Did he have short hair?"

"Who?"

"Mr. X. Did he?"

"I don't know. I told you. I couldn't see him that well."

"You couldn't tell if his hair was short or long?"

"No."

"Did he have long hair?"

"I don't know."

"Dreadlocks?"

"No. I don't know."

"Was he bald?"

"I don't know, I said!"

"Why don't you know?"

"*Because he had on a cap!*" Laya shouted.

Ariel exhaled.

Laya put her hands to her mouth, as if to seal it shut. After a moment, through her fingers, she said, "I didn't know that. I swear! I mean I didn't know I . . ."

"But you do know. It's in your head." But was it in there *straight*? "If the light was adequate to see the cap, you saw more." How could Carrie Murphy have seen a bald head, Ariel wondered even as she talked, when Laya saw a cap? Could Mrs. Murphy have had her men mixed up? Was shave-head "Big" holding Price, and "Medium" the one wielding the tire iron? "What kind of cap was it?"

"Tight to his head," Laya whispered. "What do they call those knit . . . watch caps?"

"Dark colored or light?"

"Not light."

Possibly, Ariel thought, X—Big—had lost the cap. Mrs. Murphy watched until the sirens sent the two men fleeing. Laya was long gone by then. The cap could at some point have fallen off or been knocked off in the struggle. Maybe the police had recovered it. She touched Laya's arm. "Can you remember anything else?" She almost said *Close your eyes and think.* "Think hard," she said.

Laya was already shaking her head. "That's it. That's all."

"Witnesses under hypnosis have been known to recall cars they saw parked at a crime scene, even partial license plate—"

"No."

Laya made to stand up, to escape, but then she dropped back to her knees, sitting on them. "Why did you ask about the hair? Why hair specifically? Did you know about the cap?"

"No."

"Then why?"

"I just started at the top. I would've worked my way down if you hadn't—"

"Ariel, I want the truth!"

"There was another witness."

"Another . . ." Ariel watched Laya sort through the significance of the statement. "But that's good," she said. "That's good news! Then they don't need me. They never did." She frowned, still sorting. "This witness, where was he? I didn't see anybody else."

"She. An old lady. She's who called nine-one-one."

"An old lady," Laya repeated. "It took an old lady to have the guts to call—"

"Laya, her house overlooked the alley. She saw the attack from her window. She was safely inside, no doubt with the doors locked and the lights out. The men couldn't see her. Mrs. Murphy didn't have a bloody tire iron waved in her face."

"Murphy?"

"That's her name."

"Not Carrie Murphy?"

"You know her?" Ariel's heart sank. Fervently, she wished she hadn't mentioned the name, that she'd never brought this up at all.

"I know *of* her. Everybody does. She's a local legend. One tough old bird. Did she get a good look? Could she describe them?"

Ariel told her what Mrs. Murphy had seen.

"His head was shaved?" Laya asked.

"Most likely, Max said."

"The cap fell off after I ran away," Laya reckoned as Ariel had. "Big and bald," she repeated the secondhand description. "Not much to go on, is it? God! A month, and those animals are still free!" She crossed her arms over her chest, agitated, holding herself. "You're right. I ought to try hypnosis. At least try."

"You're sure?"

"I've got to! If I could add even one thing to what Mrs. Murphy saw!"

Laya's next-door neighbor, a student Ariel had noticed before, came out onto his patio just then. Laya's head turned sharply at the sound. When he bumped into his resin chair, the twin of the one on Laya's patio, and it scraped across the concrete, she gasped.

"It's okay," Ariel said. "It's just the fellow from the room next to yours. Are you sure about the hypnosis?" she asked again.

Laya nodded.

"I'll arrange it," Ariel said.

"The police have doctors they work with, right?" Laya asked, sounding anything but eager. "I'll go back to L.A. and—"

"No! You don't want to drop out of training." Ariel sounded flustered even to herself. "I'll find somebody up here." Discreetly and privately, safely away from L.A. "If it doesn't pan out, you've done what you could, and you haven't exposed yourself to—"

"Why don't you want me to go back?"

"You said it yourself: those animals are still free."

"And Mrs. Murphy called the cops—like I should've— and she worked with them, and she's right there in the neighborhood, more vulnerable than I'd be, and she's healthy, right?"

Ariel hadn't given enough consideration to how observant—how attuned—even a blind Laya could be.

"*Right?*" Laya repeated.

34

THERE'D BE TSUNAMIS IN THE SAHARA, ARIEL VOWED, BEFORE SHE ever meddled in anyone's life again. Professional prying, fine. That's what she was paid for. If somebody got hurt, it was in the exalted name of freedom of the press. They probably deserved it. (One could rationalize that they deserved it.) But unsolicited kibitzing? Never again in this lifetime.

The conversation hadn't ended as badly as it could have. Laya had appeared almost calm on learning that the only other known witness to Price's murder had herself been murdered. "They killed her," she'd said. It had been a statement.

"It looks that way," Ariel had agreed, dying inside herself.

That was, apparently, all Laya could absorb. To ask how Carrie Murphy met her death hadn't seemed to occur to her. Ariel was grateful for small favors.

"Arrange the hypnosis as soon as you can," Laya said. Then she'd groped her way to her feet. At the door to her room, she'd paused to add, "Whatever happens, you were right to tell me." Ariel had not been relieved by the post-script.

The first thing she did on reaching B.F.'s house was call Tara Castanara. "Sorry to bother you on Sunday," she told her assistant, who immediately said, "Hold! My tomato sauce just reached simmer."

"Two things," Ariel said when Tara came back on the line. "One, do you remember the name of that really sharp San Francisco psychiatrist we used as a consultant—"

"Morris," Tara said, "Alvin. No, wait . . . Albert. What's up? You finally flip out?"

"Yes. Two, I'll be here at least through tomorrow." When they'd discussed the schedule for the following day, Ariel checked the directory for Albert Morris's number. She got his service. The psychiatrist was at a conference in Toronto through Wednesday.

She had the home number for Dr. David Friedman, her friend who'd once, briefly, been her therapist. She called, thinking to get a referral. His wife informed Ariel that Dave, too, was attending the Toronto conference; he was en route as they spoke.

B.F., who seemed always able to provide an appropriate expert, or someone who knew someone, couldn't be raised.

Ariel recalled that there'd been a psychiatrist (or psychol-ogist, she couldn't remember which) at the benefit dinner the week before. Rob Millen had introduced her. She called

Rob, who was out. The efficient Alice Manning, who probably kept a Rolodex listing every local physician, cross referenced by specialty and location, was equally out. "'Doesn't anybody stay in one place anymore?'" Ariel muttered. She considered the Yellow Pages. Then she thought of Charles Barnes. He was in the book. When he, rather than a machine, picked up, Ariel was momentarily startled.

"I don't recall a psychiatrist or psychologist at the dinner," he replied to her question. "Is your friend in, ah . . . need?"

Ariel found his delicacy sweet. His fumbling inquiry also gave her an idea: the appointment she was trying to arrange could serve more purposes than one. Laya was not in tip-top fettle. Once a shrink was found, Ariel asked herself, should she put a flea in his or her ear? Mention the patient's reveries? The, perhaps, psychosomatic cramps and dizziness? The humming thing?

She recalled her solemn vow. It wasn't an hour old; the ink wasn't dry on it yet.

"Laya's fine," she said firmly.

"Of course," Charles said. "Good."

"No, really, she's better today. In fact, there've been some new developments, *positive* new developments we need to explore, and as quickly as possible."

"So how can I help? Is it that particular psychiatrist you're trying to find, or any one?"

"What we're in the market for is a hypnotherapist."

"Hypnosis?" Charles said, his tone suggesting he thought he'd misheard. *To cure a stomachache?* Ariel imagined he was asking himself. Whatever questions he might have, he didn't voice them. He'd make some calls, and get back to her. "Leave it to me," he said.

In under two hours he called back with a name, a number, and a tentative appointment set up for the following morning.

"This is a good man," he assured Ariel. "I can vouch for him."

"He must also be your dearest friend," she said, somewhat dazed. Charles had more in common with B.F. than she'd given him credit for. "How on earth did you reach him on a Sunday?"

Charles gave a pleased chuckle. "Do call him first thing in the morning to confirm," was all he'd say.

"So, Ms. Gold, I'm clueless," said Dr. Jonathan Schell, whom Ariel called at 8 A.M. He talked fast and sounded young. "First thing I want to know," he said, "is this for your show?"

Ariel hesitated. Did he envision pontificating on camera? Or did he share Raymond Thibeau's oncologist's opinion that (certain) TV newsmagazines were "a boil on the arse of civilization"? She wanted this appointment. "If it were for the show?" she hedged.

"I'd go buy a new tie."

"If it weren't?"

"I'd take off the one my wife made me wear."

"Save your money," Ariel said. She heard a sigh, which could indicate disappointment or relief at shedding the tie, and Schell said, "Bring me up to speed on your friend. All Dad told me is she's vision impaired and seeks hypnotherapy."

"Dad?"

"Yeah."

"Charles Barnes is your father?" Ariel asked.

"Who's Charles Barnes?" Schell asked.

As soon became clear, "some old friend of Dad's" had contacted Schell Senior, a retired psychiatrist, who then called Schell Junior, whose calendar was clear because he'd planned to be at the Toronto conference. "But my wife's started to get pains, two weeks early, so here I am. It's our first, and I better warn you, if she calls, even if it's during the session, I'm outta here. That said, your friend . . . ?"

Ariel made an effort to begin at the beginning: that before the loss of her sight, Laya had witnessed a criminal attack. "It was dark," Ariel said, "and Laya—"

"When was this?" Schell had interrupted.

"A month ago."

"And loss of sight occurred . . . ?"

"Almost immediately."

"Ah!"

"'Ah'? Oh, you're thinking trauma. No, the blindness is definitely physical. What I—"

"The attack . . . a mugging?"

"Fatal beating."

"Survivor's guilt?"

"That's not the issue at the moment."

"Then?"

"Dr. Schell, bear with me here, all right?"

"What? Oh, sorry. It's the baby watch. Jitters. Speak."

"It was dark. Laya was scared. She got a glimpse of one assailant's face, but she doesn't consciously recall what he looks like." Because of her present vulnerable state, Ariel explained, her friend wished to know whether she was capable, in fact, of providing information to the police before subjecting herself to what might be a pointless ordeal.

"Thus the hypnosis," Schell concluded.

"Thus."

"I see, I see," Schell said. "Well, let's go for it. We're on for eleven?"

Schell's office was in the basement of his residence, a rambling stone-and-shingle house in Kentfield. The access street, Sir Francis Drake Boulevard, was bumper to bumper, and Ariel, who'd planned to be early, delivered

Laya on the dot of eleven. As she led her friend down
steps to a discreetly signed side entrance, she noticed ruffled pink curtains in a ground floor window. The immi-
nent offspring, she deduced, was anticipated to be a girl.

The hypnotherapist was older than he'd sounded,
probably forty, with a fringe of curling hair, a slight frame,
and restless hands that seemed to have their own agenda.
Now they grasped and pumped hers as she made introductions, and then gently took Laya's as he steered her
into his private office.

Ariel waited alone in the reception area. She couldn't
hear even a murmur. If she could have gotten hold of a
glass, she would have applied it to the wall. She had
flipped through the available magazines, and read a
series of framed *New Yorker* cartoons on one wall, and
studied photographs of an attractive brunette (pregnant
in several shots) nearly covering another wall before she
settled down and went to work on her laptop and cell
phone.

At one point she thought she heard a short, strangled
cry. Her ears strained. The *whirr* of her computer was loud
in the room. The walls were too well insulated; she heard
nothing else. The traditional fifty minutes passed, and
then an hour, and still there wasn't a stir from the inner
office.

"Have you ever done this sort of regression before?"
Ariel had asked Schell that morning on the phone.

"The very same, as a consultant with the local law.
Simple procedure. Not to worry."

At twelve-fifteen the door opened, and Schell ushered
Laya through. He looked intrigued; she looked shaken.

"How'd it go?" Ariel asked.

"Interesting," said Schell. "Very." He patted Laya's hand
before giving it up, like a doting father relinquishing his

daughter at the altar. "Think seriously about it," he said to her.

Ariel had made out a check in the amount they'd earlier discussed. She gave it to him. He hardly noticed.

When they were back in the car, Ariel asked, "Think seriously about what?"

"He wants to see me again. To keep seeing me."

"Why? What happened?"

There was a noticeable pause before Laya answered, "Nothing enlightening about Mr. X."

"Nothing enlightening for an hour and a quarter?"

"We weren't on the subject all that long."

"If you weren't on that subject, then what—"

"And Schell was on the phone part of the time."

"On the phone to . . . ?"

"See if my symptoms are all in my head."

"Symptoms? Laya, what—"

"I had stomach cramps again yesterday afternoon. The staff doctor did more tests. I told Schell that."

Ariel pulled to the nearest curb and cut the engine. "Are you all right?" she asked.

"The truth? I don't know what I am except tired."

"Can you tell me about it?"

"About going back to that alley and Mr. X?"

"If that's where you want to start."

"I can tell you it was a waste of time."

"Schell wasn't able to put you under then?"

"I didn't say that, but it wasn't like I thought it would be. I wasn't asleep, but I could see the place, the alley, and him—that man, his eyes—in my mind. It was hard to get past his eyes . . ." Laya shifted her shoulders, shivering, as if something crawled between the blades. She took a folded paper from her pocket. "Here," she said. "Schell wrote down what I said."

The notes were hastily scrawled. They weren't exten-
sive. *Five eleven to six feet tall?* Ariel read. *Big upper body. Legs
short. Knit watch cap black or navy. Clothes too.* "His clothes
were all dark?" she broke off to ask. "Completely?"

"So? What difference does that make at this late date?"

"But you saw no colors?" Ariel persisted.

"What?"

"No blue, no red, no green. That doesn't tell us who he
is, but it might suggest who he's not: a gang member."
Getting no response, Ariel said, "Making this a personal
civilian attack." She knew she was grasping at conjectural
straws. "What's this about his mouth?" she asked, reading
the last of Schell's note.

"Something was wrong." Laya touched her own
mouth, above the upper lip and slightly off center. "Here.
Split, or . . ."

"Cut, you mean? Hurt in the struggle with Price?"

"What if it was? It would've healed by now, so what've
we gained . . ." Laya stopped, thinking.

"What?"

"I don't think it was bleeding. It wasn't a wound."

"A scar, you think?"

Laya inclined her head, infinitesimally. "Maybe."

"Now we're getting somewhere!" Ariel encouraged.
"What else? Jewelry? A watch or ring. An earring?"

"Not that I saw. I would've said so."

"A nose stud? Or a tattoo, or—"

"No." Laya raised her hand, and let it fall again.
"Hypnosis or not, Ariel, how well could you describe a
man you saw in poor light—glimpsed for a few seconds—
over a month ago?"

It was a fair question. "Don't underestimate the scar,
though. That's more than the police know, and it must
have been prominent to show in that light." But how best
to pass on that information, Ariel asked herself, and the

rest of it? An anonymous phone call? A letter? She put Schell's notes in her purse. Then, remembering, she asked, "How did your stomach problems come up?"

There was a palpable hesitation before Laya said, "I told Schell about them, that and other things. Symptoms."

"And?"

"He asked a lot of questions, mostly the same ones the doctor asked yesterday."

"And decided the problem's not organic? But what made you bring that whole thing up?"

"I didn't. It came up."

Ariel nodded. Caught herself. Said "Yes?"

"A nightmare I've been having. I had it again, there. Worse."

"A nightmare?" In Schell's office? "I don't understand."

"Well, I can't explain it."

"Then describe it."

"You might as well try to describe hell." Laya strove for a normal, matter-of-fact tone. "It was when he was bringing me out of the trance. I was under, but it was shallow, like being in two places at once. I was in the alley, in the dark, but I knew I was really in the office, on the sofa, in light I could sense." She paused, as if she were reliving the sensation. "I could hear him plainly. He was saying, 'You're perfectly safe. There's nothing to be frightened of.' Repeating phrases like that, soothing. Then, right then . . ." Pressing her fists tight against her middle like someone who's taken a blow, Laya asked, "Did you ever fall and get the breath knocked out of you?"

"Not that I know of."

"All the air's sucked out of your lungs. You can't breathe. You know you're going to die if you can't get air. It was like that. No air. It's displaced by panic." Laya swallowed, steadying herself. "All of a sudden it wasn't just Schell talking anymore. It was a woman, too. *You're all right. Now come on, everything's fine,* she's saying. They're both saying. And the light was gone. No office, no sofa. A bed. Bedrails." Ariel saw that beads of sweat had formed at the other woman's hairline. "I hear Schell, but his voice is . . . like it's overlaid by the woman's. My stomach hurts, but that's not even . . . What's awful is I can't think right." A sweat drop broke and trickled. "My mind won't . . . mind. What I see doesn't make any sense."

Ariel took Laya's hand. It was icy.

"Nothing will stay what it is. I mean, everything keeps changing. Melting into something else. You can't trust anything, ordinary things, to be what they are."

Despite the determined calmness of the recitation, Ariel was beginning to be uneasy. "Maybe you shouldn't—"

"No, listen, so you'll know what I mean. This cat's on my bed? This little gray cat. Just a cat. It's purring. Warm. A skinny little thing with a sweet face. It curls around—you know how they do, making themselves a place to nap? I see this splotch of sunlight, and the cat finds it, and I feel happy. I try to reach for him, but I can't. For some reason I can't move. I'm being held down some way. I strain with all my might to move. Then he sits up, on his hind legs, and I know he's not a cat at all. And there's not just one. I can feel the *plops* as the others jump onto the bed. I can feel the weight on my legs. I don't know how many. Their teeth are bared, and they're coming after me, and there's nothing I can do to stop—"

Ariel, who had until then been rapt, recoiled. "Laya, no," she said. "This is nowhere we need to go."

"And then they're on me. I'm begging, *Let me up! Help me!* And I keep being told—this woman keeps saying—'There's nothing here, baby. You're imagining things.' But the rats are real. They're there. Feeding on me. On my belly. They're devouring my eyes. This woman, who I believed was kind, won't help. She's laughing at me, and I'm humming—"

"Humming?" Ariel said, caught despite herself.

"At the top of my lungs. She's laughing, and I'm trying to block out the noise. Block it all out. I want to be gone. To not exist. To be dead and safe."

"Laya, let it go! Stop!"

Laya flinched. She exhaled forcefully, and she was vehement when she said, "I'm all right. I am. I'm here. I'm not there."

Ariel patted Laya's hand awkwardly, casting about for something pacifying to say. She wasn't a "Now, now, shhh!" sort of person. She wished she were, but she wasn't. "Is 'there' always the same place?" she asked. "I mean is the dream always the same?"

"Close. That one was the worst."

"Did you tell Schell all this?"

"Yes. I don't know. Enough, I guess. He asked me . . . he wanted to know if I'd ever done hallucinogenic drugs."

"Yeah?" Ariel said. Damned good question. "Have you?"

"It wasn't a bad trip, Ariel. I'm not tripping, and I'm not *afraid* I'm losing my mind. I *had*. For those few minutes, caught in the hell of that dream, I am insane."

Ariel didn't need convincing. She debated returning to Schell's office, demanding some antipsychotic drug, or at least an explanation. She eyed Laya, who looked not calm, certainly, but rational. Nothing close to rabid. She'd had a nightmare, that's all; a particularly virulent nightmare.

"Fearing madness and recognizing madness are very different things," Laya continued, removing her hand from Ariel's, tucking both hands into her armpits to warm them. "Sort of like," she said, "it's not paranoia when you are, in fact, in danger."

Lordy! thought Ariel; are we back to that? But of course

we are; we never left it. She thought the dream through. The bit about the eyes was obvious enough. That Laya felt victimized, helpless to fight the predators she believed were out to get her . . . that fit. But where had all that other stuff come from? How that phantasmagoria tied in, Ariel couldn't see. It was borrowed horror.

Could the dream be prophetic? Or a memory? Ariel grasped at that straw. "Were you ever seriously sick as a child?" she asked tentatively. "Running a high fever? Delirious?"

"I'm not a child in the dream," Laya said grimly.

"True. But I wonder . . . who's the woman?"

"The woman? It beats me."

"She calls you 'baby'?"

"Did I say that? Then I guess she does."

"Could it be . . . I mean, when did you lose your mother?"

Laya laughed. It was shockingly close to a giggle. "You're wild, you know that? Always with a theory."

"What's wrong with the theory?"

"Ariel, she's not my mother."

"If you have no idea who she is, how do you know she's not your mother?"

"Well, to start with, my mother wasn't Caucasian."

"This woman is white?"

"As snow, and you know what else? So am I. I'm not just a crazy woman. In this nightmare, Ariel, I am a *white* crazy woman."

35

THEY HAD LUNCH OUTDOORS AT A BAYSIDE CAFÉ. IF LAYA'S
appetite wasn't robust, she seemed eased by the sunshine
and the normalcy. She refused to talk further about her
problems. When she asked about the status of the
Thibeau affair, Ariel recognized it for the diversion it was,
but she went with the flow. Laya listened with her old,
active attentiveness. She was relieved, Ariel sensed, to get
back to their familiar dynamics. Frankly, so was Ariel.

She was reluctant to let go of the moment and oddly
uneasy about returning Laya to school. Luckily, a class was
in progress, and a staff member took charge. Ariel was on
her way to her car when she was intercepted by a short
bespectacled red-haired woman she hadn't seen before.

"I wondered if you were *that* Ariel Gold," the young
woman said, and introduced herself as Dr. Gayle Baker.

"'That Ariel Gold'?" Ariel repeated.

"When I saw the name Laya supplied for In Emergency
Notify."

That fact shouldn't have come as a surprise, Ariel supposed, but it did. "I'm me." She smiled. "Is there an emergency?"

"I hope not," the other woman replied seriously, "but
let's talk a minute."

She led the way to a bench. It was the same one Ariel
had twice shared with Charles. Ariel sat; Dr. Baker
remained standing. "Laya seems to be getting a handle on
her dog fear issue," she said, frowning as though this were
a negative rather than a positive development. Those vertical lines between her eyes, Ariel suspected, would soon

become a permanent fixture on the pale young face. "She told you about that?" Ariel asked cautiously.

"We have to know everything possible about our students, any custom need, physical *or* emotional. She's not the first to arrive scared of dogs, and she won't be the last." Dr. Baker plunged her hands into the pockets of her white coat. With the stethoscope dangling from her neck, she looked like a girl playing doctor. "Does Laya have any history of emotional problems?" she asked.

"Surely that question's included in the *confidential* information you get from potential students?"

"It is. Laya said no. However . . ."

"Well then," Ariel said, "except for being maliciously blinded by an unknown person who's still roaming the streets, I guess she's carrying no baggage at all."

The doctor frowned again, and her fair redhead's skin mottled. "I'm not gossiping, Ms. Gold. We know the facts about your friend's tragedy, of course, and I'll be frank with you as I was with her. It's my opinion she rushed into training prematurely. She would have been better served to take time to adapt to her impairment and, ideally, to have had psychological counseling prior to coming here. However, she is here now."

"Given your opinion, why is she?"

"Because not everyone agreed with me. Since she is here, I want to see her succeed. I also want to be accurately informed. It's my job to be, and I take it seriously."

Unchastened, Ariel said, "What makes you ask about emotional problems?"

"Dizziness and stomach pains, nausea, can be symptomatic of a constellation of disorders. We don't have all the test results back—we haven't yet made every possible test—but, thus far, there's no indication that the symptoms are organically based. I suspect they're psychogenic."

"Why?"

"Psychological in origin and manifest primarily in the abdominal region."

"I didn't say what, I said why?"

"Certain observations. Our newly arrived students are often anxious, naturally, but Laya's anxiety doesn't appear to stem from the demands of training. I notice that as long as she's working, she seems well. It's when she's alone, resting in her room, for example, that the symptoms tend to present."

The woman might be inexperienced, Ariel thought, and stiff as new shoes, but she kept her eyes open.

"She's suffering from insomnia," Dr. Baker continued. "She's on edge. When I was examining her, there was a brief but pronounced lapse of attention focus. This morning I got a call from a psychiatrist, a Dr. Schell, whom she's apparently elected to consult. First I knew of it."

"That appointment concerned a matter unrelated to her . . . symptoms." Ariel realized as she said it that it was a gross misrepresentation. True, the purpose had been to retrieve details about the men who'd killed Price, but what accounted for Laya's bouts of nervous prostration or whatever *except* that incident?

"The questions he asked me," Baker said, "were directly related to her symptoms."

"I'm not saying she didn't mention them to Schell. Seemed sensible, as long as she was there. You don't have a problem with a student seeing a psychiatrist?"

"On the contrary." The frown lines creased deeply and earnestly. "I trust she'll continue to seek treatment."

Was that an implied threat? Ariel wondered—a condition of Laya's being allowed to continue here? If she opted not to see Schell, would she become a training school washout? Considered, like the "career change" dogs, to be temperamentally unsuited? Too sensitive for the program?

"Dr. . . ." Ariel's inclination was to barrage Baker with

protestations of her friend's normal, native tranquility; how courageously she'd coped with a disaster that would have brought a weaker woman to her knees; how gamely she'd placed herself square in the middle of a place populated by a lifelong nemesis, the dog. But the truth was: Ariel was as concerned as this woman about her friend's emotional health. Also, she'd sworn off interference. "Dr. Baker," she said, "I trust she will, too, but that'll be up to her."

Ariel stopped by B.F.'s for her belongings before heading for the airport. The answering machine had labored in her absence. Rob Millen's had been the first call. "Returning yours from yesterday," he'd said. "Guess you've gone home. I'll try you in L.A."

Ariel almost didn't recognize Henry Heller's voice. Had it only been a couple of weeks since she'd seen him? "Tara gave me this number. Are we still on for the big do?" He sounded crazed. "The premiere issue hits the newsstands Friday. It's . . . well, judge for yourself. I've got a copy in my palsied hand. If you don't find me in the office, check the nearest nuthouse." Ariel had forgotten the launching party for *Newsfront*. Was it tomorrow night? Ashamed, she made a note to check with Tara about the date and time.

The phone machine's last offerings were a solicitation message, a hang-up, and a return call from the office of Dorothy Thibeau's doctor, Marian Scopes.

Uncharacteristically, Ariel debated following up. She was in a hurry. She'd had her fill of doctors. She had deliberately omitted any mention of Dorothy's name when she'd left her own name and number Saturday, and she didn't look forward to questioning the "well-respected internist" who, according to Rob, "was not pleased to be second-guessed" about her diagnosis. Ariel dialed, and, to her surprise, was put right through. Bracing herself for, at

best, the sort of arrogance she'd just experienced at Gayle
Baker's hands, or, at worst, fireworks, she asked Dr.
Scopes if Dorothy Thibeau had been her patient.

"Yes," came the pleasant reply with a trace element of
some accent. (South Africa? New Zealand?) "Are you a relative of Dot's?"

Dot? "No," Ariel said, "a friend."

"Well, join the club. She was one marvelous gal. What
can I do for you, uh, forgive me. The name again?"

"Ariel Gold." Ariel waited for a reaction. There wasn't
one. "We'd been out of touch, and I just heard about her
death. It was a shock and, basically, I just want to know
what happened. Can you take a minute to talk about it?"

The doctor, who sounded as mature and relaxed as
Baker had been green and tense, said she could take whatever time it required. "I just came back from vacation, and
I set aside today to catch up on paperwork. I do hate
bloody paperwork!"

"Then tell me in detail," Ariel said, hardly believing her
luck.

Scopes freely related that "Dot" had phoned for an
appointment, complaining of low back pain, but then, presumably feeling better, she'd canceled. "You know the tale
about the shoemaker's children? Well, dear, Dot Thibeau
was a classic case. The wife of a doctor, and she was the
world's worst about going to see one. Ray used to drag her
kicking and screaming to her annual checkup."

By the time Scopes had actually examined her, being
called by a concerned neighbor two days later, Dorothy
was verging on critical, suffering from a variety of rapidly
escalating symptoms: high fever, sore throat, cough,
severe shortness of breath. "Wish she'd come in when she
first called, but we did everything we could, dear, I assure
you of that."

"Dr. Scopes, what was the cause of death?"

"Pneumonitis. You want the whole menu? Bilateral pneumonitis. Respiratory failure. Cor pulmonale . . . that's a heart condition resulting from lung disease."

"Which resulted from . . ."

"Can't tell you that," the doctor said firmly. "Sorry."

Uh-oh, thought Ariel; here comes the stonewall. "Why not?"

"Because I don't know. She died of pneumonitis, presumably viral in origin, but I can't name the specific virus. Nor could the pathologist to whom I referred the case postmortem."

"You did what?"

"Reported the case."

"She was autopsied?"

"In the event we were dealing with something infectious, or, well . . . At any rate, no luck."

"Or well what?"

"Pardon, dear?"

"You said in case you were dealing with something infectious 'or well . . .'"

"Oh, that. Nothing at all, really." Marian Scopes sighed. "Dot was in a mighty weakened condition when I finally saw her. Agitated, poor old girl. Imagining things, I knew, but I don't like loose ends, so . . . Excuse me a minute, dear."

Ariel was put on hold. She was chewing her knuckle when she was retrieved. "Sorry," Scopes said. "I hope I've been of help?"

"No! I mean yes, but wait! You said that Dorothy . . . Dot was imagining things. What kinds of things?"

"The mind works in mysterious ways to protect us from the unacceptable: the fact that disease and tragedy—*mortality*—doesn't discriminate. Even the charmed aren't immune."

"I don't understand."

"Well, you knew Dot. She was one of those people who, no matter how little care they've taken of themselves, has never been sick a day. Luck of the draw gene-wise. She didn't exercise? Stayed slim and fit. Liked her wine? Not a quiver of the liver. A closet smoker, I fear. But . . . the chickens will come home to roost."

"What was she imagining?" Ariel prompted.

There was a meditative silence before Scopes said, "I fancy she needed a grander nemesis than some piddling, invisible virus, so she created one: something she could put a name to and blame."

Ariel's heart picked up speed.

"She got it into her head," Dr. Scopes said pityingly, "that a *person* was after her."

The three-thirty shuttle to L.A. left without Ariel. So did the one after that. By then she was sitting on the porch of B.F.'s house looking at but not seeing the view. Her notes of the conversation with Marian Scopes lay in her lap.

The doctor hadn't heard her patient name a particular individual by whom she felt threatened, but Scopes would have discounted an accusation had she heard it. Dorothy had been heavily medicated and, thus, disoriented. Pressed about Dorothy's imaginings, Scopes had been brusque: "Insisted to a nurse that her food was poisoned." Since feeding had been intravenous, such ravings naturally reinforced the assumption that she was delirious.

Couldn't she remember anything else? Ariel had prodded. Any conversation at all?

Well, yes, Scopes conceded, if one counted talking to people who weren't there: a brother, she seemed to recall—some relative, at any rate. "It's not uncommon, dear, in the last days."

Ariel thumbed through her notes. The words swam.

She wasn't crying, not really; but there was a slow leak
from eyes and nose that wouldn't seem to stop. She
thought of the photo Dorothy sent B.F.: a dressed-up trio
at some forgotten party. They'd looked immutably carefree. When she'd seen the picture, Ariel remembered,
when she'd first put a face to the name Dorothy, she'd
been struck by her looks. Sleek blond hair, the blond
admittedly doctored in her later years. Dark eyes lively.
Bare shoulders elegant.

That vibrant, sophisticated woman had been reduced
in the end to frightened confusion. To the indignity of
strangers monitoring ingestion and egestion, impersonally
and methodically keeping her clean, drugging her for pain,
misunderstanding her garbled attempts to communicate.

"Did you say your name is Gold?" Dr. Scopes had at
one point suddenly inquired. "Now I wonder . . ."

What? Ariel had asked.

"It was toward the end. Dot was wanting something. I
got the word 'gold,' and guessed it was her wedding rings,
that we took for safekeeping, you know. You don't suppose she was asking for you?"

Ariel fervently hoped she had only been asking for her
rings.

The autopsy, she had learned, had been limited, a post-
mortem performed at the hospital in the presence of the
coroner who had replaced Raymond Thibeau. The objective had been to identify the microorganism that led to
death. The examination was conducted by a nonforensic
pathologist. No toxicologist had been involved.

"If there were no microorganism," Ariel had asked,
"would the autopsy have shown that?"

Just because it couldn't be identified, Dr. Scopes had
answered patiently, didn't mean it wasn't present.

"Purely for argument's sake," Ariel said, "let's say a person *were* poisoned. Would that show up in what you say

was a 'medical' as opposed to a 'medical-legal' autopsy?"

Heavy silence followed. "What an extraordinary question," Marian Scopes had commented, "for a bereaved friend to be asking."

There'd been no lessening of courtesy, but the lines of communication had been cut. It was only later that Ariel thought to pursue the comment about the imaginary relative with whom Dorothy carried on a conversation. Dr. Scopes could easily have misremembered that it was a brother; it might have been "sister" she heard. More accurately, it might have been Sis.

36

"WANTED TO LET YOU KNOW I HAD A LONG AND INTERESTING conversation with Dr. Marian Scopes." That was the entirety of the one message Ariel left on Rob Millen's machine. She called several times before leaving for the airport. He either wasn't home, wasn't taking calls, or had Caller ID and wasn't taking *her* calls. When she checked L.A. and found that he had not tried to reach her as promised, she suspected the latter.

Almost certainly, he'd lied about having contacted Scopes.

Two inquiries about a particular deceased patient within one week, Ariel reasoned, would surely have rated comment from the talkative doctor. She would have mentioned to Ariel that her call wasn't the first; she would have been surprised, or curious. She would have asked questions. Furthermore, Scopes had been away on vacation the previous week when Rob supposedly made contact.

In any event, he misrepresented Scopes. She was not defensive about her diagnosis. She was the opposite of recalcitrant. Only when Ariel asked (what even she had to admit was) an off-the-wall question, had the woman balked, and she'd been leery, not annoyed. So Rob, at the least, equivocated, obviously to steer Ariel away from Scopes. Why? Ariel could see only one reason: he wanted Dorothy's doctor to himself. He'd been unable to reach her last week, and he didn't want Ariel talking to her before he got a chance to.

What else had he been up to?

It was a good bet that he knew about the limited post-mortem on Dorothy. He would have thought to check that out while doing his research at the coroner's office. He conspicuously omitted mention of it. What would his next move be? To gather enough evidence for exhumation and a full autopsy? Maybe he had enough. Maybe the wheels had already been set in motion. By the time Ariel turned in her rental and walked to the boarding gate, she had him digging up the body himself. She was convinced that he was sitting on reams of information. Undivulged from the phone conversation he'd overheard between Raymond Thibeau and whomever. From interviews with local people she didn't know existed. From coroner's records. What he'd shared had been selective. She was a fool to leave town now!

She had no choice. There was a taping scheduled for early the next morning that couldn't be postponed. She'd already tried.

Ariel was too late for one shuttle and early for the next. She called Rob from her cell phone and hung up, again, on his machine. She paced and then settled. When a rambunctious toddler spilled soda on her shoe, she managed not to behave unpardonably. Heh-hehing reassurance to the apologetic mother, she got up to pace again. A nice-looking gray-haired businessman who'd caught the action smiled sympathy over the top of his *USA Today*. He reminded Ariel of Charles, whom she really should call to thank.

He answered breathlessly. "Just walked in," he said. "I've been thinking of you."

"Oh?" Ariel glanced at the departure monitor. Her plane was being delayed by fifteen minutes. "Terrific!" she muttered.

"Pardon?"

"Nothing." Ariel sighed and sat, a safe distance from the toddler.

"You sound upset. Are you okay?"

"I'm fine. I wanted to thank you for Schell. For getting him to see Laya."

"How'd it go?"

"He wants to work with her on an ongoing basis." Ariel slipped off her shoe and wiggled sticky toes. "To exorcise her phantoms."

"Phantoms?"

"Figure of speech. Or maybe it isn't. Laya's having a recurring nightmare, and, let me tell you, it is spooky."

Hesitantly, Charles asked, "This nightmare . . . does it have anything to do with that humming business you mentioned?"

"Did anybody ever tell you you're a major-league good listener? Matter of fact, it does."

"Whew!" Charles commented. "What on earth?"

"Yep. In this nightmare . . ." Ariel hesitated. But, she thought, if she wasn't at liberty to talk about Laya's original purpose in seeing Schell, there was no reason not to discuss this other, tangential thing. Charles was a good sounding board, and, lord knows, she had plenty of time. "Seems in this nightmare she's in a hospital—in a bed with rails at any rate." Ariel thought back. Laya had said she was being held down, that she couldn't move. "Maybe restraints, too. Judging by the state of her mind, she needs them. She's insane."

Charles, apparently, was at a loss for words.

"In the dream," Ariel clarified hastily. "Her mind plays ugly tricks on her. Like, she sees a cat that's transformed from a harmless kitty into a rat. And then one rat becomes a whole swarm, and they're attacking her stomach and her eyes, and she's . . ." Ariel made a face, her skin crawling. "You don't want to hear all this. And it is, after all, just a dream." She laughed a little, uneasily, into Charles's continued silence. "You still there?"

"Just trying to take it in. It may be just a dream, Ariel, but it seems to me that it's encroaching pretty worryingly on this lady's life."

He was as concerned as she was, Ariel thought, marveling at his empathy for a woman he'd never met. He made a good point, one she hadn't thought through at all. What did it mean when physical and mental afflictions from a dream, behavior from a dream, leached into one's waking hours? Could a dream take you over? A dream that you inhabit, and experience, and yet on some level isn't about you, doesn't include you, that features people you don't even recognize?

"You wouldn't have brought this up," Charles pointed out, "if you weren't taking it seriously. Your friend wouldn't have brought it up to Schell if she weren't taking it seriously, and he wouldn't be suggesting therapy if *he* weren't. Does she think . . . is your friend afraid she actually is losing her mind?"

"No. She's quite clear on that."

"And you? What do you think? You didn't say how she lost her sight, but I gather she's been through a lot. A terrible ordeal. Are you worried that she's becoming, ah, unstable?"

Ariel considered how to answer. The dream and the odd behavior were, unquestionably, the products of a disturbed mind. Disturbed as in unsettled, or disturbed as in cracked? She remembered Laya's icy hands, the sweat breaking out on her forehead. The inexplicable quirk of the dream's participants being white. She also remembered that Laya was able to laugh about that. "She's troubled," Ariel allowed, "but I believe she'll be okay. She seems able to distance herself. Like when she described this nightmare? It was almost as if she were reporting what was happening to somebody else."

"Are you sure that's good? Don't they call that dissociation?"

Before Ariel could answer, Charles said, "You're not thinking this dream has some real meaning, are you? Beyond what it says about your friend's state of mind, I mean? You're not thinking it's some kind of prophetic vision or whatever?"

Ariel had considered it, and said so. "I also wondered whether it could possibly derive from the past. 'All the things one has forgotten scream for help in dreams.'"

"From the past?" Charles repeated. "From *her* past, you mean?"

"Yes, a buried memory. But she says not."

Charles let out a long breath. "This is all way out of my league. Is that all, I hope?"

"Pretty much. Just . . . she feels the physical pain, the cramps and all, but that's secondary to the pain—pain's too mild a word—it's secondary to the torment of a mind out of control. She can't trust what she sees. Everything keeps changing, she said, into something else."

"It sounds to me like she's hallucinating."

"And all she wants is to be . . . How did she put it? To be 'dead and safe.'"

After a long moment Charles said, "All I can say is it's a

good thing you got Schell involved. You've got a scary situation."

Just then Ariel heard her flight being called. "How so?" she asked distractedly.

"'*How so?*' No offense, but are you joking? Am I hearing things, or did you not just say your good friend wants to be dead?"

"That's in the *dream*, Charles."

"Uh-huh. But you're the one who puts stock in dreams."

37

"INTERESTING THING," MAX NEELY TOLD ARIEL LATE THE NEXT morning in her office. He waved an officially bagged envelope in the air in front of her face.

The envelope was white, legal size, and—Ariel craned to read—addressed to Eddie Rials. Since it wasn't the one she had sent anonymously to the detective in charge of the James Price homicide, she wasn't disturbed by Max's suggestive tone, but merely curious. She indicated the chair across from her desk. "Sit," she said. "What's interesting about it?"

"Seems we got another witness to the Price beating," Max said, lowering himself into a chair. It complained of his solid weight. "Shy type, though. No signature except 'a concerned citizen.'"

Ariel managed, barely, not to react. *Another witness who'd signed his letter the same way she'd signed hers?* Even as she took in that unlikely detail, something Max said pricked. She was too busy appearing merely curious to pursue the thought. "Let's see," she said, reaching.

"Sorry. Evidence." Max retracted the envelope but kept it in tantalizingly plain sight. "I can tell you what it says though. The one who did the beating, 'Big,' as I refer to the larger of the two gentlemen, is described as a black man six feet tall. Short legs, big upper body. Wore a navy or black watch cap and dark clothes."

Ariel's phone rang; she ignored it. This wasn't making sense. That wasn't the type of envelope she'd used, that wasn't her printing she'd glimpsed, but he was quoting the essence of her letter.

"One other thing," Max said. "He has a prominent scar on his upper lip."

The light bulb clicked on. Ariel relaxed. She would've said, "Good try, but isn't entrapment illegal?" except she would've been taking the bait by asking the question. "You generally shlep evidence around with you?" she asked. "Seems kind of careless." The envelope, Ariel would've bet, was empty; the address on it, she'd further bet, was penned by Max himself, on a hunch. He crossed his legs and waited, leaving her plenty of room to talk. "Come to think of it," she obliged him by asking, "what are you doing with it anyway? It isn't your case; it's Rials's."

Max lifted one shoulder in a shrug. "Told him to call me if he got anything on this one. Envelope was dropped off at his precinct house last night, by some weird-looking woman."

"Weird-looking how?"

"Oh, kind of scruffy, the uniform who took it said. Hair hidden under a baseball cap. Heavy glasses."

Ariel kept her face neutral.

"And a raincoat?" Max laughed. "Some getup."

The mails would have been safer, but at the last minute Ariel had decided to chance delivering the note. Too much time had been wasted. She'd wanted it in Rials's hands at the earliest possible moment. She wanted the men found and off the streets at the earliest possible moment. She wanted to set Laya's mind at rest at the earliest possible moment. Laya had her worried.

Ariel had called her from the plane en route to L.A. She'd called on landing and again from home before she got an answer. Laya had been subdued. Ariel felt reasonably sure she was tired rather than despondent, but she'd called Jonathan Schell anyway. His machine apologized that he was currently unavailable (the new baby, Ariel surmised) and unhelpfully suggested a colleague in case of emergency, for which Ariel hoped to God Laya didn't qualify.

"But, Max," she said, "it sounds like good information. Don't you think?"

He sniffed. "'Prominent,'" he said.

"Pardon?"

"The type of anonymous letters we get don't usually include words like *prominent*. A '*prominent* scar on his upper lip.'"

"Oh?" What, Ariel wondered, was wrong with prominent? Perfectly good word.

"A typical unsigned communication such as we're accustomed to receiving would just say a *big* scar. If an adjective of more than one syllable should be used, it would likely be crude, a reference, perhaps, to one's female parent."

"Umm," Ariel said. She had debated using prominent; not for the reason Max suggested, but because she couldn't be sure it was accurate. But, she reasoned, Laya wouldn't have noticed the scar had it not been prominent. Behind her bland expression she tried to think if there were anything else Max might jump on.

She'd written the note hurriedly, before she could change her mind, but she'd been cautious. Using stationery from a chain drugstore. Block printing. Wearing rubber gloves. She'd felt ridiculous, like some refugee from film noir, but withholding relevant information about a murderer, the killer of two people and possible maimer of a third, was not an option. Exposing Laya to questioning in her present condition was also not an option.

"Be that as it may," she said to Max, "do you think the information's legitimate?"

He took his time scratching the side of his nose before he said, "The guys found a black knit cap in the alley."

Ariel slowly, quietly, let out a breath.

"Rials didn't know if it was connected," Max went on, "but he figured all along it was."

"Why's that?"

"It was in good shape. A practically new cap wouldn't have lasted one night in that alley. Also, no hairs. Fit with a shave-head wearing it. Plus, there was blood on it. Price's, unfortunately, not the assailant's."

Ariel nodded. "Did you come across anything else?"

"Besides vomit and rat droppings and broken Thunderbird bottles and . . . oh! A partial dental plate. Almost forgot that. So listen," Max said, his expression stern, "you ever spot a bald toothless dude about six feet tall, steer clear."

"It was his teeth? The assailant's?"

"I was kidding. I don't suppose your source noticed if either one of the men wore glasses?"

"My source?" Ariel felt her face warm; she couldn't help it. "What's that supposed to mean?"

"I'm assuming the issue here is protecting your source. It always is with you people."

That stung. Ariel didn't like the feeling of being lumped with "you people," not by Max.

"What I don't get," he said, "is why do you even have a

source with a story like this? It's not a story. News-wise, it's a nonevent. It's a *stale* nonevent. So, obviously, there's something we don't know. What is that, Ariel? And what's the deal with waiting a month to play pen pal?" In a sudden move that caused Ariel to flinch, he popped air from the plastic-bagged envelope, crumpled it, and threw it at her wastebasket. It made an ineffectual missile; it missed the target altogether. "You said you couldn't tell us anything material to this case, damn it! I believed you."

"I'd hope so," Ariel said, feigning umbrage of her own. This being wishboned between two friends was the pits. "I was telling the truth!" She hadn't known anything at the time except that Laya witnessed the beating. Laya couldn't identify the assailants then, and less could she now, unless she could accomplish it by touch. Ariel had personally paid a hypnotherapist to retrieve what memories existed, and what she'd learned, she'd promptly passed on. She'd done all anybody could expect! By the time she got through mentally justifying herself, she'd worked up a nice protective layer of genuine umbrage. "Now," she demanded, as if these unarguable facts had been delivered aloud, "what's this about glasses?"

Max studied his fingernails. "So your source didn't say either man was a four-eyes?"

There was a rap on the door, and Tara stuck her head in. "Gotta go if you're gonna make the flight," she told Ariel. "The crew's meeting you at the airport. I've got your return scheduled at five, in time for tonight." She tossed her hair, today a toxic shade of red, and, with a curious glance at Max, backed out.

"Where you off to?" he asked.

Ariel stopped shoving papers into her briefcase and stared at him. For the space of several seconds she couldn't remember. Santa Fe was next week. Detroit was . . . when? Had she already been there? "Tahoe," she said.

"Poor you!" Max was over his snit. "Hitting the tables?"

"Chatting with a sixty-year-old woman who may have dismembered the choirmaster of her church. Come on. Walk with me to my car, and tell me about the glasses."

They were in the elevator, crunched behind a rowdy party of technicians' assistants breaking for lunch, when Max said, "We picked up a piece of broken corrective lens."

Ariel shifted, breathing through her mouth to escape somebody's lethal dose of perfume. "What makes you think it's not just another piece of garbage?"

"It was under Price, and the glass wasn't scratched up the way it would've been if it was there any length of time. Former owner's nearsighted, by the way. Has an astigmatism, too."

The elevator stopped at the next floor, and yet another person wedged herself in. The doors slid to and then fro, vacillating over whether they could reach each other. Ariel was flattened against Max. Had he been in the elevator alone, it would have been crowded. "Got a partial print," he thought to add, "but no match."

"Eyeglasses," Ariel murmured. "*Spectacles.*" She couldn't reconcile the image. Even rabid killers, she supposed, could suffer from astigmatism. But why hadn't Laya, or Carrie Murphy, seen glasses if either man wore them? Or a glint of reflected light?

"Figure the specs bit the dust early on," Max startled her by saying. "Knocked off like the cap."

"Price would've fought being restrained," Ariel agreed.

"Yeah, though from what I hear, he had more experience taking on women than men."

"Mrs. Murphy saw the smaller man, the one holding Price—"

"Mr. Medium."

"She saw him kneeling down by the body, didn't you say that? Looking for his glasses, do you think?"

"And finding them. Just missed that one fragment."

"Max, . . . she got a fair look at him, right? But she couldn't pick him out of your mug shots? And you got no match on the partial print on the lens?"

"*Exactamente.* No record. A virgin."

The elevator door opened with a *ping,* and the *ping* triggered a memory, and Ariel saw him. Saw the shape of him, the bare bones memory of him.

Laya was right: how well could you describe a man glimpsed in poor light for a few seconds a month ago? Not quite a month. Three weeks. And the light hadn't been all that poor; the hospital elevator had been bright, even if the ward had been dim. Still, there had been time only for a glimpse before the young black man had averted his scowling face, and Ariel couldn't describe him now if she had to. She could only remember being alarmed because there was no one at the nurses' station and no guard outside Laya's door, and the man's behavior had seemed suspicious because he'd come deliberately to that floor, she'd believed, and changed his mind when he'd run into her. He'd scared her, although he'd done nothing more than duck his head and punch a button and wait impatiently to be taken away.

And she'd thought at the time that she'd seen him before.

"I thought you had a plane to catch," Max said, holding the door open. "What're you standing there like a lox for?"

Gazing blankly at the buttons of this elevator, Ariel willed herself to reconstruct the man. He was youngish. Not middle-aged and not a kid. He wasn't Max's "Big"; he was "Medium." Average. Not memorably light or dark. Unremarkably dressed. He'd had on baggy pants, "attitude baggies." A T-shirt? Tennis shoes. And glasses? Yes, and glasses.

"They're going to start charging you rent," Max said. She was the only one left in the elevator. The door was objecting to being held. "Did you forget something?"

Ariel stepped out into the garage. "No," she said. "My van's over that way."

He'd struck her as a student. Bookish, Ariel thought now if she hadn't formed the thought then, because of the glasses. Bad eyes equal a voracious reader equals glasses: a line of reasoning as specious as that killers can't suffer from astigmatism.

The man who'd called her house looking for Laya had been bright. No, that's not what Hattie had said; he'd "sounded educated." And polite. Not the sort of young man to have a police record—or to restrain a man while he was being beaten to death, or deliberately blind someone, or bludgeon an old lady. He'd said he—they—would "follow up" on Laya.

Max stopped her with a hand on her arm. "Where are you going?"

Ariel blinked. They were standing beside her van.

"Space cadet," Max said, shaking his head. He turned toward the exit gate but paused to add, "Oh, Gold, if you should learn anything else? Feel free to drop us a line."

38

DURING THE FLIGHT, ARIEL FOCUSED HER FULL ATTENTION ON prep notes for the Tahoe interview. She worked diligently, then and after she and the crew landed. With only a few months' on-camera experience and no shortage of qualified candidates who'd kill for her job, she couldn't afford to do otherwise. Once the interview was concluded, she

thanked the rather befuddled, white-haired interviewee
(who, in Ariel's opinion, was patently guilty of dispatching the choirmaster she claimed to have loved, but who,
Ariel knew, would look to at least half the TV audience
like a helpless and victimized old lady), and then she
unclipped her microphone, and dismissed the story from
her mind. Back in the air, she focused her full attention on
the man in the hospital elevator.

There was no defendable reason to believe he was connected to Price or to Laya. How many men in the city of
Los Angeles wore glasses? How many visited the hospital
that night for perfectly innocent reasons? He was probably
visiting his ailing mother or his wife, who'd given birth or
had an appendectomy. If, as Ariel believed, she'd seen him
before, there was nothing sinister in it; they'd happened to
visit at the same time before.

Ariel tried to recall Carrie Murphy's description of
"Medium." Close-cropped hair, she'd said. Had the man in
the elevator had close-cropped hair? Perhaps. Ariel smiled
into her hand; she was pretty sure he hadn't been wearing
a watch cap. Mrs. Murphy had placed her man's age at
early twenties; Ariel's impression of elevator man was the
same.

The old woman had worked with a police artist, Ariel
suddenly recalled. The result, Max said, was of little value:
"Mr. Generic." Nevertheless . . . Ariel unhooked the phone
from the seat. Max was out; she left a message asking to
have the sketch faxed to her house. She'd get grief for the
request, she knew—more questions, probably, than the
sketch was worth. Was it generic because Mrs. Murphy
didn't get a good enough look? Or because the man had
unexceptional features? (Ariel had heard or read that one
should be observant of ears, which were often distinctive
and unlikely to be disguised or altered; she felt sure she
would've noticed if the passenger in the elevator hadn't

had ears, but they hadn't stood out, literally or figuratively.) Nothing about his face had stood out; he'd possessed no single trait that struck the eye or lingered in the mind. If only he hadn't averted his face so quickly! Why had he? Because he'd recognized her? Hadn't expected to run into her that late at night? Didn't want to be recollected?

Ariel worried the fragment of memory until she didn't doubt she was embellishing it. It seemed as if no time had passed when the plane began to drop altitude. Through the window Los Angeles hovered in the murky distance pretending to be a legitimate city rather than urban sprawl, the tallest buildings clustered together for moral support as they tempted the seismic gods. The late afternoon sky looked sulfurous, Ariel observed, thick with a smog soup that didn't bear thinking about. She opened her handbag and took out a compact.

Maybe, she reflected, trying to fluff her hair, which was too lacquered to fluff, the man had no ulterior motive for turning his face away. He was upset, worried about whomever he was visiting in the hospital. Or he was antisocial, or shy. A . . . "shy type." She frowned at herself in the mirror. Max had said that in some connection this morning; inconsequential, but it had rung a tiny little bell in her mind.

The guard at the hospital. The phone call he'd taken. The caller who'd wanted to know if Laya would see again. A "shy type," he'd declined to leave his name. They—she, the guard, and the nurse Dinah—had been talking in the corridor outside Laya's room. Dinah had a bouquet, brought by one of Laya's students. Ariel had turned to see her, a plump black girl, barely out of her teens, she'd guessed. A "bit on the slow side," Dinah had guessed. An unkind observation, perhaps, but sound. Ariel could, vaguely, picture the sweet but vacuous face. The man with her—it had been Ariel's impression he was with her—was somewhat older. He'd looked as if he were in a hurry, or had business elsewhere, or simply wanted to be elsewhere. Preoccupied, Ariel hadn't given him a second look. One thing she did remember: the man was scowling.

The same man? That one and elevator man?

Ariel squeezed her eyes shut as the plane touched down. The thump in her solar plexus wasn't from any problem with the landing, which was smooth as satin. The pilot had "greased it."

Was it the same man or not? Images ping-ponged through Ariel's mind. Light spilling from the elevator into the twilight ward, glancing off a pair of eyeglasses. Baggy jeans riding slim hips, the hands beside them clenched like a nervous gunfighter's. A tennis shoe, a squeak of rubber against linoleum. Why had she wasted time looking at a shoe? Why hadn't she studied the face! Had the man with the girl worn tennis shoes?

"Is that fellow with her?" she had asked Dinah, but it was too late; he was already blocked from sight, getting onto the elevator, the same elevator the other man had ridden, looking cornered inside it. Was the damned elevator the only thing that brought the two men together in her mind?

Ariel forced herself to reason.

They had the scowl in common. They shared a certain furtiveness. (Or was she imbuing him—them—with that quality?) They were, she was fairly sure, of an age, both clean-shaven (she was also fairly sure she would have noted facial hair). And (significantly?) she could recall no more of one man's features than the other's. Was that not commonality in itself? Or did the commonality lie in the fact that she'd seen both too long ago and too fleetingly, and neither did one thing to call attention to himself. She couldn't honestly say whether the man with Laya's student wore glasses; she simply couldn't remember. She rather thought not, or she might have recognized him the second time.

She was making up any similarity out of whole cloth.

Maybe she should try hypnosis herself.

Surely the sketch would show her what she needed to know.

If the men were one and the same, he was connected to Laya, through the girl; he knew, through the girl, who Laya was. If he was "Medium," then the identity of the witness to his crime was known to him. Via the facility where the girl took Laya's class, or via the girl herself, he could obtain her teacher's address, follow her, devise a way to neutralize her as an *eye*witness. Via Ariel, whose face was recognizable and whose phone number was listed, he could keep tabs on Laya, could "follow up" her progress.

The hospital visits and phone calls were to check out whether she remained neutralized. Wouldn't that be what they'd do? Check whether she'd regained her sight? What the odds were she could?

Something bumped Ariel's seat, startling her. She surfaced to see the last passenger shuffling from the cabin. Her crew, who'd been seated forward and who'd been playing a video game when last she'd noticed them, had gone. She sighed and reached for her laptop. This lingering alone and bemused in public conveyances was getting to be a habit.

A thought hit. She took her cell phone from her bag. Hoping it was okay to use it on the ground, that she wouldn't scramble radio signals or whatever caused the phones to be banned in the air, she punched in Laya's number.

Dinah had said the flowers were "from the class," but Laya might recognize a description of the girl who delivered them. She would know her name. It was conceivable (Ariel's pulse picked up at the possibility) that she would also know "Medium." *He was with Mary?* Laya might say. *Then you must be talking about John, her guy.* Or fiancé or husband. If Laya did know him, she wouldn't have recognized him in the alley; she'd seen only the dark shape of the man holding Price. Feeling more optimistic than her house of cards warranted, Ariel listened, imagining the ring in Laya's little cell of a room. There was no answer.

There was still no answer when Ariel reached home, arriving to an empty house: no Hattie, no Jessie. Arthur was in residence. He suggested a snack. Ariel, busy dialing Laya's number, didn't oblige. The cat opened his mouth in soundless rebuke, and then leaped onto the sofa to take a fortifying nap. When he began to prepare the cushion to his liking, clawing at the fabric, Ariel snapped at him. He ignored her, choosing an angle of recline that suited, curling himself in a circle just like the kitty in Laya's dream, the sweet kitty that mutated into a swarm of rats. Ariel stared at Arthur, and then through him, at nothing. She'd read somewhere that a pair of rats can produce fifteen thousand baby rats in one year. She shivered. This was not a fact she needed to know. The rings went unanswered. She debated calling the administration offices, the infirmary, the competent Dr. Baker.

Visions preyed: Laya wandering, lost somewhere on the school grounds if not in a bottomless pit of hallucination. Laya lying abed, too sick to get to the phone, or (the thought came before it could be blocked) lying abed with an empty pill bottle beside her. She was, Ariel persuaded herself, overreacting. Outrageously.

Laya was probably in the dining room about now. Ariel checked her watch. 7:05. She had the vague notion that the institutional dinner hour was early, universally.

Nutritionally sound and polished off before sundown. If dinner was over, then Laya might be in the library, listening to a book on tape. Or with her fellow students, playing pinochle, or, for all Ariel knew, making s'mores around a campfire. She had no real idea what this disparate group of individuals—scientists and artists and whatever (a former teacher of yoga)—did for entertainment.

Gayle Baker had Ariel's name and number in case of emergency. There was no message from Gayle Baker; therefore, there was no emergency.

Ariel checked her fax machine. There was nothing from Max. She undressed and took a shower. And tried Laya again.

"This is all the messages?" she asked Hattie, who by then had returned from a walk with Jessie. "You're sure?" Hattie didn't bother to answer the same question a second time. She continued with what she was doing, which was tearing bits of something, rather covertly, into Jessie's bowl.

The shepherd had welcomed Ariel with hardly a trace of the reproof that usually characterized their reunions after a trip, and was now watching Hattie's food prep with an ardor bordering on religious ecstasy. Ariel had seen the pot of boiled chicken livers on the stove. If such garnishes had become a staple of Jessie's diet, they accounted for the dog's perfidy. "You're spoiling her rotten," she said, and went back to pawing through the scraps of paper on which Hattie had, in her fashion, taken messages. They hadn't miraculously altered to include any from Laya or Dr. Baker. Ariel pushed them aside, picked up the phone, and put it down again.

"What's got you so wrought up?" Hattie asked. She plunked the bowl onto the floor, where Jessie fell upon it.

"When's the last time you talked to Laya?" Ariel asked.

"Not since before you left from up there, why?"

"Has she ever talked to you about her yoga classes? About the different places she taught or any of the students or—"

"No. Stop askin' questions until you answer one."

"I've had this thought . . . this hunch. If I can talk to Laya, I might have a way of finding one of the men who killed . . ." Ariel realized that Hattie knew next to nothing about James Price or what it was that Laya witnessed.

"Killed . . . ?" Hattie repeated. She was only momentarily perplexed. "That Price man?" she asked, excited. "The one she saw get beat up?"

"She told you about that?"

"A while ago. I pried it out of her. What hunch? Is he who blinded her? What way of—"

"Where's her stuff?" Ariel said, abruptly standing. When she hurried down the hall to her study, to Laya's former bedroom, Hattie followed. "Is anything still here?" Ariel asked.

"Just a few things she didn't think she'd need." Hattie opened a closet, searched around, and retrieved a cardboard box. "She's got most everything with her," she said, handing the box to Ariel, who dumped out the contents.

She wasn't surprised to see the outfit Laya had worn home from the hospital; even blind, she'd known it didn't suit her. There was a sweatshirt ("Got a stain on it wouldn't come out," Hattie explained) and a ratty pair of bedroom slippers. "She bought new," Hattie said, raking through what was left. "What're you after?"

"That, maybe." Ariel grabbed the plastic bag Hattie had uncovered. It had the hospital logo on it.

"Nothing in there but lotion and cheap Kleenex and whatnot," Hattie said. "A thermometer."

"And the cards she got." Ariel was already shuffling through them. Of the two florists' cards, one was from the staff at the YMCA where Ariel had attended Laya's class, the other was "For my favorite patient, from Dinah."

"Who's that?" Hattie asked, taking the card.

"A nurse." Ariel was going through the get well cards. "She gave that outfit there to Laya."

"Pretty. Not much like her though."

Two of the get well cards were candidates. One was signed "Your best class," which was of no help. On the other was written in a rather childish hand: "Love from the TGIF class." There was no address or stamp on the envelope, Ariel noted, so it had been hand-delivered. "Thank God it's Friday," she said. "This is it."

"It what?"

"The card I hope came with flowers Laya got. If it is, I know which class it is. Price was attacked on a Friday night, which was when she volunteered at a settlement house near the alley."

Ariel went to her desk, and Hattie watched wordlessly, shaking her head, her expression suggesting that she'd begun to view this whole thing as senseless shenanigans. Ariel was picking through a drawer of miniature audiotapes. She selected one, and plugged it into a player. When Hattie heard the voice on the tape, her eyes widened. "What in the world—?"

"Just listen a minute."

"What I'm asking you to do, Ariel, is probably impossible," Laya's voice said before Ariel fast-forwarded to "this was a week, no, five nights before . . . before the eyedrops. The Friday before. It must've been around nine o'clock. I was leaving Martine's."

"Here it is," Ariel murmured.

"Martine Brown, I'm talking about. She runs . . . I guess you'd call it a settlement house. It's an informal kind of thing for teenage girls. Strictly volunteer—" Ariel hit Fast Forward again, went too far, and had to reverse. "It's on

Adams, a big yellow house in the twenty-one hundred block. I teach yoga Friday nights."

Ariel pressed Stop. With a grin, she said, "Fingers crossed," and hauled a telephone directory out of another drawer.

"For what?" Hattie picked up the tape player. "She describe that whole wicked business on here?" she asked.

"You can listen to it if you want to."

Hattie looked dubious.

"Aha!" Ariel said and, her finger on the listing, dialed.

"Brown House," was how she was greeted. The voice was female, a treble chirp. It sounded like a child's voice.

"Martine Brown?" Ariel asked.

"Okay." The phone was dropped, and Ariel heard "Marteeena hyeeena" being caroled, loudly, in a girlish soprano. There was distant, alto laughter, and then a screech and "Don't tickle me!" amid giggles and more shrieks.

The receiver was picked up. "Martine Brown." There was still a trace of laughter in the deep voice. "May I help you?"

Ariel introduced herself, tacking on that she was a friend of Laya. Before she could say another word, the other woman cried, "*Laya*? How is she? *Where* is she?"

"She's . . ." Ariel caught herself. Bandying Laya's whereabouts wouldn't do, especially in view of the information she was about to solicit. "She's away, in school."

"School?" A pause. "Braille?"

"Ms. Brown, Laya mentioned to me that she taught there, at . . . Brown House, did your little girl call it?"

Martine Brown laughed. She was a woman, Ariel got the impression, who'd do it every chance she got. "This devil's no child of mine! She's here with her mama, who's taking a child care class, and the Lord knows, she needs all the help she can get with the way little Miss *Keshia the Creature* cuts up."

"Ah," Ariel said. Hearing a faint giggle, she gathered that the child was at the woman's side, maybe within the circle of her arm, and that this rhyming name-calling thing was a game between them. "Laya taught on Friday nights, I believe she said?"

"Don't say 'taught.'"

"Pardon me?"

"Don't make it sound like a thing of the past. If she's in school, she's mending, and if she's mending, she can get right back on over here and get to work, and you can tell her so from me."

"I will. Tell me, did . . . does the Friday night class have a name? Something they call themselves?"

"I'm not following?"

"Do they, by any chance, call themselves the TGIF class?"

"Oh, that's right! I'd forgotten all about that."

"One student brought flowers to the hospital, to Laya."

"Uh-huh? I'm not surprised. Laya's popular here."

"I don't suppose you'd know which girl that would've been? Who brought them?"

"Uh-uh. Keshia, quit that!"

"A girl around twenty or so? Slightly, uh, full figured?"

"I just don't know." To judge by her distracted tone, Martine wasn't knocking herself out to come up with a name; the question, Ariel had to admit, didn't sound like a burning one. "She had a sweet face," Ariel prodded. "It was my impression she might be somewhat . . ." (Oh, man! Was there an inoffensive way to say this?) "Developmentally disabled?"

"Who're you with?"

"With?" Ariel repeated. The doorbell sounded, and Hattie, who'd been listening to the one-sided conversation with the bewildered intensity of a woman consulting an oracle only to hear the secrets of the universe revealed in an alien tongue, reluctantly left to go to the door. "What do you mean 'with'?" Ariel asked.

"Are you from some government . . . Ariel Gold, did you say? The TV Ariel Gold?"

"Yes, but—"

The fax machine beside Ariel rang.

"What's this all about?" Martine Brown demanded. "Do you even know Laya?"

"We're friends, truly. I can't go into what this is about, but it's nothing to do with my job." The fax machine began to yield its communication with agonizing slowness, so slowly it had to be a graphic, and the sketch was the only graphic Ariel was expecting. "Do you know the girl I mean?" she asked. The machine labored as if it were drawing from memory. "I'd like very much to talk with her."

"About what?"

Ariel heard the Call Waiting beep. Probably Max, to talk about the sketch. She ignored it. "There was a man with her when she brought the flowers," she said. "Is the girl married?"

"I tell you what, Ms. Gold. If Laya needs to know anything about . . . any girl, you get her to call me herself, okay?"

"I can't reach . . . Look, I'm not handling this very well. Let me come there and talk to you in person. I can be there in—"

Hattie was back and signaling something.

"Hold on a second, Ms. Brown," Ariel said. "What?"

"Henry Heller's out there, in a tuxedo," Hattie said. "Are you supposed to be goin' to some party with him?"

39

THE LAUNCHING PARTY WAS SLICK. ICE SCULPTURES GLITTERED and dripped. The guests glittered and circulated. The premiere cover of *Newsfront* was emblazoned on every stationary surface, on mounted posters and tasseled programs, on clever little souvenir notepads that looked like matchbooks, and on actual matchbooks. At both ends of the hotel ballroom the magazine's pages scrolled across giant screens like stadium message boards, a *2001* production extravaganza in which graphics and photos leaped into animation to the lavish accompaniment of what sounded like the Boston Pops; trumpets flourished, the cannons of 1812 boomed, and the kettledrums of Zarathustra spake.

Asking the musical question, mused Ariel: what am I doing here? She found a vacant table and sat down to people watch and grind her molars over how much she wished to be on the other side of town in a yellow house getting answers out of Martine Brown.

She'd had no choice but to be here for Henry tonight, not that she hadn't thought of every out, short of shooting herself in the foot while she made up in record time and dressed in a slinky new number bought for the party (even if she had subsequently forgotten the party)—not that Henry had noticed the dress or seemed to give a hoot in hell whether she was here or not.

He'd been whisked away, with apologies, before they'd made the lobby. Running on nerves and caffeine, now laced with champagne, he was pumping hands like a pol and laughing often, at what, Ariel didn't know, since in the hour they'd been here, she'd seldom been within earshot. He'd said precisely seven words to her: "Oh, Ariel, I want you to meet—" She'd never learned the name of the man he wanted her to meet. Henry was at that moment tapped on the shoulder by a young, beautiful, and very diaphanously dressed actress, who was lapping him up with her large dark eyes. (She reminded Ariel of Jessie anticipating the chicken livers.) *Newsfront* had reviewed her latest film. Apparently, she'd liked the result.

I could call a cab, Ariel thought, and be at the settlement house and back, with the girl's name and maybe the man's name, too, before Henry ever noticed I was gone.

She took the police sketch of "Medium" from her handbag, and unfolded it, angling it for better light. "See what I mean?" Max had scrawled across the bottom. She did. If Medium actually looked anything like this, he should be a bank robber. He wouldn't need a mask; no one would remember his face.

Earlier, in the ladies', Ariel had supplied him with crudely drawn glasses, added frown lines between the brows, and flattened the mouth into an angry line. She wasn't much of an artist, but she'd achieved a recognizable glower. That is, it was recognizable *as* a glower; it made the face no more recognizable.

"What's he so riled up about?"

Ariel jumped, and looked up to see her grandfather.

"What are you doing here?" she asked.

"You know me, Mr. Opening Night. Publisher's a buddy of mine."

"Who isn't?" Ariel kissed his cheek and thumbed off a lipstick smudge. "Why didn't you say anything yesterday about coming?" They'd spoken on the phone, Ariel calling to tell him about her conversation with Dr. Scopes, but she hadn't seen him for a week.

"Why didn't you?" he asked.

"Because I'd forgotten about it." She held out the sketch. "What's wrong with this picture?"

"Other than sorry drawing?"

"I wasn't talking about artistic merit."

He peered through the lower half of his glasses. "Who is it?"

"I don't know."

"And there's a good reason you're skulkin' in a corner, doodlin' on a picture of a man you don't know? You look pretty, by the way. Anything new on Dorothy today?"

"My theory that Sis was a patient she befriended is a bust. Since Marin General didn't work out, I had Tara call every hospital and convalescent or rehab center and hospice in the county. Her husband the doctor they knew; her they didn't. I'm temporarily out of ideas, and, besides, I've been preoccupied with something else."

He nodded toward the sketch. "Him?"

"Are you here with somebody?"

"Yeah."

"Oh."

"Why?"

"I was hoping you might feel like driving me somewhere."

"I just got here."

"We could be back in forty-five minutes. An hour." She turned to look around. "Who're you with?"

"Roy."

"Roy?"

"My driver."

"Roy! I haven't seen him in . . . I don't know when. Months. Where's he been?"

"He retired to Florida and blew his savings on the nags and the greyhounds, and asked for his job back."

"He's not too old to be driving?"

"Don't talk about old. Old is a state of mind. 'How old

would you be if you didn't know how old you was?' Who
said that?"

"Satchel Paige."

"One day I'll stump you. Where'd you want to go?"

"Do you care? Do you really want to be here?"

"Henry won't mind you goin' AWOL?"

"Take a look at him."

A minute passed before B.F. could pick Henry out of the
crowd. One eyebrow shot up. "That's one toothsome
young woman he's got hangin' on him," he said. "Who is
she?"

"Some actress. I forget her name." It was a lie.

"Efficient."

"Pardon?"

"She's already got on her nightgown."

Ariel laughed.

"Come on, sugar," B.F. said. "Let's go for a ride."

Ariel knew her grandfather hadn't failed to note that
the sketch was of the variety one finds in post offices.
She was surprised, therefore, when he didn't press overmuch about what destination she had in mind or what
business she had there. When she gave Roy the address,
B.F., who knew what brand of neighborhood it was,
merely slid her an interested look. Ariel couldn't figure it.
While he was typically up for adventure (or down, as on
the occasion of the submarine junket), he did not typically love it when she took risks. Then it came to her: he
reckoned she'd go one way or the other; this way she
wouldn't go alone.

They made quite a pair of urban guerrillas, "neither tar-
nished nor afraid," cruising down the mean streets of the
city . . . in a chauffeured Lincoln. (B.F. always bought
American.) Ariel grinned. In actuality (a realm inhabited
by those less imaginative than she), they were cruising

down the Avenue of the Stars, a broad Century City thoroughfare lined with steel-and-glass office towers and glutted with limos. 20th Century Fox Studios was coming up on their right. Mighty high cotton, real estate—wise, as were the neighborhoods beyond.

It was a balmy night, in the midseventies. Ariel opened the window to catch the breeze. "Smell the jasmine," she said as they passed a fence smothered in the fragrant flowers. The windows of the Spanish-style house were open, and Ariel caught a swell of music. It was a radio, the same oldies station Roy was tuned to, and although he had it turned low, she recognized a Gatlin Brothers number. "All the gold in California," they warned, "is in a bank in the middle of Beverly Hills in somebody's else's name." Ariel sang along. B.F. gave her a pained smile. Her musical abilities were on a par with her drawing skills. "You want to give me a clue about our mission?" he suggested.

"My mission," Ariel corrected. "Nothing perilous. Just looking for a couple of names."

"In all the wrong places."

"That we fast approach. There's no time to fill you in."

The tenor of the streets had already begun, first subtly and then flagrantly, to change. Imposing homes gave over to apartment buildings and modest but neat stucco bungalows. They became less neat. In direct proportion to their decreasing size and increasing shabbiness, their occupants tended to spill outside, killing time on concrete stoops and in dirt yards. Music blared from boom boxes; they were not tuned to the oldies station.

"Let that window up, would you?" B.F. said.

He was right. The scent of night-blooming jasmine had been snuffed by exhaust fumes. Ariel pushed a button, and the window slid closed.

Streetlights alternated now with patches of blackness, where bulbs had burned out or been knocked out. Shortly, as if they'd crossed an invisible latitudinal line, neon became the prevailing light. It flickered on bars and little all-night markets whose biggest business was done in Lotto tickets, and even on a church. It had flickered out on boarded-up storefronts with yellowed FOR RENT signs in the windows.

The particular neighborhood where Martine Brown's settlement house was located had once been a proud one, even a haughty one. Its heyday had passed before most of the current residents were born, and the big houses that remained undemolished were too often derelict. Brown House, as Ariel knew from Laya's tape, wasn't brown but yellow. Optimistic yellow, trimmed in white. Paint peeled in places, but light spilled from every window of the Victorian structure, and primroses made an effort in the window boxes.

"Right in front," B.F. ordered Roy. "Double-park if you have to, and keep the motor running." He reached for the door handle.

"This isn't a bank heist, and you're not going in with me," Ariel told him.

"*We* go or you don't," he said. "Your decision."

"Oh, come on!" Ariel gave him a shove and slid out behind him. She hadn't for a second expected him to remain behind.

They were climbing a short flight of steps to the sidewalk when a car door slammed. A man shouted. The rapid burst of words was unintelligible, but it sounded like bad news, and it was close. B.F. tensed. Ariel got ready to hit the dirt. Before the shout died, it was overridden by catcalls and laughter and muffled *thwacks!* A second before, Ariel would've been sure it was bullets piercing flesh; now she guessed it was palms slapping in greeting. She remembered how to breathe again. B.F. muttered under his breath, and picked up the pace.

"No questions while we're here," Ariel told him, "okay? And no repeating anything you hear afterward."

B.F. just kept moving.

The door was open. Through the screen they heard music, drums and electric guitar. The guitar hit a succession of sour notes. It sounded like a cat being skinned alive. Ariel knocked. A chair scraped, and a middle-aged woman shortly appeared. She looked them over, eyebrows rising when she saw the two formally dressed white people on her porch. Apparently, she found the sight amusing. "Tell me you're from Publishers Clearinghouse," she said in her rich voice, and laughed.

Ariel recognized the voice and the laugh. "Ariel Gold, Ms. Brown, and B.F. Coulter. I hope it's not too late to visit."

"I recognize you," Martine Brown said with a curious glance at B.F. She looked beyond them to the Lincoln idling at the curb. "It's way too late if you're here to ask questions without throwing in some answers." She spoke loudly, but only to be heard above the musical din. There was no rancor in the statement, and she was already unlatching the screen. "Come on in."

Ariel and B.F. were led into a spacious but sparsely furnished office. When their hostess closed the door, the music receded sufficiently to lessen the pain. "Lord help me, I'm tired of listening to that!" she said, and sat, gracefully, on one of two mismatched sofas. She indicated the other. "Sit," she said. "Talk."

Before Ariel could comply with the second invitation, the phone on the desk rang, and Martine Brown got up to answer. Ariel used the time to study the woman, who looked nothing like what the deep, jolly telephone voice had led her to expect. Instead of a heavily fleshed, motherly person, she was trim, even thin. She wore neat tweed trousers and a white camp shirt. She was probably in her sixties. Her skin was finely lined, the color of honey, and her gray-mottled hair was pulled into a tight knot.

When she hung up, having said nothing but a series of uh-huhs and "Let me know," Ariel said, "Have you given any thought to the girl I asked you about?"

The woman smiled. "I had a few things going on here tonight besides your call, Ms. Gold. Two classes, and a fistfight in the front yard, and that private music lesson we were enjoying—"

"This is important."

"So is what went on here tonight. I told you earlier. What Laya wants to know, she can ask me herself."

"That's not possible right now."

Martine Brown stood up. "I'm afraid it just got too late to pay a visit," she said.

Ariel kept her seat. She made a decision. "Can I trust you," she asked, "to keep what I tell you to yourself?" She gave B.F. a quick glance, including him in her caveat. He didn't notice, being absorbed in some literature he'd picked up from the coffee table. "Laya told me something in confidence," Ariel said. "Will you treat it the same way?"

"That depends."

"This has to do with what happened to her."

Martine looked torn. She shook her head. "I can't make any promises."

B.F. muttered something, his finger moving across a line of type in the pamphlet he held.

Abruptly, Martine said, "Are you a lawyer or what? Who, exactly, are you?"

"That depends," B.F. said.

The woman's dark eyes narrowed. She was deciding, Ariel guessed, whether she was being made fun of. "On what?"

"This information's about your place here?" B.F.

asked, his attention still on the pamphlet. "About what you do?"

"Yes."

"You're supported by private contributions." He pointed to a paragraph.

"There's enough government subsidizing going on in this neighborhood. It's a habit I'd like to break."

B.F. looked up, vague, as if he'd been lost in reading, hadn't heard a word that had been said, and realized he was interrupting their conversation. "Sorry," he said, "it's just I'm impressed."

Ariel laid a hand on his arm. "This is my grandfather," she said. "He gave me a ride here."

"What I also might be," B.F. said, and his eyes dropped again to the folder, "is some help to you, Ms. Brown. Considerable help."

Her lips parted slightly.

"Just one thing though . . ." He pressed the pamphlet against his thigh, smoothing it with his palm, as if he were ironing out any possible lack of understanding. "I don't care for publicity. I'd need to know I could trust you to keep things to yourself."

Martine didn't take long to work it out. She sat down, as ladylike as before. Leaning toward the old man, her voice husky, she said, "This room's heard more secrets than a confessional, Mr. Coulter. I don't betray confidences, and I don't sell, rent, or trade the names of our benefactors. Even those who offer bribes." She paused. Her mouth worked. Unkindly, the light picked up the minute grooves above her lips. She looked older. "I will lay down, roll over, and beg for this house."

She meant it from her depths. Ariel was out of hers. Not that she didn't understand what was happening; she just didn't know, that second, how she felt about it, not if it netted her a name.

"I'll take any kind of money I can get," Martine said, "but I won't be bulldozed. I won't make promises I don't know if I can keep, and I don't make decisions without facts."

Ariel kept her account of what Laya witnessed brief. The other woman sagged when she heard it. Ariel knew what was going through her mind: she had offered to walk Laya to her car that night. If she had insisted . . . "You obviously heard about the assault," Ariel said. "You know Price died? And you know about Carrie Murphy?"

"I heard rumors that was connected. But you hear a lot of rumors. What's all this got to do with one of my girls?"

"Laya didn't go to the cops. She can't describe either man." The half-truth was deliberate, an insurance policy. Ms. Brown had promised nothing; if this conversation got repeated, this was the message Ariel wanted spread. "But Mrs. Murphy did. She worked with a police artist." Ariel took the sketch from her evening bag and handed it over. "Do you know him?" she asked.

Some seconds passed, enough to cause Ariel to regret her amateurish modifications. "This is what I'm going to do," Martine finally said. She handed the sketch back. "I'm going to sleep on this. Let me see you out."

B.F. and Ariel were ensconced in the car when he said, "She recognized the picture."

"Oh, yeah."

"A quandary."

Ariel nodded.

"But her first allegiance has to be with her . . . constituents. If she doesn't keep faith, she might as well pack it in."

"What about keeping faith with Laya? And James Price and Carrie Murphy?"

"I meant to ask you about her. Who is she?"

"*Was*," Ariel said. She told him about the elderly victim.

They were back into fragrant jasmine territory before he said, "My compliments to the Brown woman were sincere, you know. I'm impressed with her efforts."

"It was a cheap trick, what you tried to pull."

"Cheap's not what I had in mind."

"Nevertheless."

They turned onto the Avenue of the Stars.

"That's what money's for," B.F., undisturbed, said.

Roy pulled up to the hotel's entrance, and the big car glided to a stop. Ariel checked her watch; they'd been gone an hour and ten minutes. She recognized several of the party guests waiting for their cars to be brought around. The festivities, evidently, were winding down.

"It was a bona fide offer, so why're you mad?" B.F. asked.

The Lincoln's door was opened by a doorman.

"Because it didn't work," Ariel said.

40

THE PHONE IN LAYA'S ROOM RANG THIRTEEN TIMES. ARIEL counted. Superstitiously, she let it ring once more before she disconnected. If Laya were there, she should have had time to find her way to the phone; if she were elsewhere, there was no point in waking her neighbors at midnight. The general administration number was answered by a recorded message.

Ariel huddled on her sofa, drew her knees to her chin, and tucked her robe under her bare toes to warm them.

She wished Henry had come in for a while, just to take the edge off the evening, but he'd been played out. ("Well, we're officially launched," he'd said. "I feel like they broke the champagne bottle over my head." "It was a great party, though!" Ariel had assured him, and taken his hand. Such was his state that he'd merely patted her shoulder and tottered to his car.)

She wanted somebody to talk to, to pooh-pooh her anxiety; to persuade her that there was no harm in waiting until tomorrow to learn where Laya was; to learn, from her or from Martine Brown, the name of the plump TGIF girl, the name of her sullen and (possibly) bespectacled and murderous friend. No harm in withholding, for tonight, what might be a lead in two murders and a vicious blinding assault. Tomorrow was a scant half-dozen hours away.

Where was Laya?

Ariel wished Hattie had stayed the night here instead of going back to B.F.'s condo, but she was long gone. Even if she were here, she wouldn't be up for chat. She'd be sawing logs by now.

"Where's your mistress?" Ariel asked Arthur, who blinked once, stuporously, from the other arm of the sofa.

Laya had told Ariel about a night she couldn't sleep; she had passed the hours in the dorm lounge lulled by the TV. Had that become a habit?

Ariel pulled an afghan over herself, and picked up the remote. The dog door flapped as Jessie returned from a necessary or gratuitous excursion to the backyard. She came into the living room, eyeing Arthur perched on furniture forbidden to her. "He's a guest," Ariel said and channel surfed, searching for an old movie. Jessie settled, virtuously, on the rug. *Dial M for Murder* was in its early stages. No real woman was as cool as Grace Kelly, no real man as cunning as Ray Milland, no real plot as Machiavellian as Hitchcock's.

Pleased to be distracted from real life, Ariel upped the volume.

• • •

The shrill ring of the phone came from the wrong direction. It was above and behind her head rather than where it belonged: on the table to her side. Ariel's eyes popped open to darkness. Not unbroken darkness. Perceptibly lighter rectangles in places windows shouldn't be. The ghostly shapes of objects she couldn't, in that second, identify. She focused. What was she doing in the living room? When had she turned off the TV? Why couldn't she move her feet? Kicking at the afghan in which they were entangled, she reached for the telephone.

Ten minutes later, at 4:40 by the kitchen clock, she was waiting for a kettle of water to boil.

Why, she kept asking herself, hadn't she made a bigger effort to reach somebody at the school at midnight? *"Laya's not answering her phone"* was all she would've needed to say. *"Could somebody check on her?"* She should've phoned Gayle Baker. Instead, the doctor had phoned her, to tell her Laya was missing.

Would the lost hours count? How much? What would the toll be?

Had Dr. Baker not been called to Laya's dormitory—to see a student sick with a migraine—they wouldn't know yet. That had been nearly an hour ago. When she'd passed the door to Laya's room, she'd noticed that it stood open. Looking in, she'd seen that the patio door was also open, the bed hadn't been slept in, and the room was empty. After a check of the public rooms, she'd gotten the dorm manager involved. The improvised search party had covered all communal and accessible areas before notifying the police, who were en route to the school when the doctor called Ariel.

It would be daylight soon. With daylight, they'd find Laya.

Ariel measured coffee beans into the grinder, lost count, and started over. Had Laya taken a walk and gotten

turned around? Disoriented. Or had she been lured away
by . . . whom?

"Does she have any friends in the area?" Baker had
asked. "Someone she might visit?" When had Ariel last
talked with her? Had she seemed unusually disturbed? If
she were in crisis, did Ariel think she might have called the
psychiatrist she'd consulted?

"She went out last evening," Baker had then surprised
Ariel by saying. "Do you have any idea who with?"

"You know more than I do," Ariel had replied.

"I happened to see her about six, waiting for somebody
down near the gate. She was being taken out to dinner,
she told me. A vegetarian place in San Rafael. She asked if
I'd ever been there."

Why was she surprised? Ariel asked herself. Just
because Laya had never mentioned acquaintances in the
Bay Area, that didn't mean she didn't have any. Her dinner
companion could be a former student who'd moved north
or an old New York friend who'd moved west, or an old
sweetheart—or anybody. She hadn't lived in a vacuum her
whole life. "But did she come back to the school after
that?"

She had. She'd checked in. If the police had no luck,
presumably, her fellow students would be awakened and
questioned. A school full of blind people, Ariel couldn't
help thinking, wasn't the easiest place to turn up useful
witnesses.

Should she book a flight up? Of course she shouldn't;
she should stay by the phone. She stared, unseeing, at the
teakettle. Giving lie to the adage, it began to boil, and,
shortly, to shriek.

Dr. Baker would call as soon as they knew anything.

Wrapped in her robe, sitting on her deck, Ariel drank
coffee, the pot emptying as the sky grew lighter. With a

startling suddenness, the sun crested the horizon. Forty-five minutes had passed.

It had to be that Laya was nowhere on the grounds. They were extensive. Eleven acres, Ariel thought the PR director or somebody had said. There were many houses and buildings. Still, one had to believe that if she were there, she would've been discovered by now. As nearly as Ariel could reconstruct from memory, at least a third of the campus was devoted to the dogs: the various kennels—breeding and whelping and general—and the veterinary facility; Laya would hardly be hanging out with the dogs, not at any time, certainly not in the middle of the night. So that left only two-thirds of the place to search. How long could that take?

She went inside, debated making more coffee, and opted for a glass of milk. A nice coat of insulation against future caffeine onslaughts. Drinking it, she dispensed with the previous day's mail. Fifty-seven minutes had passed. She heard the arrival of the *Times*, retrieved it, and paged through. Nothing registered except a headline about a new gun bill. California Citizens, it seemed, could now purchase only one handgun per month. My! Ariel thought. Such deprivation. How could a body get by with only one new gun every month? She shook her head. Maybe it would make sense later.

An hour and thirteen minutes had passed.

She went through her briefcase, looking for a note she'd made somewhere (on an airline napkin?) about the Tahoe murderess (or helpless and victimized old lady, as the case may be) that she needed to E-mail Tara, and found a *San Francisco* magazine, picked up at the airport. She fanned through it where she stood, the toes of one foot scratching the instep of the other, the pages riffling past her thumbnail. She was through it, back to the classifieds, before a message reached her brain. Both feet hit the floor. As rapidly, but with far keener attention, she paged backward.

The photo was in the Culture section. Rob Millen's confident, one-dimpled smile beamed from the page, tucked into a paragraph about the "local writer's work in progress."

"Bottled Spirits?" the bold lead-in inquired. The subject wasn't Johnny Walker Black or Stolichnaya, but cremains. It was an upbeat plug for the book about the Columbarium, where the ashy residue of thirty thousand people was housed. Publication was scheduled to coincide with the hundredth birthday of "the neoclassical landmark, till now one of San Francisco's best-kept secrets." Rob would fix that—if he didn't get sidetracked, Ariel thought grimly, by a book about death of a much more recent vintage.

The blurb wasn't lengthy, a single paragraph, but it was long enough to supply information of which she had been unaware, information that explained the custom-tailored clothing Rob wore and the expensive car he drove. It explained how "Mister Mover and Shaker," as he'd wryly called himself, had plenty of time to perform gratis good works, being unburdened by the need to make a living. (*"Oh, I don't think Millen's got a lot to worry about on that score,"* Charles Barnes had said. Ariel had given the oblique comment exactly no thought.)

The information wasn't stated. It was inferred by Ariel. Rob, "Robert Woodman Millen," was the only son of "the late Constance Woodman Millen." Not Mrs. John (or whoever) Millen. If she'd had a husband, his name hadn't been the one with the money behind it. Ariel wasn't familiar with the name Woodman, and no information was given about the family, which was informative in itself: apparently, credentials were considered superfluous. Tacit. One of those "If you have to ask" situations.

Well, well, Ariel mused. She studied the face in the photo, which now looked not only perfect, but patrician. Well, well . . . what? She'd already known he wasn't hurting for money. She dropped the magazine back into her briefcase. His family probably owned Rice-A-Roni or Coit Tower, or they were sourdough bread magnates, descended from some Barbary Coast gambler named Blackie. Why was she speculating about the man's pedigree at a time like this?

An hour and twenty-one minutes had passed, and so had the limits of Ariel's patience. She called the school, and got the same recording she'd gotten at midnight. Why hadn't she asked Gayle for a direct number? She called Laya's room. The phone was answered by a person who identified herself as officer somebody-or-other.

"She's accounted for," the woman told Ariel. "Let me let you talk to the doctor."

"Oh, Ms. Gold, I am so sorry!" Gayle was not her unflappable self. "What with all the excitement, you went clean out of my mind! Listen, we need to get out of here and let Laya get some rest. I'll call you back from my office in five minutes."

She must have sprinted. She was back to Ariel in two, and breathless. "I'm so sorry not to have called you immediately."

Laya had been found over half an hour earlier by Gayle herself. She'd been physically checked over and questioned, cleaned up, and put to bed. She was unharmed.

"Except for briar scratches and minor abrasions on her knees and hands," the doctor said, finishing her account of the misadventure. "Fortunately, the weather's moderate. And, fortunately, she didn't go off in another direction, like the street."

"Where was this place she was again?" Ariel asked.

"It's some distance beyond the Manse, the new dorm,

right at the end of the property. Land we'll develop if we get the funds to do it. It's fenced off," Baker added, as if Ariel might accuse the school of negligence. "How she got past that, I don't know."

Ariel was too occupied with making sense of the situation to be thinking litigiously. "She was in a *gazebo*, you said?"

"What remains of it. I didn't know it existed, it's so overgrown back there. The area will be cleared posthaste!"

"And she didn't know how she got there?"

"Says she fell asleep in the chair in her room, and the next thing she knew, she was tripping over a vine and falling."

"She was sleepwalking?"

"It seems so. Does she have a history of somnambulating?"

The word struck Ariel as funny (relief kicking in, no doubt), as if Laya had been indulging in something kinky. She pressed her fingers to her temple, and said, "No. Not that I know of."

"Sleep disorders are a feature of almost every major psychiatric disorder," Gayle said.

Ariel lost the urge to giggle. "What are you suggesting?"

"I'm not qualified to suggest anything. I'm stating a fact." Ariel heard a long, tired sigh. This middle-of-the-night scare seemed to have done Gayle good, because when she continued, her tone had changed. She sounded less like a martinet. She sounded younger. She sounded human. "I mentioned to you before that Laya's been suffering from insomnia. It's this recurring nightmare business, you know? She doesn't want to fall asleep and dream."

"She told you about that?"

"I don't think she's getting more than two or three

hours of sleep a night. The woman's got to be physically exhausted. All things considered, she behaved incredibly sensibly tonight. When she woke up, she had a moment of panic. Who wouldn't? She was on her knees in the dirt, no idea in the world where she was or which way to go. Crawling around, calling out, nobody answering . . ."

Ariel tried to imagine it. She had a sudden flashback, almost as vivid as if she were living, in that second, the morning she'd awakened with no idea of who or where she was. She'd thought the mindless, helpless terror would stop her heart. She'd been lost—but at least she could see.

"She ran into the gazebo," the doctor said, admiration now obvious in her voice, "literally bumped into it, is what I mean, and she just . . . got hold of herself. She remembered, she said, that when you're lost, you should stay put and wait to be found, so she did. She actually fell asleep again." After a moment's reflection, she added, "She's embarrassed to have caused such an uproar."

"What's next?" Ariel asked, dreading to hear the answer.

"This isn't a situation we've faced before. Having a blind student who's apt to go wandering out of her room into the night? You have to know we can't take a chance on it happening again."

It was about what Ariel had expected. What she heard next was unexpected.

"I have a suggestion that might help," Gayle said.

"You're not . . . expelling Laya then?"

"She's worked so hard, Ms. Gold! Ariel. She's overcome so much. The dog phobia, I mean, not the other fears."

"Other fears?"

"She *was* deliberately blinded. You said it: by somebody still roaming the streets. She's scared. At any rate, she's got eight days invested, just twenty to go. Twenty short days that'll make such a difference in her life. I'd hate to see . . . We've had a few conversations. She's a remarkable woman, isn't she?"

"Yes, she is."

"I get the impression she doesn't usually open up much."

Ariel let out a laugh.

"I thought not. Me either. But she talks to me. I think . . . it's more for my benefit than hers. She listens, too, you see." Gayle Baker cleared her throat. "Be that as it may. The psychiatrist . . . Schell? Maybe he'll have a different approach, like a sleep disorder clinic, but for now, it's possible that by ameliorating the psychological stress, we'll relieve the problems. Benzodiazepines might help the nightmares and the somnambulism. Diazepam—"

"What is it?"

"Valium."

"She won't go for it. By all means, suggest it, but Laya won't even take aspirin."

"Then I'm out of ideas. Do you have any?"

"Couldn't you just lock her doors? Or put an alarm on them at night? If they're opened, somebody's alerted?"

"Makes her look even more like some kind of nut case!" Gayle Baker was really loosening up. "We're not a high-security facility. I'm afraid . . . Don't quote me, but even before the events of this morning, we—we being the staff and board of directors—we'd been at odds about the way to go on this. Her . . . medical problems. I'm not the only one whose opinion has turned around, you see, only now I'm the one in Laya's corner. One board member in particular feels especially strongly that it's too great a risk—"

"What if you put her into a double room? With a roommate?"

"Put the onus on another student? Don't even think about it."

"All right, how about this: do you ever take day students?"

"Yes."

"Then that's the answer. I'll come up and stay with her tonight," Ariel promised rashly. It would cost less than hiring a nurse or a bodyguard, either of which would make Laya uncomfortable. "I'll work something out for after." Laya could live at B.F.'s. Maybe Hattie would stay with her and drive her in for classes. "Oh, doctor! With all this, I forgot why I needed to reach Laya in the first place. We might be able to do better than ameliorate the psychological stress. We might eliminate the source."

"Beats Valium all to hell and back."

"Will you leave word for her to call me? When she wakes up?"

"No problem. So, Ms. Gold . . ." After a noticeable hesitation, Gayle said, "It sounds funny to ask after all this whole conversation, but you *do* think the nightmares and so on stem from the obvious? From what was done to Laya? The trauma and all?"

"As opposed to. . .?"

"Nothing." The answer came too quickly. "Forget it. Who's Stella?"

"Who?"

"When I found Laya out there this morning, she was asleep. I told you that. I was careful not to startle her, but the truth is, she was hard to rouse. I'd swear she said the name 'Stella,' and then she said, 'Don't make me go back.'"

Ariel was at a loss. "To the school? She didn't want to go back to the school?"

"Oh, she was still half-asleep. Mumbling. But there's nobody on staff here by the name Stella, and no students either. I just wondered who she was."

41

"ARE YOU TALKING ABOUT JACKIE?" LAYA ASKED ARIEL.

"If she's about twenty, sweet face, TGIF class member, developmentally disabled—"

"You said that already."

"—needs to lose a few pounds, then, yes, Jackie's who we're talking about. What's her last name?"

Laya had called not half an hour after Ariel's conversation with Gayle Baker. Her every response was a blink slow, a frame out of kilter—pretty much what one would expect from a person who'd spent half the night wandering purgatory and wakened to helpless terror with no more idea where she was or how she'd gotten there than if she'd been dumped from a spaceship. "It sounds like Jackie," Laya said. After a pause: "Except Jackie's not overweight." A longer pause. "What about her?"

"What's her last name?"

"Grady."

"She came to the hospital when you were there."

"With flowers from the class. I know."

"You do? How? The card didn't have her name on it."

"Somebody described her to me. Dinah did."

"This Jackie Grady, is she married? Or does she have a boyfriend?"

"A boyfriend? No. I'd be surprised."

"Why?"

"Jackie's quiet, very shy. Very young for her age." Laya was sounding more alert. "What's this about, Ariel?"

"There was a man with her that day, kind of an average-looking guy a little older. Maybe wears glasses? He's—"

"Her brother probably. He takes care of Jackie a good bit."

Ariel closed her eyes. *Yes!* she thought. "What's his name?"

"I don't understand what this is about."

"Was he taking care of his sister that Friday night Price was beaten up? Was he with her at the class that night?"

"I don't remember if . . . I don't think Jackie came that night. She was sick, somebody said."

"Laya, one of the men in the alley fits his description."

"No."

"Carrie Murphy worked with a police sketch artist. I saw this man at the hospital." Stretching the truth, Ariel said, "I recognized him from the sketch."

"No. The man I saw was definitely not Jackie's brother."

"I know. He's the other one, the one you didn't get a look at. Mrs. Murphy did. What's his name?"

"This is a mistake. This kid goes to college, Ariel, on a scholarship. Do you have any idea what kind of *accomplishment* that is?" Laya's voice rose. "A kid from that neighborhood? He's good to Jackie. He wouldn't be involved in anything like that."

"You know him pretty well then?"

Laya didn't reply right away. "I know Jackie worships the ground he walks on," she finally said. And, after another pause, "She calls him Moe."

"His last name's Grady?"

"I don't think so. I think he's a half-brother or a stepbrother. I don't know his last name."

But, thought Ariel, I'll bet Martine Brown does. She folded the paper on which she'd written the names, and put it in her handbag. "Hey," she said, "tell me the truth. How're you feeling?" She had asked earlier and gotten a monosyllabic answer.

"Stupid," Laya said now. "You know about last night."

"Yes. Why aren't you resting? You're supposed to be."

"Like I'd really want to nap? Who knows where I'd end up this time."

"It's going to get better," Ariel said. "Now that—"

"Did you know I was the subject of a police manhunt? Like some child who's wandered off from mommy at the mall? I'll be on milk cartons next!" Laya laughed, a bitter snort. "And I hear from Gayle that you're coming up to sit me tonight. Oh, Ariel!"

"It's not a problem. I'll be there sometime early evening, maybe with good news. We've got our first piece of solid information now. If this works out, we could know who both men are by the time—"

"I'll tell you something. I hope it doesn't work out, because if it does, Jackie's life will be destroyed, too. This girl is . . . she's maybe ten mentally. She has a job. You know what it is? She puts labels on boxes at a factory. All day. That's what she does. She's as proud of that job as if she—"

"This is not your fault. If this brother of hers is responsible for Price's murder and for blinding you and—"

"He's the most important thing—probably the only constant thing—in her life. The father's I don't know where. The mother's an addict, which is probably the cause of Jackie's retardation."

"You're a victim, too, like Jackie, like Price, like Carrie Murphy."

"Crushing Jackie won't make it all better."

"So you want to leave a killer, two killers, on the streets? To do God knows what to the next poor victim. Because they have a sister or a wife or a mother? I know you won't like this, but 'Every murderer is probably somebody's old friend.' Come on! It's time to put this tragedy behind you. After today, with any luck, you can start to do that."

"And all the bad things, all the demons will go away? You think so? I don't. I know better. The nightmare won't be over."

Ariel closed her eyes in impatience. She remembered what Gayle had asked. "Laya," she said, "who's Stella?"

A few seconds passed. "You heard about that, huh?"

"Who is she?"

"As near as I can tell you, a nurse."

"At the school? But Gayle said there's nobody there by that name."

"Don't you remember, Ariel? In the dream, I'm not at the school. I'm at some other sort of institution entirely, because I'm nutty as a fruitcake. Crazy as a loon! And you know what? I'm beginning to believe this dream is prophetic."

Ariel laughed.

"I'm not joking," Laya said.

The day seemed old to Ariel by the time she parked her van across the street from the Brown House. It was going on seven-forty-five in the morning. Martine Brown had had plenty of time to sleep on her decision while others passed the night in less contemplative ways.

Ariel looked toward where, she thought, the alley lay. She couldn't see it from here. She couldn't see the building beside it, the scorched remains of the Asian mom-and-pop shop that hadn't survived the riots.

Brown House looked tireder by day. A patch of siding, Ariel noticed, wore a brighter shade of yellow, repainted to cover repairs or, perhaps, graffiti. On an upper window a corner of screen was torn loose, the mesh distended, bulging out as if something (a basketball? a person?) had slammed against it. Cracks rent the old sidewalk, on which a child of five or six played. The little girl (Martine's rhyming friend Keshia?) hopped erratically, mouth open, eyes glued to her feet. Ariel watched, remembering the chant not from her own childhood, but from some book or movie: "Don't step on a crack! You'll break your mother's back!"

She opened the car door and got out.

In the same moment a young woman came out of the house. The screen door banged shut, nearly catching the skirt of the shapeless pastel dress she wore. She jumped, and pressed her hands against her full breast. When she turned toward the street, Ariel's breath caught in recognition. Was that her? Jackie Grady? Or was this woman heavier? Older? Ariel couldn't be sure. It had been too long, the glimpse she'd had of Jackie Grady too casual and too brief.

"Gimme a smack, Jack!" the little girl called out, settling the matter, both of her identity and the woman's. She skipped onto the porch, holding up her palm in invitation. The slap of hands was, on Jackie Grady's part, perfunctory. She dredged up a smile; then, saying something to the child Ariel couldn't hear, clattered down the steps and, clutching her middle with both hands, hurried up the street. After only a few steps, she broke into a run.

Keshia, apparently, was accustomed to more attention from Jackie. She hunkered down on the steps and pouted. Martine Brown came out, looked up the street after Jackie, and, saying something to the child that, again, Ariel couldn't hear, went back inside. She appeared to be wearing the same clothes as last night; maybe she hadn't had such a restful sleep after all.

Ariel had watched it all as if it were a drama being played out, minus essential dialogue, on a movie screen. She snapped to, got back into the van, and, cutting a circle in the street, took off after Jackie Grady, who by then was rounding a corner.

Ariel told herself that Jackie was probably just late for

work, the job at the factory where she affixed labels to boxes. But Ariel didn't believe it. Jackie wouldn't be at Brown House at this hour unless Martine called her, and Martine wouldn't have called her unless she wanted to warn her. Well, perhaps only ask questions, but the questions themselves would be a warning, even to a girl with limited reasoning abilities, especially to a girl who worshipped the ground her brother walked on. If Jackie got to her brother, he'd be gone. So, keeping the girl in sight, Ariel drove.

The time had come to ditch the Lone Ranger act and call in the cavalry. To call Max. The explanation would be impossible, and she would be in for a world of grief, but there was no help for it. She reached into her bag for her cell phone. It wasn't in the pocket where she kept it. Her eyes on Jackie and oncoming cars, her blind hand grasped and rejected wallet, Filofax, a voice organizer she hadn't used in so long the batteries had expired, and a number of other objects her fingers worked to recognize. She knew even while she groped that the phone wasn't there; it was clamped to the recharger where she'd left it. A year ago she hadn't owned a cell phone; nowadays she couldn't function ten minutes without it.

Forget help.

They were into a commercial block now, and Ariel needed both hands and her full attention for driving. She gave serious thought to parking and overtaking the girl on foot, but it wasn't Jackie she wanted, it was the man she called Moe. Ariel was convinced they were on their way to him, on as direct and urgent a course as Moe's sister could go.

Jackie's pace began to slow. She passed an auto upholstery shop and then a liquor store with the accordion grate locked across the front. By the time she crossed the next street, she was truly flagging. She would trot a few steps,

and then speed walk, as fast as she could push herself, a
jerky marionette. Ariel kept well back. She stopped when
Jackie did.

A delivery truck passed between them, momentarily
cutting off Ariel's view. She tensed, but when the truck
passed, Jackie was still there. She was stooped over, one
hand pressed to her side, the other supporting herself
against a building. On the brick wall behind her was a
faded advertisement, painted so long ago that the smiling
face was ghostly, and the writing all but illegible. HAVE A
COKE! it must once have read. Now, all that could be made
out was HA A COK ! (It had not, Ariel realized, been altered
by time alone.) Jackie's head blocked the last word when
she leaned back against the wall. Ariel waited, van idling.
The girl breathed through her open mouth. Both arms cra-
dled her stomach now.

Two men approached, one with a toddler on his hip. A
second child, a little boy who looked scarcely older,
trailed. He stared at Jackie curiously. Neither of the men
glanced her way.

She's sick, Ariel thought. I should go to her.

A horn blew, and Ariel turned to look behind her. She
couldn't hear what the woman in the old station wagon
was saying, but she doubted she wanted to. There was no
oncoming traffic. She signaled for the woman to pass her.
When she turned back, Jackie was gone.

Ariel scanned the street. She had taken her eyes off the
girl for four seconds, and now there was no sign of her. Had
she dropped into a manhole? There was also no sign of a
place, even an illegal place, to park the van. While she was
trying to think what to do, she spotted a leather-clad motor-
cyclist sauntering out of a coffee shop half a block ahead. He
mounted a bike parked at the curb. Ariel sped to the spot.
The man was fishing through his pockets. Ariel adjusted her
rearview mirror to frame the place she'd last seen Jackie. The

cyclist extracted a toothpick, with which he explored a
bared canine. Just as Ariel decided that he intended to perform an entire prophylaxis where he sat, he harvested a
morsel, dropped the pick, and booted his kickstand.

The stores nearest where Jackie vanished weren't yet
open, so she couldn't have ducked into one. Ariel scanned
as she crossed the street, hurrying the half block back.
Could the girl have gotten into a car? Then she saw what,
from her former vantage point, had been imperceptible.
Feet away from where Jackie had rested was a space sepa-
rating buildings. It wasn't wide enough to be called an
alley, more a hole in the wall.

With egress?

Ariel slowed before she reached it, taking a few seconds to mute her breathing. If there was no egress, then,
obviously, Jackie was still there. But why would she hide?
Had she known someone was following her? Had she
spotted Ariel back at Brown House? Would she even be
canny enough to hide from a pursuer?

No sunlight found its way into the passage. It was
barely wide enough for an adult to negotiate broadside.
There was no place to hide. Not for a person. Foraging animals might find refuge, and probably did. There were
garbage cans at the far end. Which meant there had to be
access for sanitation trucks.

The odor was ripe. The cement floor looked dank. It
was too reminiscent of the godforsaken, filth-strewn alley
where James Price had known the worst moments of his
life, and Ariel didn't break any speed records rushing in.

"You lose something, lady?"

A panel truck idled at the curb behind her. The man
who'd spoken was in the passenger seat, his bulky forearm propped on the open window. His expression suggested that what she might want to lose was no time in
moving on. His tone was proprietary.

Gustavson's was painted in fancy script on the truck. Ariel couldn't see the driver, but the passenger was many shades darker than anyone she would have associated with that name. Did the logo match a sign on one of the nearby buildings? It didn't seem like the right moment to canvass the area. The alleyway, she supposed, was private property. Adjoining businesses, she supposed, must have rear entrances back there, windows barred against intruders, locks that got broken during robberies. Ariel didn't look like a burglar, and the hour wasn't conducive to successful break-ins, but there were a limited number of legitimate reasons for lurking about.

"I'm a commercial properties realtor," she said firmly, surprising herself. "Do you happen to have a cell phone?"

The man ducked his chin and raised an eyebrow. His gaze swept the crevice, the buildings on either side of it, and, from head to toe, Ariel. It lingered, for no reason she could think of, on her shoes. She resisted looking down. "Ma'am," he said, "you might want to find some listings in a more . . . compatible part of town."

She flashed a busy smile. "I'm waiting for my partner." *He's black*, she almost said. "He's late."

With a last dubious glare that suggested it was her funeral, he rolled up the window, and, infinitely slowly, the truck rolled away. Ariel watched and thought: *What's it like to live in a neighborhood where people warn people away for their own good?* She felt, not vaguely as she had for the last half hour, but pulsatingly, her whiteness. She glanced at the storefronts nearby. No Gustavson's. When the truck turned a corner, she strode into the passage. She didn't breathe until she made the other end, and she didn't look back.

She emerged into a one-way alley that ran parallel to the rear of the buildings. The parking spaces were empty of cars. Except for a large lump of rags in a sheltered doorway, a mound that was conceivably a homeless person, the area was empty of people.

Taking a deep drag of the marginally healthier air, Ariel considered the possibilities. Jackie could have turned left and gone back in the direction from which she'd come. Unlikely. She'd expended too much effort getting here. Ariel turned right. She'd gone only a few hurried steps before she spied a third option: yet another narrow passageway that intersected the alley from the opposite direction. It was a coin-toss situation. It was, by now, Ariel figured, a hopeless situation; she'd lost too much time. Simply because she didn't want to tunnel through another claustrophobic crack between walls, she kept to the wider alley.

It opened onto a commercially zoned residential street. One-family dwellings, most going to seed or already there, alternated with businesses operated out of what had once been private homes. There were signs advertising a beauty shop, and EXPERT ALTERATIONS, and, oddly, to Ariel, beads. None was yet open. There were no public telephones. It appeared that humans were in equally short supply until she caught the faintest sound of singing.

Beside the steps of the beauty shop squatted a little girl, crooning to herself. She was admiring her stubby fingernails, each hardly bigger than a sequin. They looked like sequins, painted, as they were, a deep shiny purple.

The child made no reply to Ariel's greeting. Generously, however, she angled one small hand so that Ariel could appreciate the full impact of the fluorescent enamel.

"Gorgeous!" Ariel agreed. "Like grapes. I don't suppose you'd know my friend Jackie Grady?"

Large, curious dark eyes slid meaningfully toward some point behind Ariel, and after a moment, one purple-tipped finger followed their lead.

Ariel turned. "That's where she lives? The house next to the bead shop?"

A vigorous shake of the head.

"You've been told not to talk to strangers," Ariel guessed. She knelt and sighted along the tiny finger. "That grayish house?"

A solemn nod.

"Thank you," Ariel said, equally grave. "Now, you don't have to speak, just nod, okay? Do you have a telephone at your—"

"Charlene!"

The voice came from just inside the beauty shop house, and Charlene knew serious when she heard it. She was gone in a blink, and the door was closed behind her.

And the top of the morning to you, thought Ariel. Still kneeling, she surveyed the street. *I could go house to house until somebody invites me in. Alternatively, I could just bay at the moon.* She considered going in search of a pay phone; she considered how far away Jackie and/or her brother would be when she got back; she considered what police response time would be for this area.

She got to her feet and, before she could think better of it, made her way to the small gray house that listed slightly, as if the ground beneath it had given under the weight of its burden.

42

NO ONE ANSWERED THE BELL. ARIEL COULDN'T HEAR IT; MAYBE IT didn't work. The glass inset in the door was covered by unlined fabric through which could be seen (if one pressed one's face against the pane) an empty hallway. The porch

was as bare: not a stick of furniture, not a plant, and not a
welcome mat. She raised her hand to knock, hesitated,
and tried the doorknob instead. The lock worked if the
doorbell didn't.

With a feeling she recognized as unadulterated relief,
she backed away, deciding on her next move, deciding it
wouldn't be solo whatever it was. She was hurrying down
the steps when she heard the creak of unoiled hinges
behind her.

Any number of thoughts cut through Ariel's mind.
Foremost among them was that she should put one foot in
front of the other and hit the sidewalk running. She took
hold of the handrail. It didn't offer much in the way of
support. Not unlike her knees, it threatened to give way.

The man who stood framed in the doorway was no
one Ariel could swear in court she'd ever seen before,
either in person or captured in the inadequate pen lines of
a police sketch. The glasses he wore were metal-framed,
delicate-looking, and he stared at her from behind them.
She couldn't tell if they were new, replacing a pair broken
while a man struggled for his life.

His hand made what looked like an involuntary movement, a twitch of the doorknob he held. *He's nervous,* some
hopeful part of Ariel's mind told her. And then he dropped
his hand, and dipped his head, and scowled.

Now she knew him.

He seemed to be moving in slow motion when he
stepped out onto the porch, toward her. Ariel braced herself. Her field of vision, dizzyingly, shrank to a pin dot,
and the world, as if she'd gone deep underwater, went
stone silent. It was entirely possible that she would right
here, right now, faint.

His eyes swept the length of the street. His features
twisted, not with anger but with pain. Even in her stupor
Ariel couldn't misread it. Because his mouth moved, she

knew he spoke. And then he turned and, heavily, slowly, went back into the house.

Sound, after a heartbeat, resumed. Ariel found that she had sat down; she was sitting on the steps.

"Charlene!" A female screech shattered the air. "Get over here, and I mean now!"

The little girl with the purple sequin nails had escaped again. She lurked on the sidewalk, gawking.

"Shoo home," Ariel said, her voice muffled by the dry wad of cotton that was her tongue. The child stuck her thumb in her mouth, and then, coming to a decision, struck out.

He had left the door ajar. Maybe, Ariel thought, he'd mistaken her for somebody he was expecting. Against all logic, she told herself that he didn't know who she was or why she'd turned up. And knew better. His despair was too vivid in her mind; he'd looked at her and seen fate on his doorstep.

"Oh, Lord!" she whispered as what he'd said hit with the force of a club. Ariel didn't know if she'd heard it or lip-read it, but she knew he'd said it. *"I'm so sorry."* She'd read too many stories about domestic murder-suicides. She'd covered such a story herself. Men and women, cornered, desperate, demon-plagued, who kill their family members before taking their own lives. Jackie was in there with him, Jackie who trusted her brother to take care of her.

Ariel pulled herself up by the railing, which, this time, made good its threat. The rotting stave, which was nothing but a painted two-by-two, pulled loose, hanging by one last sorely tried nail. She wrenched it free, and tested its heft. It was solid enough, about as long as her leg. A couple of rusty nails protruded evilly from one end. Ariel mounted the steps. She gave herself a second at the threshold, and then she went inside.

Off the hallway was what the builder had intended to be the living room. A sofa and TV kept faith with the plan. Just those two items. Clutching the two-by-two, Ariel forced herself to stop and listen. She heard a faint thump from the next room, and—she frowned—running water? She moved toward the sound.

His back was to the door, his shoulder blades sharp under a T-shirt patched wet with sweat. The kitchen faucet squealed as he filled a glass. Jackie was nowhere in the room.

Now, unfortunately, Ariel was.

He hadn't seen her yet. He didn't know she was there. She willed herself to back out the way she came. Her feet seemed to have no neural connection to her head.

"You're Moe?" she said.

The glass clinked against his teeth, spilling water. He wiped his chin. If he saw the makeshift weapon in her hand, he didn't react to it. "Where are they?" he asked.

Ariel almost said who, but it was obvious. He didn't think she'd be dumb enough to come here alone. He assumed cops would crash in any second. She was lucky he hadn't yanked her in the door and put a gun to her head; she'd delivered herself like a person whose ambition in life was to be held hostage.

And yet . . . he made no move that could be interpreted as hostile. He set the glass on the counter, and it occurred to Ariel that he didn't trust the steadiness of his hand, which he wiped on his pants. They were the same baggies he'd worn the last time she'd seen him, or a similar pair; they hung on him in a way she didn't remember. He was barefoot. He looked like a skinny kid, as ordinary as his plain white T-shirt. Ariel could easily imagine him in a classroom. College boy. Scholarship student. Killer.

"Where's your sister?" she asked. She noticed the evenness of her voice. She realized she wasn't afraid. More accurately, she wasn't incapacitated by fear.

There was, she saw, a back door. He could have left by it, and hadn't. Jackie, Ariel would bet, had: pushed out and told to run away by her brother before he'd opened the front door. It was why it had taken him so long. She had a sense, now a growing conviction, that, whatever he'd done, this man was no danger right now to anyone, with the possible exception of himself.

She'd been wrong before.

"Moe," she said, "she's pregnant, isn't she?" Where that knowledge had come from, Ariel didn't know. Clues. There had been clues.

The young man took off his glasses and pinched the bridge of his nose with thumb and forefinger. When he'd replaced the glasses, he said, "Not Moe."

"What?"

"Jackie's the only one who calls me that. My name is Maurice."

The syllables were clearly delineated. A young man on the way to being educated. "Polite," Hattie had called him.

"Maurice what?" Ariel asked.

"What difference does it make?" He was dripping sweat. "Thomas. Maurice Thomas." His voice thickened. "What's going to happen to her?"

"To Jackie?"

"She'll be on the streets now. She won't last a month!"

Tears, Ariel saw, mingled with the perspiration, and the sight of them, suddenly and with a force that shocked her, made her furious. "Your concern comes a little late, mister," she said coldly, as angry as she could remember ever being. "Too late for Jackie and too late for James Price and for —"

"He raped her." It was said in a whisper.

"—Carrie Murphy and —"

"That bastard raped her!" Maurice Thomas yelled.

Ariel heard him then, but it took a second to penetrate. "Price? Are you saying that Price—"

"Raped my sister!" A sob tore loose, and his fist slammed the counter, knocking the water glass flying. It shattered, fragments ricocheting into the sink. Ariel recoiled. It was all but an admission. Mitigating circumstances or not, he had killed. Because of him two people were dead. Because of him Laya was blind. She gripped the stave, ready to use it. He was oblivious. "He raped her and he beat her," he was saying, crying in earnest now, "and he didn't stop at one time. I don't know how many times because she tried to hide . . . She was scared to tell me. She was ashamed." He cried like a person who had no experience at it. He kept trying to get above it, to say what he had to say. "Like it was her fault. I didn't know till she came home bleeding." He was bleeding, too, his hand cut by the glass. He held on to himself, back bowed like the shell of a turtle. His crossed arms hugged his ribs. "All I could think of was to make him pay. To fix him so he couldn't . . . to make him stay away from her." He gave up trying to talk. Lowering his head, shaking it like a bull, he clamped his mouth shut against the sobs.

Ariel waited it out. She scowled at the blood smeared on the side of his shirt. Quiet fell. Eventually, feeling sapped of every emotion except pity she wanted nothing to do with, she said, "Why don't you do something about your hand."

He didn't move.

"Hey . . ." She touched his back. He jerked away. "Well, then just bleed."

"I wanted to kill myself," he mumbled.

Ariel started. Had she been right about his intentions?

"When Price died . . . when I heard that and the rest, I wanted to die. I couldn't do it. There was Jackie."

Ariel propped the porch rail against the counter and picked up a dishtowel. She grasped his shoulder and turned him. This time he didn't resist. The cut on his hand, she saw, wasn't deep. She handed him the towel, and said, "Sit."

The inappropriateness of her actions wasn't lost on her. She ought to be calling the law—she knew that—but she might never get another opportunity to understand how all this horror had happened. When he was in a chair, she leaned her hip against the table and, as if sheer force of will would make it happen, said, "Make me understand."

She waited. She wasn't about to tell him so, but they had plenty of time.

After a while he wiped his face on the towel, wrapped it around his hand, and said, "The yoga teacher."

"What about her?"

"How is she?"

"Laya's . . ." It was too hard a question. "Some better."

Head down, he nodded. "It's my fault what happened to her." He made himself look directly at Ariel. "Everything that's happened is my fault. But I would like somebody to know how it was."

The story started with a tragedy and got worse.

Maurice Thomas was his sister's keeper. He tried to keep his grades up and keep a part-time job and keep the landlord off his back and, all the while, keep tabs on Jackie. He'd been at it for a while. Their mutual father hadn't been seen in a decade. Jackie's mother showed up all too often, looking to scrounge.

One night Jackie had come home with a black eye, a broken tooth, and lips like raw hamburger. Maurice had gone out of his mind. Gotten half-loaded, a condition he wasn't used to. An old neighborhood hanging buddy, one who'd been around until he'd been sent away, had listened to him rant. "He needs hurting," the old buddy had said, and Maurice's blood had answered.

Getting James Price into the alley hadn't been a problem. The first blows had made the world right again. And then Laya had shown up. She didn't intervene, but reality did. The smell of fear and body fluids and the sound of bones shattering had suddenly taken on sickening reality.

"You were yelling something," Ariel said, remembering Carrie Murphy's report. "You went down beside Price, on your knees."

"He was *jelly!*" Maurice looked at her, staggered all over again by the breakability of the human body. "He was trying to crawl off. To stay alive. But he couldn't . . . I mean, he moved maybe an inch. Inches. That tire iron kept coming down . . . I couldn't make Tiny stop hitting him!"

"Tiny?" The savage who had terrorized Laya for a month—Mr. X? *Big?*—was called *Tiny?* "That's his name?" Ariel asked.

"Yeah. It's a joke, like, him being so big."

"What's his real name?"

"That's all I ever heard. Tiny Coffey. He was the last one of a bunch of kids . . ." Maurice rubbed his cropped hair in agitation, plainly feeling there was too little time to waste it on irrelevancies. "It was like nobody in his family could remember who he was."

As a kid Coffey had been mean, Maurice said. Apparently, time in stir had brought him to the full flowering of his sociopathy.

"I hadn't really hung with him since a long time ago. He was like somebody I didn't know, like some . . . Man, he *loved* what he was doing to Price! He came by here later that night. Said I better keep my face shut. If I ever got an attack of the guilts, I should think about 'baby sister.'" Maurice looked at Ariel. "Tiny's been in twice. He's got no plans for strike three, he said."

"What about Laya?"

He licked his lips. "I told him who she was."

Ariel briefly closed her eyes.

"It just came out! I wasn't thinking straight. All of a sudden there she was, Jackie's teacher, and all I could think of was . . . Oh, God! I didn't mean for any of this to happen!"

"What did he do?"

Maurice looked at her, aghast. "You know what he did!"

"I know he didn't follow her. Did you tell him where she lived?"

"I don't even know where she lives."

"Then how did he—"

"I don't know! I took Jackie and drove to San Diego that same night and just . . . hid out. A motel. I skipped a couple of days of school. Lost the job I had. I took her to a doctor. When I found out she was pregnant . . ." He was wrapping and unwrapping the towel around his hand. It began to bleed again. "Right then I wasn't even sorry about Price anymore, but when we got back, I heard he died. And then Jackie told me . . . she told me about the teacher."

"And what did Tiny tell you?"

"He wasn't around, and I didn't look for him."

"So he never said outright that he blinded Laya."

"I told you, he wasn't around."

"He never bragged about—"

"He never said he killed that old lady either, but I know he did it."

"You're saying you haven't seen him since that night?"

"Once. The day after Mrs. Murphy . . . He was outside Brown House, with Jackie. He *patted* her! On the butt." Maurice thrust out his jaw. "He smiled straight at me when he did it."

Ariel tried to put herself in this man's place, to think

what she would have done; she couldn't. "Why the hospital visits?" she asked. "Why did you call my house looking for Laya?"

"I recognized you, you know. I couldn't believe your number was in the phone book."

Ariel nodded.

"She was nice to my sister."

"She's a kind woman. That doesn't explain why you took a chance on getting nailed by trying to see her."

Maurice blinked rapidly. "At first, I just wanted nothing else bad to happen. She saw us, saw Tiny. I wanted to beg her not to talk. He'd kill her. I couldn't believe he didn't to start with.

"When she didn't talk, when nothing happened . . . it was like I couldn't let it go. I wanted to know how she was, if they could fix her so she'd see. I wanted to know why she hadn't told. I wanted her to say she wouldn't, because I didn't want Jackie to know. I wanted to *talk* to her." He shook his head. "The way Jackie made her sound, it was like she was some kind of saint or something. Like she was in some kind of a . . . state of grace or something. What I really wanted . . ."

"What?"

"What I really wanted . . . was forgiveness."

Ariel listened to silence for a moment before she said, "I feel sure Martine Brown will see that your sister's taken care of."

He shrugged, clearly not believing it.

"Where's your telephone?" she asked.

"Disconnected."

"Then I guess you'd better put on your shoes, because we're going to have to—"

When Ariel heard the back door open, she turned to see Jackie. Her heart sank. It nearly stopped when she saw the man who followed Jackie in.

43

"NO," MAURICE SAID, SO LOW ARIEL WOULDN'T HAVE HEARD IT except that the kitchen in that second was dead silent. She'd frozen in place. Jackie had been stopped in her tracks by the large hands that gripped her shoulders. The bald man had her square in front of him, a human shield. She was nothing like petite, but he loomed over her. Nothing moved but his eyes. They fixed on Ariel.

Maurice half rose, reaching for his sister. "I told you to go to Martine," he said with amazing calm. His expression said *What have you done?*

Tiny Coffey pulled Jackie against his chest. It looked like a protective gesture. "She did right," he said.

"Let go of her."

The other man frowned as if injured. His mustache—newly grown or surely Laya would have recalled it—brushed his lower lip. Then he shrugged and pushed Jackie into her brother with such force that the chair in which Maurice had been sitting skidded out from under him and slammed against the wall. His head hit the wooden seat as he went down, Jackie all sprawled limbs atop him.

"Who's this bitch?" Coffey said.

Ariel presumed—or would have, had her mind been functioning—that he meant the question for Maurice, but he was looking at her. Maurice was less functional than she was. With uncertain aim he was groping for the back of his head; the free arm, Ariel saw, had instinctively gone around Jackie.

Coffey waited to be answered. He had a gift for stillness. Lightning quick moves, and then, as abruptly, an

absence of motion. It was eerie. He stood as stone still as if
he were some machine to which the power had been cut.
A big and dangerous machine. He had disproportionately
short legs on which his pumped upper body seemed
grossly misplaced. A thick neck. The mustache didn't
quite hide a cleft lip. His inertness gave her the impression
he might be dull-witted. One thing Ariel knew. She could
see it in his half-lidded eyes. He was not sane.

The silence stretched. Then Coffey came to life.

"Baby sister," he informed Maurice casually, "come to
me. Said you need help. That you in trouble."

Jackie was whimpering. What Maurice was doing Ariel
didn't know; she didn't take her eyes off Coffey. The only
thing that kept her upright and hoping for a future was that
she'd seen no sign of a weapon. He preferred, as far as she
knew, not to dirty his hands. He preferred a tire iron, with
his victim restrained.

"I don't see no trouble," he went on. "I just see this
white bitch."

He was a coward. He'd hidden behind a helpless pregnant girl. He blinded and beat women. Later, if there
should be a later, she'd give due thought to the friendless
state in which Maurice Thomas must exist to have spent
even a minute in this psycho's company.

"What you looking me like that for?" Coffey asked.

"Mr. Thomas does need help now," Ariel said. Her lips
felt numb, yet, as if they were some new acquisition she
had no experience in using, she could feel them moving
against each other. "He needs a doctor."

"Who are you?"

"If you'll stand out of my—"

"I know you." Coffey said. "I seen you before."

"No. No, sir, I would have remembered that." Even as
she spoke, Ariel saw recognition dawn and spread across
his face.

"You on TV! Ooooh, man!" he whooped, and cackled, and the menace in his broad smile made his former cold stare seem like a benediction.

Ariel was surprised; she couldn't imagine that he watched any program more taxing than cartoons.

"What do you know about that!" he said, and then, abruptly: "What's your name?"

"Ariel Gold."

"You gonna put my man here on the tube, *Miz* Gold? Now what you suppose the brother's got to say that's worth putting on the tube?"

Ariel didn't let her eyes stray to the porch rail propped against the counter, its two precious nails protruding like rusty fangs. He'd shown no sign of noticing it. When she took one infinitesimal side step toward it (another mile, and she'd be there), she actually saw his ears move up with the clinch of his jaw. She stopped. "I'd like to hear what *you* have to say." It came out stronger than she'd had any reason to believe it would.

"Say about what?"

"What Mr. Thomas and I were discussing. The socio-economic ramifications of subsisting at the bottommost end of the food chain. I would say that you, sir, have first-hand knowledge."

Coffey pursed his lips. Ariel doubted that he understood what she'd said. (*She* didn't. She was babbling.) But he got the drift. "That right?" he asked lazily. Then, with one of his hair-trigger moves, he punched a rigid forefinger into her sternum. "You got a mouth on you, *Miz* Gold!" he said. "Shut it!"

She did.

"Now what's Mau*reece* been feeding you that you think you gonna put on your TV show?"

"He hasn't been—"

"What business you got here? What you want?"

When Ariel didn't answer, he jabbed again. That finger hurt.

"It's nothing to do with my show," Ariel got out. She could feel the bruise forming. "A personal matter."

"Personal matter," Coffey repeated. "Uh-huh. What's she want?" he suddenly tossed in Maurice's direction.

Ariel cut her eyes toward the two people on the floor. Jackie was sitting up, cradling her brother's head. From it, a stain spread on her dress. Maurice's mouth was open, but he didn't say anything. His eyes, half-closed, showed no iris. Coffey looked, too, and shook his head, as if the sight he beheld wearied him.

Ariel gained another inch toward the porch rail.

"Hey!" Coffey prompted Maurice, ungently, with his foot. Ariel flinched. Jackie yelped. Coffey drew back his foot again. "The teacher," Jackie cried. "She's my teacher's friend. She is! She was at the hospital. I saw her."

"What you talking about?" Coffey grunted.

The girl wept, mouth agape. "Laya. The one teaches— taught—at Brown House."

Ariel's heart lurched and sank. Nothing had been said until that point to indicate she knew who Coffey was or what he'd done. Wishful thinking, maybe, but there'd been a chance he might have blown the whole thing off and gone away. Instead, he'd gone into one of his power-off modes. Even his eyes went still. Ariel wondered what, if anything, was going on behind them. Doubtless it was more wishful thinking, but she could almost believe he had no idea who Jackie was talking about.

And then she saw the memory click.

"The woman in the alley," Coffey said. He gave it another few seconds' reflection. "She send you here?"

Ariel didn't see the next *click!* She heard it. It was unmistakable. So much, she thought, for having no weapon.

The switchblade wasn't long. It wouldn't have looked like much if it were whittling balsa wood or peeling an apple. Aimed at her eye, it looked like a broadsword.

She was grabbed by the lapels and shoved against the counter. "Did she?" Coffey said into her face. His breath was minty, like breath spray. "And you came, all by your little self." His upper lip, which had a twisted look in any case, corkscrewed, and his eyes took on a glaze that could only be described as pleasure. "You are a mighty stupid woman," he said softly.

Ariel knew in that second that she had badly underestimated Tiny Coffey. Because of his name maybe. In some part of her mind now rapidly shutting down, she saw that she had made him up. Who she wanted him to be. A bully. A posturer with his affected shaved head. A dullard she could manipulate.

He pricked her a little, just to see her bleed, and then he dispensed with the knife altogether, slamming a knee into her crotch with a force that shattered her into fragments of bright, pure pain. He grunted with the effort of it.

She was on her knees. She wasn't going to be manipulating anybody.

And then he kicked her in the ribs, and she went down, curling into a fetal ball as he drew back to kick again, aiming for her head. She was rolling as it connected, clipping her skull, doing less damage than he'd intended. He swore. She hit an obstruction, a solid surface. There was nowhere left to go.

When she heard the next blow, so solid it had to have found dense bone, she felt a rush of overwhelming gratitude. She was beyond pain. She hadn't even felt it.

He roared. An animal bellow that turned her insides to water. She tried to make herself smaller. She willed herself to be invisible.

"You retard!" Coffey yelled.

She opened her eyes. She saw two huge bald men looming directly above her. They were enraged, off balance, clutching their temple, from which blood flowed. The two men converged. He was one man, but badly out of focus. The porch rail struck again, and he screamed when the nails sank into his cheek.

He'd gotten hold of one end of the club, but his grip was poor, and he screamed again, hideously, when the nails were ripped from his face. Blood spurted.

Ariel flung herself against his legs, winding her body around them. He fell, flailing. A foot hit her in the kidney, but she held on. She caught sight of the switchblade, on the floor, inches from her eyes. She couldn't let go of the legs to reach for it. And then it was gone. Snatched up. And Coffey cried out. She raised her eyes. The knife was in his belly.

"Freeze!" somebody shouted.

A gun went off, and it was deafening. Ariel could hardly hear herself screech, "Don't shoot!" She howled it into Tiny Coffey's blood-soaked thighs. "Don't shoot!"

44

"YOU SOME KIND OF FOOL, LADY!"

"That seems to be the census of opinion," Ariel told the passenger from the Gustavson's van. "Census?" That didn't sound right. Her brain wasn't working too well. "*Con*sensus."

The van had been a surveillance vehicle. The passenger was Eddie Rials, the detective who'd worked the Price homicide. He'd been rendezvousing with the van on an unrelated case when he spotted Ariel earlier that morning.

When the dispatcher's call came in with Maurice Thomas's address, he and his partner had taken it. He was not a happy man.

"I should've run you off when I saw you hanging around that alley," he told Ariel, supporting her by the arm as he led her out onto the Thomas's bare front porch. "If I'd known who you were, I would've. I should've run you in."

"Should've, would've, could've," Ariel said, her eyes going to where the crude railing used to be. She wondered if a porch rail had ever been taken in as evidence before. She felt a sudden need to sit down. The steps were handy. It hurt when she sat.

"I'm still thinking about an obstruction charge," Rials said.

"I told you, I didn't know either man's name. I didn't know where Maurice lived until . . ." She looked at her watch. It said eight . . . something. Ariel squeezed her eyes shut and opened them again. The watch's hands wavered. "About an hour ago." Could that possibly be right? "He's got no phone. He was on his way in—voluntarily—when we got interrupted."

"I knew when I saw you you had no business hanging around," Rials said, unimpressed, "and you had less business coming here."

Ariel held her head. She didn't know what part of her hurt the worst. She couldn't take a deep breath without tears coming to her eyes; she had a hunch a rib was broken.

"And," said Rials, "you *are* going in the next ambulance."

Two had already left. The first took Maurice. Jackie, too. She wasn't injured, but she wouldn't be separated from her brother. The other carried Tiny Coffey. A third was on its way for Ariel. "You win," she said. She squinted out at the street; the light hurt her eyes. There were plenty of people to be seen now. All kept their distance, watching the action as if it were prime time. The woman who held Charlene was still in her bathrobe.

"Did they say how badly he was hurt?" Ariel asked Rials. "Maurice? I mean, all he did was hit his head on a chair!"

"I guess he hit it right."

"He's a good kid, Detective. A good man."

"Yeah, yeah, he's a choirboy. So we heard already from the Brown House woman—"

"Martine?"

"You didn't wonder how we happened to show up here?"

"She's who called you?"

"Recognized Thomas from one of our posters, she said. Now, what *you* haven't said is what got you mixed up in this business."

Ariel hadn't yet grappled with the fact that it wasn't Coffey who'd blinded Laya. She couldn't take it in, but she had no doubt about it. He had not recognized Laya's name. The woman who gaped at him that night and then fled, scared to death, had been of little concern to him. In Coffey's world witnesses had conveniently poor eyesight, short memories, and doors that locked out trouble. Carrie Murphy was exceptional. To him, she must have seemed suicidal. As for Laya, if he'd even heard Maurice say her name, if he'd had any qualms about her at all, they'd been forgotten with the uneventful passage of time.

Laya, as Max had believed all along, was the random victim of a crazy. Her only connection to this entire ugly business was that she had seen a crime in commission and hadn't reported it. Her punishment, meted out by fate (if you believed in it, and Laya did), far exceeded the offense. Ariel wasn't about to rat on her.

"I read about Carrie Murphy," she told Rials. "A hero-ine. I thought she'd make a great segment for my—"

"You were asking about Price before you ever heard of her."

Ariel massaged her head. "True," she said. A welt had come up just above her ear. "Okay, I blundered into some-thing that was none of my business. My new policy is butting out. Fortunately for you guys' arrest rate, the pol-icy didn't go into effect before I found your perpetrators for you."

"And you're waiting for thanks?" Rials said tightly. "When you're through at the hospital, you'll come down to the precinct house to make a formal statement. Get a better story by then."

"Detective?"

"What?"

Ariel held out her car keys. "I don't suppose you'd do something about my van before I get towed?"

Maurice had a concussion. Ariel did not. She did have two cracked ribs: hairline cracks. They felt like fault lines. Tiny Coffey was "stable"; it was probably the first time the word had ever been applied to him.

Ariel dodged reporters all day, a few on entering emergency, more on leaving, a herd at third precinct headquarters. The story made the afternoon paper. Chris Valente at *The Open File* ran her down at the police station. He barraged her with questions, starting with "Why didn't we know you were doing this story?" and ending with "Can you have it ready to air by Monday night?" The nonstory about an assault on a nobody had become a hot story about an assault on a TV news cor-respondent.

Her grandfather picked her up at the police station, his driver hustling her into the Lincoln as if she were a rock star under siege. B.F. wanted to take her to his condo for the night, if not for the foreseeable future. She insisted on going home. He insisted on having Hattie play nursemaid. "I don't need one," Ariel said, "but Laya does. Do you know if Hattie's got plans for the next three weeks?"

Henry called to check on her and offer to bring dinner, which she declined.

Max Neely called to check on her and offer her a hard time, which she suffered.

Ariel called the airline and made reservations for a late-afternoon flight to San Francisco.

Hattie, not to be denied, showed up bearing soup. When she found Ariel packing her overnight case, she told her she was crazy.

"It's not the first time today I've heard it," Ariel said. "I need to go. I promised."

"Bed's where you need to go," Hattie fussed. "You got beat to a pulp this morning." Jessie, who'd been watching the all-too-familiar routine of Ariel packing, sighed from her own bed. "Dog's got more sense than you," Hattie said.

Ariel didn't disagree, but, "I want Laya to know it's over," she said.

"Your telephone don't work?"

On cue, it rang. It hadn't stopped since Ariel got home. "Let it," she said. "The machine'll take it." This, she told herself, was do-able. She wouldn't drive to the airport. (She couldn't; her van was still at the police station.) She'd already called a cab. She'd sit on a plane for an hour, and then taxi to the school. "I have to talk to her," she said, "in person."

She explained to Hattie what she'd learned today, about who had blinded Laya, or more correctly, who had not. "So she may go the rest of her life without ever know-

ing who did this thing to her," Ariel said. "Who knows
how she'll take that?"

Hattie didn't have a ready comeback.

"The Tylenol killer," Ariel told her, "was never caught,
and that was nearly twenty years ago."

"The what?"

"Never mind." Ariel caught herself contemplating the
soft, safe expanse of bed on which her suitcase rested.
Hattie was right. She felt fragile as an egg. The phone rang
again. Without thinking, she picked it up. It was Dr. Gayle
Baker.

On the plane north, trying hard to ignore a headache,
to be coldly analytical, Ariel thought the conversation
through.

"I've been trying to reach you all day!" the excited
young doctor had said. "Listen to this!" It might be nothing, she'd qualified, a coincidence, but, "I was in the office
this morning making coffee, trying to stay awake, you
know, after being up all last night? This woman came in,
and we got to talking. Mrs. Lipton, her name is. She's a
retiree who volunteers occasionally, I think in the gift
shop. But the thing is, she used to work at the Manse, the
new dorm, you know—"

"I know," Ariel had told her. "Slow down."

"—back before it was part of the school—"

"When it was what?"

"Private hospital. Mrs. Lipton worked as a nurse there.
Anyway, she'd heard about last night, and she said it
reminded her of the old days when a patient would try to
'fly the coop.'"

"You're saying this was a mental hospital?"

"St. Luke Wellness Center, they called it the last few
years it existed. It was St. Luke Sanitarium before the days
of cultural sensitivity. Depression, anorexia nervosa, chem-

ical dependency . . . you name it, they, sort of, treated it as long as you had the money—big money—to pay. In my opinion the place was more custodial than remedial."

"This is interesting, but what's the point exactly?"

"The point," Gayle Baker had said, "is that Mrs. Lipton's first name, I found out, is Stella. The name Laya said this morning, remember? You think it's a coincidence?"

Ariel wasn't sure what to call it; freaking weird had come to mind.

Laya dreams a name, she reflected now, not an uncommon name, but not one you hear every day. The dream Stella, Laya had said, was *"As near as I can tell you"* a nurse. This Stella Lipton had been one. Now, for all Ariel knew, Laya could've met Mrs. Lipton, maybe in the gift shop. They could've talked, become friendly, and the woman turned up in her dream. That sort of thing does happen every day.

However, Stella Lipton had worked at a facility that treated head cases: patients suffering from a gamut of mental and emotional problems. *"In the dream, I'm not at the school. I'm at some other sort of institution entirely, because I'm nutty as a fruitcake."* Remembering Laya's words, Ariel felt her scalp constrict.

She shifted in her seat, and grimaced when her ribs called themselves to her attention. The drinks cart was trundled by, and she asked for water. She considered the codeine pills in her purse. She sighed. Later.

"I'm beginning to think this dream's prophetic," Laya had said.

Ariel was beginning to think Laya was looking in the wrong direction. She fought the beguilement of the notion. Yeah, okay, Laya happened to be living in a building (a building, only that: wood and plaster) that once housed people with mental problems. *And* she was sensi-

tive to . . . vibrations? Emanations? Even people with the
sensitivity of cement get vibes from places where extreme
suffering has taken place. Dungeons. Battlefields. Et
cetera. (Of course, that's when they know the score
upfront.) But go with it. Say Laya picked up something.
Pain. Desperation. Delirium.

And a specific name? Gayle Baker wanted to believe it.
The earnest doctor preferred to think that a student she
liked (and, Ariel suspected, was rather in awe of) was
inspired rather than neurotic. Gifted rather than gonzo.
Nevertheless, she'd told Ariel on the phone, she had been
obliged to apprise the school's board of directors about
last night's episode.

"Not about the nightmares?" Ariel had asked, dismayed. "Not the Stella business?" Laya, if she knew,
would be appalled.

"It was necessary to their understanding of the situation," Gayle had justified, "but I downplayed the . . . outré
aspects? I emphasized the fact that the *police* use sensitives. They have them visit crime scenes—I've read about
this—where they can gain a . . . call it 'depth perception'
about what took place."

"We're not talking about a crime scene; we're talking
about a dormitory room."

"Same principle. It's just one step beyond profiling,
really. There are documented cases of valid information,
including names, being provided through visions."

Ariel could imagine the board members' reactions.

"What I said made an impression, Ariel. The man I told
you about . . . the one adamant about making Laya drop
out? He was skeptical initially, but he listened. He definitely
took me seriously."

"Did he?" Ariel had asked dryly. She wondered how
much faith Gayle would have in "depth perception" if she
knew what Ariel knew: that Laya had been convinced

Tiny Coffey and his partner blinded her; that she'd "sensed" them stalking her, intent on mayhem, when one was oblivious to her existence, and the other yearned for her forgiveness. Laya wasn't infallible even when she was awake.

"You told them," Ariel had confirmed, "that I'd be responsible for Laya tonight? That I'd arrange for her to finish the course as a day student?"

After tonight's conversation with Laya, she thought, the whole issue might be academic.

The man occupying the window seat said, "Excuse me?" Ariel got up to let him by. She was visualizing that conversation. *The good news is the man who killed James Price and Carrie Murphy is in custody; he can't hurt you now. The bad news is he never did; your attacker's still free as a bird.*

She sat, leaning her head back and closing her eyes. Normally, she did some of her best thinking on a plane, which was a good thing, since she spent too much time airborne. Tonight she was too sore and too tired to make sense of anything. How many trips north did this make? Four in as many weeks? Her mind drifted to the first one, when she'd come up to accept an award and a challenge: to discover the identity of a one-named letter writer. Dorothy, whom she had forgotten. Dorothy, who had written in fear of her life, trying to hide it behind light turns of phrase as if fear were a breach of taste. Dorothy, who'd been buried the same weekend.

Ariel's eyes snapped open. The window seat man hovered in the aisle. It took a second to focus on what was required of her, but she got up and moved aside to let him in. Then, totally absorbed by her thoughts, she remained standing in the spot he'd vacated.

She'd had Tara check out every likely place Dorothy Thibeau might have volunteered: every hospice and convalescent home and health care facility in Marin County,

every hospital where she could have met and befriended a
patient named Sis.

Every hospital that currently existed.

Not St. Luke Wellness Center, which no longer did
exist. Which stopped existing when? The Manse, as it was
familiarly called, couldn't have belonged to the school for
long or it wouldn't still be "the new dorm." And the
refurbishing, Ariel recalled, had the fresh look, even the
new wood smell, of recent work.

Telling herself this was a waste of time, she fished in
her purse for her address book. She should stick to the
business at hand. It was as much as she could handle with
her current energy resources. She called Charles Barnes,
fidgeting until he answered.

The connection was poor, and Ariel had to identify herself twice. "Are you familiar with a hospital called St.
Luke's Wellness Center?" she asked him.

45

IT WAS A COOL NIGHT IN SAN FRANCISCO, WITH A WIND, WHICH
made it a cold night. Ariel wasn't dressed for it. She shivered as she waited outside baggage claim. When would
she ever get it through her head that Southern and
Northern California had two very different climates? The
Bay Area had more climates all by itself than most entire
states. "Miniclimates" they were called, and just because it
was May didn't mean any of them would resemble warm.

When Charles had heard she was en route, he'd
insisted on picking her up. He had no plans for the
evening, he'd said through AirFone static; he'd come get
her, and tell her what he could about St. Luke's—which

she did know was no longer in business? Ariel asked when it had closed. He had to repeat the answer. "A year or two ago," she heard before she lost him altogether.

The timing fit. It was all Ariel thought about for the rest of the flight. Sis died at least two and a half years ago. Dorothy began volunteering at Marin General two years ago. Because St. Luke Wellness Center *(where she had been volunteering?)* closed down?

The only vehicle Ariel had ever seen Charles drive was a truck, so she paid no attention to the old Mercedes sedan that rolled to the curb until he got out to open the passenger door. He must have shaved before her call. He wouldn't have had time since. He'd made it here in under an hour, but he had shaved. He smelled fresh with it. She suspected he'd canceled other plans after all.

She grimaced when she buckled herself in. He noticed. "What's the matter?" he asked.

"A twinge." Cracked ribs weren't a subject Ariel had the stamina to talk about.

"There's not a problem with your friend, I hope?" he asked as he guided the car through the maze of construction that seemed to be as permanent an airport fixture as souvenir cable cars and sourdough bread. "That's got you up here?"

Laya's latest revelations (or aberrations) were also not a subject Ariel felt up to. "Well," she said, "it's something she brought to light that got me curious about this Wellness Center."

"Oxymoronic name, I always thought," Charles said. He nodded toward a thermos on the seat. "I'd just made coffee when you called. I brought two cups." He was a man, Ariel thought, who should have a wife and a covey of children. Always prepared: a nurturer. She opened the thermos. The fragrance filled the car. Colombian, she remembered, and "leaded." It might give her a few hours' more functioning time. "This—tonight—is above and beyond," she said. "You're a lifesaver." She poured for them both, setting his in the holder. "Why're you so good to me?"

"Aside from the fact that we're friends—or I flatter myself that we're friends—how many TV personalities do you think I get to squire around?" He gave her a bent-mouth smile. "Now," he said, "about the Wellness Center. I said they closed a year or two ago? Well, it had to be two at least because the school's had the building for a year." His grin flashed again. "Time gets away from you at my age. Let's see . . . what else can I tell you?" The former owner had been an out-of-state consortium, he recalled. The hospital was old and in need of major renovation. The profit margin wasn't such, presumably, to justify the investment, since they'd sold. The buyer had donated the property to the guide dog school.

"Big gift," Ariel commented, but it wasn't the largess that interested her. "Who bought it?" she asked. "Who donated it?"

"I'm thinking it was an anonymous bequest. If that's true, the school's not going to give out a name. You could talk to somebody who was with the hospital, except I don't know if any of the staff's still in the area."

Ariel knew of one. She told Charles about the school volunteer who was a retired nurse, and asked if he knew her.

"Lipton?" he said, and shook his head no. "The only volunteers I run into are other dog walkers."

She wouldn't be around tonight, of course, and Ariel would be leaving early in the morning, long before Stella Lipton was behind the counter of the gift shop. Maybe she was listed in the phone book. Why, Ariel chided herself, hadn't she thought to ask Gayle for the woman's number?

"Ariel . . . ?" Charles said.

"What?"

"Would it be prying if . . ." He shrugged.

"If? Oh! I don't mean to be mysterious, it's just it would take so long . . ." Ariel reconsidered. They did have a ways to go, and she could hardly pump him and then refuse to explain why. "It's about this friend, Dorothy . . . Well, you knew her husband. Raymond Thibeau?" She turned to ease the ache in her side, facing him more squarely. "We talked about him."

As succinctly as she could, Ariel told him the story. He interrupted infrequently, and her edited version was probably more confusing than enlightening, but still, they were into San Rafael before she wound it up. "So," she said, "that's my theory."

"That this woman Mrs. Thibeau wrote you about, this Sis, was a hospital patient she befriended?"

"Yes."

"And you're thinking she was a patient at the Wellness Center."

"It's possible. It's the only hospital in the county at the time that I haven't checked out."

"And she was . . . murdered."

"Dorothy thought she was."

"And you suspect Mrs. Thibeau was also murdered?" His tone was politely neutral, Ariel noticed.

"You think it sounds lame?"

"I assume that a person in your line of work doesn't go off half-cocked."

Ariel laughed. "Yes, I do. A dozen times a day." She sipped her coffee.

"Well," he said encouragingly, "I expect there's more to your suspicions than you've said, right? I mean, if your show's taking this seriously."

"*The Open File* isn't involved. Not yet anyway. It's just me, sniffing around with my usual wild abandon."

"Just you? What about Millen? I got the impression . . ."

Ariel frowned. "I'm glad you asked. Tell me something. Who *is* he?"

"What do you mean, 'who is he?'"

"I read something in a magazine. His family's wealthy?"

"His mother's family. The Woodmans."

"The magazine described her as the *late* Constance Woodman Millen. When did she die, do you know?"

"Not really. Not so long ago. A few years?"

"A few? Like five or six? Or like two or three?"

"Oh Ariel, I don't . . . More like two or three, I suppose."

"Two or three," Ariel repeated, feeling a little breathless. "What did she die of, Charles? And where?"

"I wouldn't know about that."

"Rob was the only son, the magazine said. The only heir?" Ariel caught the expression on Charles's face as they passed under a streetlight. "I'm not after his money," she said. "I have reason to ask. If you'll remember, you *gave* me reason to be leery of him."

"Mrs. Millen had a brother, quite a prominent one." Charles went on to say something about a man who had owned a stock brokerage firm in the city and died when his private plane crashed.

The woman had had a sibling, Ariel thought; she might easily have been called Sis by family and family intimates. And no one gets more intimate than those with you at the end. "So," she said, "Rob did inherit. A lot?"

"Quite a bit, if you credit the talk."

"What talk?"

"There's always gossip," Charles said stiffly, "when someone comes into money."

"And, in this case, it was . . . ?"

"I don't like repeating—"

"It's important."

"There was a rumor having to do with a last minute will change."

The evidence, Ariel realized, had been quietly accumulating almost from the beginning, one item after the other, piled on like a bonfire: a volatile stack, waiting to be noticed by a spark. The magazine article had supplied it.

There was a reason Rob Millen could live well beyond the salary of a columnist for a county newspaper. He could drive an expensive car and wear custom-made clothes and involve himself in charitable endeavors (could be a *philanthropist*) because he'd come into big money. He'd come into big money because a woman died. His mother, Constance Woodman Millen. She'd died two to three years ago, leaving a lone heir, who'd "inherited quite a bit."

Ariel shook her head, sagging. Had she gone for help to the very man she was looking for? She'd fed him information about the Thibeaus. She'd kept him abreast of what she learned, her thoughts and theories. The whole enchilada. She was an idiot.

He'd probed, questions on questions, not to get a story for a book, but to find out how much she knew. He'd insisted on doing certain research chores himself, and withheld information, and lied about his findings to steer her away from the truth. To dilute it, disguise it, confuse it. He'd supplied an unsubstantiated story, an impossible *to* substantiate story, about Ray Thibeau and a telephone conversation with a mystery man. He hadn't overheard the conversation with that man; he'd been that man.

And this was all conjecture. Not a scintilla of proof.

"Ariel?"

There wasn't a place to go with it.

"Are you awake?"

The car had stopped. They were at the school. Charles turned off the engine. "What are your plans?"

"Plans?" Ariel made an effort to focus. "I need to spend a while with Laya. There're things we need to talk about." He shrugged off her thanks. "Are you staying at your grandfather's?" he asked. "I'll wait and drive you. You take your time."

"No, I'm crashing here." All that needed to be said to Laya, (let alone all that had to be thought through and acted on about Rob) was the size and weight of a mountain. A mountain range. A continent. "Charles, I'll tell you something. I hate to admit it. I may be woman, but I'm about roared out."

He smiled. "The dining room will be closed, and the vending machine coffee's undrinkable. Take the thermos."

"I can't . . ."

"Take it. I'll pick it up next time I'm out dog walking."

Dusk was settling in when he left her at the dormitory door. This was, Ariel thought, the longest day of her life, and it wasn't over yet. She'd been up since 4 A.M. It seemed like 4 B.C.

She had never noticed the tastefully small brass plaque affixed beside the entrance, and she didn't notice it then.

46

IT WAS HARD TO KNOW HOW LAYA TOOK THE NEWS. ARIEL couldn't swear she took it in. The tilt of her head suggested she was at least listening.

Ariel had found her already in bed, looking as if she hadn't slept in recent memory, drawn and heavy-eyed.

The two of them made a cute pair, she thought: Dopey and Sleepy.

"It's bad," she said, "beyond bad, that the man who did this to you may never be caught and punished, but that's not the primary thing, is it?" She wished she'd rehearsed what best to say; she was pretty sure she hadn't hit on it yet. "The primary thing is you don't have to be afraid anymore."

"The primary thing," Laya said quietly, "is I've got to talk to Maurice Thomas. Poor, misguided . . ."

Ariel was staggered. The woman finds out that she was maimed for no reason any sane person could comprehend, that the twisted evil gutless slime who did it may never even have a name, and her reaction is to worry about somebody else?

"And Jackie." Laya knuckled her forehead like a person distracted by last-minute chores before a trip. "She's got to be taken care of. If I'm not able to see to it, Ariel, you've got to."

"If you're not . . . ," Ariel sputtered. "Laya, hear me. You're safe. You never were in danger from those men. Certainly not from Maurice, and Coffey paid you no more mind than if you'd been a stray dog wandering by that alley! And—"

"You didn't say how the police came to find them."

"They just did. Who cares? Let me finish. *And* you're not in danger from the person who put acid in those drops. He didn't know you any more than you knew him. He doesn't care who you are. Your buying that particular bottle was pure rotten chance. Like being struck by lightning!"

"Which doesn't strike twice in the same place," Laya said. "Please stop raving. I understand. You don't. Promise me."

"Promise you what?"

"About Jackie."

"Okay," Ariel said helplessly. "I promise." Was she on the wrong set? She felt as if she were visiting a condemned woman on the eve of execution. Laya, she saw, was feeling around on the table beside her bed. Her fingers found the glass of water there, and then the pills beside the glass.

"What's that?" Ariel asked as Laya downed them.

"Vitamins."

Ariel smiled. People who'd given up on their futures didn't bother to take vitamins. Maybe the poor woman was simply exhausted to some point beyond sensibility. Sleep deprivation. Ariel felt like telling her to move over. She remembered the thermos, and said, "Want some coffee? I've got some."

"You've got to be kidding." Laya stifled a yawn.

Ariel poured for herself. She should go find a cot. She hadn't seen anybody to ask when she'd come in. There was hardly space for a cot in here even if she could dig one up.

Laya had once described the room as oppressive. For sure it wasn't spacious. The Wellness Center, she recalled, had catered to a moneyed clientele, but she supposed they'd been in no shape to care about spaciousness. One thing could be said for the old building: it was solid. The walls were thick or well insulated; Ariel could hear no sound beyond them. "It's stuffy in here," she said. "Okay if I open the patio door for a few minutes?"

Laya roused at that. "Don't!" she said. "Please." She turned toward the sliding door as if she could see it, and something unwelcome beyond it. "Are the draperies closed?" she asked.

"Yes."

Laya relaxed somewhat. "A friend put a good lock on it for me today. Nobody will be getting in."

More like out, Ariel thought, as in somnambulating,

and wondered what prompted Gayle Baker to reconsider her suggestion. She took a sip of coffee, which, she was glad to find, was still hot. "I'm going to use your phone book, okay?" she asked.

"Ariel."

"What?"

"Why would I have a phone book?"

"Oh. Right."

"You can get the number from information."

Not a good idea, Ariel thought, to go looking for Stella Lipton within Laya's hearing. "I'm going to round up a cot or a rollaway bed or whatever," she said.

Although a radio had been left on in a room down the hall from Laya's, the place seemed deserted. No one was in the lounge. Ariel went looking for the dorm manager, but the office was locked. She went back to Laya's room. "Where is everybody?" she asked, startling the other woman out of a doze.

"In the city still, I'm pretty sure. What time is it?"

"You need a watch." Ariel consulted her own. "Not quite eight-thirty. In the city doing what?"

"Somebody donated tickets to a concert. A busload went."

"The whole student body?"

"I don't know about that. I just knew I wasn't up to it."

"What about the dorm manager?"

"He gets off at seven."

"But who's in charge?"

"This is not a kindergarten, Ariel."

"Yes, but . . ."

Laya smiled, on the verge, Ariel thought, of being offended. "A lot of the students live all by themselves in the outside world, you know? When we leave here with dogs, more will. I will."

"Of course. I wasn't thinking." Ariel went to the patio

door and pushed aside the drapery. She could see no sign
of life in the other dorm, but that didn't mean much. Only
students who retained some vision would be expected to
have lights on. If she weren't here, the light wouldn't be
on in this room. The grounds were bright enough. She
couldn't see the other buildings from here.

"If I can't find a cot," she told Laya, "you may have a
bunk mate."

A glance into every unlocked room that wasn't obviously that of a resident revealed brooms and mops and
assorted like items, but no furniture. She did locate a
phone directory in the lobby. In it were eight listings for
Lipton, none preceded by Stella or an initial S. Ariel
sighed, unpocketed her phone, and went to work.

J. Barton Lipton of SR, San Rafael, was the lady's husband. J. Barton, who answered, called his wife to the
phone.

Ariel dropped Gayle Baker's name right away to estab-
lish her legitimacy. It got a little trickier after that.

"Dr. Baker said you worked out here at the Manse, the
new dorm, when it was still St. Luke Wellness Center,"
she said, pacing the lobby, dropping, unconsciously, into
her sympathetic, coach-cultivated, I-wouldn't-ask-but-it's-
important voice.

"Yes?" said Stella Lipton. Leeriness was blatant in *her*
voice. She was waiting for a pitch or some other come-on.
She hadn't recognized Ariel's name. More probably, she
hadn't heard it. Who listens when "courtesy callers" give
their names?

"Would you have had any contact with people who
volunteered?" Ariel asked. "Like a Pink Lady kind of
thing?"

They never had a volunteer program at St. Luke's, Mrs.
Lipton informed her.

"Oh," Ariel said, sails deflating like flaccid balloons.

"What exactly are you wanting to know?"

Ariel leaned against a wall. She felt like sliding down it, into a puddle on the floor. "I had a friend," she said, "named Dorothy Thibeau. Dr. Raymond Thibeau's—"

"Yes?"

Ariel's ears pricked. That "yes" wasn't dismissive. "You knew her?"

"Yes."

"How?"

"From St. Luke's. She used to visit."

"Yes?" The parroting wasn't deliberate; it was all Ariel could get out.

"One of our patients, a lady she knew from back when she worked at . . . some big job at I. Magnin. Store's gone now, did you know that?"

"Yes, I know. And Mrs. Thibeau visited . . . ?"

"She came pretty regularly, yes."

Ariel held her breath. "To see Sis?"

"Sis? Oh, that's right! I'd forgotten all about . . . You knew both ladies, then?"

Ariel felt as if she'd come to the end of the rainbow.

"Sis, yes," Mrs. Lipton was saying, "toward the end that's all the poor thing would answer to. A childhood pet name, was it? Like a family thing, huh?"

"The Woodman family," Ariel murmured.

"Woodman?"

"Her family name. Her maiden name."

"Oh. Well, I wouldn't know about that."

"Did her son visit often?" Ariel imagined that he must have. It would look bad if one didn't make an effort when one was in line for the family money. The uncle, mom's prominent stockbroker brother, was deceased, wiped out in a plane crash. Mom was ill. As it turned out, terminally. The heir would do the right thing, if only to allay gossip.

"I don't recall seeing any children."

"There was just the one," Ariel said. She was truly surprised. Bad form, Rob. The rich, she supposed, were different.

"Well, shame on him . . . What, Bart? Hold on a second." Ariel heard disjointed conversation. "I know that," Mrs. Lipton said, presumably to her husband, "but we've got Call Waiting, all right? Now, where were we? Oh, yes. Children. They can be callous, can't they? The husband, now, he was faithful."

Ariel hadn't considered whether Rob's father was still alive.

"In good times and bad and oh, honey! The bad times were an ordeal. Worse than the DTs, and I saw my share of those!"

"This was a chemical dependency problem?"

"Why, no." Mrs. Lipton hesitated. "Schizophrenia. Chronic. I thought you said you knew—"

"Oh, I did! When you said DTs, it just threw me off for a second."

"Oh. Well . . . it was pitiful. Hallucinations. You'd know it was going to be a bad day when you'd come in and hear that humming."

"Did you say *humming?*" Ariel dropped into the nearest chair, trying to absorb what she was hearing. She felt as if her own neural connections were snapping.

"Makes me shiver to remember," Mrs. Lipton said, "especially when she'd start with the snakes! I, personally, happen to have a thing about snakes, so—"

"How about rats?" Ariel interrupted to ask.

"You do know, I see. Oh, yes, ma'am, we got rats, too. All species of vermin, some of them human."

Mrs. Lipton was a talker. She went on chattering, something about restraints and "the great escape," which culminated at an old gazebo. She wasn't talking about last night, and she wasn't talking about Laya.

Ariel's gaze swept the pleasant, deserted lobby. Here, in this place, a woman had once suffered a sickness of the mind. And here, inexplicably, through some crack in time, Laya had caught a glimpse of it. Had picked up on it. Suffered it. All Ariel's concern had focused on what those nightmare visions said about Laya's state of mind. It was a whole new thought that the woman in them existed . . .

Constance Woodman Millen. Called Sis in her childhood, and Sis again at the end.

There had to be some reasonable, some *acceptable* explanation for this. Ariel's head reeled. Had her own preoccupation with Sis somehow fed into Laya's receptors? Or . . . Laya had met and talked to Rob the night of the benefit dinner; had she, like some kind of highly sensitive radio receiver, picked up signals? Ariel grimaced. Guilt rays? That made no more sense than to think that exposure to a place could be responsible, but . . .

"Hello?" Stella Lipton asked.

"Let me ask you . . . ," Ariel said. *A thousand questions!* "Which room was it? That she was in?"

"Which room? Honey, I worked with I don't know how many patients, for fourteen years! And that one's been dead and gone . . . three? I don't . . . It was what we called C wing."

"Which is where?"

"You go in the front door, and . . . Have they changed things around much? I haven't been in there since they remodeled."

"I don't know either, but keep going."

"Turn right, and you go down a long hall. The room was in the middle somewhere."

Laya wasn't in the middle, but she was closer to the middle than to either end. "Mrs. Lipton," Ariel asked, "how did she die?"

"RDS."

"What is it?"

"Respiratory distress syndrome. Adult RDS. Only experience I ever had with it. I'd anticipated some digestive-related disorder. She complained of stomach problems, but I guess they were really head problems, if you know what I mean."

"Was there an autopsy?"

"Always. Well, I mean all deaths required a coroner's ruling. In a place with depressives—suicidally inclined, some of them—and anorexics and substance abusers and . . . well, you can imagine how strict the protocol was. Is that your phone beeping?"

"No."

"Oh, that's me! It could be . . . My granddaughter's expecting, and . . . Sorry! Call tomorrow."

Ariel clicked off. Then, quickly, rashly, she looked up Rob Millen's number and dialed it. She had no notion that she could intuit guilt from his voice; she just wanted to hear it. She had a gut-deep need to remind herself that the subject of her abstractions was real, that he was where hands could be laid on him.

She was about to give up, to hang up, when he answered. His voice was husky. There was laughter in it, the tail end of a lazy, intimate chuckle. She was as sure of what she'd interrupted as if she were there to see it.

"Hello," he said again, and then, "Go away, whoever you are."

After the click, Ariel dropped her head into her hands. She had to do something. She needed to sort things through, rationally, and decide what to do. Whom she should talk to. What she could possibly say. She'd sound like a crackpot. The type who got alien messages from rabbit ears and bedsprings. Who'd sniffed one joss stick too many. From the bedlam of her thoughts came one pure, fine idea: the deck might be full of jokers, but she held the cards.

Rob Millen didn't know she knew. He knew next to nothing about Laya, and nothing at all about her revelations. He didn't know Laya was here at the school, that she was here in this building, maybe in the very room, where he had, somehow, caused his mother's death. He also didn't know where Ariel was, and, judging from the way he'd ignored her calls, he didn't care.

And, obviously, he was all tied up.

There wasn't one thing to worry about tonight except how fast she could, finally, go to sleep.

47

SLEEP WASN'T THAT EASY. THERE'S A NEUTRAL ZONE BETWEEN fatigue and shut down, where cognitive thought stops. Rumination isn't cerebral; it's bovine. Ariel drifted in the limbo, slouched in the room's one chair, her stockinged feet propped on the bed. She could barely see the inert mound that was Laya, who slept like the dead.

With the draperies closed, the darkness was nearly absolute. Ariel sipped tepid coffee and, basically, woolgathered. Listened to silence. She tried to imagine a like silence of vision. No form, no color, no light. If you couldn't see where you were, where were you? Nowhere. If you were nowhere, you didn't exist. But she could see, and she was here. Her ribs were proof. She felt the dull ache, drumming with her pulse. The codeine she'd finally taken was beginning to kick in. Her back itched. She didn't move. Laya used to tell the class during *shavasana*, the corpse pose, to be still. Let the mind

scratch the itch. Ariel hadn't been able to grasp the concept then; she had it now.

The sound of her exhalation was loud in the silence.
She set the cup on the floor and clasped her fingers on her
stomach, and listened to herself breathe. She began to
have a sensation of floating, which was very strange,
because she was incredibly heavy. She ought to get up.
Get into her gown. Curl up at the foot of Laya's bed. She
would in a minute.

When the door was opened some time later, neither
woman stirred. There was no light from the hallway to
disturb them, as the lights had been turned off. The turn of
the lock made only the smallest click. The closing of the
door was soundless.

Jessie looked miserable beyond words. Ariel felt sorry
for her. "I thought," she told the dog, "you'd learned your
lesson about skunks." The odor was worse than the last
time this happened. It was acrid. Not the muskiness of distant roadkill. Up close, at full, potent strength, it was caus-
tic, burning the throat and stinging tears from the eyes. An
electrical stench, like scorched wires. "Stop whining!" she
said.

It was hard, even, to breathe.

Jessie whimpered. Ariel lost patience. "Stop it, I said!"
How was she supposed to sleep? *Please let me sleep.* Jessie
was crying. Ariel hadn't known dogs could cry. She
coughed, and one foot slid off the bed onto the floor, jarring her into a coughing fit.

Her eyes were streaming. They were open, but she
couldn't see. This place was too dark, too close. There was
no air. Where was this? She pushed herself up from the
chair. Immediately, she fell across something. A bed.
Somebody. *A body.* It moved under her. Ariel gasped, jerk-

ing away, rolling. When she hit the floor, the pain in her ribs was shocking. She lay there, fighting dumb panic. There was more air down here. She would stay here.

Jessie moaned.

Jessie? Not Jessie. That was a dream. She was awake now. But why couldn't she breathe? Why couldn't she see? Had she gone blind?

"Oh!" Ariel cried as reality hit. "Oh!" She pulled herself up by the bedcovers and felt for flesh. She grasped an arm. "Laya," she said. She couldn't say "Fire." Laya would panic. "Wake up!" Laya barely stirred. "Please!"

Which way was water? Towels to wet. She scrabbled on all fours, colliding with something. She deciphered it with her hand. The desk. Which way was the bathroom? She crawled around the obstruction, and, when she bumped into a wall, she stood, feeling along it to a door frame, and then a light switch.

The light came on, a dull flare wreathed in smoke, and then, with a pop, went out.

Coughing violently, Ariel located the towel rack and sink. When she was breathing through one wet towel, she groped for another, finding one draped on the tub, drenching it under the tub faucet.

Still only roughly oriented, she hit the bed faster than she'd expected. She fumbled the towel around Laya's head and face, and pulled at her shoulders. She was deadweight. "Wake up!" Ariel yelled, her voice muffled by cloth, her throat feeling torn. She shook Laya, who offered no resistance and no help.

"Outside," Ariel muttered. It was steps away. She pictured where the patio door would be, and stumbled to it, ripping the draperies aside. She could see now. Laya had been mistaken; there was no extra lock. (What kind of lock could you put on a metal-framed sliding glass door?) The door, however, wouldn't budge. Moving her hand to the top of the frame, she found the guard. It slipped out easily, yet the door was still frozen shut. She grasped it, shaking it in its frame. *Why won't you open?* her mind shrieked. The towel was nearly dry around her nose and mouth, and, for the first time, she was aware of heat. She could hear the fire now. She dropped to her knees. There was no guard at the bottom of the door.

What else could be holding it?

She was gasping. This was incredible! How could they make it so hard to get out in a place where blind people lived? And, my God, the sprinklers! There had to be sprinklers. Why hadn't they come on? And smoke alarms? And where was everybody? She pressed her hand against the glass. It was cool. The fire was the other way. They couldn't go out the other way.

And what else could be holding the door?

A bar. Some kind of rod in the track would stop the door! Ariel put her fingers on it, and wrenched it out. A metal pipe from the feel of it. The door opened.

Laya was total deadweight, her trunk dense, heavy as wet cement. She seemed to have an impossible number of limbs, all flaccid, all in the way. She landed on her knees as Ariel dragged her off the bed, bringing them both down. Ariel bit the towel against a scream. Her side felt speared. She took a second, and then struggled for a better grip. Three feet to the door, then two, and then they were on the patio. She stopped, huffing, and with a last monumental effort, dragged Laya to the grass.

She sucked in air. She could breathe. She could see. She heard the sound of sirens.

She put her fingers to Laya's neck. Her hands were slippery with sweat, and shaking too badly to feel a pulse. "Laya!" she said, and patted at her face. There was, she was almost sure, a flutter of eyelid. Ariel slapped her. "Laya," she said. "Oh, God!"

She pushed herself upright, gauging the distance of the sirens. They wouldn't see the two of them here, not right away. She had to draw their attention. But someone was already coming on foot from the other direction, from behind her. *Thank God!* she thought. Before she could turn, something was thrown over her head. Cloth. The towel. She was blind again. And then she was choking again, a forearm vising her throat, a body against her back. Her mind had yet to grasp what was happening, but she was already clawing and kicking. The arm was rock hard, crushing her windpipe. She tried to reach a face. Her nails searched for an eye, hair, anything to hurt. Her foot found a shin, slid up and found a knee. Ariel kicked backward as hard as she could. Had she been wearing shoes, the kneecap would have snapped. Even barefoot, she'd done damage.

The grip abruptly, marginally loosened. She had air! If he'd cried out, she couldn't hear it above the roar of blood returning to her brain and the noise of her own frantic wheezing. She made a fist, clutched it with her left hand, and jammed her elbow back, using the combined strength of both arms. She hit soft flesh. That brought a gasp she could plainly hear.

She also heard a shout, not from her attacker but from somewhere else.

"Help!" she screamed, shocked when nothing came out of her throat but a rasp.

And then the arm was gone from around her neck, and she was shoved forward, onto Laya. She sprawled. She ripped away the towel. Two people in firefighter gear were running toward her. A single man fled in the opposite direction. He was already obscured by bushes. Ariel pointed. "Get him!" she tried to say. It was a whisper. And then she passed out cold.

48

"HOW'S MY FRIEND?" ARIEL ASKED THE EMT.

"She's in the ambulance ahead of us," he said. "Her vitals are good. Don't worry."

"Was anybody else hurt?"

"Guess not, ma'am. Just the two units were called."

"Funniest thing," Ariel said hoarsely.

"Ma'am?"

"You go for months on end without seeing the inside of an ambulance, you know? Then boom! Twice in one day."

"Yes, ma'am. Lie back down please."

During "observation," for which the hospital insisted on keeping her, she kept falling asleep or passing out or zoning out, she wasn't sure which. All she knew was she kept losing chunks of time. Her head ached, and whenever somebody roused her to check vitals or take blood, she'd discover a new place that did.

Then the police came with their questions. "I don't know," "I can't say for sure," and "I didn't get a look at him" told them less than she could guess, but as much as she was in any state to say. Her throat gave out quickly, and she was forced to nod or shake her head or write down her responses, as well as her questions, which were mostly sidestepped.

She did learn that no one else had been hurt. The fire had originated in a broom closet directly opposite Laya's room (Ariel knew exactly where it was; the door had been locked when she'd tried it, looking for a cot), and it had been contained in that one wing. There had been only two other people in the building. One student, in a separate wing, had been awakened by the fire truck sirens, and the other had made the call that brought them. Both had, calmly, walked out of the building.

The police were unwilling to share what, if anything, they knew about how the fire started. Ariel didn't have to be told that it was deliberate. She had to believe she had been its target. When the fire failed to do its job, the man who'd set it came after her. That was an unplanned move. An act of desperation. The fire, however, had been thought through. Water must have been cut off at a main, or the sprinklers would have gone into action. The smoke detectors had obviously been disabled. Both things done, she was sure, by whoever put the metal bar in the door track, and none of the three would be difficult if you had access and a willingness to kill.

That she might have been the cause of three other people's deaths was horrifying to Ariel. That anyone was so inhuman as to risk it was appalling.

She was patted on the head about Laya's condition. "Not to worry," she was told; "we're taking good care of her." What did that mean? "She's fine." "Fine?" Ariel croaked. Then why was she unconscious?

What if she had gone away again? Back to the exosphere or wherever she'd retreated after she was blinded?

At one point Ariel found herself awake and alone simultaneously, and so parched she thought she'd die. She sucked on ice that had been provided. It had to be nearly daylight, she thought, but her watch said it was a few minutes before two. She wanted to go see about Laya, but she didn't know where Laya was. She'd rest a minute, and then go find her. The next she knew it was after seven.

She needed to call Tara. And Hattie, who was scheduled to fly up today. She yearned for aspirin, a throat lozenge, oblivion. She buzzed for a nurse, and then lay still and tried to make sense of what had happened the night before.

She hadn't mentioned Rob Millen to the police. She had been in no condition to explain her theories, which hung by tenuous threads from flimsy premises.

How could he have known where she was? Was it the call she made? She'd used her cell phone. With Caller ID he could know who she was, but not where. And he had been occupied at home. "Go away, whoever you are," he'd said. How long between then and the setting of the fire? One hour or closer to two? Time enough to arrange for her to go away permanently?

A man who's murdered once can't be counted on not to do it again, Dorothy had written. And yet again? As often as necessary?

But why would he consider it necessary? How could he possibly know she had learned who Sis was? Learned who and what *he* was? How could he know she even suspected him? Then she thought of another call she'd made: the snide message she'd left about having talked to Dorothy's doctor. She had thrown her mistrust in his face.

Still unanswerable was: why Laya? Was she, like the other two students in the dorm, simply expendable? Too bad they might have to go, too, but them's the breaks? Unless . . . Ariel sat up in bed.

She'd paid no attention to one thing she'd heard several times. From Gayle Baker. A member of the school's board of directors had wanted Laya out. Been adamant about it, presumably because she posed a liability problem. *"One board member in particular feels especially strongly that it's too great a risk,"* Gayle had said. And later, when she told the board all about the visions and about Stella: *"The one man I told you about . . . maybe he was dazed, but the point is, he listened. He definitely took me seriously."*

Gayle had been discreet. She'd never mentioned a

name, Ariel was sure of it. Rob? *"You do good works?"* she had once asked him. *"Just call me Mister Mover and Shaker,"* he'd said. In addition to gleaning vegetables for poor people and supporting the arts, did he move and shake on the board of directors of the guide dog school? The fire was set by a person familiar with the school and its layout. Who, more than a board member, might have that knowledge as well as easy, unsuspicious access to every area? If she could put Rob in that boardroom, it would answer every how and why.

He would know where Laya was and what was going on with her.

He would know from Dr. Baker that Ariel would be with her last night.

He'd know about the revelatory visions because Gayle described them to the board, and he'd know that the doctor, for one, took their content seriously. Would he? Hearing about profilers and how the police use sensitives to solve crimes, the hard nuts, the ones orthodox methods couldn't crack? Hearing that this blind student who lived in or near his mother's old room had visualized her symptoms and hallucinations—and a name. Stella. A real person, unknown to Laya, who turned up in her visions. If she could divine one name, he'd ask himself, why not another? Why not Mother's? Constance Millen. Sis.

And Laya had the ear of the one person searching for Sis's identity. Ariel. Who, Gayle had informed the board, would be up last night. And expecting Ariel, Laya would not go along with the other students to the concert in San Francisco.

Had the fire been planned for last night because the other students would be safely away? Take it a step further: had that been set up? The concert tickets had been donated, Ariel recalled Laya saying. By whom? Rob could well afford such a gesture.

The door opened, and a balding man in a white coat strode in. Dr. Gross, his nametag said. Ariel hadn't seen him before; that's a name she would have noticed on a man dealing with the sick. He pressed her call button to turn it off. "You feeling better this morning?" he asked, wrapping on a blood pressure cuff and sliding a thermometer into Ariel's mouth almost simultaneously. "So," he said, "you had the cracked ribs before last night, I was told."

Ariel nodded. "Laya?" she asked around the thermometer.

"Your friend?" He pumped the bulb, squinting at the numbers. The cuff was ripped off with a *scritch* of Velcro. "We're concerned about lung damage," he said. "Prognosis looks positive, though."

"Is she conscious?" Ariel rasped out when he'd removed the thermometer. "Is she awake?"

"Still pretty groggy. Confused as heck." Gross folded his arms, watching Ariel when he said, "What with the barbiturates and benzodiazepines in her."

"Barbiturates?"

"Seconal and Valium."

Valium? Ariel stared. Gayle Baker had talked Laya into taking it after all? Had she somehow taken too much?

Gross waited, as if he'd asked a question.

Ariel cleared her throat. It felt like gargling steel wool. "Did you say Valium *and* Seconal?" she asked.

Gross nodded. "Interesting pharmacological soup, the blood we got from you ladies. A party?"

Ladies? Ariel remembered the pill she'd taken. This was the sort of innocent situation that got twisted into headlines people remember after the paltry revisions were forgotten. "Codeine," she said. "The ribs. The prescription bottle's in my . . ." She was looking around for her purse when she realized it wasn't there. It was in Laya's room at the school. Possibly burned to a cinder.

"Your levels," the doctor was saying, "weren't nearly as high as your friend's, but—"

"Stop!" Ariel held up her hand. Neither she nor Laya had ingested anything illegal. They hadn't operated a vehicle or "dangerous machinery." (That pill bottle warning had always struck her as superfluous; would a person really be likely to down a few Demerols or whatever, and then rush out to thresh some wheat?) "Let me ask you something." What they needed to be talking about here was why two separate sedatives would be prescribed.

Somewhere on his person Dr. Gross beeped. "Excuse me," he said, and pulled out his pager. "I'll be back," he said, already going out the door.

Ariel got out of bed and found her clothes. They were filthy and smelly, but the peek-a-boo hospital gown wouldn't make a good traveling outfit. Dressing as she dialed, she called Charles Barnes. There was no answer. She found a phone book in the nightstand drawer. After arranging for a cab, she called Tara at home.

"I won't be in until late today," she said, looking in vain for her shoes. "Tell Chris—"

"Ariel? Is that you? My stars, you sound sexy."

"Go suck on a bonfire and you will, too."

"Do what?"

"Tell Chris I've been delayed." The shoes were still in Laya's room with the purse and suitcase. "Tell him *interestingly* delayed."

Tara, for the only time since Ariel had known her, seemed to be at a loss for comment.

Hattie, when Ariel called her, had plenty to say.

"Where are you at? What's the matter with your voice? You sound like you got the croup."

"I'm all right. Laya's all right—"

"What do you mean y'all are all right? Why wouldn't you be? What's happened?"

Hattie heard "fire," and, presumably, Ariel's hasty reassurance: "I'm not hurt in the least." If she heard the suggestion to stay put until further notice, she ignored it. "I'll get an earlier flight," she said and hung up.

Laya's room, it turned out, was two doors from Ariel's. She was lightly snoring when Ariel looked in. Thanks to Dr. Baker's combination of drugs, Ariel thought grimly. The word "overkill" occurred to her. With a last worried look, Ariel let her be, made good her hospital escape without attracting notice, and beat her taxi to the curb by seconds.

The theory that had neatly dovetailed fifteen minutes before no longer did. The pills queered it. Why, Ariel asked herself, would a doctor prescribe two different sedatives? Especially to a person she knew was unaccustomed to taking any form of medication? Gayle probably had a good explanation, but the ride to the school wasn't long enough to fathom it. Ariel couldn't get past the fact that Laya had been under Baker's care ever since she began manifesting symptoms and having nightmares. It was Baker who conducted all the tests Laya had undergone. She who was privy to the results. She who'd said there was no physical reason for the stomach pains.

So what? Raging paranoia, Ariel admonished herself.

The cab driver, she couldn't help noticing, was eyeing her in the rearview mirror. It was no wonder. She looked like a vagrant. She sat up straighter. Wait till he found out she had no money.

Random thoughts, insubstantial as gas bubbles, kept popping into her mind. She had only Gayle's word that she had defended Laya to the board, that there had even been a need for defense. It was Gayle who discovered Laya missing from her room, or claimed she did, and she who found her, and she who said she'd seen Laya waiting for some unknown friend earlier that same night, and . . .

Ariel's eyes narrowed. The only "friend" Laya had ever mentioned was whoever, supposedly, put a lock on her door, whoever had, in actuality, barred the door to make it harder to escape the fire. Gayle Baker? The school doctor would have totally free access to every nook and cranny of the grounds. She could come and go at any time, could do anything, and not be questioned.

But so what? She had no motive for harming Laya.

Ariel tried to open the cab window, to get some air to clear her throbbing head. The button didn't work.

Furthermore, Gayle was the wrong sex. She had nothing to do with Sis, with Constance Millen. She had nothing to do with . . . Rob?

Handsome, charming, wealthy, single Rob.

Maybe she wasn't the wrong sex after all. And, being a doctor, she was in an ideal position to do . . . whatever had been done to Sis. The wrong drug. An overdose.

"Where did you want out?" the cab driver asked.

They were at the school. "Drive on around," Ariel said. She directed him to the Manse, and asked him to wait.

From the front the old building looked perfectly normal, untouched by the near tragedy of the night before. Bright morning sunlight lent its gingerbready facade a cheerful aspect.

The hallway outside Laya's room bore the scars of battle. The room itself was a mess of smoke and water damage.

"Ma'am?"

Ariel jumped at the sound of the voice. A man dressed in the uniform of a security guard came in through the patio door. "Can I help you?" he said.

When Ariel explained who she was and what she was looking for, he told her that her belongings had probably been taken to the administration offices for safekeeping. Nodding, eager to be out of the room, Ariel spotted her shoes. Aside from being covered in soot, they were undamaged. She took them and left.

The cab driver eyed her as she emerged from the dorm, relieved, perhaps, to see she was no longer shoeless. She dumped out debris and popped the shoes together, sending up soot clouds and setting off a coughing fit. He'd be more relieved, she imagined, when he saw something that looked like money.

"Ma'am? I found this."

Ariel turned, squinting in the sun's glare. The security man stood in the doorway, holding out her overnight case. "No purse, though," he said.

Ariel wished it were her purse, with aspirin in it. Her head hurt. Sunlight glinted off his glasses and the shiny brass plaque affixed to the wall beside him. She took her bag, and turned to leave. And stopped.

49

GRIM-FACED, THE CAB DRIVER INSISTED ON ACCOMPANYING Ariel into the administration building. Now she was not only dressed like a street person and showing no signs of being able to pay the fare, but she was also acting mental. She had stood forever outside the dormitory, staring at a spot on the wall as if she were mesmerized. When she'd finally gotten into the cab, he'd had to ask "Where to?" three times before she came out of her trance.

The same super-efficient blind receptionist manned the front desk. She had custody of Ariel's purse and Laya's as well. Ariel paid the fare, added a tip that split the cabbie's face into a jack-o'-lantern grin, and said, "Wait, please."

Dr. Gayle Baker jumped up from her desk at the sight of Ariel, all solicitation. "I called the hospital first thing," she said. "They told me you'd disappeared. What in the world—"

"I have two questions," Ariel said. "First, did you give Laya sedatives?"

"What?" Startled, Gayle sat down. "No."

"I see," Ariel said. It had been the "vitamins" then. What a vicious trick to play on a blind woman.

"What are you doing here?" Gayle asked. "Shouldn't you—"

"Excuse me, but I've got one other question. Who was Narcissus Barnes?"

"Who was . . . ?"

"Narcissus M. Barnes. The new dorm was donated in her memory, it says on that little plaque. 'Presented to Marin Guide Dog Academy to Honor the Memory of Narcissus M. Barnes.' Who was she?"

"The wife of . . . Actually, I'm not at liberty—"

"The wife of the man who gave the property to the school," Ariel said. "Charles Barnes." She'd known since she saw the plaque, but after being so wrong, so consistently, so absurdly, she didn't trust herself to draw any sane conclusions. "Sis," she said to herself, and groaned. "Narcissus."

"Ariel, shouldn't you go back to the hospital?"

Ariel smiled vaguely, said "Thanks," and turned to go. "Oh," she said, "one other thing. Is Charles on your board of directors?"

"No. Why?"

Not a problem, thought Ariel. He got a hell of a lot more from me than he would ever have picked up in a board meeting.

Laya has a way of knowing things, she'd jabbered. *Things she has no explainable way of knowing.*

Conversation after conversation, Charles asking, her digging Laya's grave with every reply.

"She can tell the future?" You betcha, pal! *"And see the past."*

"You believe in this?" ... *"I've seen it."*

"You're not thinking this dream has some real meaning?" ... *"I wondered whether it could derive from the past."*

"You wouldn't have brought this up," he'd accurately observed, *"if you weren't taking it seriously."*

She had kept him right up-to-the-minute.

"This sounds strange, but I was talking to her, and she started humming." And ... *"In this nightmare she's in a hospital ... insane."* And ... *There've been some new developments we need to explore, and as quickly as possible."* And ... *"It's something she brought to light that got me curious about this St. Luke's."* And on and on. She hadn't known about Stella Lipton one full day before Charles knew, too, that Laya had reached back into the past and pulled out a name. Only the first, perhaps; more to come. It was a risk he couldn't afford to take.

"Well, I guess that explains that," Gayle said.

Ariel blinked. Had she spoken out loud? "Pardon?"

"I take it you know Mr. Barnes. If you and he are friends, that's how he knew about Laya. Why he wanted her admitted."

"What are you talking about?"

"When he heard there was a last-minute dropout, he *suggested* her as a replacement." Gayle made a face. "Which meant she was in like Flynn."

"Because he's an important benefactor?"

Gayle chose her words. "He's a friend to many worthy causes. Money, time—"

"Concert tickets."

"As I said, he's a generous man."

• • •

The receptionist was deep in conversation with another woman as Ariel passed the front desk on her way out. Ariel wouldn't have noticed if she had been in conversation with a zebra, but the woman called her name.

"Ms. Gold?" she asked. "Excuse me? Would you mind too much signing this for me?"

She was white-haired, chunky, dressed in slacks and a shirt with the school logo on the breast pocket. She held out a sheet of paper and a pen. Reflexively, Ariel took them. The paper was blank. It took several seconds to grasp why this stranger was asking her to sign a blank piece of paper.

Fidgeting like a child in need of a bathroom, the woman said, "Just write 'To my friend Stella,' okay?"

Ariel actually began to write before the name registered.

The retired nurse smiled happily. "You know, I didn't realize who you were last night? Didn't take in the name? But Polly there was telling me about the fire and that Ariel Gold was one of the women injured, and bang! I realized—"

"I've seen you before," Ariel said.

"In the gift shop, probably. I volunteer."

"On the grounds. I was with Charles Barnes. You spoke to him."

"Oh, a couple of weeks ago, right! I didn't notice you. Is he the nicest or what? And devoted to that poor wife? Like I said last night, in good times and bad . . . Ms. Gold? Wait! My autograph!"

The taxi ride to B.F.'s house passed in a haze. Ariel felt too stupid to think. By the time they arrived, she had passed from numbness to heartsickness. She went into the house, into the nearest bathroom, and undressed. She turned on the shower, as hot as she could stand it.

He's a killer.

The cold fact of it was too staggering to take in. The hows and whys irrelevant. Cognizance came in small, sickening, visceral bursts.

He kills people.

She stood under the water, letting it pound her, wanting badly to feel anger, outrage, anything other than ill.

He killed his wife. She couldn't make it real in her mind. *And Dorothy.* She couldn't even picture it. *And, too nearly, Laya. And, too nearly, me.*

The betrayal felt real enough.

"Why're you so good to me?" Ariel could see herself smiling, asking the question. When had that been? Days ago? Last week? Last night? They had talked so much in such a short space of time.

"I wish you'd tell me about what you do, Ariel."

Kind, empathetic, helpful Charles. Nurturer. Murderer. The words chased themselves. Became meaningless. Empty, like everything he'd ever uttered.

"We're friends—I flatter myself that we're friends."

As if the act of bathing were a complex operation, Ariel focused on each individual step. Soaping, meticulously, every inch. A soot mark on her arm didn't want to come clean. Her elbow stung. She must have scraped it last night, when he pushed her down onto Laya. She lathered her hair. The shampoo leaked into her eyes.

His crinkled when he smiled; she had particularly liked that about him.

Had he manipulated everything from the first day? Working her strings and pulling strings? Getting Laya into the school. *"If she weren't here, Ariel, I wouldn't be having the chance to get to know you."* Arranging the psychiatrist appointment. *"Just leave it to me, Ariel."*

Never mind. Let it go.

She rinsed herself, taking time to get every trace of shampoo out of her hair.

He was, of course, Laya's "friend." The mysterious friend with whom she'd had dinner the night Gayle saw her waiting by the gate. The helpful friend who'd removed the batteries from the smoke alarms, and turned off the water at the main, and barred the door, and set the fire. Oh yes, and substituted sedatives for vitamins. It occurred to Ariel that she should retrieve the vitamin bottle; recover the evidence. It didn't seem pressing.

She turned off the water.

For the first time she could remember, she wished she had remained ignorant of the almighty answer. Where was it written that every crime had to be solved? If she had left Laya alone, the nightmarish visions would never have happened. Last night would never have happened. Poor Narcissus Barnes could remain peacefully dead, as she had wanted to be. As Dorothy felt she had wanted. As Laya confirmed she had wanted.

But Dorothy had wanted to live.

"Are you doing a story about our late coroner, Ariel?"

Chill bumps raised the hairs on Ariel's wet arms. She reached for a towel.

She hadn't answered Charles's questions about the Thibeaus, it struck her; not until last night. Nor had she mentioned Stella Lipton—the nurse who'd cared for his wife, the woman about whom he'd lied and said he didn't know—until last night. After the fact, surely, of the lethal arrangements he'd made. Curious.

Ariel sat on the side of the bathtub, the towel around her neck, the enamel cold on her buttocks. She began to dry her hair.

Vaguely, she imagined how he'd gone about befriending Laya. Waiting until she was alone. A kind word. A helpful hand over a rough patch of ground. It would have been the easiest thing in the world. God knows, he was comfortable as an old shoe. Ariel felt as if she'd known him for years. "Tell me about what you do," she could hear him saying to Laya, as he had said to her.

He might not have given Laya his real name. No one need be aware they'd ever met. He could say he was a gardener, an instructor, anybody. What would a blind woman know? He would just be a sympathetic voice and a strong arm. "You look tired, dear," he might have said; "are you feeling okay?" Or "I had the strangest dream last night. Listen to this!" I'll tell you mine if you'll tell me yours. And he was a person who knew how to listen.

Laya could have told him about Stella, and sleepwalking to the gazebo, and any number of unnervingly accurate details from any number of variations of the dreams about which Ariel had yet to hear. Maybe she had divined another name. Maybe his name, having no idea of its significance. He might know more about Laya's dangerous dreams by now, Ariel thought, than she did, and . . . Ariel's hands slowed on the towel. She had chatted with Laya about the Thibeau business, more than once. How hard would it be for Charles to introduce that subject? "Was that Ariel Gold I saw you with the other day?" he might say. "Now, that's exciting, a TV star for a friend. Is she up here working on a story?"

When she heard her name called—she thought—Ariel went still. She listened, heard only the loud silence of the huge old house, and decided she'd imagined it. The shower gave a last dyspeptic gurgle. Ariel relaxed, sighing. She had to take steps about Charles. What first?

Somewhere, a floorboard creaked.

Ariel came to her feet. Hattie? Here already? She wrapped the towel around herself. It couldn't be Hattie, not yet. Was it anybody? Then there was the unmistakable sound of footsteps, crossing the hardwood floor of the foyer.

Ariel flew the few feet to the bathroom door, closing it quietly, and turning the old-fashioned lock. She put her ear against the wood. It was solid; it was also thick. She couldn't hear anything. Had the person stopped, or stepped onto a rug? Who besides Hattie and B.F. had a key? The people who took care of the property? Of course! She had no car here; they wouldn't know there was anyone in the house.

"Ariel?"

The property managers wouldn't call her by her first name. She jerked away from the door. The voice, male, muffled—not B.F.'s—came from just beyond it. She backed toward the window. It was easily big enough to crawl through. She was on the ground floor; there would be a slight drop, nothing dangerous.

"Are you in there?"

The window was painted shut. Struggling with it, Ariel looked about wildly. What kind of weapon would be in a bathroom?

"Are you all right? It's Rob."

Rob? For the space of a second, Ariel couldn't connect the name to any person she knew.

"Please answer me!"

Ariel clutched the towel against herself.

"Say something," he said, "or I'm calling the police!"

"How the hell did you get in?" Ariel yelled, as furious as she was frightened.

"I walked in. The front door was open. Look, I'm sorry if I scared you, but when I saw the door open, I was afraid—"

"Get out of this house!" Ariel opened a cabinet. Tissue. Safety razors. She grabbed a bottle of rubbing alcohol.

He sprung backward at the suddenness of the door

being snatched open, his eyes widening at the sight of
Ariel, poised to fling the alcohol into them.

"Hey!" He raised his hands in surrender. One, incongru-
ously, gripped an umbrella. Ariel hesitated, distracted. The
umbrella was purple, florid with a scarlet print, what
looked like cabbage roses. In other circumstances, he
would have looked comical. "Like your outfit," he said,
and grinned.

Ariel recognized the umbrella; it was from the stand in
the foyer. She grabbed it. Considered beating him to death
with it. The towel slipped. Rob gaped, thought better of it,
and, deliberately, turned his back.

"You want to put something on?" he asked. The amusement in his voice was more than Ariel could take.

"Get out!" she said, righting the towel, nearly choking
on outrage. Her raw throat closed.

"I will. I'm going."

"Then move!"

"You sound awful. Are you all right?"

"I'll be fine when you're gone. How did you get in
here?"

"I told you, the door was open."

"I did not leave the door open."

"It was ajar."

Could it be that she hadn't closed the door properly?
She had no firm memory of entering the house. She had
no firm memory of coming to the house.

"After what happened last night . . . ," Rob said. "I
heard about the fire when I went into the office this morning, that it was arson, that you were attacked—"

"Oh, turn around. You look ridiculous, like you're being
held up at gunpoint."

He turned, keeping his eyes, pointedly, on hers, no
longer sounding amused. "I heard they didn't catch whoever did it. When I saw the door open and you didn't

answer. . ." He nodded toward the umbrella in her hand. "It was the only weapon that came to hand."

"You were going to rescue me."

"Let us be eternally grateful I wasn't put to the test."

"Why are you here?"

"They said at the hospital that you left, without being discharged. I thought you might have come here."

"I mean what do you want? If you think you're going to get a story, you can go—"

"Your neck's bruised."

"Yeah?"

"Shouldn't you be in the hospital?"

"Oh, shut up." Ariel set aside her various weapons. "Go sit down someplace."

She hadn't brought a robe with her; she went looking for one. No wrap in the closet of the master bedroom, what had been Jane's bedroom, was appropriate to the occasion. That these things hadn't been disturbed, cleaned out, or, apparently, touched in all these months struck Ariel as morbid. Something ought to be done about that. She found trousers and a light sweater. Her slender sister's pants were only slightly tight. She wasn't too preoccupied to notice it.

Rob was sitting in the living room, his hands between his knees, contemplating a painting inspired solely, as far as Ariel had ever been able to see, by the concept of red. It was the one jarring note in the room. Jane, she absolutely knew, hadn't chosen it; it had been a husband-pleasing compromise. "I've got to get back to the hospital," she said.

"To see your friend Laya?"

"What do you want?"

"To confess."

Ariel's heart thumped, a single jolt of uncertainty. It wasn't possible; she could not, once again, have gotten it all wrong.

"I was going to rip you off," he said. "The Thibeau story. I sort of misled you on a few points. I had a book in mind."

"Oh." Ariel exhaled. "That."

"But it became increasingly clear there was no book in it."

"Oh, really?"

"A one-shot story, possibly, your kind of thing. Frankly, I doubt there's even that. But definitely no true-crime opus."

Ariel crossed her arms and let him talk.

"And I lost interest altogether when my wife came back."

"Your . . . what?"

"She left me nearly a year ago. Ten months, two weeks. To find herself. She came back this week, all found. I'm the greener grass after all." He smiled, a big, dopey smile, the most genuine expression Ariel had ever seen cross that fine face. "I would've called you, but I've been busy."

"It's okay," Ariel said. "I went ahead without you."

"You'll have to meet her." Rob came out of his blissful fog. "Went where without me?"

"To a fire. Now I'm going to the hospital. Excuse me, I've got to call a cab."

"You don't have a car? I'll drive you."

"Suit yourself." Ariel was already in the foyer. An envelope lay on the hardwood floor. "What's this?" she asked, bending to pick it up.

"Your mail, I guess. It was there when I came in. What about the fire?"

The envelope was thick, business size, buff colored. The color blended with the floor. Ariel hadn't seen it when she came in, but it could have been there, dropped through the mail slot. There was no stamp or address, only her name, typed, and the word PERSONAL.

50

ROB MADE GOOD TIME REACHING A KENTFIELD ADDRESS ARIEL had gotten from the phone book. She didn't do any talking on the way. He, after a barrage of questions to which he got no answers, shut up and drove.

"The Barnes house?" he said when she told him to stop. "This is Charles Barnes's house."

The three-story Edwardian would have been hard to miss. A black-and-white was parked alongside the ambulance in the circular driveway. "What's going on?" Rob asked. Tears sprang to Ariel's eyes. Despite everything, she had wanted to be wrong.

A young uniformed policeman eyed the car as it slowed and stopped. He approached the passenger window, saying, "Unless you folks have business here, you need to move along."

"What's happened?" Ariel asked.

A more experienced officer would likely have claimed ignorance and sent them on their way. This one turned somberly to look at the house. "Accident, looks like," he said.

"Fatal?"

"Uh . . . did you know the man that lived here?"

Ariel considered the question. "No," she said; "I didn't." She raised the window, and Rob backed the car, and drove them away.

He parked a block away. "What's going on?" he asked.

Quietly, Ariel said, "Rob, I can't think of a solitary reason why I should give you the time of day, can you?"

"No," he said, and, after a while, "well, if Barnes was a friend of yours, I'm sorry."

"He wasn't."

"Right. I can see you're not at all upset." When he got no response, he said, "A lot of people will be. Kind of a mystery man, Barnes was. Came from nowhere, married old money . . . raised some eyebrows, that marriage. He got more than he bargained for, grief-wise, but he stood by it. And what he's accomplished since she died . . ." He frowned. "I've forgotten her name, the wife."

"Narcissus," Ariel said.

"Oh, yeah, I knew it was something floral . . ." He frowned. "Narcissus? Not . . . Sis?"

Ariel handed him the envelope.

"This is from . . . ?"

She nodded.

He hesitated. "Are you sure you want to let me . . . ?"

"It's yours. Do whatever you want with it."

Rob pulled out the several typed pages, smoothed them, and began to read.

Dear Ariel:

I expect things have begun to fall into place for you by now. I know you; well, I believe, for short acquaintance. You'll dig till you find what passes for truth. I prefer you have the real thing.

My wife, Narcissus Madeline Barnes, was a wealthy woman. She was also the most tormented human being I've ever known. Only sporadically did we share any-thing resembling a normal life. Medication helped, but only when she took it, and she wasn't reliable. I loved her. Because I loved her, I honored her wish.

Her life, through no fault of hers, was pointless, her death tragic. The use to which her money goes has lent both dignity. And, after years of sitting helplessly by while

*a person I loved suffered, I've had purpose. In my church
it might be seen as penance. I haven't been assuaging
guilt; I've been carrying out a legacy. I've given, and realized, great joy.*

*Let me tell you about it. Kids who would have been on
the street are studying to become teachers and doctors.
One I know of will be a priest. People who would likely
be dead live healthy lives. All because of me. I don't have
to tell you about the blind, what the school means to them.
Getting Laya in, like much of what I've done, has been
behind the scenes. That is exhilarating. Changing lives,
Ariel, is exhilarating. The power is intoxicating. You can't
even imagine. This week it became clear you would
destroy it all.*

*I don't fear a courtroom. Visions aren't evidence. The
power you hold is more insidious. You would see me
judged in the court of public opinion. Prime time. You had
stumbled onto a story, and, exploiting your friend's divine
gift, you'd wreak havoc for no good reason except to satisfy your curiosity—and for the sake of a television show!
"Mystery Solved by ESP," or some such tawdry thing. A
circus! It seemed to me so obviously unfair. God wouldn't
allow it to happen. My failure proves that I was wrong.*

*I have one regret: your friend and my late wife's, Mrs.
Thibeau. Her husband was a reasonable person. She was
not. She was less easily discouraged than I thought, and
more resourceful. Had I known she would bring you into
the picture, I would've taken her more seriously.*

*I told you once I don't believe in coincidence.
Everything happens according to a plan. You, for reasons
I don't understand, must be His instrument. Wield your
power carefully. He will guide you.*

Rob whistled, scanned the letter again, and said, "He's
crazier—was crazier—than his poor wife ever thought

about being. Last night . . . that was him?" At Ariel's nod, he shook his head. "It's true what they say. Power corrupts."

"'Power does not corrupt. Fear corrupts . . . the fear of a loss of power.'"

"Whatever. What are you going to do?"

"Nothing. I told you, it's yours."

"No, not this time." He studied her. "There's no point being bitter, Ariel, or hurt. He wasn't sane."

"He was crazy as the proverbial fox. Notice how carefully the letter's worded. Do you see any confessions there? Notice it's typed. Notice there's no signature."

"Maybe he thought the Almighty needed a little help guiding you in the right direction."

"Call your paper, will you? See if they've got anything on what happened."

The paper had the story, but there were few details yet. "A fall," Rob said when he hung up, "from a third story widow's walk. A 'tragic accident.'"

"Good God!"

"Looks like he was repairing a railing. There were tools up there."

Ariel's jaw set. "Notice this couldn't be construed as a suicide note either." She gave a little laugh. "Hallowed ground, tearful tributes . . . Maybe he'll get something named after him! My God! Two murders and two attempted murders and—"

"What *two* murders? You don't still believe he killed Mrs. Thibeau? Did you read this letter?"

"I read it." Ariel opened the car door to get some air. Some distance. "It's hardly a deathbed confession."

"I've talked to the pathologist who autopsied Mrs. Thibeau, Ariel. Natural death. That letter she wrote you? Could it be—"

"That's none of your business."

"—she was setting the stage to sell you a story?"

"What!"

"You can't tell me you don't ever pay for stories."

"She wouldn't—"

"Take money? She did once. Isn't that your theory? Or Dr. Thibeau did, with her knowledge."

"That was different."

"Somebody who'd take hush money wouldn't take money to talk? Hello?" Rob jabbed the appropriate paragraph in Charles's letter. "'Her husband was a reasonable person. She was not. She was less easily discouraged than I thought, and more resourceful.' Did you get that? 'More resourceful'? She hit him up, Ariel. She had another go at Barnes. He didn't 'take her seriously,' but—"

"She was terrified of him!"

"—but, she thinks, the information's marketable, and if I spice it up a bit—i.e., I'm desperate to do the right thing, to tell all, but he's threatened my life, well . . . she's no longer a shabby blackmailer, she's the heroine of the piece."

"No," Ariel said. *A man who's murdered once can't be counted on not to do it again, can he?* The obliqueness of the question had never struck her before. Dorothy hadn't actually said he'd made any threat at all, had she?

"More importantly," Rob said, "it makes a better story. It ups the price."

But Dorothy was convinced on her deathbed that it was Charles who'd put her there! Drug-induced delirium? Had she come to believe her own tale? Snatches of the familiar letter came back. The banter . . . Ariel had seen it as gutsiness disguising fear. Was it a pitch? As carefully worded as the letter Rob held now? "No," she repeated, but she couldn't help remembering the very first line Dorothy wrote: *I caught your show last night.* Inspiration for a scheme? *It's an intriguing twist, isn't it?* Dorothy had asked. Had it been a genuine question, or a hook?

Ariel had wondered so many times what sparked their long- ago, forgotten meeting. Dorothy's initial approach. She had been pawning her belongings at the time, desperate for money. *How often I've thought of our conversations and resisted contacting you. I don't think you'll be surprised to hear that.* She would have told me just enough to pique my interest, Ariel thought, to make me want the rest, to make me coax her. *You did warn me. "There is only one way to achieve happiness on this terrestrial ball, and that is to have a clear conscience, or none at all."* Enough to get an offer. But *The Open File* didn't have an unlimited budget; Charles had come in with the high bid.

The omission of his name . . . "She left it out deliberately," Ariel said. "It wasn't that I was supposed to know it already. She never told me his name."

"What?" Rob asked, baffled.

"She was still holding out. No freebies." *The man. The do-gooder. The executioner. And Sis with no last name. Impossible to follow through on without Dorothy's information—which was available at a price?*

"Rob," Ariel said, "is there any question at all—I mean at all—about the cause of her death?"

"Not as far as her doctor's concerned, or the pathologist, or me. She wasn't young. She wasn't particularly strong. She got sick. It happens every minute of every day."

After a time Ariel blew out air, a tired exhalation. "Do me a favor, Rob," she said. "Don't ever, ever write me a letter."

"Okay," he said agreeably.

"In one day I've lost two friends, two people I thought were friends."

"With friends like those, you don't need—"

"I'll bet you money," Ariel blurted, "the vitamin bottle's gone from Laya's room. No sedatives left in evidence, and no thermos. That wasn't just 'unleaded' in that thermos. One codeine pill wouldn't have made me that groggy last night. It was 'interesting pharmacological soup.' I'll bet you the thermos is gone, and . . . You don't know what I'm talking about, do you?"

"No."

"Whatever he composed this bloody letter on will be gone as well; count on it. Damn it! One thing I can't help wanting to know . . ." Ariel heard herself and made a wry face. "I guess I'm unreformed."

"Pardon?" Rob said.

"'Four be the things I'd been better without: love, curiosity, freckles, and doubt.'"

"Dorothy Parker," Rob said. "What one thing?"

"What did he use to kill his wife?"

"One thing I can't help wanting to know," Rob said. "What did he mean by a 'divine gift' and visions and so on?"

Ariel looked him in the eye. "It's a mystery to me."

They sat in silence then, thinking their separate thoughts. After some minutes Ariel said, "So he just gets away with it."

"Three stories straight down . . . Does that sound like winning to you?"

Ariel shuddered. "He'd probably established a foundation for the money, to immortalize himself."

"It'll do the same good, no matter whose name's attached."

"If the police come up with anything, with the arson or the fake suicide, I won't lie. I'll cooperate."

"Sure."

"They won't, though. He was a careful man." Ariel closed the car door. "Give me a ride to the hospital, will you?"

51

"So, is your vision restored?" Ariel asked Laya.

"What kind of question is that?" Laya spoke carefully, her hand at her throat.

"Well, that's what happens in the movies. A near-death experience, and Presto! *'Praise be! It's a miracle! I can see again!'*"

Laya grinned. "Then I guess your memory came back."

"Oh, everything! Clear back to the womb."

Seriously, Laya said, "What happened, Ariel? I haven't been able to get a straight answer out of anybody around here."

"What do you remember?"

"I was in bed in the dorm. I woke up here."

"Laya . . ." Ariel wondered where to start. How much to say. She contemplated the other woman, a very strong woman who had made it clear she didn't need punches pulled. "You said someone put a lock on your door for you? The same person, I'm guessing, who took you to dinner night before last?"

"Yes? Gabe? What about him?"

"Gabe?"

"Gabriel. He's a school maintenance man. Do you know him?"

Ariel didn't think anything Charles could come up with would surprise her at this point, but *Gabriel?* The messenger of the Lord? She plunked into a chair beside the bed. "Some interesting things have happened," she began, "while you were sleeping."

Laya's lunch was brought in while Ariel talked. When it

was taken away, untouched, she was still talking. Her throat, she thought, would never be the same. She dreaded getting to the part about Charles's—Gabriel's—death, and fully expected that Laya would react as she had on hearing about Maurice Thomas: poor, misguided soul, or some such pitying remark.

"The man was a total lunatic!" Laya said.

"Well, yes," Ariel agreed.

"And I," Laya said, horrified, "blabbed to him like a fool! He wormed information out of me like a priest in a confessional!"

"I don't think priests actually worm—"

"I nearly got us both killed!"

"Hey, what you didn't blab, I did."

"The great sensitive. The brilliant visionary." Laya covered her face with her hand. "I didn't have the first clue."

"You? I had everybody in the county except him all but convicted. Rob Millen, your doctor—"

"Dr. Baker? Why would you suspect her?"

"Because I'm an idiot."

"Good lord, Ariel!" Laya shook her head, still trying to take so much in. "That was really and truly the man's *wife* I've been dreaming about? That poor, wretched woman!" She faltered. "I don't . . . I was beginning to believe it was me. A prophecy."

Ariel grinned. "I believed it was Rob's mother."

"What is this, one-upmanship? At least you weren't shaking in your boots about some madman blinding you and coming after you when he didn't know you existed."

"Yeah, well, you didn't spend the last month trying to solve the murder of a friend who wasn't a friend and wasn't murdered. Top that!"

Laya thought a minute. "I can't. You win."

"Thank you. Look, Laya . . . I want to ask you a serious question. Honest answer, okay? Does it bother you too much that the person who did blind you might not be caught? I mean ever?"

"When I think he might hurt other people? Sure. But I'm with Barnes on one thing: everything happens according to a plan. Whoever and wherever this person is, he can't escape his karma."

"You're kidding, right?"

"Absolutely not." Laya was grave. "As 'His instrument,' you ought to know that. Now, I need to tell you something."

"If it's more philosophy, I don't want to hear it."

"I'm not going back to the school."

"Oh, Laya, no! You'd be in a different room if that's what's worrying you. The one you were in is too damaged—"

"I've decided to see about another transplant."

Ariel smiled.

"If it doesn't work this time, so be it. I'll have tried."

"Who am I talking to?" Ariel laughed because she felt like crying. "Whatever happened to 'I can't afford it'? 'I can't go through it again'? Whatever happened to Laya, the omniscient, who *knows* 'another transplant would go the same way'?"

"Ariel, come close." Laya was grave. "I want to be able to see you when I tell you this."

"See me?" For a second Ariel thought her joke about the miracle of a near-death experience hadn't been a joke after all. Laya's fingertips touched her face to read the expression there. "What?" Ariel breathed, a little frightened.

"You, my smart-ass friend," Laya said, "ask too many questions."

Epilogue

Dear Ariel,

Greetings from Corfu. We've been here a month. Second honeymoon. I know you said never write you a letter, but I figured you'd hang up on me if I told you this over the phone. I'm doing the Thibeau-Barnes book after all.

Don't freak! It's not true-crime. It's a novel. A mystery. As these days, I'm feeling more Cartland than Capote or Christie, it's a romantic mystery. (You remember Libby Vail? She compared the Thibeaus to Ronnie and Nancy. I'm doing them more as Edward and Wallis, and my Charles and Sis have a certain Scott and Zelda quality.) Worry not; the names are changed to protect the guilty. (The Thibeaus and Barneses, I mean, not Ronnie and Nancy, et al.) I've got a dandy contract. If I dedicate the book to you, will you not be mad anymore?

Fiction or not, I've done my homework, and that's why I'm writing. I may have the answer for which you yearned. As you may know, Mrs. Barnes was autopsied. The death certificate cited adult respiratory distress syndrome. Routine toxicology screens were all "noncontributory to a diagnosis." Lung slides, however, were sent off to a pulmonary pathologist. I've been corresponding with him. "Similar findings with which I'm familiar that could cause the indicated changes," he wrote, "are associated with the pathology caused by paraquat." You ever hear of it? It's a herbicide. His report didn't go to the original lab; it went to Thibeau.

*I won't go into a bunch of details (do your own
research if you're so inclined), but a victim isn't likely to
know she's being poisoned; hot liquids or spicy foods can
mask the taste. And "the constellation of symptoms often
lends itself to being interpreted as influenzal in origin."
And (get this) "No cases of conviction of homicidal poi-
soning by paraquat have been reported in the United
States." As you said, Charles Barnes was a careful
man.*

*By the by, I got my answer, too. Before I left, I vis-
ited the guide dog school. I know about the visions. I
heard all about your amazing friend Laya, the "sensitive." I know one thing you don't.*

*After talking to Gayle Baker, I also talked to one of
her nurses. Seems this nurse, Janet, has a buddy named
Stella. They were yakking one day a couple of months
ago in the school infirmary. Stella, who apparently likes
to hear herself talk, was holding forth about the good
old days when she worked at St. Luke's. Janet remembered one story in particular: "this poor crazy who suffered awesome hallucinations." (Yes, I heard about
them, too: the nasty creatures and the humming and
"the great escape," etc.) So, Ariel, here's where it gets
intriguing.*

*Per infirmary records, your friend was a patient that
day. It was the first time she reported sick. They put
her to bed. She was zonked out in one of those
curtained-off cubicles. Even asleep she must have
heard the ladies talking, don't you think? I'd guess it
was right after that that her nightmares began. Not to
take anything away from her; some people truly do
pick up vibes, which she, obviously, had already begun
to do. (You did know she was assigned Mrs. Barnes's
old room? I went there. Maybe it was because of what*

*I already knew, but I'll swear it made me feel
depressed as the dickens!)*

*The enlightening infirmary scene won't be in my book.
My readers will be romantics, like me. We believe in
magic.*

Warmest regards,
Rob

Visit
❖ **Pocket Books** ❖
online at

....

www.SimonSays.com

....

Keep up on the latest new
releases from your favorite
authors, as well as author
appearances, news, chats,
special offers and more.

SIMON & SCHUSTER
A VIACOM COMPANY
www.SimonSays.com

Pocket
Books

2381-01